All for Anna

By Nicole Deese

This book is a work of fiction. Names, characters, places and incidents are products of the author's imagination or are used fictitiously. Any resemblance to actual events or locales or persons living or dead is entirely coincidental.

Copyright © 2013 Nicole Deese

Okay Creation Designs
© Sarah Hansen
www.okaycreations.net

DEDICATION

All for Anna is dedicated to those who have known the heartache of loss, the heaviness of guilt or the hopelessness of shame.

May the healing that comes through recovery find you as it has found me.

PROLOGUE

The church was packed; standing room only.

Who would have imagined a child could affect so many lives in only six years? I stood toward the back, shoulder to shoulder with my sister and Jack. They practically pinned me in with their close proximity. It was almost as if they knew my plans of escape. My heart pounded loudly; the beat seeming to come from within my ears, drowning out the music that played over her slide show.

Anna.

I knew she had been beautiful; though the body I remembered looked very little like the healthy girl who was pictured here on ponies and scooters or wearing pjs and tutus. Her smile had been mesmerizing and her eyes so full of life and future dreams. Her blond hair, long like Cinderella, was shiny and spotless, bouncing with each move she made in the home video.

The video was a stark contrast to the mud splattered, bloody hair that I had pushed off her face before administering CPR. The innocence that same face and body exuded on the screen was unbearable to watch, at least for me. I felt my knees start to give out, but willed myself once again to stand strong. It was the least I could do to honor her memory.

As the screen faded to black, the pastor introduced several family members to take the stage. My breath caught when I saw her: Johanna, Anna's mother. She made her way to the top of the platform. The movements of her crutches were slow and precise. Guiding her carefully up each step was the man I presumed to be Anna's father.

I shrunk down a few inches to conceal my identity in the crowd. The whispers and finger-pointing during the last couple of days had been hard to swallow, but as the only guilty party in this horrible tragedy, they had not been misguided. Even so, I would not allow for that distraction today.

Johanna took the stage.

Though I had been invited by her, I felt like an impostor the second she addressed the crowd, reading from her letter on the podium.

"Dear loved ones; family and friends of Anna..."

I was neither of those things

She read on, making note of the kind gestures that the community and church members had provided for them in the last week; the week her world had been turned upside down. Her sweet smile was behind every word she spoke, even though tears flowed down her rounded cheeks. Briefly, I envisioned a rainbow captured by the slightest hint of sunlight and unhindered by the dark rainstorm still present overhead. That's what Johanna was: a rainbow amidst a storm. Something raw and contagious tugged at my heart as I watched her. More than mourning or grief, she seemed to have a rare discernment, one that made me deeply uncomfortable and claustrophobic.

I was the wolf in sheep's clothing.

I looked up for just a moment from the stain on the carpet I'd been staring at, when Johanna found me and held my gaze. I was frozen.

"Though our sweet Anna is gone...we know where she now resides. May her life be a reflection of love, forgiveness and grace. Even in the darkness there can be light, and even in the hardest circumstances we face, there can be hope."

In an instant, I was breaking free from the hold of Jack and Stacie and running for the exit door. The usher opened it for me quickly, but even in the fresh April night air I choked with panic. My body shuddered and convulsed with insurmountable force. Breath could not fill my lungs quickly enough. My heart slammed against my chest over and over to the point I wished it would just explode, taking me with it.

A minute later, hands were on me, pulling me to the curb.

"Tori, what's going on? What's happening?" Jack asked, helping me sit as he pulled me closer to him. Stacie smashed herself onto my other side.

I couldn't answer; my body was not my own.

She shouldn't have died.

Why was I spared? Why wasn't it me?

"You're fine now Tori, you're safe. It will be okay, you *will* get through this," Stacie lulled in my ear.

No...Anna is gone—dead!

I couldn't save her.

I let her die.

Another wave of hysteria ripped through my body, this time

bringing fresh, hot tears with it. My body shook with sobs that did not seem human; sobs that I could not control. Sobs that would never change the outcome of the innocent life lost. I knew in those few intense moments of clarity that life as I had known it had forever changed. My tears would only serve to obstruct the pain and hold back my will to survive.

Guilt has a way of replacing one's natural survival instinct with a purpose of its own; a purpose that can never right the past, but if allowed, can dictate the future.

There was but one purpose to the future I now called my own: to give it *all for Anna*.

ONE

- 17 months later -

I sat picking the invisible lint off my perfectly pressed indigo scrubs. The waiting room was like any of the others in the hospital, except smaller and more isolated. To my left were a private staff lounge and a large conference room that held discussions of lengthy experimental procedures and drug trials, or the occasional lecture given by some uppity doctor with more letters after his name than I cared to count. To my right was a hallway. I leaned my head against the wall and recited the mantra that I had practiced for every interview Human Resources had scheduled me for.

This was my last hurdle to get over. Though I had already been guaranteed the job, thanks to my good references and resume, interviews made me anxious. I wondered, briefly, if a psych interview was standard for every Trauma RN who was hired at Dallas Northwest. But even if it was not, I would do as I always did, regardless of what she asked: minimal answers, facts only. I breathed in deeply, already feeling the perspiration on my palms.

Only facts, I can do this.

A loud clicking sound echoed in the hall to my right, stopping in front of me. I lifted my head.

"Victoria Sales?"

"Yes?" My throat was suddenly dry and scratchy.

"I'm Dr. Crane, please follow me. Next time, feel free to come right in through this door at your appointment time. I have a private waiting room attached to my office. There's a couch inside that I think you'll find much more comfortable than the chairs out here."

"Thank you." I followed her obediently.

Two things I learned from Dr. Crane in that short introduction: that she was already planning a second appointment, and that she seemed to pretend my level of comfort was her utmost priority.

Passing through the "couch room", I entered a dimly lit office full of modern furniture that I was positive came from IKEA. The white-noise machine was set to a low hum in the corner and was almost hidden by the overgrown plant that reminded me of something I'd seen in the movie *Jumanji*. In the other corner stood a long, chrome light that was bent in a very unnatural way, defying gravity as it swooned over a hard leather sofa.

Her chair was a perfect fit to what I had observed of her thus far. A mirror image, if there could be one between human and chair: tightly fit, perfectly proportioned, no frills, no cushion and no flexibility. She sat and cleared her throat, forcing a tight, awkward smile.

"Well, Ms. Sales, it's nice to finally meet you. Dr. Bradley had many wonderful things to say about you when she called me a couple weeks ago regarding your transfer. I was sad to see her relocate to Arizona Medical after all her years here at Dallas Northwest, but she seems to be quite content there in Phoenix," she paused momentarily nodding in my direction. "I hope your transition to Texas is as beneficial."

Her eyes were kind, but her voice indicated that there was much more than my list of positive attributes she would be discussing with me.

"Thank you," I said, trying to calm my rapidly increasing heart rate.

"Dr. Bradley and I met way back in med school and strangely enough, we both ended up here in Dallas to do our residencies. It's actually quite an interesting story..."

She stopped short as my expression apparently did not change enough for her to recount it to me. I was relieved. I had no interest in hearing about her *glory days* with Dr. Bradley—although on second thought, maybe it would be better to keep *her* talking so that I wouldn't have to. I opened my mouth to ask her more about her reminiscing, but it was too late. Her hand had already reached for my file and it now lay open on her lap.

"The important thing, Ms. Sales, is that Dr. Bradley has recommended that you see me before starting your new position at this hospital. Although she spoke highly of your abilities as a trauma nurse—which is really saying something for a woman of your age—she also had some concerning observations," she said.

"Concerning observations?"

"Yes. Not only is it a priority of mine that the staff at this hospital be in a place of mental and emotional well-being, it is a necessity in a position like yours. After reviewing your file and speaking with Dr. Bradley, it is my recommendation that you complete a minimum of six sessions with me."

Her words felt weighted; hitting me like a surprise punch to the gut. I worked hard to process them. My mind was in overdrive.

"I'm just a little confused, Dr. Crane. I was told I have the job. I was already given a start date. Is this a new condition to my hiring?" I asked, feeling my face flush with heat.

She leaned in, studying me carefully before she spoke. "This may not be standard protocol in the hiring process Ms. Sales, but it's my job and my responsibility to make sure that all medical staff at this hospital are in a healthy place in regard to their mental and emotional stability. To hear anything contrary to that, especially from a colleague I greatly respect, is to put this hospital, its staff and its patients at risk."

The heat that had warmed my cheeks now burned hot in my chest. The logical explanation she gave was not the reason for my fury, but the person behind it was: Dr. Bradley. I could say nothing, but inside my mind a battle raged.

Why did she do this to me?

She was the one who pushed me to move back here—to the only place on earth I had hoped to avoid. She was the one who had told me to put Stacie first...and then she sabotages me once I'm here?

"You may start your first shift on Monday as planned, but you will not be fully released with privileges at this hospital until I sign off at the end of our sessions. That means, specifically, that you will not be allowed to work any extra shifts or hours in the meantime. It sounds like that will be quite an adjustment for you," she said, a faint smile on her lips, "I have the time right now if you'd like to begin your first session today?"

I took a deep breath. Looking around her office I avoided her gaze like the plague. Whatever game she was playing, I would play it better.

"Fine, what would you like to know?"

A cold, eerie feeling washed over me as I spoke. I knew what I had to do.

Stick to the facts, Tori, just stick to the facts.

****

"Well, first, I'd like to get to know you a bit before we dive into the obvious. Can you tell me a little about yourself and your family?" She smiled as she rolled her pen between her thumb and index finger.

I swallowed hard and exhaled once again.

"Well, as I'm sure you know, I recently turned twenty-three. I'm an RN and have worked in the trauma unit for the last fourteen months at Arizona Medical. I graduated from UT Southwestern in the spring of 2010. I have a sister who's five years older than me and expecting her first baby at the end of the year, and my folks are both real estate brokers in the area. I think that pretty much sums it up," I said, working hard to keep the cynical tone out of my voice.

"And your sister…Stacie, is it?" she asked while looking down at my file.

I nodded.

"She's the reason you came back to Texas? Can you tell me a little about that? Why did you leave Phoenix to move back here?"

"Yes, her husband received a promotion in his company and had to fulfill a six month contract in Australia. She asked me to transfer to Dallas and live with her during her pregnancy. They have an extra room and offered to cover my expenses so I could pay off my school loans. Stacie didn't want to be alone and Jack isn't scheduled to fly back until she's in her eighth month of pregnancy," I answered without inflection.

I felt pleased with myself for throwing in those extra details where I usually wouldn't. But I knew that the more I added to this part, the less time there would be for questions later—at least that's what I hoped.

She looked at me for what felt like an eternity and then said, "That sounds like a great offer. Were you quick to say yes? Or, was this decision something you had to process through when you decided to move back to Dallas?"

I never wanted to come back here.

"It was fairly quick; my sister needed me. I wanted to help her."

At least wanting to help Stacie was the truth.

"How do you feel about being near your parents again? You moved so soon after your graduation."

Her tone was far more accusatory than inquisitive.

I narrowed my eyes at her. "It will definitely improve my commute to family dinners—so I suppose that's a plus."

I wiped my wet palms on my knees slowly shifting my gaze to

the floor, wishing it would open up and swallow me whole.

"Mm-hmm, I see," she said, adding more quick scratches on her note pad. "Victoria—may I call you Victoria? Was your plan always to move to Phoenix after graduating from nursing school?"

I froze for a moment, not quite prepared for that question.

"I had several options I was considering, but Arizona Medical Hospital was the best choice for me," I said, pushing down the truth that was burning in my throat.

"When I reviewed your file…it looked like you had already taken a job at our sister hospital in east Dallas prior to your graduation—in Labor and Delivery," she said, "Only you quit just weeks later to be re-hired in Phoenix, in the Trauma unit, is that correct?"

More information from the traitor I assume.

"Yes, that's correct."

"Would that have to do with what occurred the evening of April 9th, 2010, just eight weeks before your graduation?" she asked, leaning in to help close the gap between us. Only it wasn't a gap, it was a chasm that stretched the three feet between my couch and her chair.

I leaned back and pressed my body against the cold, hard leather knowing full well the line of questioning that was going to be asked next. I prepared for the mantra to come out just as I had recited it in my head.

"On April 9th, 2010, there was a bad storm and I was involved in a car accident that resulted in one fatality."

A light chiming sound went off near the *Jumanji* plant in the corner indicating our time was up. She didn't move and neither did I as she said, "Next session I'd like to talk more about what your life looked like before the accident, Victoria. It will give me a baseline to judge how you're doing now."

I stood then, turning my head toward her.

"There is no before—only after."

And that might have been the only real truth spoken in that room today.

TWO

Commuting into the heart of suburbia was going to take some adjustment on my part. I had grown very fond of my little apartment in downtown Phoenix. It may have been cramped, but it was just my style. Space was a luxury I did not require.

Pulling into my sister's driveway, I took a deep breath and prepared for the whirlwind of questions she was sure to ask about my day. That was precisely why I had already decided to get my running shoes on as fast as humanly possible. I needed to think—or maybe not to think, I wasn't quite sure which. Whatever the case, one thing was certain: the pressure building inside me would soon explode if I didn't combat it first.

"Tori, is that you? I'm so happy you're home! I just got back from Home Depot and grabbed some swatches for painting your room. I thought we could decide on a color together," Stacie said from somewhere in the monstrous upstairs, her sing-song voice filling the house.

"Oh? And *who* will be doing this painting project, Stace?" I asked, mocking her. I knew the response even before she answered.

Stacie may have décor vision, but her inner D.I.Y. superstar got the pink slip a long time ago. The girl couldn't craft, color, paint, glue or finish any project without creating a disaster zone. A few years back there was a sit-down intervention after she glued her fingers to a messy Mod-Podge frame. We made her promise to let someone else execute her design ideas from then on. I'm still unclear as to why superglue had been a part of that equation.

"Very funny, I'll hire it out, I promise. Even if I *wanted* to paint, it's against the pregnancy rules. Hey, how did your last interview go?"

I climbed the stairs to my bedroom where she stood waiting for me. Her short blond curls bounced as she spoke. I looked beyond her into my room where several boxes and Hefty Bags sat in the corner, needing to be unpacked.

"It was fine," I quipped.

One benefit of my small apartment in Phoenix was there wasn't much to move back. My room at Stacie's was large enough to fit nearly all of the contents that were once contained within the walls of my old living quarters. From the doorway I could see my couch, coffee table, TV, bed, desk, and dresser. I also had an attached bath, fully equipped with a soaking tub, shower, and two sinks. Overkill? I think so.

"Do you ever give any other answer than, *'fine'?*" Stacie asked, rolling her eyes.

"It was an interview, Stace. Boring. Routine. It was...fine," I said shrugging.

As I walked past her, my heart tugged a little at the lie, but I didn't want to talk. I *needed* to run. I changed quickly and pulled on my shoes as she stood in the door frame watching me curiously.

"What...are you doing?" she asked.

"I'm going for a run."

"A run? *You?* Is that what you've been doing each morning before I've gotten out of bed?"

"Yep...sorry, I'll try to be quieter," I said slipping past her into the hallway.

"No, that's not my point." She turned and followed me as I made my way down the stairs. "When did you start running, Tori? You *hate* exercise, you *hate* sweating...I don't even think you like nature!"

That's the point.

"People change, I guess," I said as I reached the front door.

"Well, I've been meaning to tell you that your body looks really great," she called after me.

Stacie was known for her innocent quips and positive nature. Opening the front door, I shook my head and smiled sadly. I could picture her standing in the entryway trying to figure me out.

Give it up, Stace. You'll never figure me out.

I can't even do that.

I started to jog, throwing my shoulder-length brown hair back into a ponytail. I could see a few rogue pieces poking out of the side in my peripheral vision as I re-adjusted my sunglasses. I picked up the pace. The September heat filled up my lungs and burned my skin with its unforgiving rays. Texas was brutal, but so was Arizona. If I could run there, I could run anywhere.

I rounded the corner near the man-made pond in the middle of the neighborhood and saw a group of children laughing as they ran through sprinklers. In the northern states, trees were already losing their leaves, but in Texas, kids would be enjoying pool days for at least another month. I watched the kids play and shove each other over the water stream and instantly I was there again, sucked into the dark places of my mind which blinded me from the present.

I can feel her limp body in my arms, her small frame sagging under the weight of her blood and rain soaked clothing. I see her mother stumbling out of the car in shock as she moves toward me. She gasps for breath and then sinks to her knees, unconscious. I push harder on the gaping wound that used to be the side of her abdomen—once smooth, skin-covered, and normal. I won't let go, I can't let go. I know how to help her! But then I'm lifted up—pulled away. The hands on me are too strong and I am too weak to shrug them off. I struggle, screaming something...and then it fades to black.

It is always the same, always.

Every pore on my body was sweating.

I pushed on, propelling my feet forward. I wouldn't feel that pain again; I couldn't feel that pain again.

Why did Dr. Bradley have to stir all this up? What is the point?

I was doing fine—managing.

I had been an excellent employee and she knew as well as I did that none of this would interfere with my job—I would never let it.

I didn't even need her recommendation!

I sincerely regretted asking her for it now.

She spent all that time gaining my trust, watching me work...only to sell me out to a shrink to "fix me" in the end.

I slowed my pace, wiping perspiration from my eyes. I realized the irony of that simple, automatic gesture. Most people burdened by pain wiped away tears, but my pain would only ever yield sweat.

I no longer had tears to cry.

As I stood in front of Stacie's large, rustic front door, a reflection caught my eye within its framed glass. For a moment, I couldn't even place who this red-faced, athletic impostor was. And then I saw it, the five inch scar that traced the side of my forehead and curved its way down below my left temple: a permanent identification mark.

"Mom called you again, Tori," Stacie said the second I pushed open the front door.

I grabbed my water bottle off the kitchen counter and chugged it until I had no breath left at all. Stacie walked in.

"Dear God, Tori! You look like—I don't even know what! I don't think running in this heat is healthy."

"Its fine…I ran in…Arizona…I can…run…here…too," I said, panting.

I leaned over the sink and poured the excess water on my face and head.

"Well, okay. Just be careful. Dehydration is a real thing, you know?"

"Really, Nurse Stacie? Please enlighten me on the body's response to dehydration."

"Fine, sassy pants, but don't say I didn't tell you when you drop dead from heat stroke one day."

I smiled at her to make nice, though we both knew who would win this battle of wits. "Well, in that case I'd be dead, so I probably wouldn't be sayin' too much. What did Mom have to say, anyway?"

Stacie rolled her eyes at me as her hand rested on her growing baby bump. "She said we are invited to a dinner at their place tomorrow night. There will be a few friends, lots of cook-out food and the pool, of course. I may have accidently told her that you weren't scheduled at the hospital until Monday…which kinda turned into an accepted invitation. I'm sorry, but she has called *three* times already! I couldn't keep making excuses for you."

Stacie sheepishly bowed her head. She lifted her eyes slightly to peek at my face, preparing herself for a verbal beating. I was simply too spent to give her one, though. I laced my fingers together and gripped the back of my neck, exhaling hard.

It was time.

I had been dreading seeing my parents since the day Stacie asked me to move back. She was right though. I'd been home for almost a week and hadn't yet made time for the inevitable guilt trip I'd receive when I saw them—as if I didn't carry enough guilt for one lifetime already.

THREE

Hefty Bags gone, boxes unpacked and paint swatches chosen, I was beginning to feel a bit more settled while living in Stacie's brick mansion. A big part of me was still in denial that my perfect plan to stay in Phoenix forever had failed. I had liked working in the number two trauma city in the nation. But, perhaps, I had liked the distance even more. Maintaining relationships had been off my priority radar for some time now.

If there were an upside to living in Dallas, it certainly wasn't the close proximity to certain family members, but rather the promotion to *first place* on the trauma rating scale. The work would keep me busy and the busyness would keep me sane—I hoped.

I sighed, thinking again about the therapy sign off with Dr. Crane. If anything would bring into question my level of sanity, it would be the hours of talking with her. I wasn't much of a socialite. Talking seemed useless to me, unless there was a patient involved. That, at least, had a purpose.

I pulled on my jean capris and black tank top and brushed my hair back into a low twist. I secured it loosely with a few bobby pins. Glancing in the mirror, I surrendered myself to the help of my makeup bag that often sat unused. This was merely an attempt to ward off the "Tori, you-look-too-tired" speech from my mother. I had never been a girl who cared much about makeup or fussed over the perfect accessories, handbags or shoes. Powder, concealer, eyeliner, mascara and lip-gloss were about all I owned in the makeup department.

My brown, slightly auburn hair, was almost always worn up in some simple style that was quick and easy. I applied the concealer under my eyes and dusted the powder over my face to set it. The contrast of my olive skin tone to Stacie's fair, almost translucent skin had been a running joke in my family for years. Born five years after my sister, I questioned for nearly a decade if I had been adopted.

My mother could have been Stacie's twin in practically every way, including their matching blond hair. My eyes were dark green while theirs were a brilliant blue. It was yet one more area I didn't fit the *Sales' mold*.

Stacie's car was already running in the garage with the air

conditioning blasting. Pregnancy had given her less tolerance for heat as it had been a relentless source of nausea during her first trimester. Her job as the Marketing Director for the Sales Real Estate Company our parents owned had been flexible enough, allowing her to work from home during the worst part of the summer. That also explained why her house was an unchanging 69 degrees inside.

"You ready to go, Sis?" Stacie asked in her usual perky tone.

Is a cow ready for slaughter? No…not ready, just hopeless.

In the twenty-minute drive to our parents' house, Stacie filled me in on the latest news regarding our family friends. She also included the nicknames that she and Jack had made up for the people they could never remember names for. I laughed lightly and saw her smile at me, knowing the feelings she couldn't hide. She was glad I was here with her.

My mind slipped away as she gave me an update on the family company. She explained how business had started to pick back up again after the industry had slowed due to a recessed economy. Her bubbly personality was the perfect match to any kind of depression one might face in life. Whether it was economical or emotional, Stacie was unrelenting in her positive vibes.

We passed the acres of farmland and corn stalks that were as tall as a full grown adult. A memory of Stacie and I running in such fields flooded my mind. We had loved to play hide-and-go-seek in the fall just before it was time to harvest. Farmer Johnson, who lived next to my parents, had given his blessing for us to play in his fields as long as we helped sell his corn on the side of the road for a couple weeks after school was out. He had even paid us, although I was sure we took home more corn than any monetary wage we might have earned during our two week employment. There was nothing tastier than fresh, sweet corn on the cob.

One fall in late September, Stacie called to me just a few feet into the stalks. Her voice was high-pitched and frantic. A jack rabbit lay on its side, very still, breathing slow quiet breaths. It had obviously been hopping for a long time with the trap attached to its right hind-leg, and was too exhausted to keep up the fight.

Our dad had never been a hunter or trapper. He was too involved in the business world to have a hobby like that. Yet somehow, I figured out how to release it.

Stacie was crying and stroking the wild rabbit, beside herself with grief. Once the rabbit was freed I told Stacie we needed to find it a place to rest so it could heal. I carried the rabbit home and then found an old cat carrier in the garage to put him in after wrapping the bloody leg with gauze and tape. Salad scraps, water, and some newspaper were put inside its new shelter.

Our dad was very proud of our efforts with the rabbit we eventually named Snowcap, but felt it needed extra medical attention. After a visit to the vet, antibiotics and lots of rest, Snowcap was ours to keep. Stacie and I had bonded that day as more than just sisters, but as partners. We had worked together to save a life.

Stacie reached for my hand as we pulled into the driveway.

"Tori, I know this is…difficult, but I am so happy you are home. Jack would have never agreed to go overseas this long if you hadn't decided to come. I'm…I'm just so-"

Her eyes welled up with tears.

"It's good to be with you too, Stace. Let's go in and get this over with, okay?" I said, not wanting to be stuck in the car with an emotionally-charged pregnant lady any longer than I had to be.

****

If Stacie's house was a mansion, then my parent's house was a kingdom. Right in the middle of twenty acres stood an enormous estate. It featured: six bedrooms, four baths, an in-home theater, chef's kitchen, three formal dining areas, a driving range and a large outdoor swimming pool and spa retreat. The land was meticulously maintained and manicured down to the minutest detail.

There were rocks, plants, small bridges, koi ponds, outdoor grills and patio furniture to seat an army. Japanese lanterns were strung everywhere. It was a spectacle for sure.

The home was built for a magazine cover, not for real life. But that was my mother: proud, pretty, and perfect, a southern woman through and through.

I saw her immediately as I stepped outside onto the patio, my breathing paused with apprehension. I looked across the yard at the huge crowd that had apparently been invited to this *intimate* affair. A glass clanged in the distance and my mother floated over to me in her A-line skirt and heels. She hugged me dramatically in front of her guests. My eyes darted to Stacie who mouthed, "I'm sorry," as she hid behind the food table.

Apparently, I'm in this alone.
Awesome.

"Everyone, everyone, may I have your attention please! Our guest of honor has arrived. Please help us in welcoming our daughter home from Phoenix and in congratulating her on her new job at Dallas Northwest," my mother said. Her voice had carried over the crowd that filled the patio and yard. People I hadn't seen in years and some I had never seen clapped and hollered, "Congrats!", while I stood there completely speechless.

I turned to my mom, who wore pink pearls and a silk sleeveless blouse, and stared blankly. She pulled me in for another hug. This time I felt weak in the knees. I hugged about as much as I went on coffee dates with my girlfriends— never.

"Victoria, can you say something to the crowd please? They all came here for you dear," she whispered.

Does she really believe I'm that stupid? These people don't even know me! Inside I shook with anger, embarrassment and shock…yet somehow, I managed to speak.

"Uh, wow. Thank you everyone…for coming out this evening. It's…nice to be back."

I forced the last of the words out of my mouth. What I really felt was quite the opposite. I wanted to be back in Phoenix, alone in my small cramped apartment, the apartment that was only large enough to fit me. If I could click my heels and be transported, I would have in a heartbeat. I heard the toasting and cheers and within seconds I was headed inside, the unmistakable sound of my mother's heels coming after me quickly.

"Were you surprised darling?" my mother asked.

Calm down. She doesn't understand me. She will NEVER understand me.

"Yes Mom…pretty surprised," I said, feeling flushed and shaky.

"Well, I know you don't like people fussin' over you, but I thought it would be so nice for everyone to get a chance to see you. It's been so long since you've been back, Victoria, and people ask about you all the time," my mother said through her southern grin of hospitality.

I'm sure they do, Mom. Most people don't know many child killers, especially one who is the daughter of two wealthy, church-going realtors.

I took a deep breath, searching for the words to say, when I saw my dad walk through the doorway. At the sight of him I wanted to crumble. He had always been my rock, my pillar, my calm within the chaos of the storm that raged inside the Sales house. As such, he had made the rare effort to understand me for who I was. He seemed to understand that although I wasn't a show-stopper the way my mom and sister were, with their high dramatics and socialisms, that I still held an important place in this family—or used to, anyway. He smiled hugely as he neared, never taking his eyes away from my face.

He shook his head slowly in admiration, "Tori...I've missed you baby girl."

He waited for my silent permission before extending his long lean arms around my shoulders, pressing his cheek to the top of my head. In that instant, the anger I held toward my mom vanished.

"Hi, Dad."

Emotion filled me in a way it hadn't in over a year. I swallowed hard to fight it back down.

"Your mom was pretty excited about seeing you tonight darlin' and throwing this big bash for you and all. I hope you can take one for the team here, Sis," he said. He winked at me as he spoke. He was always respectful of my mother, even when he knew she was over-the-top.

"Yes, of course. Thank you, Mom," I said, obediently.

"Great, well let's get you back out there then." She gave me a playful shove and said, "And Victoria, you look *real* good sweetheart."

And there it was: looking good was worth far more than feeling good. That's the magic ticket around these parts.

For the next couple of hours, I was surface deep with three types of people: those who knew me before the accident, those who knew my family and heard the reports of the accident, and those who were curious about how a twenty-three year-old girl survived one of the most well-known tragedies to happen in this small town just east of Dallas. I could feel my panic surfacing with each new face that approached me during the evening, but no one mentioned the accident (thank you Dad for laying down the ground rules).

I heard a loud splash followed by rounds of laughter as I watched several young men dive into the pool. I didn't hesitate for a second at the crowd's distraction. I barreled quickly through the yard glancing around briefly for Stacie. I found her alright. Feet propped up—laughing hard—with a cup of ice on her lap.

Note to self: Drive my own car next time.

I looked for an escape and saw a hint of my beloved bridge to the far left of the house. I walked swiftly and with purpose, doing my best to avoid a probing parent or nosy neighbor. I needed to sit, decompress, and get centered—whatever that meant. As I approached the bridge, the dusk lighting shifted around a tall shape. At first I thought it was a tree, but it didn't move like a tree. I got closer and realized my idea for finding peace was not that original. I was not the first to make a claim on this bridge tonight.

"Oh-" I said startled, "Sorry, I was just…uh-"

WHAT? What was I just?

"Leaving," I said.

I started to turn; embarrassed as the man I thought was a tree stepped into the shadowy light. His features were strong and he had piercingly dark eyes, which, like his hair, shimmered in the glow of the moonlight.

"Victoria, right?" he asked, with a voice that was as rich and smooth as decadent chocolate.

"Uh, do I…know you?" I asked, peering into the darkness.

"No, but you're the guest of honor, so I guess everyone knows you now, right?" he joked.

"Oh…right. Forgot I was *announced* earlier," I said.

I looked away to break the awkwardness I felt standing alone in the dark with this stranger, a very good-looking stranger at that.

"Was I in your way out here?" His tone sounded amused, as one corner of his mouth lifted slightly into a smile.

"No, I just…I just like to take a little time to walk and enjoy the property when I come out here. This is one of my-favorite spots," I lied, but at least it made sense…*maybe?*

"Yeah, your parents have a very nice property out here. It's hard to believe that we're only twenty minutes away from Dallas. Feels like true Texan country." His eyes searched mine for longer than I felt comfortable, and I broke the gaze again to stare at the dark ground, "Although, it's got to be kinda hard to *enjoy* it when it's too dark to see where you're walking, don't you think?" the man asked, repressing a laugh.

I did not find his joke funny, but I did find something else—my voice. Good looking or not, I would not be his punch line.

Okay Tree Man…you're on.

"Well, I don't really need much light since I've been out here a thousand times. I can understand though, how it might be a little harder for a guy who's at a party for someone he's never even met until now. Excuse me; I need to go check on my guests."

My voice shook and my face burned from embarrassment as I turned away. As I headed toward the patio, begging my eyes to adjust to the darkness, I thought I heard him say, "That's not entirely true."

But I didn't care to banter with him, not at my expense anyway.

After another round of hugs and false promises to stay in touch now that the prodigal child had returned, Stacie and I left the party. I was utterly exhausted. And for the first time since the accident, I thought about something other than that horrible night while riding in a car after dark.

I thought about the stranger at the bridge.

FOUR

After a lengthy process at security, I left with my new hospital ID badge in hand and took the elevator up to the 6th floor. Today was session two. My long weekend of thinking and rationalizing made me realize these sessions were just a means to an end. If I wanted to work—and I *wanted* to work—then I had to get through them. Facts only, of course.

The first half hour was filled with mindless information regarding my high school hobbies, my college experiences, roommates and a lot more detail about my relationship with my parents. At least the church history was easy enough—it was just that, history. I was feeling strong, capable and apathetic as usual, ready to take on the firing squad of questions that was sure to come next. Dr. Crane sat across from me, her legs crossed. After busily scratching on her notepad, she looked up, perfectly poised.

...and armed with her secret arsenal.

"Victoria...I know it must be difficult to talk about the events of April 9, 2010, but I want to hear them from you—in your own words. Take as much time as you need and I will only interject with questions if necessary. Please start prior to getting in your car that night. Let's just see how far we can get today. If we need to continue at a later date we will."

Her voice was gentle as she spoke. I wasn't sure why, but that seemed to cause me to feel quite unsettled. I rubbed my hands on my knees.

Despite all my preparedness, the facts that circled in my head were difficult to separate from the relentless dreams and flashbacks that had made this nightmare my constant reality. It was a nightmare I had revisited every day for the past seventeen months. I took a deep breath and closed my eyes, shoving down the vividness that had not lessened with time. My only goal was to try and speak from a place on the sidelines.

You can do this, Tori...tell her. Tell her the facts, then you can get back to work.

"It was a three day weekend in April, eight weeks before graduation. I was working at Dallas East, and studying for my Boards. That night was my sister's birthday dinner held out at my parents' house in Middleton. I got off late, so I was running behind schedule, but I made it in time for the dinner."

Just in time to be seated and avoid the dirty looks from my mother. She would see my tardiness as rude, even though I had been awake for nearly twenty-six hours straight. She had no clue that I had just aided in an emergency C-section where both mother and baby were in critical condition when I left.

But there are no excuses in the Sales house.

"The party went well into the evening. After the cake and gifts, the guests started to leave. I had only had one day off, and I really wanted to get caught up on sleep so that I could study. When I left, I noticed a change in the temperature outside, but chalked it up to the weird weather patterns of Dallas. About two miles down the road, Stacie called and said there was a severe weather warning issued for all Collin and Dallas Counties. She told me I should turn around and go back and stay with them for the night."

I paused; reflecting for a moment on what was my biggest regret from that night, and likely my whole life.

I had ignored her warning. I did not turn around.

Why didn't I just turn around? I was too selfish and self-centered; I thought I was immortal.

Unfortunately, I was.

"But the roads and sky were clear, and I saw no immediate threat. I just wanted to get home. I thought I could get back to my apartment before the storm hit, but a few minutes after I hung up with Stacie, I heard the sirens start."

"The tornado sirens?"

"Yes. Just seconds after I heard them I saw the first lightning flash, and then felt the rumble of the thunder."

I paused again. This time it took longer to push the memory down and find the facts.

What were the facts?

"You're doing great, Victoria, please continue," she said, leaning into my space.

The hail came next.

"The hail started. It came down hard and fast. I slowed my car some, but the tornado sirens urged me to find shelter as quickly as possible. The hail continued to get more intense and larger in size. I thought it was going to come right through the roof of my Honda. The buildup of hail on the ground made it slick and I couldn't see anything. The power on the road had gone out and I couldn't even see the yellow divider between the two lanes anymore. There was no shoulder to pull off to and no shelter nearby."

I shifted uncomfortably on the sofa, rubbing my palms on my knees, creating friction.

"As I approached a slight curve I saw the headlights of an oncoming car. I was trying to pull over to the far right of my lane, but had barely started to slow when the back of the oncoming car appeared out of the hail. It all happened so fast."

Dr. Crane sat looking at me intensely, no longer writing on her notepad. She waited for me to continue.

"As my front bumper slammed into the rear wheel of the driver's side, both vehicles spun to opposite sides of the road. I got out of my car the second I came to and crawled across the road to the other vehicle. It had spun completely around and was pointing back in the direction it had come from.

"The hail had shifted back to hard rain when I reached up, opened the front passenger door and looked inside. When my vision focused, I saw the driver slumped down in the seat, unconscious. I crawled across the seat, assessed her injuries and was able to support her neck with a jacket that I found on the floor. I looked in the back and noticed the passenger door was ajar. That's when I saw the empty booster seat."

"Victoria...I hate to stop there for today, but we are almost out of time and I have a patient right after you. We can pick up there during our next session, but I am curious as to your own injuries sustained that night. You said you *crawled* across the road? Why was that, were you in shock?"

I still am.

"I didn't care much about my injuries. I'm a nurse, I'm trained to help others," I said quickly, the hardness of my tone breaking my voice.

"But you did have injuries, correct?" she asked, again.

"Yes. I sustained two cracked ribs, a laceration to my forehead along with a concussion, but nothing major."

I stared at my shoes, not wanting to see any sign of sympathy or pity on her face. My injuries were minor in comparison, but as we both knew, there was no comparison to death.

"I wouldn't call that minor," she said, "And you still went after the other victims and treated them? That sounds a bit heroic to me, wouldn't you agree?"

Heroes don't let innocent children die.

The chime broke my silence.

Dr. Crane snapped my folder shut and took a deep breath, as if cleansing my aura from the room.

"I'd like to see you back Friday morning prior to your shift. Please don't let yourself shut down, Victoria. I know this must be painful, but it's an important step to retell the details of what happened that night. It's then that we can work through the *aftermath*. I have spoken with your charge nurse, Meg Holt, regarding your schedule. You are set to work three 12 hour shifts a week, rotating weekends like the others. The only exception is, of course, no on-call hours or extra shifts until I sign off. It's important that you let yourself rest and reflect as we go through this process."

"And what process is this exactly?" I asked, looking up for the first time.

I could not even begin to contemplate what *four* days a week of no work would do to me. My brows furrowed, pushing down the scream welling up inside my chest. I knew though, it wasn't meant for Dr. Crane.

It was meant for Dr. Susan Bradley, my *friend* in question.

"Well, let's get into that on Friday, shall we? I'd rather have more time to discuss it with you properly. Enjoy your first day back in Trauma, Victoria."

I felt the pressure rising again in my chest as I left her office. I walked quickly to the restroom, once there I turned on the cold water. Soaking my hands and wrists, I stared at the woman reflected in the mirror. I leaned in to examine the *aftermath* on my face. It was my scarlet letter, reminding me and everyone else of the hideous debt that forever marked my life. No amount of powder or cover-up could erase it entirely.

It *was* me now.

I closed my eyes, seeing her again.

Anna.

I brush her long, blond, blood-stained hair off her face; her lips and cheek already swelling from where she hit the ground just minutes before. She is limp and unresponsive, and there is so much blood. The trauma that sought to tear through her innocent body, however, had failed to mask her beauty. I have never wanted anything as much as to see her breathe. I have never prayed for something so hard.

I rip off my shirt, using it as a compress for the wound on her side. I try in vain to do CPR. I keep going until I can't see, can't hear, and can no longer feel.

And then I'm lifted. The strong hands pull me up—pulling me off of her. I scream until my world goes dark. I have failed.

I found my reflection again in the mirror.

Only four more sessions…and then I can bury this back down and never talk about it again…to anyone.

The clock told me I had exactly 45 minutes until my first shift started. I exhaled deeply and headed toward the elevators. All first floor Emergency Rooms have the same general look no matter which city in the U.S. one lived. Emergency was Emergency.

The smell greeted me immediately, like a long-lost friend coming to visit. Other people might be repulsed by the smell of hospitals—a mixture of sweat, urine, vomit, and bleach—but to me it was *home*. My first couple of weeks would be spent shadowing a senior Trauma RN while learning the protocols and layout of Dallas Northwest Hospital. Due to my age, I was still considered "green" in the eyes of any Emergency Staff team. To me that simply meant that saving lives could not be my only purpose; I also needed to prove myself.

My "initiation" into the ER in Phoenix was so far beyond anything I had ever seen or experienced prior. I had done some work as a tech in Urgent Care during my first couple years of nursing school. That was probably the only reason my resume and application were accepted so quickly. That and the fact they were desperate for help.

The supply and demand for trauma nurses was well matched with its position as second highest trauma city in the country. They didn't seem to mind that I had been a CNA in Labor and Delivery the year prior to graduating, nor did they question my drastic switch from wanting to specialize in birthing babies, to stabbings, broken skulls and overdoses.

That first week in Phoenix had been mind-blowing, and my fear so intense that I was often paralyzed by it. A trauma nurse could be wrapping a broken arm one minute and the next be assisting in pulling a lead pipe out of someone's chest.

What happened in the Emergency Rooms of large metropolitan cities were the nightmares your nightmares had while they slept. People who came through Emergency lived to tell their stories of horror. Those that didn't leave often died after living out their worst-case scenario. That's what Trauma was, a world of worst-case scenarios.

After a month of cowering behind the more experienced nurses and pretending to be busy with paperwork, IV's, and administrative tasks, I was called out of hiding. A bus full of high school football players had crashed on the interstate. All hands were needed, including mine, "green" as they were.

I had watched the trauma nurses work quickly and effortlessly, setting shoulders, bandaging open wounds and applying burn towels to the students who had been closest to the engine when it caught fire. All were busy when my patient was rushed in with a severely mangled leg and arm. He was unconscious and receiving CPR by the EMT. I ran to meet them, shaky and uncertain. But then it happened, a rush of adrenaline like I had never experienced before. It was all-consuming.

The EMT who was using the manual resuscitation bag pointed and yelled for me to do chest compressions until we got to the defibrillator. In an instant I was the breath for his lungs as we raced to bay one. Dr. Bradley met us there as the EMT went over his vitals and injuries.

I lifted the paddles and charged them to life, positioning them on his chest. Feeling the power and the terror of death that hung in the balance, I stood with him at fate's door. And just like that, he had a heart beat again.

"Good job today, Green," Dr. Bradley had said later that day.

"It's Tori—and thanks!" I corrected, smiling at her.

"Ha! I'll tell you what, *'it's Tori'*, I'll call you that after you've survived six months here...until then, it's Green," she said.

Though it wasn't as dramatic as pulling a lead pipe from a chest, I had helped a boy come back to life...and I was hooked. The fear would still come, but I no longer hid from the unknown. The adrenaline rushes were more addictive than anything I had ever encountered, and I needed and wanted more.

When adrenaline pumps, every other thought and emotion takes a step back. You are a slave to it; willing to do whatever it asks, no matter what the cost.

And if that cost threatened to make me forget who I was…then I would be a slave to it forever.

FIVE

Noon to midnight was a surprisingly good shift for a newbie in Emergency. It was one that I suspected was not entirely left to *chance*, but I couldn't let myself dwell on the things I couldn't yet control. Soon it wouldn't matter anyway. Once Dr. Crane signed off, I'd be back to working 70 to 80 hours a week if I could just put up with a few more sessions. Last night's shift was pretty much what I had anticipated: tours of the floor, introductions met with unfriendly exchanges from female nurses and overly friendly exchanges from male counterparts who saw me as another fish in their sea.

It had been a relatively slow evening; nothing too dramatic had been called in, which always made for an interesting balance. On the one hand, emergency nurses were happy when the general public didn't break any stupidity meters by getting caught doing something crazy, illegal or dangerous. On the other hand, it was slightly depressing when we couldn't be a part of any extreme lifesaving efforts.

Stacie had been online with Jack for the majority of the morning, which was his tomorrow afternoon in Australia. I could hear her contagious bouts of laughter even through the layers of drywall in between us. They had been high school sweethearts and a couple I had secretly hoped to emulate one day.

Fat chance of that now.

Broken and damaged didn't usually make the top of the list for best life partners.

For almost as far back as I could remember, Jack had been a part of our lives. His jovial personality and big brother-type attitude made him impossible *not* to love. He taught me to drive, ski, and even how to hold and shoot a gun. He was a computer nerd by trade and an over-achiever to any and all experimental feats and activities. He could master almost anything he tried; whether it was fixing an electrical issue, learning a new instrument, or mastering mixed martial arts. He knew how to dissect whatever was at hand and break it down to steps and strategies, overcoming it mentally before he even laid a hand on it. I poked my head in quickly and said hello to him. Then I went to my room and pulled on my running shoes.

"Tori…if you are thinking about running you should go tonight when it cools down a bit! There is a heat advisory out—supposed to be a hundred-and-four degrees by this afternoon!" Stacie called to me from behind her door.

Urgh…it's almost mid-September for crying out loud! Aren't temps supposed to be decreasing instead of increasing already?

"Thanks, I'll be fine!"

I shut the front door before I could hear her argument and then I was off. The air was hot—stifling really. It was like running head-on into an industrial sized blow-dryer, set to high. I avoided the street where the kids had played the other day and headed down to an area with an open field. It was being groomed for yet another street of mirrored brick houses, each of them the size of a city block.

I rounded the corner past the crews of construction workers eating lunch under their makeshift shade. They gawked at me as I ran by. Perhaps they were wondering why anyone would be out running in this heat today.

I was starting to ask myself the same thing.

I became more purposeful with each stride, pushing myself to go on. I had never been one who cared much about the time or distance of my runs. That was not why I had started in the first place. I never had a goal to achieve some physical greatness, or a long distance record.

Running was just a way to deal.

I'm sure there were lots of other ways to cope. Alcohol, for instance, which was good at numbing, seemed too easy and never lasted long enough. It also required more each time I drank, in order to get me to a place of forgetfulness. And was that really what I wanted, to forget Anna? *No.*

Some people in my position with access to pharmaceutical drugs might become pill-poppers, but I had seen how that ended up and I knew that it would only jeopardize my career, and ability to work. There was no room for mistakes in trauma. So, that left me with physical outlets only.

I chose what I hated most: running.

Fighting emotional pain with physical pain made sense to me when not much else had, so I stuck with it. I imagined I had run as far as ten miles on a single jaunt before, and most likely averaged closer to around four or five now. I wiped at my forehead and fanned my shirt in vain trying to vent myself, but to no avail. The sun bore down on me and for a second I thought of the Australian desert.

Had Jack seen it?
I bet it feels just like this…dry, hot, and no mercy for anything living in it.
I pushed on.
Only five blocks to go. You can do this Tori, PUSH!

I ran diagonally through the tall grassy field. I had to get back on the main path which led to Stacie's block. It was then, while I was in the grass, that the ground started to shift.

Right to left.
Left to right.

I shook my head to clear my vision, but it was unrelenting. Everything was distorting. The ground kept moving beneath my feet.

Is this an earthquake?

I tried to run toward the cement sidewalk, but my legs were like rubber and trembled under my weight. My head felt as if it were being pulled down by some invisible rope. It no longer seemed attached to the rest of me.

Regaining balance was impossible.
The ground was coming fast.
Right before I hit, I heard myself utter, "Oh, crap."

****

I heard it long before I could see it, the loud obnoxious sound of a siren. It wasn't too long before I felt myself being lifted up off the ground. The surface I laid on actually seemed harder, if that were possible. I couldn't open my eyes or respond, yet I could still hear in this foggy black world that engulfed me. My head ached, as did my left hip.

I must have fallen on my left side.
Why? Did I trip?

I could hear two distinct voices talking—both male. I felt a tight grip on my upper left arm that was growing more intense with each passing second.

Blood pressure.

Someone is taking my blood pressure.

I tried to lift my head, but it was pushed down.

I tried again, but it was pushed back down. This time I worked to open my heavy eyelids, slowly. Fuzzy shapes were swirling around, dancing before my eyes. If I weren't so desperate to understand what was happening, I would have tried to reach out for them. It was like a freaky side-show. It was then that I felt a prick in my left wrist.

"Ow!"

I swung my right arm in front of me trying to hit whatever or whoever it was that was holding me down. This time, I heard the voice that was attached to my wrist yell, "Okay Mike. Let's take her in to Dallas Northwest."

No...No Please! Stop!

I forced my eyes to focus. I was blinking rapidly when I saw him.

"*Tree Man?*" I asked, completely confused as my head was pushed down yet another time.

"Please relax, Victoria. You have heat exhaustion from running in a hundred degree weather. Did you just call me 'Tree Man'?" he asked, sounding almost as confused as I was.

I felt the ambulance lurch to life and then remembered what was happening.

"Please, no! Don't take me in. I'll be fine, I promise. No more running today. Just take me home, I can rest there!"

"You are dehydrated, overheated and need more fluids than what I have on hand. There were other...*geniuses* like you out there today, believe it or not," he said.

Hey...is he mocking me, again? What's with this guy?

"Please, I can't go there. I just...can't. I'm a Trauma Nurse and just started work there yesterday. I can't let them see me like this. Please! I'll do anything!"

My voice was high and squeaky, very out of character for me, but it came out that way nonetheless. I was desperate. This was not the impression I needed to make at my new place of work. This kind of thing could stick with me for the duration of my nursing career. I could just imagine the nicknames I'd be called...and I just got rid of "Green".

He looked down at me, "Is that a promise?" he asked grinning widely, raising his perfectly groomed eyebrows at me in question.

"Uh, will you take me home?" I asked again, still desperate, but nodding in response.

"Okay. Mike, turn left in two blocks on Baker Ave. It's the third house on the right," he said to the driver.

"How did…who are-"

My head started to pound again before I could finish my question.

"Shhh…just rest. Lay your head back. The home remedy won't be nearly as enjoyable for you, though," he said, chuckling lightly to himself.

We pulled up to Stacie's house.

If being carried in by an EMT while sweaty, hot and delirious wasn't embarrassing enough, seeing my sister in a full-blown panic attack on the sidewalk was.

"Oh. My. Gosh! What happened? I told you not to go running, Tori! It's heat stroke isn't it, Kai? Oh. My. Gosh!" she said again, sounding like a teenager caught up in a MTV drama.

Kai? So, he has a name.

"It's just heat exhaustion for now, but she does need to get cooled off quickly. Where's your nearest shower, Stacie?" he asked, carrying me through the doorway and heading down the hall.

What? He can't possibly mean-

"Sure, of course. Right this way," Stacie said, leading us both to the nearest bathroom.

"Take her shoes off and turn the water to cold," Kai said.

I was the one in a full panic now, "Is this really necessary?"

"Yes!" They both said in unison.

The next thing I knew I was lying in a bathtub, fully clothed, with freezing water sheeting down on me. I gasped and cried out for air, flailing my body around the tub like an octopus on the loose. No one seemed to care though, and no one offered me any help. In just a matter of seconds, I was fully alert and angry as ever.

"Get me out of here!"

Kai turned the water off. I sat shivering in the bath, looking at them both with what I hoped were eyes of pure fury. Realistically, I'm sure I just looked pathetic. Stacie moved quickly, handing Kai a towel. Then she left to get me some dry clothes. He just stared at me, lips pursed, as if calculating his next move.

"Just give it to me…please," I said, pointing to the towel while avoiding his gaze.

He took my wet arm and pulled me up in one smooth motion, steadying me cautiously. He wrapped the towel around my shoulders.

"I did tell you this way was *less* pleasant," he said.

Stacie walked in with shorts and a t-shirt for me before I could respond. Kai excused himself momentarily while I changed. I was still shaking when I emerged in the hallway. Kai placed one hand on my back and the other on my arm, leading me to the couch. I felt an unfamiliar warmth surge through me. Stacie busily worked to re-arrange the millions of throw pillows she had accumulated, making room for me to lie down. Kai propped my feet up and gave Stacie instructions for my fluid intake.

I was humiliated.

"I'll make sure she stays down. Thank you, Kai. I'm so glad you were the one who responded," Stacie said.

He knelt down in front of me then, just inches from my face. I startled back a bit, surprised by his lack of personal bubble…and mine.

"Now Victoria, I'm gonna take you up on our deal, but first I need to make sure you're gonna be a good patient. Listen to your sister, drink lots of fluids and I will be back to check on you when my shift is over tonight."

He winked at me once and then stood.

What is happening here?

Who is this guy?

Everything I thought to say was stuck somewhere between my head and my mouth. I didn't quite know how to feel. Flattered? Upset? Angry? Grateful? Who knew heat exhaustion came with so many mixed and conflicting emotions.

I watched him turn toward Stacie.

"Her blood pressure is fine, but if you notice anything unusual at all call me immediately, okay? I'll come back and check her again for signs of a concussion," Kai said.

"Okay, thanks again, Kai. I'll tell Jack you stopped by. He's really missing home, but he loves the sights of Australia. I'm a little jealous…"

Jack? Kai knows our Jack?

The door clicked shut and Stacie was back in the room with me in two seconds flat. Her look was one of a mom who had already counted to three and was now ready to dish out the punishment. I winced a tad and her face broke. Her soft demeanor returned, leaving just a hint of disappointment.

She will make a great mother.

"Victoria Grace Sales, you already know what I'm about to say. No more running in this heat, okay? Find a treadmill if you must, but please don't be dropping on the sidewalk anymore…the baby and I just can't take it," she said. She sat halfway on the couch, close to my mid-section.

"I'm sorry Stace; I didn't mean to upset you."

"I know. I'm just glad someone saw you and called."

"Yeah…who is that guy anyway? Why was he at Mom and Dad's the other night…and how does he know you and Jack?" I asked, still dazed by the recent events.

"Oh, Kai? I forgot you don't know him. You must have moved before we could introduce you. He's pretty good friends with Jack now, actually. They met a little over a year ago," she said, "There was an *incident* at Jack's company softball game."

"Incident?"

"Let's just say computer nerds aren't always the best at sports coordination."

She laughed and rolled her eyes. I laughed too. It felt good—strange—but good. Stacie left the room to get me some water.

"Ya know, Tori…Kai is a great guy. Like a *really* great guy," she said, from the kitchen.

Oh no.

"I don't know why I never thought about that before. Maybe because he's Jack's age…but surely that's not a big deal now. Tori, you should-"

"No Stacie. Don't even start. You're not playing match-maker with me. I didn't move all the way back here for you to *play house* with my life."

But the twinkle in her eye remained, "Fine, whatever you want, Sis."

SIX

By the time Kai came back, I felt completely restored. When I heard the knock at the door I contemplated pretending to be asleep, but I knew Stacie would give me away, which would only mean more humiliation for me in the end. He was in shorts and a t-shirt now, and looked freshly showered. I wondered how long this last shift was for him today, but then remembered...I wasn't supposed to care.

"Well, someone's looking better now," he said, strolling over to me on the couch.

"Yes, thank you. I feel just fine now," I said, hoping to make the exchange as quick and painless as possible.

"Kai, can I get you something? Ice water? Or maybe a Coke? Please feel free to sit down," Stacie said, glancing at me and smiling.

Urgh...this is going to end poorly for me.

"Thanks Stacie, I can't stay long, but I would love a Coke," Kai said.

I sat watching him silently. I refused to be the one to speak first. This wasn't a social occasion after all. It was just a simple medical checkup by an EMT who knew everyone in my family but me. As I assessed him, he seemed unfazed by the strangeness of the day.

Maybe this was all normal for him?

Picking up his friend's sisters and throwing them in a cold shower before a proper introduction had been made.

I always knew EMTs had to be a tad quirky in order to deal with the crazies they saw during their day—before those same crazies were brought to me in the ER, of course.

Wait...was I one of those crazies now, too?

Stacie handed him a large glass of Coke with an abundance of ice and walked into the next room, too far to be in a conversation, but close enough to still be within earshot.

"So, you're a runner, huh?" Kai asked, his bright white teeth standing out from his naturally tanned brown skin.

I tried to place what nationality he was. As I thought about the South Pacific, I flipped through maps in my head like an old Rolodex: Guam, Papua New Guinea, Tonga, Samoa? Dallas had a large mixture of Islanders who had settled within the city. Vast diversity was everywhere here.

"Uh, something like that," I said, swallowing hard.

"Well, I could recommend a good gym down the road from here. Might be a better alternative for the hot days that are left in September," he offered.

"Thanks, I'll probably just wait it out. I prefer to run outdoors."

"Alright, I just don't want to get another call about you lying in a field somewhere passed out—not that I mind picking up pretty girls—but still, there are other ways to get a workout in."

He laughed lightly and took a gulp from his drink.

'Pretty girls?' He thinks I'm-
No, don't even go there.

"Yeah, you won't. I promise."

I snapped my mouth shut after my last word, remembering. *Promise.* I was delirious when I had begged him to take me home. There was no way he would actually take a stranger up on any promise while she was strapped down to a gurney, right?

He smiled wide. It was that same smile I remembered seeing in the ambulance.

Maybe I'm wrong.

"I believe that's the second promise you have made to me today," Kai said. "How am I to know if you're even trustworthy enough to keep just one of those promises unless I take you up on your offer?"

"I don't recall making an offer..." I said, shaking my head slightly in denial.

"Oh, I do...and since I'm the one who *wasn't* suffering from heat exhaustion, I think it's safe to say I'm a little more reliable in the memory department...at least for today."

My mouth gaped open a tad at his bluntness.

Guess he's not exactly a beat-around-the-bush type.

"Well then, please enlighten me with my *exact* words?"

"Let's see, *I* wanted to take you to the hospital and *you* wanted to come here. Your exact words were, 'please, I'll do anything', and I do believe I kept my end of the bargain."

His eyes glimmered at me in a way that sucked the breath right out of my lungs. I wanted him to be ugly and repulsive in that moment, but he was definitely not either one of those things. He just might have been the most attractive man I had ever conversed with, and that was saying something. I had talked to a lot of good looking men in the medical world.

Kai trumped them all—easily.

"What did you have in mind?" I forced the question out, dread filling me.

"Let me take you out. I'm a pretty resourceful guy, and I can promise you we'll have fun. How does this Saturday sound? I can confirm a time with you later in the week."

He beamed as he put his empty glass down on the side table and walked toward me. I swallowed hard as he got closer. My programmed response had always been to say *no*, but…

"Okay," I said.

He leaned down over me then, taking my face in his hands. I exhaled sharply as he stared deeply into my eyes. If I could have been sucked into a giant sink hole in the earth, I would have been far more comfortable than I was in that moment. I was quite sure I was no longer breathing at all. My body surged with electric jolts and I was actively telling myself to *calm down*. He let go in a matter of seconds, but held my gaze.

"No concussion, just like I thought. I'll see you on Saturday, Victoria…until then stay out of the sun, okay?"

He winked again and walked out of the living room, saying goodbye to Stacie.

And just like that he was gone.

I could hear Stacie laughing to herself after she shut the door. I waited for her teasing to start, but it never came. That, was a far worse fate I was sure.

****

I arrived early at work Wednesday, grateful to start a shift without a probing therapy session first. My mind was clear, or mostly anyway, and ready to take on whatever challenges would to come my way—or so I thought. After checking in with Meg Holt, the charge nurse, I was immediately handed a chart by an elderly nurse.

She looked like she had started her career in an era long past. The name on the chart read "Henry Albert, Jr." and he was waiting to be seen in pod three. I thought I saw a smirk on the nurse's face as she passed me.

I pulled back the curtain to the third pod and saw Mr. Albert. I understood immediately why I was given his chart. Mr. Albert was most certainly homeless, and his aroma could not be missed. I breathed through my mouth as I entered.

"Ooh, I get a young pretty nurse today, huh? You must be new!" Mr. Albert said.

"Hello, Mr. Albert?" I asked.

"That'd be me little missy, but you can call me Henry."

His smile was almost toothless, but there was something sweet and genuine about it.

"It looks like the doctor has already seen you Henry. You are here for...immersion foot, is that right?" I asked, knowing this was going to be difficult to stomach, no matter how trained or immune I had become.

"That's right, Ma'am. Does your chart also tell ya I have had this three other times this year?" he asked.

"Yes it does, may I take a look, Henry?"

There was not a lot of skill involved in diagnosing or treating trench foot—or immersion foot as it was sometimes called, but rather in its prevention. The difficulty was found in keeping it clean, dry, and elevated so it could heal. Dry socks and shoes were a must.

Henry's foot wasn't the worst I had seen, but it wasn't far off. I gathered the foot tub and made preparations for him to soak it in the hot water. As I worked to roll up his dirty pant leg, it hit me that cleaning this small area was a futile effort when the rest of him was filthy.

"Henry, can I ask when the last time you were able to shower or bathe was?"

His eyes dropped along with his head. "I'm sorry, I must be pretty stinky to you little lady, my apologies. The lake is quite a hike from where I sleep and my foot's been in too much pain to make it there lately," he said.

"Well, that's quite alright. I'm just thinking we could get you a shower today instead of just a foot soak. I think you'll feel better and then we can do the hot soak for your foot afterward. How does that sound?" I asked.

"Ah, ha! I knew you were gonna be a good one little lady! That would be terrific!"

"Great, well they are just down this hallway here. I will wait for you outside the door. Pull the cord if you need anything. Soap is in the shampoo dispenser. Take your time," I said.

I couldn't help but smile. That such a simple thing could create such joy in someone was pretty amazing. We walked slowly together down the hall as Henry limped, wincing at the pain with each step he took. He saluted me before entering the men's shower room and I immediately returned the gesture.

"*What* do you think you're doing?"

The drill sergeant nurse was back. Her eyebrows were so furrowed; I struggled to identify even one of her eyeballs.

"Mr. Albert is just cleaning up in the shower before we do his foot soak," I said.

"Oh, for cryin' out loud! Of all the ridiculous ideas…that man has been homeless for twenty years! One little shower is not going to magically make him stop needing medical treatment here. That's like giving a dog a bath during a rainstorm; you just know he's gonna go roll in the mud the second you let him out. All it does is *waste* our time," she said, hands on her hips.

"Mr. Albert is not a dog, and though it may not make a difference long term, it will make a difference for him today." I did my best to stay respectful, but I could feel my heart rate quicken as I spoke.

"Huh…talk to me about that in thirty five years sweetheart, you won't be doing anything for the difference of one day!"

She started to storm off, when I called to her.

"I didn't get your name? I'm Tori."

"Stormy," she yelled back, not bothering to turn her head as she spoke.

The most appropriate name for a person I might have ever heard.

****

It was as if a new man had emerged when Henry came out of the shower. Freshly washed, shaved, and smelling like soap, we walked back to the pod. I prepared his foot bath by heating the water to 104° and set the timer. It had to first soak and then completely dry in order for any healing to take place. The hardest part for Henry would be keeping it clean and sanitary so no more infection built up.

"Henry, I know it will be difficult for you, but your foot needs to be checked once a day and soaked in warm water. Are you able to get to a place to do that, or will you need to come back here?"

"Well...I don't have anything fancy like this, Doc," he said pointing to the plastic foot tub. "But I can probably get back here if that's what I need to do."

"The problem is if we don't get this under control now, it will fester and spread and could ultimately lead to gangrene, or amputation. I will go and find you several pairs of clean socks, but just make sure you are never putting the same ones on twice. Don't sleep in them, and try to keep your feet dry as much as you possibly can, alright?" I asked.

"Sounds good to me. I always listen to pretty ladies," Henry said, smiling.

He winked at me when I got up to go find him the hospital socks in the supply closet. For a moment I thought of Kai— of his wink yesterday before he left the house.

Had I really agreed to go out with him?

"Here you are Mr. Albert, now make sure you change your socks, and come back to get checked for the next few days so we can soak it and make sure it's getting better and not worse," I said, handing him six pairs of hospital socks.

"Thank you," he said.

His eyes welled up with tears, dangerously close to spilling over onto his cheeks. "You helped an old man feel dignified again. It wasn't always like this for me ya know, my life used to be different—normal. But there are things that happen in life and in war that can rob you...I let that happen to me," he said. "You're a special gal, Nurse. I'd see you any day over nurse *Stick-in-the-mud*. Tell her I said that, too!"

He stood up, grabbed his cane and backpack, and tipped his hat to me as he left. I watched him go. Strangely, I felt more connected to him than I did to most people I knew.

What robbed him twenty years ago?

****

The patient stream was steady after Henry left. There was almost always a long wait within Emergency. Patients were treated by medical need first, not by arrival time. It was an interesting balance and often caused a lot of stress for the triage staff who did the initial assessments.

The beginning of fall was always filled with soccer injuries, football fractures and concussions, along with flu bugs that got out of hand during the newness of the school year. The twelve-hour shift was full, to say the least. Sleep was all I could think about when I climbed the stairs to bed that night.

Just as I drifted off, I heard a low rumble on my night stand. A new voicemail blinked on the screen of my phone, begging to be heard.

It was the one Phoenix number that I wanted to delete: Dr. Susan Bradley's number.

SEVEN

Rolling out of bed the next morning, I checked the outside temperature on my phone before dressing in my running clothes. I may have promised I wouldn't run in the heat wave, but I never promised to stop running. The low 80's were a huge improvement to the 100 degree weather that had oppressed Dallas just days ago. I wasn't about to let the temperature drop go to waste. I needed to plan out my next move, running would help me do that. The anger that I had gone to bed with after hearing Susan's message was still seeping from my pores.

"Tori, I know I'm probably the last person you want to talk to right now and I get that. I know you've been meeting with Dr. Crane. As upset as I'm sure you are about that, I don't regret my recommendation for your therapy. I care about you...I hope you can make the most of the sessions. Take care."

My sister was asleep when I left the house. That made my escape much easier this time around—no one to answer to, just how I liked it. There was a time when authority had made me feel safe, cherished, and even loved, but that time had passed away like the ending of my childhood. Dr. Bradley had just proved that point all over again. No one could be fully trusted with who I'd become.

So much of who I used to be had either died from pure starvation or from suffocation. Those who had been close to me, either as a friend, colleague, neighbor or family member, were the first to be pushed aside in the weeks that followed the accident. Stacie was the only exception, but even she was kept at arm's length. I hadn't anticipated the gossip, whispers, or awkward conversations that seemed to linger wherever I went.

Death's wake had a way of unleashing the worst in people.

Leaving Dallas had been my most logical choice, despite the protests of many. Ironically though, it was that same *many* who spoke carelessly about the irreversible damage that had been done to me: the survivor of such a horrific tragedy. *They* did not get a vote.

There were no goodbyes.

My conscience had stayed quiet until the evening of my departure. I had sworn Jack and Stacie to secrecy days before I left, knowing when I did that they would not let me take a taxi to the airport like I had wanted to.

I finally agreed to let them take me, after much debate. Truthfully, they were the only two people I could count on. As they drove me to the airport, I stared at the one-way ticket to Phoenix in my hand.

After overhearing my mother sob that I was "wrecked for life" to my father who consoled her, I kept the date a secret. I would call when I arrived.

My pain was like a car in overdrive after hearing that. It raced around recklessly, oblivious that it hit every speed bump at maximum capacity. It never stopped to check for damages.

I was certain I would never get ahead of the pain, but I had to try.

Leaving was my only option.

Jack had carried my luggage to the ticket counter. Quietly, he walked me to security as Stacie lagged behind us, crying. We had never been apart. Even through my college years I had chosen to stay close to home, for her.

Stacie reminded me often of how long she'd prayed for a baby sister when she was young. My mom had told her she just needed to be happy as a "lucky only child". But as *luck* would have it, the answer to her prayers came in the way of an unexpected pregnancy. Stacie was given a baby sister, and my parents were given a second child. Though we had our drama moments growing up, she had always been my one true confidant in life.

She was my best friend.

"You're sure you want to go through with this, Tori? It's not too late to decide to stay. You can live with us and take as much time as you need to...figure things out." Jack squeezed my shoulders with his hands as he looked down at me.

"I know. Thank you Jack...but I'm sure."

I was sure I needed to leave, but doubted that time would fix anything, much less help me to 'figure things out'.

"I love you little sis, more than I could ever say," Jack said, emotion thick in his voice.

Stacie moved to stand in front of me then, her eyes red and swollen. They were puffier than I'd ever seen them, including the night before her wedding. The night she had blubbered hysterically through her rehearsal dinner speech over the "great catch" she'd found in Jack. Public speaking did that to Stacie.

Microphones were kept far out of her reach after that.

This tearful moment, however, was certainly not spurred out of a grateful heart. Her sorrow had filled every inch of the air around us. I hated that I was causing her pain, but I was trapped in my own pain-prison, and there was no way to get out.

She grabbed my hands as she sobbed for what felt like an eternity. Finally, a strong resolution filled her face. She had pulled it together—one last moment—for me.

"I love you, Tori. I'll be praying for you every day…don't forget that."

Her voice was surprisingly strong for how hard she'd just been crying only seconds earlier. She leaned on Jack for support. I could sense another round of emotions coming for her so I hugged them both quickly, and turned away to join the long line at security.

I had to force myself not to look back at them. As much as I hated to see the hurt in their faces, it wasn't the worst thing I had come to know in the eyes of my family members. Just below the surface of their heartache was a resolve that made my stomach churn: disappointment.

Not only had I failed Anna, I had failed all of them, too.

I ran now, along the track near the lake. I focused on the rooftops while keeping my breathing in check and thinking about Phoenix.

Those first few months in Phoenix were the loneliest months of my life. Sure, I had been asked out on dates, or drinks after work, but I had turned them all down. Once the guys figured out I wasn't the *good time* they'd hoped I'd be, I stopped getting asked.

I took Stacie's calls more often than not, due to the fact that I knew she'd show up on my doorstep if I didn't. I kept our conversations brief, only skimming the surface when we did talk. She had tried several different tactics to get me to "open up", but as I told her, I just didn't know what she expected me to say.

I didn't even know what to say to myself.

My folks only received a call from me at times when I was almost certain I could leave them a voicemail update. Mostly though, I relied on email as our main form of communication. It was safer that way. The latest sights and sounds of Phoenix were a common theme in our email correspondence. Discussing local real estate was a topic I was well versed in and quite comfortable with.

I had truly become an expert in the art of deflection.

The first time I went out for the sole purpose of socialization was about four months after moving to Phoenix. Early one morning, after working the entire evening prior, I headed out the back doors of the hospital. The tram was located just a block away and was only a ten minute ride back to my apartment. I was desperately longing for sleep.

As I walked through the parking garage I heard a frustrated scream rip through the large cement tomb. Due to my lack of sleep, my nerves caused me to jump. I turned instinctively in the direction of the cry I'd heard. I spotted her then, slumped over her trunk. As I neared, I could see her tire was flat. I could also see how tired she was.

The feeling was mutual.

"I can try and help you put on a spare. I saw my brother-in-law do it a couple of times," I had offered, trying to sound much more enthusiastic than I actually was.

"No, I'll call my insurance and have someone come out. It will just be an hour or so wait. Hey, you hungry, Green?" Dr. Bradley asked. Her face seemed to perk-up at the thought of breakfast.

I wasn't hungry for food, but in that moment, I was hungry for conversation—*real* conversation. It was as if the months of living in my hole of social silence had finally reached maximum capacity.

"Sure, where to?" I asked.

"I know just the place; it's only half a block away. Let me call my insurance hotline and get this tire thing going. Then we can walk there."

Twenty minutes later we were sitting at a local diner with a large order of flapjacks and coffee. We talked about what it was like to move from Dallas to Phoenix, and the differences in people, climate, weather, houses, and even food. We laughed about the culture and how it compared to the *high society* back home. It had felt good—really good, almost normal.

That had started an almost once a week tradition at the pancake house on 5th Street. It was strange at first to think about eating with a doctor of her position and caliber, but neither of us spoke about it outside of those mornings. It soon became familiar, routine, and even downright homey. She had become a *friend*, the only one I had outside of those that were obligated to me through blood.

Susan and I had shared a lot with each other over pancakes and coffee. Things I hadn't felt compelled to share with anyone—even Stacie. By the third month of our breakfasts together, I finally stopped avoiding the questions surrounding the *real* reason behind my move. The hardships with my parents and friends back home and the major shift in my career focus had been a suspicion of hers for a while.

As I retold the story of the accident, I kept only to the facts. It had been the first time I had told it. I didn't shed a tear; I didn't deserve to shed a tear.

Susan slowly began to chip deeper into my hard exterior, asking me questions that even my own subconscious had been afraid to ask. Though I had once been concerned about her sympathy toward me and how it could affect my job, she never coddled me. Instead, she pushed me harder, especially at work. Sometimes I wondered if she was deliberately trying to break me, to see if I would throw a fit of rage or some other kind of nonsense, but that never happened.

In my eighth month of working under Dr. Bradley, she pulled me aside in a staff lounge with a very concerned look on her face.

"Green, I want a truthful answer. I have given you the benefit of the doubt for some time now because I always see you eat a hearty-sized meal at breakfast, but I just can't let this go on any longer. You need to be honest with me, starting right now."

I was shocked at her accusatory tone. Panic ripped through me, trying to identify what she was referring to. I came up with nothing.

"I...I'm sorry, but I have no idea what you are talking about," I said.

"Your weight, Green. You're shrinking by the second and I need to know what is happening with you. The staff is noticing too, and there are many suspicions going around about an eating disorder. I want to believe that we are friends enough for you to confide in me if you need help," she said.

"No, no I promise Susan—I mean, Dr. Bradley—I swear to you I eat! I eat normally. It's...it's not the eating, it's the running I'm doing. I run... I run..."

I couldn't finish.

Why did I run? To lose weight?

No. That may have been a nice side effect, but that wasn't the reason.

I hadn't stepped on a scale in years. I stood puzzled by my own lack of thought.

Dr. Bradley broke the silence.

"You run *from* the pain, right, Tori? You run *because* of the pain. When you said you had taken up running, I thought it was for health reasons or even a new hobby since you're low on companionship here," she said, pausing before looking into my eyes again. "How much? How much are you running?"

I had never tracked the distance—not even once. The trail I ran on was at least a 12 mile loop, but I had only just recently mastered that. My runs seemed to be much longer after stressful days at the hospital, the days where I aided children—young, sick children.

"I'm honestly not sure. I don't really keep track of the distance. I just go until...I can't go anymore," I said.

The truth was powerful.

That admission, even to me, was one of great magnitude. Susan opened and shut her mouth twice before speaking. Concern and something else I couldn't quite place registered on her face.

"That's your cope Tori, you see that right?" she asked.

She wasn't looking at me now. It was more of a rhetorical question, her own personal "ah-ha moment" that I was watching unfold before my eyes.

"All these months I've been trying to stir something in you, something deep and real. Any emotion at all would have been encouraging to me, but you are shut down, locked out of your own grief. I pushed you, harder than any new RN or young resident on this floor. I was trying to get you to break, to crack under the pressure so you'd release what's behind this dam you've built up. But nothing breaks you. I couldn't figure out how you were able to keep it all in, but it finally makes sense now. You don't keep it in...you fight it *with* pain," she said, turning to me again. "Show me your feet."

I could feel my mouth gape in surprise as I stared at her. After a second of processing I said, "Dr. Bradley, I really don't want-"

"Show me your feet, Green."

This was no longer my friend Susan, but my attending doctor

who spoke to me.

She locked the door to the lounge as I sat in a chair and slowly took off my shoes and socks. Her face contorted in what could only be described as horror, which quickly shifted to pain and then finally to what looked like understanding.

We both stared down at the torn flesh, red swollen scabs, and blisters. It was the first long look I'd given them. My socks and shoes had almost always covered them, so the moments for scrutiny were short-lived, during my shower time only.

No words formed in my head. I had never told a lie to Susan. She was too smart for my deceptions, too quick for my diversions.

"I won't scold you, Tori. I refuse to be your mother, but I *will* be your friend. I know that I am almost twenty years your senior, but I get you. I *really* get you. Our stories aren't so different, you know? I didn't have a tragic accident that ended in the death of a child, but I lost my husband almost fifteen years ago and I know what it is to grieve a loss. I've grieved the loss of the life I loved and the loss of the lives I'll never know—the ones he could have fathered if I hadn't been so selfish about the timing of our family," she said, taking a deep breath before continuing. "I'm alone, Tori. This job is my *whole life*, and sometimes it's a very sad and lonely life. Don't waste yours on this. Don't waste yours on what you can't earn back...guilt doesn't fade with time. Take that lesson from me."

With that, Susan opened the door and walked out. I sat staring at my ugly, disfigured feet, replaying her words in my head. Susan had allowed me to think she'd always been single. Hearing her speak of a husband was a shock, but hearing her own words of grief and guilt were even more mind-blowing.

Susan *knew*.

She understood.

Our connection had been based on more than just our Texan heritage, but on what could have been the greatest common denominator of all: death.

EIGHT

Friday morning had come too soon. I watched the second hand tick on the far wall of Dr. Crane's office. With each rigid movement my anxiety increased.

Today I would tell her about Anna.

"Victoria, I've made quite a few notes during our last two sessions together. I've compared them with some notes from your file, but before we talk more about those, I'd like to hear the last part of what happened the night of the accident. You had stabilized the driver of the other car and noticed the empty booster seat on the passenger side, is that correct?"

Wow, well I guess we'll just jump right in, then.

"That's correct," I answered.

"Where did you find the little girl, Victoria, and what was her condition?"

"The six-year-old female was found about five yards away. I was able to get to her quickly because the headlights were shining in the grass where she...landed. Her condition...was critical," I said, focusing hard.

"Was she breathing when you got to her? Go ahead...tell the story in your own words. I'll hold any other questions until the end."

I didn't hesitate this time. The longer I paused, the worse it was to re-tell. I wanted to detach, to speak the words without having to think about them.

I can do this.

"It was difficult to find her breath because the rain was still coming down hard. I checked for a pulse and couldn't detect one. She had a severe puncture to her right side and lacerations on her forehead and left leg. I took off my shirt and used it as a compress, and then started CPR immediately. I tried to keep pressure on her side in between chest compressions," I said, pausing only briefly before continuing on. "When I heard her mother open the car door I was hopeful she could assist me. But, as soon as she took a step out, she cried in pain and fell to the mud, unconscious. I don't know how long I was out there. I had no phone to call for help...it gets fuzzy after that."

I stopped then, unsure of what to say next. Dr. Crane sensed my uncertainty, and filled in what she knew from the report.

"The ambulance came then. The report said a rancher was out looking for livestock in the storm when he heard the impact and called 911. All three of you were transferred to Mercy North. It was there that Anna Watson—the little girl—was pronounced dead on arrival. Her mother was treated for a severe concussion, a broken ankle and minor abrasions. You were both released on the same day, is that correct?" Dr. Crane asked.

My mind skipped over the scenes that haunted me the most: the EMT who pulled me off Anna, the moment I awoke in the hospital room with full recollection of what had happened, and the doctor who told me Anna's fate. Those were the worst. Those were the hardest for me to think about, much less talk about. I fast forwarded my memory to the day I was released from the hospital. I nodded in response to her last question.

"Was there any *interaction* between you and...Johanna Watson, Anna's mother?"

The question rattled me as a shiver traveled down my spine.

No one knew about that—no one.

I hadn't told a soul about the conversation I'd had with Johanna—not even Dr. Bradley—so where was this coming from?

Intuition, maybe?

A mere coincidence since we had both been released on the same day?

"No."

I wasn't willing to be pushed any further, not on that one. There were some things that no amount of therapy tricks could get me to reveal. Dr. Crane's head snapped up in attention as she assessed my stiff posture. I could practically hear the debate going on inside her head. I held my ground.

She was too smart to press me on it.

"Victoria, you asked me last Monday what it was that we were doing here—you and I. I didn't answer you due to our time restraint, but I wanted to be fair to you and answer that today. I'm a big believer in trust-based therapy. If I'm not open with you, then I shouldn't expect it in return. Wouldn't you agree?"

"Sure," I said, still a bit miffed at her last line of questioning.

Though a big part of me wanted to tune her out, my curiosity had already been sparked. What impending diagnosis could she possibly reveal?

I'm a lost cause.

"As I stated before, I've taken a lot of notes. Most of them are not on *what* you've said, but *how* you've said it. How your body responds as you speak is actually more important to me than *what* you say most of the time," she said.

I nodded, though I didn't understand.

"The brain is a very unique organ as I'm sure you know from your anatomy studies. There are so many parts of the body that it controls: our speech, our sight, our hearing, our heart-beat, our emotional well-being. Its ability to connect it all is what keeps us in balance—in sync. You, Victoria, are *not* in sync. The trauma you've experienced has left you in a state of disconnection. Your life prior to the accident looks very little like your life today." She shifted in her chair and put my folder back on her desk.

"You've mastered—for now—a complete compartmentalization between your emotional responses, your mental responses, and your physical responses to what happened that night. This kind of response to trauma can be expected anywhere from a few days to even a few weeks after a traumatic event has occurred. Once that initial response period has passed though, the brain should settle and the shock should dissipate. I think you and I both know that is not the case with you, Victoria. Would you agree with that statement?" she asked.

I knew there wasn't a chance I could deny it. Every word she said was not only accurate, it was nauseating. It was like watching a horror movie and stopping it in the middle of the climax. Would the heroine be rescued? Could she still be saved?

I was more afraid than ever to hear the answer.

Too much time had passed. I couldn't even remember the Tori *before* the accident. A different kind of death had claimed *her* that night. It was the kind of death that no pulse could conquer, the kind of death that stalked its prey like a dark, hungry shadow. That Tori was gone.

"Yes. It never dissipated," I answered, stunned by the sound of my own voice.

"Victoria, when was the last time you cried? Can you remember?" She was leaning in toward me again, getting closer by the second.

Is she waiting to add my answer to her clinical calculations?

"About a week after the accident."

Anna's funeral.

"That's about what I had figured. I'm certain that what you're dealing with is a form of PTSD—Post Traumatic Stress Disorder," she said.

My ears felt like they were stuffed with a hundred cotton balls. I couldn't understand her words.

"What?"

What did she say? PTSD...like a war veteran? That can't be what she means.

No way.

"PTSD. And yes, it happens more than you realize, in everyday people who experience the worst that life can throw at them. It's not just a post-war diagnosis. So many people walk around with it thinking it will lessen with time, but it doesn't. Those people just find ways to cope. Usually, very unhealthy ways like abusing drugs or alcohol, or isolation from family and friends. They can also develop other mental disorders, as well. Some have even been known to commit suicide as a way of escape, but it doesn't have to be that way—not for you."

Dr. Crane spoke with such conviction that if I hadn't known any better I would have sworn I was in church.

"It will take some hard work, Victoria, to un-hinge the compartments holding back your emotions and your ability to feel, but I am willing to guide you through that process. I think you're an extraordinary young woman who has far surpassed any heroic validation I could offer, but I also know that if you're not helped...the trappings of PTSD will consume you. So, let's make a compromise, shall we?"

Compromise?

"I'm not sure I understand what you mean, Dr. Crane?"

My head was spinning in a million different directions.

First she tells me I have PTSD like I just got back from a bloody war field in Iraq, now she wants to play "let's make a deal"?

"Having you here against your will only defeats the progress we can make together. So, I am willing to sign off on your overtime hours, if you are willing to agree to treatment. That means that you will be the one making the appointments with me, doing the homework I assign, and showing up here willing to work. I know this is a lot to think about, but I can't help you until you decide for yourself that you want my help."

She pushed back her chair and stood up. I was still in a daze when she placed her hand on my shoulder and looked at me with deep sincerity.

"Anna doesn't have a choice to make, but you still do. Her death doesn't have to mean your death. There is no even exchange, Victoria. If you won't do it for yourself...think about doing it for Anna."

NINE

"There is no even exchange...do it for Anna."

There had been several diagnostic claims made to me or about me over the last 17 months, mostly by disgruntled family members or co-workers. I had been called: cold, detached, withdrawn, ice queen…and worse. I had easily ignored every one of them. This one, however, struck a chord that resonated through the entirety of my body. It was a low blow to involve Anna's legacy, but Dr. Crane had a point.

Did she really, though? Is therapy for PTSD—if that's actually what I have—really going to help honor Anna's life?

It was a question that I didn't know how to answer. That fact alone gave me pause. As tempting and appealing as working overtime was, the flip-side to her compromise was downright bone chilling. The idea of more therapy was like looking into an abyss, strapped into a harness, and being told to jump. Sure, the harness provided some sense of security, but without knowing the depth of the free fall, what good was a harness at all?

What if I lose what little control I have left?

I may live in a prison now, but at least I know my way around it.

I knew I needed time to make this decision, but for the next twelve hours thoughts on PTSD and therapy compromises would have to be placed on hold. Nursing did not mix well with mental and emotional distractions. I tucked the thoughts away and hurried down to the locker room to change into my scrubs.

My stomach was suddenly aflutter as I pushed opened the door and rounded the corner to my locker. There, taped to the dull metal locker of #44, was a folded note. My name was written on the front.

I pulled it off slowly.

Tori-
I realized I never gave you my number, must have been too caught up in "playing doctor". I'll get yours from Stacie later today and text you to confirm a time for tomorrow. Everything is planned—just pack a bathing suit and a change of clothes. We'll have fun!
PS. Don't worry, no hot tubs are involved…I promise.
555-298-4463

Kai

Note still in hand, I slumped down hard on the bench.
This day is just chock-full of surprises. What had I gotten myself into?
And why did the idea of swimsuits and Kai make my heart race at a hundred beats a minute?

The idea that he had been in this very locker room looking for me, caused my anxiety to simmer. But there was something else mixed in with the anxiety, something that I hadn't felt in quite a while: excitement.

My smile—even though I couldn't see it—was ridiculous.
No, this is ridiculous!

Deal or no deal, family friend or not, it was obvious that Kai's charming ways seemed to get him what he wanted, but that would change soon enough. Though his gesture was undeniably flattering, I knew it was misdirected. Stacie was the type of girl who ended up with a guy like Kai. He needed a girl who would giggle and swoon, one that was well-mannered and polished. He needed the type of girl that seemed to be created with some sort of magical "girlfriend pixie dust" that I didn't possess.

There was a nagging voice somewhere in the back corner of my mind that seemed to disagree with my judgment. The fact that he had pursued me even after my less-than-gracious-moment at my parent's house, and after my drowned rat exhibit in Stacie's bathtub, did lend some credit to the opposition. But even with those truths in mind, I had no choice but to dismiss the notion that my judgment could be off.

There was no use playing a game that would ultimately end in disqualification before it even began. If he was hoping to get a *Stacie Jr.*, he would be sorely mistaken. Our apples may have fallen from the same tree, but they had rolled in opposite directions.

****

Meg Holt, the charge nurse in Emergency, was sitting at the nurses' station buried in paperwork when I checked-in for my shift. Though my encounters with Stormy had been interesting at best, Meg seemed like she enjoyed her job and liked her staff. I had interviewed with her when I first arrived back in Texas a couple weeks ago. It had been a fairly short interview compared to my detailed overview with Human Resources, but I quickly gathered that she was a down-to-earth type of gal. Though very capable of managing a demanding work environment, she was absent of the typical stress-case attitude that was usually married to it. When she told me she was from the Northwest—Oregon, I believe—the dots connected.

Meg partnered me with Bev Hatty for the day. Bev was a thirty-something socialite who, in my opinion, was far too interested in the lives of each and every staff member we passed. Though she wasn't exactly instructional or helpful, she wasn't a total stick-in-the-mud like Stormy had been either. Bev's main focus was on a doctor by the name of Thomas, a doctor who I was fairly sure was married.

I wondered how much longer I'd have to be "supervised" as I administered my third IV for the afternoon while Bev stood in the doorway and texted on her phone. Apparently whatever was happening on that tiny screen was far more important than the lady who was crying from her kidney stones. Thankfully, the woman's morphine kicked in within twenty minutes and she was now resting peacefully, waiting for the doctor.

The last six hours of my shift were filled with college students who were drunk beyond measure. Many needed treatment for alcohol poisoning, while the other obnoxiously noisy frat brothers filled the waiting room. Hospital security was higher on evenings and weekends, usually due to this exact scenario. Drunks didn't seem to follow the rules as well as the old lady with a rosacea flare-up did. Being surrounded by several universities came with its perks—and its annoyances.

"I really don't think I need to be here...I'm just a tad woozy." One twenty-something frat boy had slurred to me. He had practically passed-out on me before we even got to his outpatient room.

"Just lie down right here, if you need a bucket-"

Too late.

Vomit was now all over the floor and bed. Thankfully, I was standing a good three feet away at that point.

With breath like a sewer plant he said, "Whoops, I'm think I'm gonna need a-"

I gave him a vomit-catcher just in time for the next round. After I administered his IV and the CNA cleaned up his mess, he looked almost gray in color. He was also sweating.

His story was similar to the other ten-plus college students who had arrived here via car or ambulance. A Ping-Pong binge drinking game at one of the frat houses a few miles away had been their demise. Though this guy was still conscious and breathing, it was quite obvious he had consumed more than *just a few* shots. I hooked him up to the necessary monitors.

Trying to make him as comfortable as I could, I gave him an extra pillow. Time and fluids were the only antidote for him at this point. He was beyond any other intervention we could offer.

I checked in the hall for Bev a few times to ask where various supplies were located, but she was nowhere to be found.

I'm sure Dr. Thomas knows where she is...

I made do fine on my own though, as usual. Turning to leave so I could update the doctor on my patient's condition, my wrist was yanked behind me. I stumbled to find my footing. In an instant, I was pulled to the bedside of my inebriated patient. My wrist ached under the strain of his tight grip.

"Nurse, you sure are a pretty little thing."

He breathed hard in my face as his head wobbled left and right. His eyes were still glazed-over, but even still, they held in them a sickening focus.

"Thanks, now please release my wrist...Travis," I said, trying not to agitate the look of aggression on his face.

I learned once that using a person's name could shock them back into reality, but now I questioned if that logic worked on drunks. I doubted it. His grip didn't loosen in the slightest. The strength of the intoxicated never ceased to amaze me. "If I wasn't so attached to these ma-chines, I'd show you a real good time darlin'," he said. His emphasis on the word machines sounded like rocks in a dryer—hideously annoying.

His face contorted as he spoke, not like that of a predator per say, but of a boy who had played the field at least a few dozen times and wasn't used to rejection.

"I'm not interested, please let go of my wrist."

My voice was stronger now—more intense. I pulled and twisted, fighting for release. Suddenly, he was sitting upright at full attention. His other arm came around my backside, bringing with it the monitor wires and his IV bag.

I was trapped—pinned-in—completely immobilized.

His arms were a vise, squeezing all life from my lungs.

"Let me go!" I growled with the last of my breath.

I dodged my head away from his sloppy mouth as it made a bee-line for somewhere between my neck and chest.

"Stop fighting me! You'll like it!"

He was completely immune to my panic and my disgust.

As I made one last desperate attempt to break free, a large shadow passed over me. In the split second that it took for the man to burst into the room, my struggle was over. Kai threw Travis to the bed.

The quick release forced me backward. I caught my balance against the wall, sparing myself from the hard collision that awaited me. Kai pressed into Travis holding him down easily.

"I believe the lady made herself *very* clear. Touch her or any nurse again and you won't be here for alcohol poisoning next time, capishe?" Kai's voice was hard and unflinching. The contrast in his tone was shocking.

Travis nodded, stunned by the turn of events. I could see his mind trying to connect the missing pieces, but Kai didn't wait for him to process. With a hard shove to the chest, he released Travis.

His eyes found me then for the first time. Whirling around with the speed of a superhero, Kai took my elbow and ushered me from the room. Together, we ducked into a hallway.

I leaned into the wall, trying as best I could to stand.

"Are you alright, Tori? Did he hurt you—touch you?" Kai asked.

Kai's face was shockingly concerned for a man I had only known for a week.

"No, I'm...I'm okay I think, just kind of stunned," I said, shaking my head slightly before resting it against the wall.

"That guy's a real piece of work. I transported him and several of his buddies here earlier. I thought I heard a struggle when I walked by a second ago, I'm glad I came back to check...I'm sorry I wasn't there sooner." Kai's voice was starting to calm to a normal level again, but his eyes still burned with outrage.

"Well...thank you. I was trying to break free when you came in.

It just happened so fast," I said, my face growing hot under the scrutiny of Kai's gaze.

A puzzled look stared back at me while he processed my words. Then, he leaned in and softly asked, "Tori…why didn't you scream for help? There are plenty of armed security guards all over this floor."

"I…I don't know. That didn't even cross my mind."

I was surprised at how easily the truth had slipped through my lips, completely unfiltered. He stared down at me for a few more seconds. A look I couldn't quite place crossed over his strong masculine features.

"You're a rare one, Miss Sales," he said, a hint of amusement returning in his voice. "I'm gonna have to report this, though. You'll probably be asked some questions. If anything like that ever happens again, please call for help. There is no reason you should ever be treated like that."

I nodded, too stunned to speak. I was certain only caveman-like utterances would have escaped my lips if I had tried.

Why does he have to be so handsome?

He took a few steps to the side then, as if to release me back into my reality. I exhaled loudly, not realizing I had been holding my breath.

"Did you find the note I left for you?" His smile confirmed the ending of *Intervention: Save-The-Helpless.*

"Yes, I did…swimsuit?" I asked, giving him an I'm-not-so-sure-about-that look.

Amazingly, his smile grew even wider. "Well yes, but it's most likely not for the reasons you're thinking. It will be…a little more *adventurous* than a casual swim. Correct me if I'm wrong, but I doubt you're the dinner-and-a-movie-type."

That smile—the one that reached all the way to his eyes—was infectious.

Every witty remark I could have made was lost. Still unsure what exactly I was agreeing to, I nodded. Slowly, I peeled my body away from the wall and took a few steps toward the main hall. I needed to get back to work. He placed a hand on my shoulder as I moved to pass him. I followed his dark muscular arm up the eight inches or so to his eyes.

"I'm glad you weren't hurt today, Tori," he said, shifting his gaze away momentarily. "Can I pick you up tomorrow at eleven?"

My heart hammered against my ribcage.

How does anyone say no to him…ever?

"Sure."

It wasn't my most eloquent response, but it was the best I could do under the circumstances—Kai touching me.

"Great…see you then." He turned, and started walking toward Security.

Ironically, it was in that exact second that Bev-the-socialite chose to "find me".

"Oh, there you are!" She was looking at Kai, but speaking to me.

"I've been looking all over for you, Tori…I didn't realize you two knew each other."

Her voice was like a canary—a tone-deaf canary.

I opened my mouth, but Kai beat me to it as he walked back over to us. "Hey, Bev. Tori and I are actually family friends, she's gonna make a great addition to the staff on this floor, don't you think? We were just going over some safety procedures." With that being said, he gave me a quick pat on the back before strolling away again.

"Hmm…Seems like that's not all you two were going over."

I gawked after him, unwilling to respond to Bev's nosiness, or give her any more ammo to support what she thought she had seen. Something told me that if there was a romantic relationship going on within this hospital Bev knew about it—all about it. But I wasn't as bothered by her as I wanted to believe.

I finished out the rest of my shift irritable and testy, not fully realizing why until I laid my head down at the end of the night. It was then it surfaced, the line that echoed somewhere in my head like a clanging cymbal.

"Tori and I are actually family friends…"

I guess that confirmed my suspicions. I could stop wondering *why* Kai would be interested in a troubled girl like me. He was doing me a favor. He was simply being a friend because Jack and Stacie were *his* friends. It all made perfect sense now.

Well, I didn't need any more friends. The solo life fit me just fine. At least it had, until about four days ago when some hot islander had checked me for a concussion.

Tomorrow is going to be a long day…

TEN

"Knock, knock!"

Stacie opened my door as she was knocking.

What a great sense of privacy I have in this house.

I met her inquiring gaze, refusing to give her the information she was seeking—unsolicited anyway.

"So...when is your date with Kai?" Stacie asked.

"First of all, it's *not* a date. And he'll be here around eleven."

"Oh, well *s-o-r-r-y* Broom-Hilda. I didn't know you would be waking up on the wrong side of the bed on *date day*...maybe I should tell Kai you'll meet him there on your broomstick," she said, laughing at her own lame joke.

I chucked a pillow at her, purposefully missing her rounded belly. She threw up her hands in mock surrender.

"Now, what ever will you wear my dear Tori?"

Stacie loved fashion. No, Stacie was *obsessed* with fashion. Whenever she spoke of it, her eyes lit up all crazy-like and she changed her speech to sound like she had been born a Brit. I sighed deeply, remembering my bathing suit dilemma.

I had one of course, but the body it fit was quite different than the body I had acquired with all my running over the last year. Downplaying the matter for my audience, I told Stacie of my issue.

"Oh my, now that won't do! No one needs you losing any clothing on your first date," she said, sounding far too much like Mary Poppins.

"Oy...Stacie, please!" I grabbed another pillow to chuck at her.

"Truce! Truce! Okay...fine. Come into my closet and let's see what we can find for you."

I followed Stacie into her gigantic walk-in closet. It was lined with the kind of shelving I had only ever seen in magazines. She had at least seventy pairs of shoes, all of which were perfectly organized. Her color-coordinated wardrobe boxed me in on all sides.

On the back wall were pull-out drawers, all evenly spaced with a hand-sized cut out for easy access. Inside one near the top, lay roughly ten bathing suits.

"Obviously, I won't need any of these suits in the near future. This baby is not really helping my figure out these days," Stacie said, patting her tummy.

Her fourth month of pregnancy had only accentuated her gorgeous figure, causing her to glow with what looked like a fairy-like sparkle. She was stunning, no doubt about it.

Oh Jack, I'm sorry you're missing this.

"Your figure looks better than ever, Stacie. Stop being ridiculous," I scolded. I put my hand on her belly like I'd done a couple of times this past week. Hugs might have made me uncomfortable, but touching this new little life—even just through the skin of Stacie's tight abdomen—was simply amazing.

I wonder what you are little one?

Rifling through her drawers I found a suit that fit almost perfectly. It was a coral and lime tankini with matching board shorts. I could be comfortable in that. I put them on while Stacie raved in approval, complimenting my skin-tone and trim legs.

I pulled on an additional white tank and threw a change of clothes in a beach bag. Checking my face and hair in the mirror, I decided against eye makeup. Most likely it would have ended up everywhere but my eyes by the end of the day anyway; water and makeup didn't mix so well. I'd never been a fan of the *raccoon-eye*. I pulled my hair up into a messy bun and met Kai downstairs. He had already made himself at home, talking to Stacie.

He is just a family friend, keep that in mind.

"Hey Tori," Kai said as I hit the bottom of the stairs.

Stacie turned toward me and winked.

"Hey," I said, ignoring Stacie as best I could.

"Have you recovered from last night?" Kai asked. The concern in his voice was unmistakable. My eyes screamed a warning at him, while Stacie looked at me inquisitively.

"What happened last night?" she asked me.

"Uh-"

"It was just a really busy evening. Lots of stupid college students drinking too much. It made for a bit of a madhouse in the ER," Kai said.

At least he's quick on his feet.

"Oh, phew! Don't scare me like that," Stacie said, swatting at his shoulder.

"Sorry, won't happen again," Kai said, his eyes never straying from mine.

I was grateful he had understood me. I didn't need mother-hen-Stacie giving me any more grief on when, what, or how I lived. If she even knew half of all I'd been exposed to, she'd lock me away in a closet till I was forty.

"Ready?" Kai asked, extending his arm so I could walk out first.

I doubt it.

"If you are," I said.

****

The drive to Rockwall had always been one of my favorites. It wasn't far from central Dallas, yet it felt like a world away. Surrounded by water and trees, the setting was simply beautiful.

I was definitely surprised to see two Jet Skis on a trailer behind Kai's truck. I had never been on one before, and I hoped I wouldn't make a total idiot out of myself. Kai, as usual, seemed confident, happy and relaxed.

"Sorry about that back there. I didn't realize you wouldn't want Stacie to know what happened last night with that college punk," he said.

"That's okay. The less she knows about my job hazards the better—for everyone."

Kai looked like he wanted to say something more on the matter, but re-directed instead.

"So, ever been on a Jet Ski before?" he asked.

"Nope, this will be my first time." I tried to sound nonchalant. I doubted I'd pulled it off, though. I wasn't a very good actress.

"Great! It's not hard to learn, I promise. Once you get the hang of it, it's really fun. My buddy Briggs, from the station and I take these bad boys out several times a month. It's kind of nice to operate something so compact every once in awhile."

I looked out at the lake from my window as his truck slowed to a halt.

Before I knew it, Kai was helping me out of my seat. The skin he touched below my elbow seemed to radiate with heat as tingles crawled up toward my shoulder. I moved out of his grasp quickly, willing the sensation to stop.

I helped him untie the Jet Skis and get them into position, pointing them out toward the lake. I felt a flop of uneasiness in the base of my stomach, but tried to focus on the rush I would soon feel instead.

"So what do you think? Should we ride then eat? Eat then ride, or ride, eat, and ride some more? It's ladies choice today."

He laughed as he gestured widely with his hands. I couldn't help but smile.

Lunch? He made us lunch?

"Hmm...Well, since you put it like that, I'm up for doing my first lesson before lunch. Lead the way," I said.

"Now that's what I like to hear!"

He threw me a life jacket.

In the mere seconds it took me to get my tank top off, he was already buckled-up, ready to go, and waiting. My fingers fumbled with the latches. Giving me much resistance with each tug, I tried in vain to pull the straps tighter. I bit my bottom lip in concentration. Hearing his low chuckle, I narrowed my eyes at him. Kai was unfazed by my evil glare. Instead, he leaned back casually on his Jet Ski and watched the show of my complete and utter failure at *Life Jacket 101*.

"What are you laughing at?" I asked, kicking sand in his direction. My stubborn determination was beginning to break down. I sighed heavily.

"May I?" Kai asked as he stepped toward me. With one quick draw of his arm, he cinched each buckle tight. Smiling, he tipped his imaginary hat to me and bowed.

"Is that your specialty move for all the girls you take to the lake, Kai?" I asked. Now that my pride had already been damaged, I didn't feel an urge to repress my sassiness.

Kai busted with laughter, "Ha! Oh Tori, you kill me. First of all, I don't take girls to the lake. Secondly, *if* I had a specialty move it wouldn't be getting a girl into a life vest!"

His laughter continued and I found myself wanting to join in. Amused as I was by his response, I realized his admission only reaffirmed his thoughts about me. If he didn't bring his dates to the lake, then his explanation to Bev had been quite accurate yesterday. I was just a *family friend*. The good news was that family friends shouldn't make me nervous.

If only these stupid butterflies in my stomach would follow that same logic.

He just wanted to be a friend. Better yet, he wanted to *befriend* the younger sister of his friend, to be the nice guy—the hero. That was part of his genetic code after all, wasn't it?

With new determination I sat down on my Jet Ski. Kai explained the four main points of driving. He leaned over me to demonstrate as he spoke, securing a safety lanyard to my life jacket. If I crashed, the Jet Ski would shut off immediately and the key would stay attached.

"First, plant your feet on the foot wells like this. Second, always keep your both hands on the handle bars whether going straight or making a turn. Third, you'll want to ease into the throttle or it will take off from underneath you. Try and keep it at less than twenty miles an hour until you're comfortable. Fourth, lean into your turns. Feel ready to try it?"

His instructions whirled around in my mind. I hoped they would come naturally when I was out on the water. I nodded in agreement as he pushed me in. Then he jumped onto his beside me. We sat afloat for a few seconds until he gave me the gesture to turn it on. The engine roared to life and all my senses came alive with it.

I pushed the throttle slowly, feeling a jolt of energy rush through me. Suddenly, I was driving on top of the water. My first few turns were shaky at best, but Kai kept giving me a thumbs-up. He stood effortlessly, circling my path while seeming to keep an eye on every move I made. The steering handle didn't have much play in it, so that took some getting used to. But once I was comfortable, I pushed the throttle deeper, increasing my speed.

THIS IS AMAZING!

I glanced back at Kai. He was beaming like a little boy on Christmas morning. Obviously, he loved this hobby and was happy to share it with someone. I was happy, too. At least as happy as someone recently diagnosed with a brain disconnection could be.

Kai signaled for me to come over to the middle of the lake where he idled.

"Race?"

He both yelled and signaled the guidelines for our race. Our finish line was a tree on the far side of the lake, he pointed to it. He also indicated that 40mph was our cut-off speed. I nodded.

We were off a second later.

We raced on the water over and over, Kai winning every time, although he would usually let me get ahead at least once during the lap. After a good solid hour of racing and spraying each other with lake water, it was time to eat.

Kai had brought a blanket and a cooler filled with Subway sandwiches, chips, drinks, and fruit. I had to admit—even if just to myself—that this type of kindness didn't exist in my life outside of Stacie. It was a strange feeling to be the one being served—a bit of an uncomfortable one.

"You were awesome out there," Kai said. "I think you were lying to me earlier. You've definitely done this before."

"No, I swear, that really was my first time. It's a lot of fun…being on the water like that is really amazing," I said, surprised at the ease in which I spoke to him. He handed me a sandwich bag.

The water must have knocked something loose in my crazy brain. Did I just really say the words fun and amazing in the same sentence?

Kai smiled at me as he took another bite of his sandwich. He leaned onto his left forearm, propping his body up at the elbow as he ate. He extended his legs on the blanket casually, lying on his side. My eyes grazed briefly over his bare chest and arms. He had the kind of body I had only ever seen on a protein shake advertisement.

Photoshop had nothing on Kai.

I averted my gaze quickly, shifting to stare down at my apple instead.

"I knew you'd like it," Kai said.

"*What*…like what?"

Embarrassment burned my face and neck. A second later, I realized what he was referring to.

Oops.

"Whoa there…I was just agreeing with you. It really is quite breathtaking."

Which part, your arms or your chest?

"Uh, yes. The *lake* is gorgeous," I said.

I smiled weakly, ashamed of my internal dialogue—okay, maybe ashamed was too strong a word.

Family friend…keep that in mind, Tori!

"I grew up on the water. On my island in Samoa there's not much distinction between land and water. You live on both. It's funny to see older kids here getting swim lessons for the first time, I swear the parents on my island just throw their little ones in and hope they'll figure it out."

Kai laughed, and handed me a soda.

"When did you move to the States? How old were you?" I asked, briefly touching his hand as I grabbed the drink.

"I was twelve...so about fourteen years ago now. My father passed away when I was ten, from cancer. He had always wanted his only son to be in medicine. He and my mother saved for years so I could be educated in the States. Before he passed, he made her promise that she would still take me. It was a pretty hard transition at first, but we're both happy to be here now," he said.

"Your mom lives in Texas, then?" I asked.

He sat up straighter, clearly pleased by my interest.

"Yes, she bought a house in Richardson. She has a great community of friends at her church and has found peace with herself and with God. She's a remarkable woman, very strong and brave. She's my hero in more ways than one."

My heart pounded hard in my chest. Hearing a son speak that way of his mother was not just uncommon, it was touching—even for the emotionally disturbed like myself.

"What about you, Tori? Tell me about your family."

My family?

What do I say after that story?

"It seems like you know them already. I don't have much to say, I guess. It's just my parents, Jack and Stacie, and me."

He smiled knowingly and said, "But that's more than double the amount of family I have, so I'm sure there's plenty more you *could* say."

No, because relationships make family...not just warm bodies.

"Tell me about how you know Jack and Stacie," I said, redirecting.

"Let's see...Jack and I met at a softball game when both the umpire and the batter ended up with bloody, broken noses. Jack was the one who led us to the dugout to assess their injuries. We struck up a conversation and it turned out we both went to the same church. It's just so large we had never met before. I saw him there a few times after that. I guess our friendship just grew from there. Stacie was always inviting me over for dinner...I think she must have felt bad for me being a bachelor and all. You really have a great family, Tori."

And there it was again, beating me over the head.
My family.

I stood up, ready to be done with this conversation in every way possible. I challenged Kai to another round of Jet Ski races. He did not refuse.

ELEVEN

Back on the water I was free.

We circled the lake several times, jumping each other's wakes. I pushed the throttle harder feeling the rush of adrenaline surge through my veins. My hair whipped violently in the wind, having lost the tie that once held it back. Each minute I drove, my inhibitions dissipated.

With a newfound bravery, I stood, like I had seen Kai do earlier. I could see him now to the side of me, pushing his Jet Ski forward to keep up with my increasing pace. Soon the world around me started to fade. There was no Kai, no motor sound, no trees, no rocks, no boats, and no water.

There was only me. Alone.

In an instant, I was trapped, reliving my nightmare again.

Alone, I sat up, dazed by the buzzing and the lights around me. Cords tugged at my body and my ribs were aching from my shallow breaths. I tried to place my surroundings.

Looking down at my hands, both bandaged and taped, I threw the blankets off my legs in a panic. I was in a hospital. The confusion was overwhelming, but not nearly as overwhelming as the memories that flooded just seconds later when the doctor walked into the room.

He was followed by Stacie and my parents. Their voices were muddied and thick, asking questions as they pet my hair like some stray animal.

I ignored them all. Reaching out my hand to the doctor, my mind burned with only one question.

"How is she—the little girl?" I asked. My throat was so dry and scratchy, the words were hard to force out.

No one answered.

Their efforts to distract me were futile. I pushed them off me with every bit of strength I had, and asked my question again. This time my voice broke with violent emotion.

"How is she? How is the little girl?" I demanded.

The doctor came to the side of my bed, his head bowing low, eyes down.

I didn't hear his words; I didn't need to.

My body went limp and cold all over. I closed my eyes, sobbing into my bandaged hands. I willed myself to fall asleep, hoping I'd never wake.

I wanted to stay in the dark, where I wouldn't have to feel—ever again. But the nightmare stayed with me no matter if I was awake or asleep. It was always the same, always.

The Jet Ski was at its peak speed now, zipping through the blurs around me. I wanted it all to be over. I wanted the nightmare to end. No matter how many lives I had hoped to save in the future, it would never replace the one I took.

Anna was gone...forever.

I heard a muffled scream somewhere in the distance, but I couldn't find its source. Instinctively, I turned the Jet Ski—sharply.

And then, I was flying.

The flight itself was only a few blissful seconds in length. Then gravity pulled me down onto the wet concrete-like surface. The water slapped every part of my exposed skin as I tumbled end over end.

I missed the rock wall at the water's edge, but just by a couple of feet. I tried to cry out in pain but only managed to swallow a mouthful of water. Even though I survived, I was certain my skeleton was all that remained. No skin could possibly be left intact after such a beat-down.

My life jacket kept me bobbing on the surface while ten thousand stinging needles poked at me. My ears throbbed as I coughed over and over trying to catch one full breath without tasting the lake. With my eyes pointed up toward the sky, I waited for the fog around me to clear.

Stop running.

My head snapped up in attention.

Who said that?

I looked to my right. Kai slowed his Jet Ski as he got close.

"Tori...are you okay? What on earth happened?" he asked as he slipped into the water in front of me.

"Did you...did you say something a minute ago?" I asked softly, just inches from his face.

"What? Yes! I said lots of things...I've been screaming at you to slow down for the last five hundred yards. What happened?" he asked again, this time his tone much firmer than the last.

Oh, it was Kai?

Or am I hearing voices now, too?

Stop running.

I grabbed his upper arm tightly.

Panic overwhelmed me, trumping the pain that my body was still recovering from.

"I'm sorry, Tori. You must be scared. I was scared just watching you. How's your neck? Do you feel, okay? Do you think you can ride back with me to the shore?" he asked. "I'll come back out in a minute and pull your Jet Ski in. Let's just get you settled first," he said touching the back of my neck gently.

"I...I think so. Will the Jet Ski be okay?"

"Don't worry about that, it's fine. That's easily replaceable...you are not," Kai said.

If my body hadn't been so red from hitting the water, I'd swear I was blushing. Kai boosted me up onto his Jet Ski as gently as possible, and then climbed on after me. He steered easily from behind, never exceeding 10 mph. I winced a few times as my legs thawed, but the nearness of Kai was a nice distraction.

How long has it been since I was touched longer than the briefness of a handshake or greeting hug?

I couldn't remember.

It had been over a year at best.

Kai drove the Jet Ski up onto the shore and hopped off. He started to un-buckle my life vest, but then hesitated, as if waiting for my permission. My arms were still so stiff from my landing though, that I nodded without a second thought.

In an instant, I was freed of its constriction.

"Let me help you over to the blanket, Tori."

He lifted me off the seat and braced my unsteady walk over to the blanket, the same blanket we had sat on an hour earlier.

"Thank you...and I'm sorry, Kai. I'm usually not this dramatic of a person. You've seen me at my worst and you've only known me a week!" I said, mortified.

His expression was soft, kind, but it held something else in it as well that I couldn't identify. He was quiet for a few seconds longer than felt comfortable before he shook his head.

"Maybe it's me, then? Maybe I'm a bad luck charm?"

His smile spread from ear to ear, as he knew that was the farthest thing from the truth. If anything, Kai had practically rescued me on three different occasions now. Odds were not working in my favor lately.

I'm turning into a helpless victim around this guy.

But even as I thought it, it wasn't reason enough for me to stay away from him. That, was the scariest thought I'd had all day.

Kai's eyes skimmed over my body, doing his best to look like the professional he was. He pointed out the bright red spots that would most likely bruise. Ultimately, he decided that there was no serious damage done. I was a tad disappointed when the injury inventory was over.

You are going to feel pretty stupid when he tells you you're just like the little sister he never had.

"If you're okay here for a minute, I'll go pull in the other Jet Ski so it doesn't float too far down the lake."

I nodded.

While Kai was retrieving my Jet Ski, I laid my head back and tried to process what had happened. It took a second, but then it all came back.

I had crashed because I couldn't switch back to reality from the memory of the doctor telling me about Anna. I swallowed hard.

PTSD was riddled with flashbacks, wasn't it?

Wasn't that what I'd heard about veterans after coming back from war?

Though this was far from my first flashback, the intensity had been much stronger. If I couldn't control when they happened, I could potentially be a *danger* to anyone at any time. Given the right set of circumstances—or wrong—I was nothing short of a walking, living hazard.

Stop running.

My eyes flew open as I looked from left to right.

No one.

Chills climbed up my spine.

God?

No answer.

Of course there's no answer, don't be stupid!

Laying on the shore waiting for Kai, I knew I really only had one option left. If I didn't want to go completely insane before my twenty-fourth birthday, I would have to take it. Hearing voices and having movie-type flashbacks were among the short list of things that would be cause for new concern, but honoring Anna was still at the top of my list.

Maybe it was time for a compromise with Dr. Crane after all.

****

Our drive home felt shorter than the drive out to the lake earlier that day. Kai hummed softly to the music on the radio as I laid my head against the window. He had some *God station* tuned-in. I didn't care what music it was though. His voice was soothing; I wished I could hear more of it.

Ultimately, I knew there wouldn't be *more* of anything when it came to Kai and I. Our time together had meant one thing: nothing.

Even still, I wanted to cherish the last of it. If I was destined to play the role of *little sister* within this mix of family and friends, then I only wanted a few minutes to pretend otherwise.

Just a few minutes to dream that in some past life things might have been different for us. That broken didn't have to mean eternally lonely. That a man like Kai could find a woman like me interesting and attractive. I held onto my fantasy all the way to Stacie's driveway.

It was late afternoon when we pulled up to the house. The sun was getting lower on the horizon and a soft breeze blew in from the east. Kai beat me to my door again, helping me out of his large Ford truck. As I stepped down, I could feel the bruises forming on my thighs.

"I had a really nice time today, Tori—with the exception of your death-defying crash. I wish you could have said the same. Today didn't really work out for you like I had hoped it would," he said.

His tender smile caused the butterflies to awaken inside me once again.

"I can...I mean, I did have a really nice time today—with the exception of my bad driving skills and depth perception," I said, rolling my eyes.

He chuckled then, stepping closer. He reached his hand out toward my face. I was a mixture of both fire and ice as he skimmed the curve of my scar with his thumb. I was frozen, yet my skin blazed from the heat of his touch.

He withdrew his hand quickly, a look of uncertainty flashing in his eyes. It had happened so quickly that I wondered if I had imagined it. I was known for my vivid imagination, after all.

But I could still feel the flush of my cheeks.

It had been real, right?

"I'd like to see you again, Tori. Maybe we could do something a little less *dangerous* next time," he said, his eyes locking onto mine.

My stomach flipped wildly as my palms began to sweat. This had to end now; I had to stop this before all my dignity and control were lost forever. There was no *magic pixie dust* for me. I wouldn't ever be a girlfriend. I could barely be a friend.

The role of *little sister* would have to suffice.

The only other alternative…was to be nothing at all.

I stared down at my feet.

"Thank you Kai for being so willing to befriend me with no questions asked. I'm sure Jack will be really happy to know that he could count on you. I'll tell Stacie to ask you over for dinner soon," I said, my heart racing.

"Oh…okay," he said.

Kai took a step back and looked at me inquisitively. I stood motionless, not quite sure what my next move should be.

Why did he look so…disappointed?

I had just invited him to hang out at my family dinners, he should be thrilled!

"Have a good evening, Tori. Please say goodbye to your sister for me." He turned and walked to his truck. His back faced me as I watched him grip the handle of his door.

Then, he stopped.

My heart stopped, too.

In that second I wished more than anything that I could be *unbroken*. I envied all those normal, carefree girls that knew nothing about shame, or loss, or heartache. The girls that wouldn't think twice about saying *yes* to spending more time with a guy like Kai.

"Tori?"

Kai stared at me, a look of confident determination on his face.

"Yes?"

"For the record, Jack never asked me to befriend you. That was all my doing. Have a good weekend."

He winked at me before closing his door and driving away.

For once my mind was blank. No thoughts, no sarcasm, no witty banter. Kai had pursued me all on his own, and I had just pushed him away.

A teeny, tiny shred of a feeling that I hadn't known in quite some time was pushing its way up through the cracks of my past.

Please don't let me go so easily, Kai.

TWELVE

"It's so nice to hear from you Victoria, what did you decide?" Dr. Crane asked.

I was surprised when she answered her phone on a Saturday afternoon, until she explained that she'd given me her cell number. She told me I was welcome to call her anytime a need arose.

Do I have Dr. Bradley to thank for that courtesy?

"I would like to schedule an appointment," I said.

"Okay...how does ten o'clock work for you next Wednesday morning?"

"That would be fine. I'm only scheduled to work Wednesday and then the weekend of next week, so I'd like to pick up some on call hours once you sign off," I said, reminding her of the bargain she'd made.

"Sounds good. I'll have your paperwork ready for you Wednesday morning. Take care...and Victoria? Your first homework assignment is to *connect*. Try to connect with at least one person and we'll discuss how it went at your appointment," she said.

After hanging up the phone I replayed her words in my head.

Connect?

So pretty much the opposite of what happened today with Kai, then.

Awesome. Just awesome.

I slumped back on my bed. It would be a long week if I didn't pick up any extra hours. Wednesday couldn't come soon enough. I needed that paperwork ASAP.

I was exhausted both mentally and physically from my time at the lake. I heard Stacie pass by my open door while talking on the phone. She paused, as if wanting me to overhear her conversation. I closed my eyes and pretended to be asleep; too bad she knew my trick.

"...Yes, I'll ask her. She just needs some time," Stacie said.

I could guess what was being said on the other end of that call. I chose instead to picture the calm of the lake, the blue of the sky and the beautiful Samoan I had just watched drive away.

You'll have to deal with her sometime; You can't ignore her forever.

I heard Stacie come in my room. I peeked out through one eye and saw her standing with her hands on her hips.

"So that was Mom on the phone. I was trying to help her understand that pushing you isn't going to work..."

I hope she heard you, 'cause she never seems to hear me.

"Thanks," I said, opening my eyes fully. "What does she want?"

"She wants me to ask you if you'll go shopping with us this evening...for the baby. We are going to narrow down our choices for both boy and girl—for the nursery. That way after the ultrasound we can get to work. I would really love for you to come, too."

Stacie was so sincere when she spoke. Her sweet demeanor was impossible for me to ignore. I thought for a few seconds, and then looked back at the clock. If I could rest for an hour, would I be willing to go?

Since one of my connection opportunities had already failed, maybe this was my second chance?

I agreed, but only on the stipulation that I could take a nap first. Stacie, of course, was thrilled. I hoped I had made the right call. Her reaction scared me, but that was fairly normal.

For every one thought I had, Stacie had about ten emotions that could match it. Her passion scale started where mine topped-out. Pregnancy had made that gap between our personalities even more extreme.

"Great, I'll let her know. We can leave here around six thirty. Let's get some Chinese for dinner...the baby and I have been craving it for weeks! And Tori...you will tell me all about your date today, right?"

I sighed as I waved my hand in the air before turning over to position my head under my pillow. I heard her leave a few seconds later. Stacie was nothing, if not persistent. I knew that wouldn't be the end of it.

****

Mom looked like she was dressed for a photo shoot with *Southern Living* when she entered The Baby Warehouse. Everything was a perfect match with her: her french-tipped nails, her nautical handbag and her navy and red pumps. She was the perfect combination of color and class.

If I hadn't known this woman, I would have thought her

striking and confident. Nobody ever believed that she was fifty. Often, people assumed that the three of us were sisters when we were all together—an assumption I was quick to correct, even under my mother's disapproving glare.

"Hello my darlings! How fun that we all get to be together again, and shopping, too," she said, announcing her greeting to the entire store.

I hugged her quickly, hoping it would have a calming effect on her. I did not want more cause for commotion. She walked close to me throughout the store, picking out every piece of cute baby paraphernalia that she saw. After awhile, it all kind of looked the same to me. This crib or that crib, this stroller or that stroller, this highchair or that highchair, etc. But I was happy for Stacie. I knew it had to be hard on her with Jack away, so I decided I would keep my mouth shut and take it all in stride. I would try to *connect*.

Did this count as connecting yet?

I sure hope so.

After nearly two hours of listening to, "Oh my word! That's soooo darling," or, "Isn't that just so precious?" It was time to eat. I did not complain.

The Chinese restaurant was fairly crowded, but they managed to seat us in just ten minutes. Stacie's baby bump gave us a slight advantage.

"So Tori, how's work going?" my mother asked after our order was taken.

"Pretty good, just learning the hospital's protocols for now and job shadowing," I said.

If I couldn't be completely honest with Stacie about all that went on in Trauma, I had to be even more guarded with my mother.

"Ya know, I still have a friend in Labor and Delivery that would be happy to hire you if you ever wanted to switch floors," my mother added. Good intentioned as she was, she was completely oblivious to any specifics about my life or career. "Thanks Mom, I'll keep that in mind."

Switch floors? Like that's even how it worked.

Connecting is way more difficult than I had anticipated.

"Stacie told me that you went out earlier today with Kai Alesana. How did that go? He's sure a sweet young man." My mother looked at me, waiting for a response.

I turned to look at Stacie who was suddenly very focused on her appetizer.

Connect. Connect. Connect.

"It was fine. We're just *friends*. I actually see him around my hospital, so we're more like *friendly* co-workers," I said.

Good one.

"Well, if I were a young single woman, he'd be the kind of friend I would want to have. That's for sure."

She winked at Stacie who giggled into her drink.

"I didn't realize you knew him that well, Mom?"

The second I asked the question, I wished I could take it back. I didn't want to encourage a discussion about Kai, but my curiosity proved stronger than my logic.

"Oh, well...I wouldn't say I know him too well, but he has come over a few times for family cook-outs. Actually, he and Jack built our latest deck renovation last spring. He was quite the handyman. They made a pretty good team, wouldn't you agree Stace?" she asked.

"For sure, although I think they did it more for the free baked goods and daily diving competitions," Stacie said. She laughed as she set her drink down.

"Diving competitions?"

"Tori, you should have seen them! Because it was so hot out, they would dive into the pool the second they were finished working. There was this whole rating system they came up with; how did it go again, Stacie?"

Stacie jumped into the story as if right on cue. Full of animation, she threw her arms in the air and laughed loudly.

"They would only get a ten if they could complete the crazy obstacle courses they laid out for each dive. If neither of them could complete it, then neither would score. One that Jack set up involved our two lawn chairs. They had to jump over them both, spin around three times, and then dive backward into the pool perfectly for it to count. It was like the Olympics for the testosterone-challenged!"

I laughed, picturing the comedy show that must have been. It seemed strange that I hadn't known Jack and Kai as friends, but I could imagine they got along quite well. My mother's face changed as she watched me laugh with Stacie. I tried to place it her look.

Was it relief?

"I don't think I told you, Tori, but Dad and I have been visiting Stacie and Jack's church for the last few months," my mother said.

Now that was surprising. My parents had attended the same church since before I was born—at least on important holidays or to meet their clients before a lunch date. The idea of them gracing the doors of another was downright revolutionary, especially after my mom's initial reaction to Stacie's church transfer years ago.

"What? No, I hadn't heard that," I said.

"Yes, it's been really nice seeing them there," Stacie added.

"Why the change, I don't understand. Did something happen to Pastor Howard?" I asked.

"Oh heavens, no. We haven't made anything official quite yet, but change is necessary sometimes. It's been really good to feel challenged again after such a difficult season."

Difficult season?

"Tori, are you going to join us tomorrow? I would sure love for you to come and meet some of our friends," Stacie asked.

Oh no. Think of something...think of anything!

"Tori?"

"I, uh...can I let you know in the morning?" I asked.

I didn't want to talk about church, or anything it involved. This last year and a half had been hard enough for me; I didn't need any more complications. God and I seemed to have a mutual understanding now. He didn't ask anything of me and I didn't ask anything of Him.

It was working out just fine.

Was it really?

The question seemed to jump out of thin air, sending goose bumps down my spine.

It wasn't that I held any disrespect toward those that wanted to believe in God, or even the idea of *church community*. I had finally realized though, that I was no longer the type of person that needed church. Nor was I a person the church needed.

I could grasp the concept of desiring acceptance from seemingly spiritual people. I also understood that there were folks who looked to the church for balance, support and comfort. But *religion* could offer me none of those things now.

My guilt overshadowed them all.

Dodging Stacie the last two Sundays had been fairly easy. I knew that wouldn't be the case forever though. The truth would have to come out and I would rather it be sooner than later. I knew she wouldn't want to hear it, but that didn't change the fact that her God and I hadn't shifted out of neutral in a very long time.

Thankfully, the conversation moved on to the baby. That was always a safe and welcome topic for me. I sat back, shifting into listen-only mode. They discussed everything from nursery décor to co-sleeping, breast-feeding vs. bottle feeding, and the most-debated topic, "cloth or disposable diapers?"

I ate my Chinese food silently. Since I was momentarily under the radar, I found myself day-dreaming about another foreign food, one that I had never experienced—authentic Samoan.

Did Kai cook it?

Did his mom cook it for him? Did he even like it anymore, or was McDonalds his type of food now since he was an American?

Mom paid the bill before we said goodbye in the parking lot. The night had been relatively painless—almost enjoyable. My mother had seemed different. Not in personality or social mannerisms necessarily, but different nonetheless. It bothered me a great deal that I couldn't identify what it was. In the end I chalked it up to the length of time we had been apart.

How arrogant I was to think that *my life* was the only one that could have changed over the last seventeen months. I made a mental note to inquire about it later to Stacie, after a good long sleep.

I was exhausted.

THIRTEEN

Sunday.

It wasn't like I had blatantly lied to Stacie while I was living in Phoenix; I just hadn't offered her the whole truth. She believed the reason I had worked every Sunday was because I had no other option, but in reality, I had requested that shift. I figured as long as I worked on Sundays, the church questions would stay on hold. I had been right.

Though I had prepared an excuse for why I couldn't attend this morning's service, I hadn't been prepared to get a call from my dad.

"Hey Dad, how are you?" I asked, answering the phone on my nightstand.

"I'm good, Sugar. Your mom told me all about your great time last night and I was so happy to hear that you three were back together again, breaking the bank no less," Dad said.

"Yeah, it was good," I said.

"I know Mom told you that we've been attending church with Jack and Stacie the last few months and I was hoping to see you there this morning, kiddo. I've been doing my best to give you space, but I miss you like crazy."

Why couldn't I be working today? Or have the flu?
Was it too late to fake the flu?

My dad was a man who didn't ask for much. He worked hard, earning everything he had and giving even more than that away. There were few people I couldn't say no to, and he was at the top of the list. Exceptions, though, had to be made.

This area of my life was off limits.

I opened my mouth to tell him that I'd rather meet him somewhere after church, but it was then that he hit me with another low blow.

"I probably shouldn't tell you this…but your mom's been on her knees praying for you a lot these last few months. She's been praying specifically for you to join us at church, so we could be together as a family. I know you two have had your issues in the past, but she really wants to make things right. It would mean a great deal to both of us if you came."

Oh come on! For crying out loud!

Is there no shame left in these people at all?

"Oh Dad...I don't know. It's different for me now. I'm not so sure that church and I are really a fit anymore-"

"Nonsense. If you don't like it, you don't have to come back, but at least come today," he pushed.

I blew out an exaggerated sigh. He knew he was winning. I rolled my eyes and smashed my head back into my pillow.

"Fine, but I make no promises on anything in the future. Are we clear on that, Dad?" I asked.

"Clear as mud, sweetheart. See ya at eleven, and plan on lunch at our place afterward."

Click.

I looked at my phone, stunned.

Did that really just happen?
Bullied by my own father into going to church?
What had the world come to?

Stacie purposefully stayed out of my way as I got ready. I could feel her watchful eye as I moved about the house, but she knew better than to try and talk to me. It was one thing to give in under pressure; it was another to admit it. After my shower I stood in front of my closet for what felt like an eternity.

What do I wear to the one place I dread going most of all?

I sighed.

Maybe I was looking at this the wrong way. How hard can it possibly be to tune out a two hour church service?

I'll just think of it as a job—one that I hate doing, but have to get done in order to move on with my day. That's all it is, a chore, nothing more.

I worked hard to believe that logic pounding in my head as I grabbed a simple navy maxi dress out of my closet. I layered it with a short gray cardigan, and slipped into some matching gray ballet flats. The length of the dress would hide the large bruises on my thighs. I was grateful for that at least. I styled my hair down, an unusual choice for me, but why not?

It had already proved to be a strange day, and it was still morning.

****

Stacie waited patiently in the car for me. She complimented my outfit as I buckled my seat belt. I nodded in silent recognition. That was the extent of our conversation on the drive to church.

There was nothing that could make me see this day differently than the chore that it was. Nothing, until I saw Kai enter the worship center. There were possibly three thousand people in this large dome-shaped room, and I had to see *him*. Stacie waved at him wildly, like a pregnant lady who had gone completely mad. He smiled in reply and headed our way.

I wanted to die, but I wanted to take Stacie out first.

"Hey," Kai said, smiling.

"Hey," I replied.

"Do you want to sit with us, Kai? My folks should be joining us shortly, but there should be room on the other side of Tori," Stacie said, as if she was doing him the world's biggest favor.

Yep, I would definitely take her out first.

"Sure thing," he said.

Kai headed down the row to sit next to me just as my parents showed up.

Great. Now I get to explain why Kai is sitting next to me during our family lunch today. This day just keeps getting better.

My dad's embrace was tight, but quick. He winked at me as he moved to find his seat. I was sure it was his way of approving my decision to show up. My mom reached across Stacie's belly to squeeze my hand and tell me how happy she was to see me. She was sincere. I could see it in her eyes, though it was hard for me to admit it, even if only to myself.

As the band started to play, everyone stood.

My stomach lurched violently with nerves.

"Your hair looks really nice that way."

I jumped at the sound of Kai's voice in my ear.

"Thanks," I said.

I heard him laugh as he started to clap along with the music. I stood awkwardly, unsure of what to do. I'd been in church hundreds of times: stand up, sit down, sing, greet, sit, share, listen, and leave. It had always been the same structure, but today was the first time since...the accident.

The old familiar was no longer familiar.

Jack and Stacie had changed churches a few years ago, which was quite the drama in our family at the time. I had been so busy with school that it didn't seem to faze me in the slightest, though.

Church was just church. Who cared where they went? However, my mother did not see it that way.

To her it was a betrayal, an utter disgrace that *her* daughter, who had practically been born on one of those padded pews, could ever consider leaving. It was simply unimaginable. One would have thought that Stacie had started sacrificing animals to idols the way my mother had first reacted.

But Jack and Stacie continued to rave about the ways they had grown during that first year at their *mistress church*. Stacie began serving in the community, at the poorest schools in Dallas, bringing meals to the teachers and working in after-school programs. They had spoken mostly, though, about the small groups they had been a part of. Words like accountability, acceptance, and encouragement were heard often. Although they had invited me many times, I was always too busy to attend. Besides, I had friends at my parent's church.

Where were those friends now?

Nowhere.

My mind was scattered, but my ears couldn't help but hear Kai's deep, strong voice next to me. I had been right; the humming I'd heard in his truck was just the tip of the iceberg. His voice was beautiful. Soon, I focused on it alone. The words flowed tenderly from his lips, and I wondered if he really believed the words he sang. I had never heard these songs before. They were different from what I remembered.

The songs I had sung in an old ancient language, to an old ancient God, were a far cry from these.

I looked to my left, all three people to my left were signing, eyes closed like in a prayer.

The sight was bizarre. I had never seen them like this at church, and I had twenty-three years of history to think back on.

What was happening here?

I had often felt like the outsider when it came to my family. Mom and Stacie were a pair, and Dad was the hard-working entrepreneur. I had opted out of the family business to pursue nursing—a career choice that was foreign to them all. Even still, some things were foundational.

Church and religion were two of those things.

So your feelings can change, but theirs can't?

And there it was again, the voice that quickened my heart rate. It seemed to come from somewhere…*within?* Is my PTSD getting stronger?

Wednesday was just a few days away.

What would Dr. Crane think about these voices? Maybe I'm further gone than she thought. Maybe it was already too late for me? I shuddered at the thought. Envisioning a lifetime of voices talking in my head was hard to swallow, even for me.

Kai seemed to sense my uneasiness and gave me a wayward glance. His brows were raised in question. I tried to smile; I failed miserably.

Sorry Kai, but you're standing next to a crazy girl.

The music ended.

Much to my relief, we were seated just after the extended meet-and-greet time was over. Stacie and Kai seemed to know many people around us, all of which were full of questions and kind remarks. To say I felt awkward was an understatement.

There was a Sesame Street song that sang it best, "One of these things does not belong here…"

Yeah, ya think?

A middle-aged man who dressed like he was in college, wearing jeans and a polo, made his way to the stage. Kai leaned over to me and whispered his name, "Pastor Mark."

We are down to using first names in church? And wearing jeans? My grandmother is probably rolling over in her grave right about now…

The sermon was titled, *Our Need for a Savior*. It wasn't like I wanted to hear it, but as it turns out, it's pretty hard to zone-out in a room that's so largely focused on the one thing happening up front: the message. I sighed, trying to will myself to relax.

Kai gave me a quick pat on the knee, while never taking his eyes off Pastor Mark. Stacie nudged me gently. Even out of the corner of my eye I could tell her smile was ridiculously huge. She had not asked me again about *lake day*, but by the looks of it, her optimism hadn't died.

"…How easily we grow weary in our pain and suffering, in our shame that imprisons us, in our need to control every circumstance we face. But all along, God has given us one answer to all of these dilemmas. He is the only One that can bring light to our darkness.

We must recognize that our need for a Savior came before we even existed on this earth."

A warm sensation radiated through my chest.

Geesh, this guy is good.

Pastor Mark was a passionate man. He paced back and forth on the stage, but never pointed to the crowd with looks of condemnation. Instead, only kindness seemed to flow from the words he spoke.

It was obvious he believed every word.

Maybe I had heard this before…*maybe*, but if so, never like this. I was suddenly very envious of Stacie and Kai and their ability to *simply believe*. I wished I could be a person that needed church, a person that felt comfort from it the way they both seemed to.

It dawned on me then, that maybe there was more to this whole faith thing. But just the idea alone was far too over-powering. I knew the ending before the question was even formed in my mind. Nothing ever could or ever would erase what had been done to Anna.

My debt was a mountain I could not climb, and a bill I could never pay.

FOURTEEN

As soon as the last prayer ended, the room was in motion.

I was acutely aware of Kai's presence behind me. He gently touched my arm, and said my name. I turned to look at him, surprised again by the handsome face that stared back at me.

"Can we talk for a minute?" Kai asked.

"Right here?" I looked around at the crowded space. My parents and sister were very close in proximity to us. More importantly, they were all within earshot.

"No, let's go this way."

Kai led me through the crowd. Gently, he pressed his hand to the small of my back. My knees felt weak as I reminded myself how to walk. We exited through a side door that took us outside onto a patio. A few over-sized flower pots framed the doorway behind us. Kai dropped his hand as we stood to face each other.

He stared at me for one long, uncomfortable minute. As usual, my heart rate quickened.

"Tori...last night I did a lot of thinking about our time together at the lake. I went over our conversations..." he said, pausing to search my face.

Okay...and realized what?

That I'm not the girl you hoped I'd be? I could have told you that, pal.

"I was trying to figure out where I had misread you—or worse, where I may have misled you."

Oh God...that is what he's about to say. That he was wrong to ask me out, that it was a mistake.

"That's okay Kai, really. I get it. Can we just forget about everything? I need to go find Stacie, she's my ride."

A wave of rejection crashed over me—fighting me as I desperately tried to take back control. I started toward the door, but his hand met mine first, pulling me away from it.

"Tori, no,"—his tone was almost frantic—"that's not what I'm trying to say."

He pushed back his thick black hair, ruffling a few stray pieces in the process. The familiar spasm in my stomach was back. I worked hard to ignore it.

"Then what *are* you trying to say?" I asked impatiently, raising my voice.

"That I *like* you. That I don't know how or where the signals got crossed, but I'm not doing anyone a favor by wanting to spend time with you. If you don't feel the same way I can deal with that, but I won't let you think that I don't have feelings for you. And I don't mean feelings like a big brother," he said, taking a step closer to me.

Shocked at hearing him address the concerns of my inner-dialogue, I could do nothing but stare at him. I blinked, trying to make sense of his words.

"Kai, I'm having a hard time understanding why, or how, you could be saying that to me. You only think you know me because of my family, and I'm not like them. I'll never be a Stacie."

The words flew out of my mouth, in one rushed flow of consciousness.

Kai reached for my hand then, bringing it close to his chest. Instantly, I felt a calm wash over me. I had no explanation for why that was, but I knew I didn't want him to let go of it, either.

"Can you do me a favor, please?" he asked.

I sighed, nodding as I stared at our hands.

"Let me worry about the *why's* and *how's*, okay? You don't need to question that. Those aren't the questions I'm asking myself when I'm near you. But I can assure you, I don't want you to be your sister, Tori. She's great and all, but you're...you're something very special."

"Oh."

It was a stupid response, but no other words came. My voice was with the rest of me somewhere, somewhere floating further away from everything I knew to be real.

He reached out for my face then, his thumb lightly tracing the edge of my scar. The moment was surreal. Every thought I had was put on hold as I concentrated on the warmth of his touch. He followed the raised, curved line as it trailed under my left cheekbone. My breathing faltered when his thumb neared my lips.

He stared at me intently.

The door behind me opened and slammed back against the wall, killing the magical moment completely.

"Oh, there you two are! I was just about to leave you, Tori. We're having lunch out at our folk's place, you're more than welcome to come, Kai," Stacie said.

Kai gently dropped our joined hands. He took a step back before answering her. "I'm sorry. I already have plans with my mom this afternoon for lunch. I'm helping her with some yard clean up, but I'd love to take a rain check," Kai said, looking at me apologetically.

"Okay. Well, I'll see you in a minute then, Tori. I'll head out to the parking lot and let Mom and Dad know I found you."

Kai turned back to me, his eyes mysterious and charming.

"I'm bummed I can't spend time with you and your family today. I start my forty-eight hour shift tonight...so my next opportunity to see you won't be till Wednesday. What's your schedule this week?"

Dang.

"I actually work a twelve on Wednesday, then I work the weekend shift with another possible shift or two in between," I said.

Irony was standing here with Kai, questioning if I really wanted those extra hours or not. I had just agreed to the compromise with Dr. Crane yesterday, but yet spending time with Kai seemed even more appealing than work. No one would be more surprised by that internal revelation than I was.

"Hmm...well that poses a bit of a problem. It might be kinda hard for me to get to know you better if I can't spend time with you?" He laughed, and then focused on me again, as if remembering something important. "Are you free Thursday evening by any chance?"

"I think so. Why, what did you have in mind?" I looked at him suspiciously, unsure why he suddenly looked nervous.

He hesitated.

"There's this work function, actually. I hadn't decided if I was going to attend yet, but if you'd be willing to go with me...I'd be happy to take you," Kai said.

"What sort of work function?" I asked, mirroring his look of uncertainty.

He laughed again and cleared his throat.

"It's an annual fundraiser for the firemen, EMTs, and paramedics of Collin, Denton, and Dallas counties. It's a pretty formal dinner, but afterwards there's dancing, karaoke and an auction. Most of my station will be there."

"And you weren't sure if you were going?"

"It's uh...it's not as fun to go solo," he said.

I couldn't make sense of him. Here he was: smart, kind, funny, and *gorgeous*. Why would he *not* have a date? I would be willing to bet there was a line of women just waiting for Kai to notice them.

"Hmm...that does sound like a predicament," I said, torturing him a little longer. "I suppose I could work something out. I'll just have to black-out Thursday evening on the on-call schedule. What time should I be ready?"

Kai smiled, confidence returning in spades. We walked toward Stacie's car where I'm sure she sat waiting for all the juicy details. Details she'd be sure to ask me the second my car door was closed.

"Let's say five? And, it is formal. I hope that's okay?"

"I do own more than scrubs, ya know."

My insides were flipping wildly with nerves at just the *thought* of dressing up for this event.

"Great, I'm really looking forward to taking you, Tori. Can I call you this week?"

I stared at him.

What was happening to me?

"I think I'd like that," I said.

"Well I *know* I'd like it," he said smiling, "Until then, Tori."

Kai winked at me before walking away.

Stacie looked like she might explode from excitement as I opened the car down and sat down inside. Her smile could have spread across the United States. It was embarrassing.

"Just drive Stacie...I'll tell you everything, I promise."

****

The way out to my parent's house was like a high school slumber party. Stacie wanted every detail of my time spent with Kai. Though it was my nature to hold back information, I wasn't sure I wanted to—not with this.

I hadn't felt *happy* in a very long time. I wanted to marinate in it, to allow it to saturate the sad and lonely places that had taken up residence in my heart. *Happy* was short-lived. It wouldn't last, I knew that. But I would be a grateful host for however long it chose to stay.

Good feelings were fleeting.

"So what did he say after you told him to just forget about it?" Stacie asked. She practically dripped with curiosity.

"He...he told me he *liked* me. He said I was special." I blushed at the admittance.

Did that really happen?

Stacie squealed in delight.

I told her then about the upcoming dinner on Thursday evening. She was beyond excited, immediately discussing plans for my attire. Apparently, she had that part under control. When she started describing the different fabrics and color options, I started to fade out, allowing today's events to flood my mind instead.

What am I even doing? The girl Kai thinks he knows is a fraud.
If he knew my past...what would he really think of me?

I pushed the depressing thoughts away and tried to focus on what was directly ahead: lunch with my parents. Unexpectedly, the mental picture of them at church flashed in my mind. What had been the cause for such a dramatic change in their church demeanor? And why had they really switched churches?

"Stace?" I asked, interrupting some new rant about how beige pumps could make a woman's legs look longer.

"Yeah?"

She shook her head slightly, as if coming out of a fashion-fog.

"Why did Dad and Mom *really* change churches?"

Stacie was quiet for a minute. She seemed to be thinking hard about her answer. While never one to beat around the bush, she always tried to be careful with how she worded things—especially the important things.

"That's a difficult question for me to answer, Sis. It would be better coming from them I think, but I can say that a lot has changed with them since you left. I've seen things in both of their lives that have been hard to watch...but ultimately, those things have grown them as people, and as parents."

Stacie's voice was low and smooth. She concentrated on each word she spoke.

"*Grown?* What do you mean?"

"If you really want the truth...then I'll tell you. It just might be hard for you to hear, and I want to be sensitive to that."

I nodded at her, but I was suddenly filled with dread. I didn't think there could be anything more difficult left for me to hear in this life, but maybe I was wrong about that. I swallowed hard, waiting for her to go on.

Stacie took a deep breath.

"Tori, after you left I know I told you Dad and Mom were okay—that they understood after you had called them from Phoenix, but that wasn't the whole truth. I was afraid to tell you everything because you were already dealing with so much. I didn't want to add to your suffering, so I tried to tread lightly."

I was surprised at how much she sounded like me.

"When you left without saying goodbye, it was *very* painful for them. I saw them cry many times over that—over you. They even went to counseling, trying to process through how to deal with their loss."

How to deal with their loss? Was she joking?

Anger rolled off me in droves.

"I didn't *die* Stacie, don't exaggerate!"

"You might as well have. They were beside themselves for weeks—months even. Their daughter had completely pushed them away while in the midst of a horrible tragedy, and they couldn't help you! You wouldn't even let them *try*," she snapped.

"They couldn't help me! No one could help me! What were my options really, Stacie? Stay here and suffocate under all their pity? Force them to look at a daughter who overnight had traded a promising future for...the guilt of a *child-killer*? No way! I didn't need that reminder from our mother—I live with it every single day!"

Stacie drew in a sharp breath at my words. I had never allowed myself to be quite so honest. My internal thoughts as *post-accident Tori* were still too raw, too real. No one could understand them. Stacie pulled into my parent's driveway a minute later, parking several yards away from their front door. Silently, she put her head on the steering wheel. For a second I thought she might be in real physical pain. I felt my hard expression soften as I thought about the baby.

Is she having a cramp?

Stacie lifted her head and looked at me, tears streaming down her perfectly made-up face. In a voice barely above a whisper, she spoke.

"You can't possibly think that, Tori. Please tell me you don't really think you *killed* that little girl? All this time I thought you were angry because of the accident. Because it had altered your life plans, robbing you of the joy of some of your best accomplishments. I never, ever saw it as *guilt* though—until now. I...I don't even know what to say to that."

I sat quietly.

I didn't know what to say either. I wished I could rewind time and erase my last big blurt. But it had happened. Stacie now knew a portion of the shame that I had tried to keep hidden. I could no longer deny it.

"I'm sorry, Stacie. I shouldn't have upset you."

"Stop it! Stop it right now, Victoria! I am sick and tired of you trying to protect me. That's *NOT* your job!" Stacie hit the steering wheel hard with the heel of her hand, "I am *your* big sister, and at the moment I feel like a pretty crummy one. I guess we've both been trying to protect each other over this last year and a half, but look where it got us? Nowhere. Starting today, I want the truth from you, no matter how painful or ugly it is. I can promise you that it will stay between us, but I can't promise that I will always say what you hope to hear. Can you agree to that?"

I was leaning on the arm of the passenger side door when she asked. I had only seen Stacie erupt like that a few times over the course of my childhood, but never had it been directed toward me. The reality of her words hung in the air between us like heavy smog. I had a hard time seeing through it, much less taking a breath.

This week had been determined to choke-me-out.

It had started that first day in Dr. Crane's office. Dissecting the details of Anna's death piece by piece had been brutal, but learning I was at the root of my parent's odd behavior was just absurd. Now Stacie wanted to make an honesty pact with me?

She doesn't know what she's asking for.

"I don't know if I can do that, Stacie."

She sighed and took my hand.

"We'll do it together, then. You're not alone in this anymore."

FIFTEEN

Sunday lunch was interesting, to say the least. My *honesty pact* with Stacie had come about unexpectedly, but it had also opened up a whole new set of issues. I found myself watching the way my parents interacted with each other, and with me. I was on edge, waiting for the other shoe to drop at any moment.

With each question they asked me, that sinking feeling in the pit of my stomach grew. It was difficult to look them the eye. The knowledge that my absence had been difficult for them was one thing, but the fact that it was at the root of several major changes in their lives, was quite another. I tried to wrap my mind around what Stacie had said. I wondered about their counseling sessions, had their marriage been in trouble?

It would have hurt them more if I had stayed—I did the right thing.

During lunch, my dad gave me an update on the family business. He told me all about the new marketing plan that Stacie had been developing, and the properties my mother had recently sold. My parents were a well-known couple throughout the region, their faces on billboards all over the city.

Sales Real Estate was definitely a household name. Their long history of success was based mostly off referrals, an old-fashioned approach in today's economy. They had made it through the troubled years, worked tirelessly through the boom of the first-time home buyer's era, and were now strong, steady and growing.

Before I was accepted into nursing school, my dad had taken me to lunch. He had asked me to consider joining the family in the real estate arena, but he knew I would decline his offer. My heart had never been in business; I belonged in health care. I had known it since I was a child. Though he accepted my answer graciously, I knew he was disappointed.

Little did he know that was just the first of many disappointments to come.

My one recognition by the Sales Real Estate team however, was the slogan I came up with as a senior in high school, "Let the Sales guarantee your satisfaction!" My dad had beamed with pride. He had called to order new posters and signs that very day. It'd felt good to contribute, however minor. It had also eased my guilt of turning down his offer.

If only slogan-writing could do that for me now.

****

I continued to watch my parents throughout the day. They worked side by side cleaning up the lunch plates, telling us to go enjoy the pool. Neither Stacie nor I felt like swimming though, so we sat together on the deck, drinking sweet tea. Our mom joined us when she was done. She had that look on her face again, the one I couldn't quite place. It made me uncomfortable.

It was like she could see me—the real me, the one I had hidden from her specifically.

She smiled and touched my hand as Stacie told us the latest update on Jack. This gesture to anyone else might seem normal, but that kind of affectionate touch was *not normal* for us. Stacie and Mom were that way with each other, but not Mom and me.

Greeting hugs were one thing, but not intimacy. Intimacy meant: common ground, connection, understanding, willingness, and vulnerability. We did not have intimacy.

My heart ached as I stood up, sliding my hand out from under her touch. I told them I needed to stretch and walk a bit. They nodded in response to me, remaining in their lounge chairs. I was grateful.

I walked deep into the landscaped yard, finding the bridge where I had first seen Kai. I stood on its highest point, leaning over to stare down at the koi fish below.

Their brightly colored scales were hypnotizing as I watched them swim. I could stand on this bridge for hours watching them, thinking. This bridge was a great spot to seek peace and serenity—not that I really believed in either of those things anymore. I heard footsteps approaching as my dad found me. He leaned onto his elbows, peering over the wooden rail beside me.

My dad was a calm man, relaxed in manner, but strong in principle. Even the most difficult workday ceased to bring him stress, he simply didn't believe in it. We stood silently for a few minutes, mesmerized by the beautiful scenery around us.

'Do you know that you're one of only two people who really appreciates this little spot out here? Mom was gonna have me fill it in last year and move the fish to the pond on the other side of the house, but I remembered you loved this spot," he said, still gazing downward.

"Yeah, it's a great spot. I'm glad you kept it," I said.

"Darlin', I can't tell you how happy I am that you're home. I know you hate the gushy stuff, so I'll keep it short. It just feels so good to see your face again. Thanks for coming to church this morning, too. What did ya think of that? Pretty different, huh?"

His eyes sparkled in wonder as he spoke, as if this church conversation was actually exciting to him.

Weird.

"Uh...well, yeah it was *different*. I hope you aren't expecting me to make a habit out of going though, Dad."

"Oh Tori, hold your horses. No need to get defensive on me. I'm just asking a simple question. Your mom and I have discovered a lot in the short time we've been attending there. We just wanted to share it with you," my dad interrupted, never getting above a firm whisper.

"Yeah, I keep hearing that, Dad," I said sarcastically.

"Ya know, pumpkin, it sounds like you have some stuff to sort out with God."

His body still faced the pond. Though his eyes were still focused on the water below, I felt smothered.

"No Dad, I really don't. It's pretty well sorted out already," I said.

"There are only two paths we can be on with God: moving forward or moving away."

I didn't speak. The words in my head were too hard and angry to be directed toward my father. My battle wasn't with him. I tried to remind myself of that.

"With either, heartache will still come. It's not life's circumstances that separate the two paths...it's the ability to hope. That's the game-changer, sweetheart."

Hope?

"Come on. Let's get back to the house. I think Stacie might be ready to head home for her afternoon nap."

We walked close to each other, my dad's hand on my shoulder nearest him. Before he slid the glass door open, I remembered a question from earlier.

"Dad? Who's the other person that loves my spot at the

bridge?"

His eyes twinkled mischievously as he grinned.

"I believe you've already been formally introduced to him. It's Kai Alesana."

****

Kai's call didn't come until Tuesday afternoon.

Although I tried to pretend I wasn't waiting for it, the amount of times I had checked my phone during the last twenty-four hours was embarrassing. His voice was confident, yet kind as we talked.

I could hear plenty of male voices in the background, yet he never diverted his attention. He confirmed the time for Thursday's dinner and my stomach rolled in anticipation. I couldn't even imagine how good Kai would look in formal wear. That thought brought yet another dip in my stomach.

What were his expectations for me?

****

After a long run to prepare my mind for my upcoming session with Dr. Crane, I left for work. Stacie had asked why I was going in so much earlier than my scheduled shift, but I didn't tell her. The words were not ready to be said.

I had planned to tell her about my therapy, yet there was something stopping me that I just couldn't get past. If I admitted it to her, then there would be no going back. It would all be real then. I wasn't quite ready to give up the safety of my denial.

I would tell her though, in my own way and time. Because of that, it didn't count as a breech in our *honesty pact*. Of that, I was convinced.

****

Dr. Crane seemed to be a very pleasant mood when I arrived at her office. She offered me a bottled water as I sat on the hard leather sofa. She smiled as she held my file on her lap, yet she made no move to open it. Instead, she observed me.

I felt like I was being graded on a test I hadn't even taken yet.

"Tori, how have the last few days been for you?"

This was the first time she had asked me about *present-day Tori*. I was intrigued.

"Pretty good, I guess," I said, straightening my shirt.

"That's good to hear. I'd like to ask you how your assignment went. Did you find someone to connect with?" she probed.

Uh, I'd say so.

I'm like a professional connecting machine now.

"Yes, definitely," I said with confidence.

Maybe getting fixed would be much easier than I thought it would be. Although, I couldn't figure out how this idea of *connecting* with people would help with my flashbacks. But hey, she was the expert, who was I to question her tactics?

"Can you tell me about it?" she asked.

She sat back, making herself comfortable as she picked up her sweet tea. Apparently she thought she was in for a long story. I cleared my throat.

Who do I start with, my parents, Stacie, or Kai?

Gosh, I really am a connecting machine!

I launched into the story of the lake day with Kai, then dinner with my mom and Stacie, and finally, my visit at my parent's house. I looked around the room as I recounted the facts of the weekend. Pride filled my chest like a balloon as I spoke. At the end I took a deep breath and waited for her praises.

A second later however, my pride balloon popped. Her expression lacked the enthusiasm I had expected from her. There was no standing ovation for my great efforts, instead I saw only the narrowing of eyes and a head tilt.

Nothing good ever came from a head tilt like that.

Did she not hear all my connecting? I did exactly what she asked of me!

"Tori, in no way do I want to discourage you. It sounds like you made some great social strides over the last few days. In comparison to what I assume was a fairly anti-social year in Phoenix, what you shared definitely shows some progress. However, in all of your recounting, I never heard any real conversation from *you*."

Seriously?

I had loads of conversations! Was she not listening to me at all?

I scowled. "I don't understand what you're calling *real* conversation, Dr. Crane. I had plenty of conversations! I am exhausted just from thinking about them all!" I said.

She took a deep breath. "Tori, please remember I am on *your* side. I am only trying to help you. This exercise wasn't about filling time with social activities; it was about letting someone in. Real *connection* happens when we share ourselves with someone, when we allow real vulnerability and authenticity in our conversations. Even if you can only let your guard down a little at first, that is how it starts," she said leaning forward in her chair and staring at me intently. "It's about letting someone reach you, that part of you that's been closed off for the last year and a half. It sounds like you could get there with your sister if you pushed yourself a bit more."

I sat thinking about the conversation Stacie and I had had in the driveway of our parent's house. If that was the closest I had come to this *connecting* thing, then I was way out of my league. My talk with Stacie had been very uncomfortable for sure, but the truth was, that wasn't even the tip of the iceberg.

Could I really share all of me: my thoughts, my shame, my fears, my insecurities?

Could I do it the sake of sanity?

Could I do it for the sake of honoring Anna?

"I'm sure this is a lot to take in. It's normal to have fear, Victoria. It plays a big role in how we learn to be open and vulnerable after a tragedy occurs. This idea of sharing and connecting may seem pointless to you, but it's what will ultimately begin your healing. It will take some time, but your loved ones— the people you can trust—are the key to working through your PTSD. They are the ones who will help expose the dark places in your mind and bring them out into the light."

"And what if I don't want to bring them out?"

"Then they will continue to grow darker. They'll start to seep into the other compartments of your life. Let me ask you, Victoria, are the flashbacks you experience always the same? Is it just one scene, or have they expanded into multiple scenes?"

The chill that went through my body was enough cause for me to shiver. The flashbacks had started a week after my accident. Originally, it was just one single image of Anna in my arms that would hold steady in my mind. Now though, it was a slew of memories.

My flashback while on the Jet Ski was evidence enough that she was right. This train wasn't going to stop on its own; its destination had to be the equivalent of Hell.

"Multiple. And they've been happening...*more* often," I said, looking at the floor. I hesitated to make eye contact with her after such a confession. I felt more broken just by admitting it.

"I see. I have some literature I'd like to send home with you, Victoria. For a nurse such as yourself, I think you'll find it very informative. It deals more with how the brain functions under stress and duress. It might help to educate yourself as we continue processing this from the inside out," Dr. Crane said.

"Okay, I'll read it."

"Before you leave here today, there are two questions I want to ask you to think about for our next session: what is the common denominator in your flashbacks? And what feeling can you identify in them?"

When she was done speaking, she leaned forward in her chair and reached her hand out to me. It hovered in the space between us. I stared at it.

I felt weak.

The overpowering pull was back, calling me a fool. It was ludicrous for me to hope I could be anything more than the woman that had killed a child—the woman that had ruined a family. The dominant voice of resistance pulsed through my body. Every beat of my heart was begging me to leave, to walk out and never come back. I needed to exit this office and leave Dr. Crane and her therapy discussions behind. If I could just bury the pain back down it would all be over.

It would all be over and I would be...*safe.*

But something stopped me.

It was something small—yet fierce—that rose inside me. My fingers reached across the gap and met hers with a grip that surprised me. She held my hand tightly while laying her free hand on top, sealing me in.

"You will recover, Victoria. You will learn to process through this pain and regain your mind again. You will be free again to think and feel. You're not too lost and you're not too far gone. I know you don't trust me yet, but I believe you can trust in the science if you commit to understanding it. I'm here for you day or night. Call me when you learn your schedule next week."

****

Fatigue worked through my body, even in the midst of a very full and demanding twelve-hour shift. There was never a dull moment or break that took me away from the hustle and bustle of the ER. My mind though, was somewhere else.

I couldn't shake the feeling that deception was feeding on my reality and robbing me blind, yet I couldn't pin-point where or how it was happening. I was anxious to study the books and print outs that Dr. Crane had provided me. That was one thing I could do; I could study. If there was an answer then surely it would be in science.

I could stake my life on that alone.

I tried to step quietly as I felt my way up the dark staircase. It was well past midnight when I arrived back at Stacie's house. My normal routine of showering after work and getting into pjs was dismissed as my body fell flat onto my bed. I heard a slight crunch underneath my shoulder as I made contact with the comforter. I lifted the small piece of paper up into the light of my cell phone.

Tori-
Can't wait to show you what I found today! Your outfit for tomorrow will be smokin' hot, yet gracefully elegant. I have it all planned out.
Sweet dreams...hope they're of the Firemen's Ball!
Stacie

Though my eyes were closed, my mind was now fully engaged with the promise of Thursday evening.
I would see Kai again.
I fell asleep while thinking only of that.

SIXTEEN

I woke to find a text from Kai on my phone.
Kai: *Looking forward to seeing you tonight.*
Though I told myself it was foolish to get nervous, my body had a mind of its own. Waves of anxiety filled me from head to toe. I could hear Stacie stirring in her room and decided before the fashion preparations were unleashed that I needed to run. I slipped my shoes and quietly headed out the front door.

It was hard to fathom all the events that had taken place since my return to Dallas. I hadn't even been back a month, yet so much had happened within that short of time frame. Life in Phoenix had not been nearly as versatile or socially taxing. Though the majority of my days had been filled with working at the hospital, there was little else that I had allowed into my schedule outside of my daily runs.

I thought back to last night's fatigue. I knew full well that it had little to do with the twelve hours on my feet and everything to do with the mental strain of my appointment with Dr. Crane. The interactions I'd had with Stacie, my parents, and even Kai had forced a new level of energy from me lately. I may not have *connected* in the way Dr. Crane defined it, but it was still draining nonetheless. I wondered when—if ever—I would feel energized by the company of others.

I ran outside of the housing development onto the overpass. It was lined with new, made-to-look-antique lampposts. I thought again of Kai.

It had been a long time since a boy had been in my thoughts this much. My one and only romantic relationship had ended right after I graduated from high school. He had hoped we could keep it up long distance—Boston to Dallas—but I knew I needed to focus on getting into the nursing program.

Boyfriends were ultimately expendable.

Ian had been a funny mix of cowboy and jock. He knew ranching well, as he had worked as a ranch-hand in his grandfather's stables every summer, but he was also an elite soccer player. He'd received a full scholarship to Boston University.

We dated for almost two years.

During that time, there had been many sit down talks with Jack. Everything from Ian's intentions to keeping curfew was discussed. Even though my dad had asked Ian those same questions, Jack took it upon himself to go the extra mile when it came to me dating. Ian had often joked about being the only guy he knew who had to get the blessing of two dad figures in order to date one girl.

I was such a different girl back then. One that was free to joke, laugh, and tease. Ian was always reaching for my hand and introducing me as his girlfriend. My heart would swoon over his words. He had been my first real kiss, awakening in me feelings and desires I didn't even know existed.

One night, on a blanket outside on his grandfather's field, things went way too far. Ian knew my limits. He knew, yet he tested them relentlessly. Something was different that night though; it was more than just a test. He ignored my protests countless times.

Stricken with panic, I pushed him off me, gasping in shock at his forcefulness. Every bit of trust that had been built in those two years had come crashing down, the demolition taking only seconds.

His apologies were numerous on the car ride home. There wasn't a doubt in my mind who he was so afraid of. *Jack.* When he walked me to my door that night, he said the only four words I'd ever wanted to hear from him.

"*I love you, Tori.*"

But they fell on deaf ears. No longer were they sweet and pure. No longer were they right and true. The only meaning found in those words was the admission of his guilt.

His shame had tainted them completely.

Soon after that, I started to pull away from him. Though he had apologized many times, I couldn't forget. As his plans for Boston became more concrete, I broke it off completely. Ian had emailed me many times during that first year while he was away at school. He begged me to reconsider a long-distance relationship with him.

I never did.

Kai is different. He is not Ian.

I rounded the corner into the high school parking lot several miles from Stacie's house. I made a wide U-turn and headed back in the opposite direction. I knew Kai was *different*. He hadn't taken or expected anything from me. Instead, he was respectful and kind.

There was no guilt clouding his judgment. He had made his intentions clear each time he had spoken to me, wanting my company for reasons I was yet to understand.

****

The second I opened the front door I knew something was wrong. She was directly beyond the entryway on the couch, but said nothing to me as I entered. Her head was down and her eyes were spilling over with tears.

My heart sank to the floor.

"What's wrong, Stacie? What happened?" I asked, running to her side.

My strides were long and quick. In an instant I was sitting next to her, willing her to speak. She lifted her head, opened her mouth, and then burst into a new round of sobs. My mind was whirling in panic.

The baby?

Mom and dad?

Oh...Jack? Something happened to Jack!

"It's nothing terrible...it's...it's my appointment. It was moved from this afternoon. My doctor had an emergency with one of his patients," she cried, sniffling every few seconds.

Oh goodness...pregnancy does make you crazy.

"Okay, help me understand, Stace."

I treaded carefully, not wanting to wake up the *anger beast* that could be lurking in the shadows of all this emotion.

"It's Jack. He was going to be able to video chat with me during the ultrasound today so we could find out what we're having together. But they had to move it to tomorrow morning. He doesn't think he'll be able to get on then. It's just so hard being away from him. He is missing EVERYTHING!"

Stacie cried now with tears I understood.

Jack *was* missing a lot. In all the years they had been married—or even just dating—I'd never known them to be apart from each other. Suddenly, I felt like a jerk. I hadn't thought enough about Stacie's feelings, especially in light of her pregnancy. These tears were less about a rescheduled appointment and more about the milestones that Jack wasn't here for.

Suddenly, I had an idea.

"What time is your appointment, Stacie?"

"Nine." She sniffled, meeting my gaze.

"I can go with you tomorrow; I think I have a plan, actually. Are you willing to wait to find out the gender until Jack can get online with you?" I asked.

"What do you mean...*wait* for Jack?"

"Stacie, what if I recorded your ultrasound? When it's time for you to find out, the tech can just turn the screen and not show you. She can tell me instead, or the camera that is. That way you can still learn the gender together once Jack is free to video chat with you."

Stacie lit up like a firework and hugged me tightly.

"That is a brilliant idea! I would love for you to come, Tori! I have an even better plan though, how about *you* tell us? Let the tech tell you after you record the ultrasound appointment and then you can be the one that tells us what we're having!"

Stacie was ecstatic now. I was relieved.

"I would be honored to do that for you both, I'll think of a fun way to do it," I said.

"I'll go call Jack and tell him the news while you go and take a shower."

"What...you don't like my sweaty shirt and shorts?" I joked, looking at my pitiful attire.

Stacie turned her nose upward and squinted at me.

"The look is hardly as bad as the *smell!*"

She squealed up the stairs knowing a pillow was sure to be thrown her way.

A shower would be nice and frankly quite necessary. I smiled thinking about what tomorrow's big day would hold for Jack and Stacie. For the first time since my move, I was thankful for living in Dallas...and nowhere else.

****

"You done in there yet?" Stacie called from outside my bathroom door.

Here we go...someone's all better now.

"I have a few outfit choices laid out for you in my room—with shoes...but you'll have to try them on to make sure they're going to fit right."

Stacie's overwhelming selection of *options* made me question her spending habits. There were short, long, strapless, full-skirted and halter dresses strewn about on top of her mattress. It was a store, not a closet selection that lay on her bed waiting for my approval.

"Where did all these come from?" I asked, mouth gaping.

"You know: weddings, dances, work parties, social events, theater..."

Stacie rattled off the list in a casual manner.

"Oh...is that all," I said rolling my eyes.

She smiled and then immediately launched into details about what would look best on me. She had thought of color, shape, style, and length. She held each one up, finally narrowing it down to only two. I could have slept and been more of a help to her.

"Okay, so it's navy short or dark blush long. I'll have to see them both on you and then we can decide."

We? Really?

I laughed at her as I entered the bathroom, but she paid no attention to me. Her head was swimming with plans and details. She wouldn't have heard me if I had screamed, "Fire!"

The navy dress—although beautiful—reminded me of a bad prom night, one that ended with cheap beer and a hotel room. Stacie agreed. It wasn't quite right for me. It was then I tried on the "dark blush long", as Stacie had called it. I had little hope for that one as my appreciation for pink in *any* shade was limited at best. But when I felt it fall over my hips and hit the tips of my toes with its silky touch, I was taken aback.

"Oh...my...lanta! Tori, that is positively breathtaking! That dress was *made* for you. Look at yourself!" Stacie said, pointing to the tall mirror by her dresser.

I stared at the image it reflected as if detached from it somehow. The strapless, sweetheart neck-line flowed like a waterfall over my body to the floor. It pulled together in the center of my chest and dropped a pleat of layered fabric from below my breast bone to just above the natural hem-line.

It was exquisite.

The color brought out the olive in my skin—as Stacie pointed out—and my hazel eyes were bright in contrast. I slipped on the silver, strappy heels that Stacie gave me seconds earlier. The shoes made the ensemble complete—or rather, made me completely aware of the fact that I was a *fake*.

This isn't me.

"Stacie, it is *beautiful*...I'm just not sure," I said, looking down at the heels on my feet.

I felt nearly naked in this dress.

I looked at myself again in the mirror. My shoulders, neck, and arms were exposed. I was exposed.

"What do you mean? You are *gorgeous*, Tori! This is *your* dress. Heavens, you were in a swimsuit in front of him last week, remember?" she exclaimed.

"I feel more exposed like this than I did at the lake, though," I said, reflecting back on the day at the lake. I had been in swimwear, but my swim shorts had never come off and the tankini top had straps.

"That's nonsense. This dress is *not* immodest; you are just trying to find a reason to back out. You *are* wearing this, Tori. It's beautiful on you. Besides, we don't have time for your second guessing...I already booked us both appointments for a mani-pedi. We're going to be late. Now, go get that dress off and lay it out so it doesn't wrinkle. I'll meet you in the car!"

Stacie left before I could argue. The idea of getting my nails and toes done did sound nice. I hadn't done anything like that in a very long time. I took one more glance in the mirror and wondered what Kai would think of it?

I would know the answer to that soon enough.

****

I heard him before I saw him, chatting it up with Stacie downstairs. I stole a few extra minutes at the top of the stairs to try and calm my nerves. Currently, they were out of control. I took several deep breaths, and then walked out onto the landing. The mirror on the wall grabbed at my attention, glimmering in my peripheral vision. I turned just for a second and saw what Stacie had created.

My face was perfectly made-up with eyes that popped from the shimmery metallic shadow and long dark lashes. My lips were complete with a soft pinkish-pearl lip gloss. Dark hair cascaded down my back in loose curls from some pinned-up knot at the crown of my head. I grabbed the silver clutch Stacie had given me, tucked the gloss and my phone inside, and took my first step down the stairs.

A smile tugged at the corner of my mouth as I saw him take a step toward the center of the floor near the bottom of the staircase. The room was silent, except for the loud gasp that escaped his lips. I couldn't bring myself to look into his eyes, not yet. I didn't like being the center of attention, but I couldn't help but wonder what he was thinking. I saw his hand reach out for mine on the last step, feeling an electric surge race through me as we touched. I looked up then and saw his face.

Wonderment.

"Victoria...you're...stunning. You look...you look amazing."

Kai's voice was soft and sincere when he spoke. I felt myself flush instantly at his words. I looked away from his eyes, they were too intense.

"Thank you. You look great too, Kai," I said, stepping back to admire his tux. He offered me the flowers he had set on the side table.

"These are for you my lady," Kai said, holding them out to me.

My stomach clenched again, butterflies releasing everywhere inside of me. I noticed then that Stacie also held a bouquet of roses.

He brought Stacie flowers too? Is this guy for real? Can one man actually be this amazing?

Stacie grinned and nodded at me as if she had read my mind. She took my flowers from me and hugged us both goodbye, letting me know she wouldn't wait up. Kai led me out of the house, his hand never leaving my back as we walked through the driveway.

He helped me up into his truck, letting our hands linger a few extra seconds as he smiled up at me. I took a deep breath once he shut my door, trying to release the anxiety I felt by being so close to him. If there was ever a doubt that Kai was the most attractive man I had ever known, tonight obliterated it. He was gorgeous.

The drive over was nice. He filled me in on what the evening would consist of. I noticed how trained his eyes were on the road when he spoke. Though he would respond to my questions, he never glanced in my direction…not even once.

The line for the valet was about ten cars long as we approached the convention center. It was then that he finally turned his head and looked at me. My heart hammered within my chest instantly.

"I'm not sure I want to take you in there," he said. His eyes shimmered with mischief as he nodded his head toward the building.

My breath caught at his statement.

What does he mean?

"I don't want to share you tonight, Tori. You're gonna be quite the distraction among all those guys in there. I had to *make* myself focus on the road just so I could drive us here," he said, laughing to himself.

Though I was sure he meant it as a compliment, a rush of insecurity blocked my mind from its comprehension. Slowly I reached across my body and gripped my opposite shoulder. I wanted to cover up as much of my exposed skin as possible. I hated myself for forgetting to grab a wrap from Stacie's closet.

Kai gave me a puzzled look as we inched our way closer to the front of the valet line. I looked out the window at the couples walking through the large revolving glass doors. I tried to keep my face neutral—pleasant even.

A young valet attendant opened my door. In a second Kai was there, helping me down and pulling me close. I diverted my gaze.

This is a mistake. Why did I ever agree to this?

"Tori? Did I say something wrong?" His arm encircled my waist, creating fire where he touched as he whispered the words.

The feel of his breath on my neck sent tingles down my spine as we walked toward the building.

"What? No, not at all," I lied, shaking my head and trying to smile.

Apparently, it was less than convincing.

Kai dropped his arm from my waist and slid his hand down past my elbow, pulling gently on my wrist. Carefully, he led me to the wall near the center's entrance.

"I didn't mean to make you to feel self-conscious when I said you'd be a distraction tonight. I realize that a girl like you doesn't aim to be the center of attention, but that's exactly what will make you one. You're stunning, Tori. There is absolutely nothing you should feel self-conscious about."

He spoke with such sweet conviction; I almost believed him—*almost*. I lifted my eyes to his and flashed him a timid smile. He smiled back while reaching for my hand. Together, we walked into the building. I took one last deep breath and silently prepared for a night full of people.

****

The room was beyond anything I had ever seen or could possibly describe. The details were astonishing. The banquet hall had been transformed into a midnight garden wonderland with trees, flowers, lights and candles. The ceiling and walls were covered in fabrics that were perfectly matched to the theme. Vines and trellises bordered every corner. An outrageous number of small white twinkle lights swooped and draped everywhere I looked. It was positively breathtaking.

The tables were emerald and silver, each with a large twinkling topiary tree in its center. Place cards were written in calligraphy and small white truffle boxes sat on each plate. I looked at Kai who was equally as impressed. We laughed together in amazement.

He linked his arm through mine. Leaning down he whispered, "Shall I escort you to our table, Miss Sales?"

SEVENTEEN

The four-course dinner was served in between the evening's scheduled events. As a comedy duo introduced each speech or act, we enjoyed some of the finest food that Dallas had to offer. The silent auction had taken place in a separate room and the results would be read aloud toward the end of the evening, prior to the dance. I had met at least a dozen EMTs who worked with Kai, each having been familiar with who I was—knowing my name before it was spoken.

Briggs had been my favorite introduction of the night. He was quite the character, and he was also Kai's best friend. He teased Kai relentlessly as he told me just how much Kai talked about me during their long evenings at the station. I knew I had blushed, but I had also laughed at his funny antics.

I watched as Kai and Briggs pretended to have a boxing match just a few feet from me. They were nothing but grown-up boys in suits. In the end they man-hugged (one swift hard pat on the back), and I could easily see just how strong their brotherly-bond was.

"Has Kai told you about the camping trip next month?" Briggs asked, smoothing out his ruffled dirty-blond hair.

"Uh...no," I answered, unsure who I was to be addressing.

Kai shoved Briggs away playfully, and took a step closer to me.

"Well, I wasn't sure if you'd be interested, but I was planning to mention it later this evening, that is if Briggs will let me get a word in."

Kai scowled at him. I laughed again at the show they put on.

"What is it exactly?" I asked.

"It's an annual trip that a bunch of the guys from the station put on...out in hill country. We try to do it in early November when the weather is cool and the hiking is good-" Kai started.

"And sometimes ladies join us. Wives, girlfriends, random strangers...you know what I mean," Briggs interrupted.

"That's it. You're *done* talking to her," Kai joked. He lunged toward him as Briggs ducked just out of his reach.

I watched them, laughing, as they dodged small pockets of people around the floor. Several older women glared at them as if they were behaving like disobedient children.

I felt a tap on my shoulder and turned, ready to say, "No thank you" again to the waiter carrying champagne.

But it was not the waiter.

"Victoria?" the petite woman asked.

No.

Oh God, no.

This can't be happening.

"It is...it's you!" the woman exclaimed. She attacked me, embracing me in a hug so tight I could hardly breathe. Her presence alone was enough to suck the air from my lungs.

"Johanna?" I whispered. I was shocked I could even speak her name. Everything in me wanted to shut down entirely—cease to be.

"Victoria, you look beautiful! I can't tell you how good it is for me to see you here, honey. I've prayed for you so much during this last year. I didn't know you were back in town."

Oh God.

What do I even say?

"You look...you look good too, Johanna. Why...are you here?" I stuttered. My head felt as it was floating away from my body. Black spots were interrupting my vision. I blinked several times trying to focus.

"My nephew's being honored tonight. He invited me. I'm sorry I startled you. I thought I saw you earlier, but I wasn't sure. I never got a chance to talk to you after the memorial service...and then I heard you'd moved from Dallas."

My heart rate quickened, my eyes darting for ways of escape.

I can't do this.

I can't talk to her.

This isn't supposed to happen.

I saw Kai walking toward me then and felt instantly conflicted. Would he add to my distress or relieve me of it? He had no idea the magnitude this conversation held for me. With easy, carefree steps, he walked straight into my worst nightmare.

I was a blinking orb of guilt; he was the victim drawn-in by my toxic light.

"Yes, I moved to Phoenix for a while...for work," I said slowly, seeing Kai's sweet, innocent smile as he walked up to us. He extended his hand to Johanna like a gentleman.

"Hi, I'm Tori's date, Kai Alesana. How do you two lovely ladies know each other?" he asked.

Johanna laughed lightly at the compliment. I didn't move a muscle.

"I'm Johanna Watson...an old friend of Tori's."

"Oh, well that's great, it's nice to meet you," Kai said.

Kai smiled, but it wasn't his usual happy-go-lucky smile. This one looked odd and out of place. He looked how I felt, like he wasn't sure what was supposed to happen next.

I couldn't wait a second longer. I *had* to exit.

I excused myself, leaving them behind in a cloud of awkwardness. Without looking back, I increased my stride as I rushed through the banquet hall toward the ladies room.

You're okay; You're fine.

Just get to the restroom...you can sort it all out in there.

"Victoria! Wait, please!"

How did she catch up to me so fast?

I stopped just outside of the restroom door. Johanna was next to me then, tears rolling down her cheeks. My heart ached unbearably.

"I'm so sorry. I didn't think that seeing me would upset you like this, please forgive me for being so insensitive," she said reaching her arm out and touching my hand.

"Forgive *you*? Johanna, yes...seeing you is a bit of a shock, but there is nothing you ever need to ask *my* forgiveness for."

I was surprised at how easily the words flowed, but they were truth. For all the words I couldn't say, somehow I had found the courage to speak those. She reached for my hand, holding it firmly.

"You still haven't accepted it?"

I stared at the floor knowing full well what she was asking. It was then that my courage disappeared.

"I meant what I said at the hospital Victoria, and I mean it here tonight, so please hear me. You are *not* responsible for what happened to Anna. I forgave you for even the slightest bit of blame that you could place on yourself for *our* accident. You did more for her than anyone could have. I hope that you can see that," she said, tears streaming down her face.

"No, I can't see that," I whispered back. I was shocked at the emotion swelling in my throat.

"I have prayed for you, Victoria, that you would receive grace in place of guilt."

I looked at her, but I could not understand her. Why would this woman—this mother who had lost her child—be praying for the person who caused her death? Her words were as surprising now as they had been three days after the accident. Words I had tried so hard to forget.

She had come into my room just minutes before Jack and Stacie were to arrive to take me home. I was frozen with fear, afraid of what she would say to me. I had killed her child.

She leaned onto her crutches and slowly made her way over to where I sat on the bed, pulling on my shoes.

"Victoria, I'm Johanna Watson. I heard what you did to try and save my daughter's life. I hope you know how grateful we are to you for that," she said. Though her eyes were red-rimmed and puffy, she tried to smile. "I also know that this next season will be hard—for both of us."

Her tears started then, flowing in one continuous stream down her cheeks. Her next words were piercing as she held my gaze. "I do not blame you. I wanted you to know that."

Pain radiated in my chest, causing my guilt to exploded from my lips.

"I shouldn't have been driving...I should have turned around. I'm so...sorry. I'm so sorry...I tried..."

I couldn't go on.

A second later she was next to me, sitting on the edge of my bed. We wept together. Her sobs were filled with unspeakable grief; mine were filled with undisputable regret.

"I forgive you. For whatever you think you should have done and didn't, I forgive you. Guilt will get us nowhere."

I wanted to hear her.

I wanted to believe her.

But then I went to Anna's memorial...and my want just wasn't enough.

"I...I don't know what to say to that, Johanna."

"You don't need to say anything. You just need to *accept* it. I pray you will," she said, wiping her eyes and smiling again. "I hope you can still enjoy your evening tonight, it looks like you've found a very nice man."

Kai.

Where was he now?

Johanna gave me a quick hug, and then she was gone, leaving me alone to unscramble my thoughts. I escaped into the bathroom and locked myself inside an oversized stall. Leaning against the cold tile wall, I closed my eyes. I focused on my breathing the way Dr. Crane had showed me, trying to visualize my exhalation like blowing away the anxiety within. I hoped it was enough to stop the flashbacks. I was desperate.

Suddenly, I felt a calm come over me.

Stop running.

And there it was, the voice that seemed to stalk me, the insanity that would not leave me alone.

I stood frozen for several seconds, waiting for more to come. I waited for the horrible movie to start in my head, for the pictures of Anna in my arms, for the memories that would never heal. But nothing more came.

I opened the stall door and went to the sink. Seeing the reflection of my dress in the mirror, I remembered where I was—what I was here for.

I remembered Kai.

I won't ruin this night for him...if I haven't already.

I left the restroom, trying to readjust my eyes once more to the dim lighting in the banquet hall. There was someone speaking up front, some award for bravery being given out, but I didn't want to listen to that. I didn't want to wonder if that young man was Johanna's nephew.

I searched only for Kai.

I felt a hand on my arm.

"Tori?" Briggs asked, his face full of concern.

"Oh, hey, Briggs. I'm trying to find Kai. Do you know where he is?"

"Ha, well join the club. He's looking for you, too. I think he just walked outside thinking you may have gone out for some fresh air?" He looked at me skeptically.

I nodded and turned to walk away, but my arm was caught and pulled back. I stared at Briggs. There was no trace of his earlier light-heartedness on his face. He was all business now.

"Tori, I meant what I said earlier. I've known Kai for a very long time and he has never talked about a woman like he has talked about you. He cares a lot for you and you should know he doesn't play games. He's the real deal," Briggs said, dropping my arm.

I suddenly knew how it felt to be on the receiving end of one of Jack's *big brother talks*. It did not feel good. I could appreciate his concern for Kai. I had similar concerns for him, and yes, I was at the root of them all.

"I understand. Thank you," I said, looking at the floor.

I wasn't a game player, but little did Briggs know, that there were worse things out there than toying with a man's heart. The darkness I carried around was much graver.

"Good, then you and I will be great friends, then."

He patted my arm and walked away.

I opened the hall doors into the lobby, not sure which outside exit I should try first. My decision though, was easy. I saw him, or what I hoped was his shadow, behind the large glass door which led out to a deck.

As I approached, I could see him pacing. I hesitated at the door, unsure of what I would say to him. But then he was there, opening the door, as if sensing my presence.

"Tori, are you okay? You looked really upset earlier, and then I couldn't find you anywhere. I was starting to worry," he said, reaching for my hand and pulling me toward him onto the deck. I could no longer hear the noise from the banquet hall.

He was worried about me?

"Yes, I'm fine. I'm sorry that I caused you to miss some of your party. No more interruptions from me tonight…I promise," I said, forcing my best smile.

"I don't care about the party. I care…about you. If something's wrong, I hope you know you can trust me."

That was the second time Kai had told me I could trust him.

Could I?

But something told me I already did. I trusted him. I remembered what Briggs told me and my stomach clenched.

"I wish *trusting* you and telling you the *truth* were the same thing. If only it could be that simple." I walked over to a wooden bench that overlooked the rose garden and sat down. The sun had almost set and the petals were radiant with color.

I took a deep breath.

You can't actually be thinking of telling him…

But as quickly as the thought came, I suppressed it, squelching its power over me for the first time since I'd taken Dr. Crane's hand. I would keep my promise to myself and to Briggs. I would not hurt Kai. I was not a game-player. He had a right to know who he thought he cared about.

"That woman...that woman is..."

Fear was a tourniquet around my chest, squeezing every last trace of air from my lungs. I fought it, while trying to piece together my thoughts. I had to speak, but I also needed to prepare for the inevitable: rejection.

"You can trust me," Kai said, sitting down next to me and putting his hand on my knee, stabilizing the pain that hung on my next words.

"That woman...is the mother of a little girl who died in a car accident just over a year and a half ago." I took a deep breath. "An accident...I caused. I'm not who you think I am, Kai. A child died because of me, an innocent, beautiful child and nothing will ever change that fact."

My eyes were closed by the end of my statement, but even still, the absence of warmth beside me was unmistakable. He stood and walked toward the railing. A cold wave of shame washed over me. I was convinced in the seconds that followed that outright rejection was a far better fate than the deafening silence that enclosed us now.

I couldn't expect Kai to handle it. *I* couldn't handle it and it was *my* life, my cross to bear. His quiet presence was numbing. Whatever fairytale I had dreamed up for this night had long since expired.

Why I sat there waiting—or what I waited for—I wasn't sure. But I didn't move. The voices that were usually so quick to rush in with their guidance—the voices I had silenced—refused to offer me any help now. I was alone, sitting silently in my shame.

Kai finally turned toward me, his face anguished and hard.

For a brief second I feared him; the fire in his eyes was so intense. But as soon as his eyes found mine, they softened. He didn't speak. Instead, he strode toward me, each step purposeful and determined. In one quick motion, he pulled me to him.

Placing his hands on my face, he brought his lips to mine, kissing me so passionately that I thought I might fall over from the sheer force of it. My body responded in kind, without thought, without struggle. Heat that had started at my lips was coursing through my body, growing hotter by the second.

He broke away for a just an instant to search my eyes, making certain that I understood him. When he found the answer he sought, he kissed me again. This time his kiss was sweeter, softer, taking my breath with it.

When it ended, he touched his forehead to mine. His hands had moved to my bare shoulders. I stood, speechless.

"Thank you, *Pele*. Thank you for telling me," Kai whispered, full of emotion.

"*Pele?*" I asked, pulling away slightly to search his eyes.

"It means something similar to *sweetheart* in Samoan," Kai said.

Every cell in my body felt raw and exposed; the kiss lingered on my lips, imprinting itself on my heart. My mind was reeling, struggling to comprehend what had just happened between us. I was so confused.

"Kai, do you understand what I-"

"Yes, and there is nothing more to say about that tonight. It's not how I see you and it doesn't change how I feel about you. Do you need more proof of that?" he asked, a smile tugging at the corner of his mouth.

He cradled my face again and stared into my eyes before finding my lips once more. I stood there stunned, captivated by this man. I did not understand him, but I knew in that moment I did not want to lose him. Something was *happening* inside me.

That kiss was more than just a romantic gesture…it was *connection*.

"Are you up for a dance? I'm sure it's started by now," he asked.

"Yes, I think I am," I said, smiling at him.

****

The banquet room had doubled in size. A large wall had been pushed back, opening up the largest dance floor I had ever seen. The band that played was incredible. It was hard to take it all in.

Kai led me to the floor. Holding me tight we swayed together to the music. The comfort I found in his embrace was unmatched to anything I had ever experienced before. He was an anomaly.

The emcee announced the karaoke contest and suddenly people

were applauding like crazy. The singers were asked to audition at a side panel for about sixty seconds before competing on stage. The live band would accompany them in their song choice.

I saw several people around us walking toward the front to claim a space in the try-out line. The emcee went into more detail about how the winner would get to sing at a New Year's Eve event at some fancy venue downtown. The proceeds would benefit local fire stations.

In an instant, two men from Kai's station were on either side of him, pulling him away from me. They pushed him toward the try-out line, apologizing to me for his abrupt exit. I watched them, thinking again of how easy and natural their relationships seemed.

Kai passed his voice test and had entered the line to perform on stage. He was only third from the front, but already I missed his company. Briggs joined me then, standing at my side. He clapped along with the music that accompanied the first contestant. It was honky-tonk country.

Briggs tipped his imaginary hat to me and winked. I was grateful to be in his good graces for the moment. I wondered if the reason he stood beside me now was for Kai.

Was there some sort of protection clause in their friendship?

Briggs pointed out a few crazy dancers who had obviously had way too much to drink, but were trying to line dance nonetheless. I laughed till it hurt as Briggs imitated their unique moves. The next song was a ballad from a Broadway show I had never seen, and she was amazing. Her notes held and peaked at just the right moments giving me goose bumps. For a second, I felt bad that Kai would have to follow such an act.

Briggs must have sensed my unease for Kai. He laughed and said, "Just wait, Tori, he'll be fine."

Kai took the stage. He was confident as he picked up the microphone and stared into the crowd.

"This is for you, *Pele*."

My breath caught in my throat. I recognized the tune as soon as it started. It was a pop hit by one of my favorite artists. I knew the song well.

Kai started it flawlessly, moving to the beat and singing in a way I couldn't have imagined. Even though I had heard him sing next to me at church, nothing I had heard compared to this. This was a performance. He was more than gifted, he was absolutely incredible. People all over the room watched him and participated. I was mesmerized. When he got to the last chorus the room went wild.

I could feel Briggs looking at me for a reaction, but I couldn't take my eyes off Kai. He walked toward me, looking like a superstar. Dozens of people were patting him on the back and praising his talent, but he never once diverted his eyes. He hit Briggs on the shoulder, as if indicating his approval for standing by me, and then took my hand.

"You ready to get out of here?" he asked me.

"But...don't you want to see if you won?"

"Nah. That's not why I did it. Come on, there's something I want to show you."

The valet brought Kai's truck around and we headed in the direction of Stacie's house, although I knew that wasn't our destination. It was already past ten, but I didn't want the night to end. We parked at a playground and walked together on a paved path, our hands brushing as we strolled.

There were several street lights that illuminated the old wooden play structure and swings, but beyond that it was pitch black. I slowed my steps, thinking we would stop somewhere in the light, but he kept walking. I followed.

When the path ended, I paused. Stacie's heels would not be fond of walking though the grass. Hitching my dress up a few inches, I took one careful step forward up on the balls of my feet. My foot never made contact with the ground however, Kai lifted me up into his arms before it could.

How does he do that so easily?

"I'm very capable of walking Kai," I said, embarrassed.

"I know, but that takes all the fun out of it for me," he said, laughing.

After just a few yards of walking he set me down. A large tree with a trunk as wide as four men stood before us. I touched it, making sure I was seeing it correctly in the darkness of night.

"This is my spot," he said.

"Your spot?"

"Yes. I teased you the first night we met at your parent's house, about finding the bridge in the dark, remember? You'd gone there to get away from your party, I'm guessing to think and re-group, but I also have a spot I could easily find in the dark," he said, touching the tree.

I remembered that night well. It was the first time I had seen him, which now felt like ages ago. So much had happened since those first days in Dallas.

"Why do you come here?" I asked softly.

"To think, pray...talk to my dad," he said, reflecting.

"When did you find it?" I asked.

"A few years ago, after a bad call at work. I needed to process, spend some time alone—pray," he admitted.

I knew I should have felt uncomfortable or awkward by his statement of faith, but I felt neither. I knew he meant it. I also knew he really believed he could talk to and hear from God. Who was I to judge that?

"It's a great spot, Kai."

I walked around the base of the trunk, careful not to trip on the large exposed roots that rose above ground.

"Well, it's not just mine anymore...I want to share it with you. It's much closer to Stacie's than your parent's bridge, and I know how important it is to have a place to get away to and think, in quiet."

I looked up at his face in the moonlight.

"That's incredibly thoughtful. Thank you," I said.

"It's only two miles from Stacie's—an easy distance for you to run," he said, smiling.

I laughed. He knew I hadn't intended to stop running after my brush with heat exhaustion. He picked me up again, and carried me to the path.

Once at Stacie's he turned off the engine and walked me to the door. I hated that this night had ended.

He held out his hand to me, I took it willingly.

"Tori, may I ask your dad for his blessing to date you, officially?" he asked.

When will this man stop surprising me?

It took me a few seconds to process his words, but when I did there was nothing but clarity that remained.

"Yes," I said.

Kai leaned in and kissed me tenderly.

"Good-night, *Pele*".

I walked inside the house and closed the door. Peeking through the fogged glass I watched him drive away. The second he was gone from view, I let the giddy squeal that had built up inside me escape. It was then that I realized I was not alone.

My squeal was not a solo, but a *duet*.

Stacie was right behind me in the dark entryway.

EIGHTEEN

After hitting snooze several times, I opted to skip my morning run. Chatting with Stacie until the wee hours of the morning had been my undoing. *Girl talk* was still alive and well between us.

I told her everything I could remember: the decor, the lighting, the food, the entertainment, the kiss, the dance, the song. Stacie "oohed" and "aahed" like I was the best storyteller in the world, though in reality, I was a terrible one. Good story tellers didn't need the continuous prompting of questions in order to keep talking…I did.

I hesitated only once during the course of our conversation.

Deciding *if* I would tell Stacie about seeing Johanna was an internal battle, to say the least. However, without that information, the climax of my evening with Kai never would have happened. Honestly, I still wasn't sure why it had happened, but I wouldn't trade that kiss for anything—well, almost anything.

In the end, I told her, although I deflected her immediate sympathetic responses. I didn't want to go back to those feelings. Two conversations with Johanna in one lifetime were enough. Her words haunted me.

I had quickly forwarded the conversation on to what I knew Stacie would classify as "the good stuff". That was indeed what she had called it. She was a sucker for romance. Hallmark had nothing on her.

Stacie covered her mouth with one hand, letting her tears fall freely as I retold the scene on the deck. It had been a magical moment, a dream. Kai knew the ugliest part of me—who I was, what I'd done, yet instead of running from me, he pulled me closer.

He was a walking conundrum.

****

The wait in the Obstetrician's office was relatively short. Once Stacie fulfilled her duty to donate a urine sample, we were escorted back to the ultrasound room. Stacie's nervous chatter ended when the wand began roaming over her belly. I held her hand.

Once Stacie was comfortable, I started the recoding for Jack. The baby was full of energy. We laughed several times as we watched this little gymnast perform.

The tech went over each measurement with quick precision and clocked Stacie at exactly twenty weeks. She was half way, which meant Jack would be home in just over three months. Sometime in early February, a baby would be welcomed home as well.

As Stacie cleaned herself up and got dressed, the tech took me into the hall and whispered in my ear. My smile was automatic when she told me the gender. I'd never had a preference of course, neither had Stacie, but there was something about this knowledge that made it even more real. The naming, planning, and nursery colors would all fall into place with that one bit of information.

I made Stacie drop me off at Target on our way back home, telling her to stay in the car while I ran inside. My plan had developed into a mini masterpiece. I would find an appropriately gendered outfit, wrap it, and let Stacie unwrap it with Jack on the video call. It was their moment to uncover. I was happy just to have played a part in it.

I purchased the outfit and took a minute to arrange it in the non-descript gift bag, then walked back out to the car. Stacie was chomping at the bit with anticipation. I couldn't blame her.

She waited—semi-patiently—for Jack to call once we arrived back at the house. When I handed her the bag, she screamed in delight and quickly waddled her way upstairs to the computer. I waited downstairs; excited to hear them discover the news together. I had exactly thirty minutes before I needed to leave for work, so I busied myself by packing my bag and changing my shoes.

Then I heard it (so did the whole neighborhood I was pretty sure).

"A girl! We're having a GIRL! Get up here, Tori!" Stacie yelled from her bedroom.

I ran up the stairs into her bedroom. The picture of this man and wife was priceless. Jack was full screen, choking back tears while Stacie was a full-fledged mess of excited, crying energy. Jack thanked me for helping them have this moment together. I was overcome by his sensitivity—my *brother*. He adored Stacie, just as he would adore his new daughter. The thought was beautiful.

Stacie grabbed at my hand and pulled me front and center now.

"Jack, guess what else?" Stacie asked him.

Oh gosh. Really, Stacie...now?

"Tori has a *boyfriend!*" Stacie squealed like a teenager.

Okay. Wow...Thanks, Stace.

"I know," Jack said, a huge smirk developing on his face.

"What? What do you *know?*" I asked sarcastically.

"Kai wrote to me. He wanted to make sure I was cool with him hitting on my little sister. I assured him I was, but that he would still get my *special talks* even from Australia," Jack said, laughing.

I was dumbfounded.

Kai asked Jack before he'd asked me?

"He's a good man, Tori. You couldn't do better if I hand-picked him myself," Jack said.

"When...when did he write you?" I asked.

"Maybe a week ago or so, before your date to the lake," he said.

I couldn't help but feel a tad miffed by this information. "Wow. He's pretty *confident* in himself. We only just talked about dating last night."

"Tori, don't get all bent out of shape, he didn't want to start something he couldn't finish. He was just making his intentions clear, at least to me, and wanted to make sure he knew how to read you."

A sick, creeping feeling came over me. My throat felt instantly tight as I strained to speak.

"What do you mean?"

"I explained to him that you'd had a very difficult year and that you were just getting back on your feet in Dallas. I told him to give you some space if you needed it."

I felt like I had just been punched in the gut by his words. I would have gladly traded the feeling for a physical blow.

"Oh Jack," Stacie whispered, a worried look on her face.

"*What?* What am I missing here?" Jack asked.

"Nothing, absolutely nothing. I need to go to work," I said, walking out the door.

I heard Stacie call out to me, but I waved her off.

If Kai already knew about the accident, then why did I have to re-count it to him like he was hearing it for the first time? Was that why he was so quick to move on with our evening—kissing me like a man who hadn't been bothered by my confession in the slightest?

By the time I arrived at work, my confusion level was at an all-time high. A part of me wished I had asked Jack more specifics about his conversation with Kai, but it was too late for that now. Though I knew Jack was only trying to protect me the way he always had, this was *my* business. It should have been mine to share—when, how, or with whom I wanted.

I wanted to call Kai—confront him outright with what he had known prior to last night, but I was out of time. I was running late as it was. Mentally I worked to find a scenario that would make it alright—make it okay—that he knew before I told him. I came up with nothing.

Was this yet another failed connection? No.
I had done my part this time.

****

My escape was work.

For the next three days I did nothing but work and sleep. The overtime hours filled every nook and cranny of my day. I didn't have time to talk to Stacie, Kai, or anyone else. Instead, I tried in vain to sort out my thoughts alone.

By Sunday night I was beyond drained—both mentally and physically. My shift had started early, but had ended just after midnight. I'd left the house while Stacie was in the shower, avoiding yet another conversation. Her texts had blown up my phone during the last seventy-two hours, to which I responded I was *fine* and needed at the hospital. I told her we would talk Monday—tomorrow—though I still was unsure what should be said.

I was too tired to think any more about it tonight.

As I dragged myself to my car half asleep, I saw him standing there, waiting. I wasn't sure how he knew when I was off or where I had parked--those questions were too hard for me to process at the midnight hour. Despite my latest conspiracy theory regarding him, I couldn't stop the wild flipping in the base of my stomach or the way he made me want to free fall into his arms and forget *everything*.

His face was conflicted as I approached.

"Hey," I said.

"Hey," Kai said, standing there, hands in his pockets.

At his casual stance, my irritation was quickly re-kindled. I wanted to strangle the girl inside me that was so willing to give in without explanation just seconds ago. I pushed her down and silenced her.

"What's up?" I asked, keeping my distance.

"I'm hoping you can tell me. I've called you several times, Tori, and your sister doesn't seem to know what's going on with you either," Kai said.

My sister, of course! Naturally, he would call my family.

"Well, maybe I can start by telling you to stop going to my family members to snoop out information on me!"

My voice was hard and angry. Stewing for three days was probably not the best way to have a calm and rational conversation. His head jerked back a bit as his eyebrows shot up in surprise at my accusation. I held my ground, crossing my arms over my chest.

"What *information* are you referring to, Tori?" Kai asked.

"Jack told me about your little *conversation* before our date last weekend. You *knew* about my accident even before the lake day and yet I was the idiot who had to recount to you at the fireman's ball. No wonder you didn't want to talk more about it that night! You already *knew* everything!"

I threw my hands up in the air, adrenaline coming alive in me like a charged bull. There would be no reason to start pretending with him now. If a relationship wasn't based on truth, then there was no relationship. For once I had actually followed those guidelines. I had taken the risk, laid it all out there and I wasn't about to let that go unnoticed.

"Are you finished? Or is there more you need to say?"

Why can't he just yell back like a normal person?

The fight in me deflated as he waited patiently for my answer.

Confused, I put my hand on my hip and shook my head slowly, "No, not at the moment."

"Okay, then. Jack *didn't* tell me about the accident. He told me you'd had a very hard year, and not to pressure you if you weren't ready to talk to me about it. He said he'd watched you pull away from a lot of people and that I needed to give you space to breathe, allow you to decide when to trust me—if ever," he said.

Oh wow. I am an idiot.

I leaned against my car with a thud wishing again that I had the power to rewind time, to take back the ugly things I had said, and how I had said them. I grimaced, thinking about how I had treated Jack. He did have my back—just like he always had.

"Jack *didn't* tell you?" I asked again, my voice so weak it was hardly audible.

"No. *He* didn't tell me, but Tori, I-"

"No, I'm sorry. I was way off in my thinking. You may as well know the *rest* of it," I said, throwing my hands up and slapping them back down on my thighs.

"The rest?" he asked, looking startled.

I might as well tell him.

"Yes...I'm seeing a therapist here for PTSD. I guess I'm semi-insane or *something*, but you should know that before you decide to take this any further with me—if you haven't already seen enough that is."

He nodded, absently. I wasn't sure if he'd heard me.

"I have a form of PTSD, Kai. Post Traumatic Stress Dis-"

"Tori, I know what it is. I suspected something was up the day you didn't scream for help when that punk tried to violate you. It's not as uncommon as you think it is. I have a lot of buddies who have walked that same path. It's a hazard that comes with jobs like ours, but it doesn't mean you're *insane*."

"Well, I'm still trying to wrap my head around it. I haven't...I haven't told anyone yet, except you," I said, realizing the weight of my words.

I really did *trust* him.

I trusted a man that I hadn't known for longer than a month.

"I'll help you, Tori...if you'll let me. You're right, your family is *your* business, but I do think you should at least tell Stacie about this. The more support you have, the sooner and fuller your recovery will be," he said, taking a step closer to me.

"Yeah. That's what my therapist keeps telling me," I said.

"Good, I like her already. Now, I do have one favor to ask you," he said, leaning in.

My nerves grew wild in anticipation. As he inched closer to my face, our lips were just shy of touching when he turned his head and whispered into my ear instead.

"Can I get a ride home?"

I laughed and pulled back, hitting him in the chest. His laugh bellowed though the parking lot.

"You were *that* confident we'd make up that you actually had someone drop you off here?" I asked, mouth gaping.

"Well, I would say I was pretty *hopeful*, yes. I knew that Briggs wouldn't be nearly as patient to wait for my hot girlfriend to get off work as I would be. There wouldn't be quite the same pay-off for him," he said, winking at me.

This time he came closer and pulled me into a hug. I rested my tired head on his chest and listened for a moment to his heartbeat. There was safety with Kai, a concept that had been completely lost on me for quite some time. As he pulled back, he slipped my keys out of my fingers.

"May I drive, please?" he asked.

I gawked at him, doing my best to act appalled.

"What? You're against women drivers?"

"No, but I am against drivers who almost fall asleep on me when I hug them. You look like you haven't slept much this weekend, am I right?"

I smiled weakly, refusing to verbalize how right he was. He kissed me then on my forehead and I was gone—gone to a happy place where boys like Kai could fall for girls like me. Girls, who had made mistakes beyond repair, were certifiably insane, and were entirely too stubborn.

He drove me home, calling a buddy from the station to pick him up from Stacie's after we arrived.

And that was the night he called me his *girlfriend* for the very first time.

NINETEEN

I sat up, soaked in cold sweat.

My sheet and blankets lay twisted on the floor. It had been nearly four weeks since my last flashback episode on the Jet Ski and I was beginning to grow quite accustomed to dreamless slumber. This one though had been bad, really bad.

It wasn't full of the usual gruesome details that were looped on repeat. Instead, it unleashed a new kind of horror. Anna wasn't the only victim that lay helpless in a field, but Kai, Stacie, and Jack were there as well. All had critical injuries. I couldn't move fast enough.

None of them could be saved if my efforts were split.

Stacie had been the logical choice. Saving her would be saving *two* lives. When I got to her though, her eyes filled with terror and she screamed so loud I had to cover my ears against the sharp shrill pain. It was then my own fear began. My ears were wet with a thick, sticky substance. I felt my face and head in a panic. Nothing was dry.

I didn't want to see them, the hands that were now covered in red—my hands—but it was too late.

My eyes focused.

Blood was everywhere—on everything.

I woke up screaming.

I was grateful for the fan that Stacie used in her room at night, also for the two closed doors in between us. It was only five in the morning, but I couldn't risk going back to sleep. I walked downstairs through the dark house and flicked on a lamp by the fireplace.

It was then I remembered the books that Dr. Crane had given me two sessions ago. Guess this was as good a time as any to crack them open.

At my last appointment she'd mentioned them again, giving me a stern yet professional reprimand for my procrastination. She had also encouraged me to journal my feelings as they came to me.

Journal? Right.

Wonder what she'd think about the nightmare I just had.

Dr. Crane had continued to prod and ask questions about what my flashbacks entailed—their themes—but until this morning I was still unclear about their *common denominator*. This nightmare though, proved what she had suspected all along: fear.

It was my fear that recycled through each flashback, my fear of not being enough to save her—or in this case, anyone—myself included.

Kai told me more about his friends that had experienced PTSD—both from work-related incidents. We had walked together around the pond about a week ago as he recounted the details of each of their stories and their "paths to recovery" as he called it. Though I knew he was trying to be helpful and supportive, there was one glaringly obvious fact that I couldn't seem to overlook. Neither of them had been the *cause* of a death. Sure they had both seen horrific tragedies, but at the end of the day, the blame was not theirs to own.

I kept that fact to myself.

As I read now in the quiet of the morning, I struggled to focus. I'd never had an issue studying in the past. Learning was one of the only true passions that had stayed with me when all else was lost. Page after page I tried to lose myself in the words and descriptions. I even tried to read it like I was helping a patient, but I wasn't fooled by my own deception.

I was the patient.

The issue wasn't that I didn't believe in the diagnosis or even in the *process of recovery*. The diagrams and explanations of the brain were all medically sound and logical—nothing I could deny. But I also couldn't deny what I knew I would never find in a book: the remedy for guilt.

I decided after skimming through the stages of recovery, that I would keep my expectations low. Regaining sanity and living life functionally, without further decline, was all I was after. If the walls in my mind had been built up, then I would have to tear them down, piece by piece. If isolation and withdrawal had cemented my stubborn will of self-reliance, then I'd slowly have to open up my circle of influence.

This, of course, was easier said than done.

I searched for an answer to rid my mind of the flashbacks and nightmares, but the only help offered was continued therapy and time. I wanted desperately for that to be enough, but my gut told me otherwise.

If my flashbacks were indeed tied to my guilt, my mind might never be my own again.

****

A little after seven o'clock, I headed up the stairs. I passed Stacie's room where I hoped she had slept well. We'd been on good terms for the last few weeks, moving past my impulsive blunder that had occurred on *ultrasound day*. I had apologized for storming out of the house, and for my anger toward Jack.

I also shared with her about my therapy appointments with Dr. Crane.

I made her promise she would keep that information confidential. She was happy to oblige, relieved I'd taken our honesty pack seriously—or at least as seriously as I could take it.

I sorted through my laundry in search of clean running shorts, planning to make a date with the washing machine later in the day. I was grateful for a day off, a feeling that surprised me. Kai unfortunately started his forty-eight hour shift today, so I'd likely not hear from him until this evening when he called.

Buzz. Buzz.

My phone vibrated on my nightstand.

It was a text from Kai.

Kai: *Up for a run? Want some company? I can be ready in 10 minutes.*

I smiled as I considered his proposal. I had never run with anyone before. Kai was hardly *just anyone*. Kai was a man who didn't lack in strength or endurance. Proof of that claim was evident to anyone with eyes.

His body was solid and muscular. I had heard stories about the workouts at the station and they were nothing short of intense. I felt quite unsure about my ability to keep up with him, but ultimately my desire to see him was greater than my pride.

I replied.

Tori: *Meet me at the bridge on Elm in 20.*

My run to the bridge was fairly short. As I neared it, I could see him stretching. A rush of energy pumped through me. While one second he was stretching, the next he was doing some kind of strange combination of bobbing and weaving. I hoped it wasn't a new dance move.

As I got close he smiled, matching my pace as I approached. Within seconds though, I was doubling my cadence just to stay in stride with his long legs.

"Good morning, beautiful," he said, looking at me with the grin I'd come to know quite well over the last six weeks.

"Good morning. What was that little jig you did on the bridge back there?" I asked, trying not to laugh.

"Oh, ha! You saw that, huh? There was a bee next to my hand, I was just trying to get away from it," he laughed.

"A bee, huh? Is *that* your weakness, Kai? Big, strong fireman is afraid of an itty bitty bee?"

He laughed again before answering, "Actually, I'm pretty allergic to them. I was cornered by a whole nest of them once when I was ten. I had over thirty stings that day. I have to carry an EpiPen now wherever I go. Kind of a bummer," he said.

I punched his shoulder.

"Or...kinda great that you won't die from a bee sting," I said sarcastically.

"True, if you want to be all glass-half-full about it."

"And if I was ever charged with a life perspective...that would be it."

This time his laugh was more of a loud, air-sucking bark.

I smiled and shook my head.

****

We ran past the park and the high school, turning left onto an old country road. I had been on it just a few times before. The greenbelt that spanned for a good couple of miles made for nice running scenery. It was some of the only green land left that hadn't yet been capitalized on by greedy builders or investors.

I worked hard to match Kai's never-ending stride, but didn't complain.

"So, we haven't really talked about the camping trip since the fireman's ball," Kai said, breathing heavily.

"No, I guess we haven't. When is it?" I asked, sweat dripping from my forehead.

Kai turned his head toward me, "Weekend after next. Do you

want to come?"

"I'm not sure, Kai. I mean, it does sound fun to hang out with you in hill country, but I don't know anyone else. Don't you think that's weird?"

Kai laughed. "What? Don't be crazy. You know Briggs...and Mike."

"Uh, I only know Mike because he drove me in an ambulance after my not-so-graceful fall. We're not quite BFF's yet," I said.

Kai pushed me gently on my shoulder and laughed again—or tried to.

"There will be at least three other women there. I promise they'll all love you, Tori. I have an extra tent and everything else is taken care of already. All you need to do is just agree to come. Do you have your schedule yet?" he asked.

"No, but I put in my November calendar requests tomorrow," I replied.

"Great, it's settled then. You're going," he said, grinning wide.

I rolled my eyes at him, but couldn't help but feel flattered.

"Fine, I'll go."

We kept running.

Kai's talkative nature had grown quiet. The only sound I heard was our breathing. Somewhere in the last mile I had found new motivation to keep pushing myself forward. I'm sure Kai's presence had something to do with that. The new pace he'd set had finally stuck; it was no longer a conscience battle.

I felt good.

It was right about then though, that I realized Kai's stride was no longer matching mine. He was stopped and bent over, sweat pouring from his face onto the broken, faded concrete.

"I surrender! I surrender!" Kai said, holding up one arm. He was still bent in half and breathing hard.

I jogged back to him, trying to make sense of his declaration. His head lifted and his eyes met mine.

"You won, woman. You didn't have to kill me though...I would've surrendered miles ago if only I'd known you were going for a long-distance medal," he said panting.

"Oh. Sorry, Kai, why didn't you say something?" I asked. It was then he gave me a look that I could clearly identify as *male ego*.

Kai looked at his watch and pressed several buttons in sequence.

His eyebrows shot up as he read the tiny screen. He stared at me in surprise.

"What?" I asked.

"Is this normal for you? Your *normal* distance of running?" he asked, shock still registering on his face.

"Yeah I think so...I don't really keep track of the distance," I said, wondering what he was getting at.

"Tori...we've almost ran 6 miles....in one direction," he said flatly.

"Okay...well, you don't exactly look like a guy that's out of shape, Kai," I said, moving my hand to my hip.

He grinned and stood upright.

"Have you ever heard of guys that can bench press two-fifty, but can't do an hour of cardio to save their life? Well, you just met one."

He laughed heartily now. I laughed too, even though I knew he was exaggerating. I felt self-conscious under his gaze in the seconds that followed. I shifted my weight back and forth, trying to ease my anxiety.

"Thanks for the lesson in humility, *Pele*," he said, looking around at the road we were on. "We're probably a good three miles out still if we take this short cut through the field, would it *pain* you to walk with me a bit?" he asked, his eyes amused.

"No, of course not. I really am sorry...I should have paid more attention."

We headed toward the dirt trail that ran diagonal to the street. While walking in step with one another —both sweaty and hot —Kai turned to look at me again.

"So, what do you measure them by?" he asked.

"What do you mean?"

"If you don't go by distance, do you measure your runs by time or by land mark?"

I swallowed hard, thinking about how to respond. I didn't want to lie, but the truth was unconventional at best. He waited for my answer, his eyes still glued to my face.

"I guess I go by how I feel," I said quietly.

"I'd make it to mile marker one if I measured it by how I *felt*," Kai said, laughing.

I was grateful for his humor; it seemed to break up these serious conversations so much better than my angry defensiveness did. Dr. Bradley had been the only one who knew why I ran. Consequently, she was also the one who had helped *me* understand it. Kai took my hand in his, giving me the courage to continue my revelation as we walked.

"I always hated running. I hated anything that made me hot and sweaty, actually," I said.

"Could have fooled me," he said, winking.

"Yeah, I've probably fooled a lot of people over the last year. I started running to deal—*cope* is what they call it in recovery lingo. I would run when I couldn't handle it anymore: the stress, the pain, the...the memories," I confessed.

Kai's face changed again. This time I saw nothing but compassion. I hoped it wouldn't turn to pity. I hated pity.

He nodded, freeing me to speak again.

"There were times in the beginning I could only make it a few blocks, but I'd push myself till I either threw up or was forced to sit down, afraid I was going to pass out on the sidewalk. Then, as I pushed through one level of pain, I'd push past the next and the next. One day I ran for close to two hours straight, all the while focusing on ridding myself of...the images."

"Did it work?" he asked.

Kai's question was soft, thoughtful, yet his grip on my hand grew tighter. His jaw was tense.

"That depends on how you define *worked*, I guess. If running kept me from other ways I could have chosen to cope, then yes. But as you see, this is only a temporary fix. Nothing will take it away forever," I said, refusing to make eye contact with him.

Kai was quiet then and so was I.

I'd never said those words aloud—I wasn't even sure I had actually thought them inside my head. Hearing Dr. Bradley's theory of me was one thing, but it was entirely another to admit it to someone else in full transparency. He stopped walking, pulling me to a stop as well. I searched his eyes in question.

"That's not true you know," he said softy.

Confused by his seemingly cryptic words I asked, "What's not?"

"Tori, I know you're trying to figure out a lot of stuff right now and I admire you so much for your courage and willingness to be honest, but I think you're missing what could be the biggest part of your recovery if you let it."

Please don't say it, Kai.

I stared at him, hoping that he would change the direction of this conversation, hoping that he would give me space in this one area.

"God. He is more than a temporary fix, Tori. He's the only one that we can trust completely. I don't know where you stand with Him right now, but I do know that you hold the truth inside you," he said passionately.

I held his gaze for a few moments more, and then broke out of his grip. I walked ahead without him. This was one conversation I wasn't ready to have—with Kai or anyone else.

"I'll give you space to think on it, but I won't pretend that faith isn't the answer you need. Sure, there is tremendous value in therapy and support from your family and friends that *love* you," Kai said, letting his last words hang in the air between us before continuing, "but I'd be kidding myself and you if I pretended that you could possibly find hope anywhere else, but *in God*."

I kept walking, processing his words before throwing them out. I knew he believed them, but that wasn't enough to make me believe them, too. Again I found myself wishing it were different—wishing I were different. He caught up to me and put his hand on my shoulder, stopping me gently.

"Tori, this is who I am. I won't apologize for it. I am a man who makes plenty of mistakes, but I know what I believe and *who* I believe in. I hope you can understand that, because this is the one area I won't make any concessions in," he spoke firmly now, searching my eyes for understanding.

I nodded, letting my still posture melt under his gaze.

"I do understand that your faith is important to you, Kai. I would never ask you to change that, nor would I want you to." I took a deep breath before continuing, "But don't expect me to agree with you. My convictions aren't the same as yours."

He reached out and touched my face, grazing his thumb over my scar. No one before Kai had ever touched that tender, raised skin on my cheek. But that simple gesture brought more comfort than I wanted to acknowledge. Comfort was something I had all but forgotten.

"How do you sort the truth from the lies, Tori?" His eyes were both tender and soft when he asked.

I swallowed. "I don't know."

Kai's smile was sad, but he didn't move his hand away from my face. "Thank you."

"For what?" I whispered.

"Your honesty."

Kai pulled me in for a sweaty hug before we decided to pick up the pace.

We ran back to the bridge in comfortable silence.

TWENTY

Halloween: possibly the worst night to work in a medical facility.

Aside from the many acts of ridiculous stupidity, the word *creepy* didn't even begin to describe what happens in hospitals during the course of this twenty-four-hour holiday. Nurse Holt had agreed to "limited decor and costumes" throughout the emergency floor per her memo, but there were those that pushed the limits. Take Nurse Bev Hatty for example: her platinum blond Marilyn Monroe wig, her ruby red lips, her spider-leg-long false eyelashes. That was just the start. Over the top of her black scrubs she wore a red sequined lace-up corset, which I was quite certain she would have worn solo if not for the "Nurses, only wear scrubs" rule.

There were a few doctors who took extra liberty with their Halloween garb, but for the most part, the staff's festiveness entailed funky headbands, face paint, and Halloween printed scrubs.

I wore simple black cat ears and drew on whiskers with black eyeliner. Though the day had been very busy with dislocated shoulders via bounce houses and allergic reactions to cupcakes with mystery ingredients, it would be nothing compared to the night shift. The staff nearly doubled by five o' clock and the waiting room began to fill with many strange looking characters—and not just strange due to costume choice.

People were odd on this holiday. Unusual and unappealing stunts were often tried, tested, and proved harmful on this day. The difficult part was that Halloween messed with the most important sense a nurse had: the ability to visually assess a patient's need and distress level. On this night, that sense was blinded by fake blood, painted scars, and layers of makeup and clothing (or sometimes no clothing).

Kai had sent me a text earlier in the day asking me to be *careful of the crazies* and to call him before I left work. I smiled at his thoughtfulness. He was one person who truly knew the freaky details that often went along with a shift worked on Halloween night.

I had already seen several emergency vehicles come through. At this point, their loads were mostly drunken high school students, but there was also a group of pumpkin smashers who'd been brought in as well. Apparently, their last house didn't go as planned. A group of black ninjas had jumped out and retaliated on them by way of BB guns. Guess that was the last house with smashed pumpkins on that particular street.

The floor was frantic by nine. I still had three hours left. At least my remaining time would go by quickly. I made a note to tell Kai about my glass half-full mentality.

Hey, maybe I am a positive person after all.

I laughed out loud.

After releasing my last patient--a man hit in the face with a baseball bat at a haunted corn maze—I walked to room 104. I checked the chart briefly on the outside of the door and knocked twice as I entered. My eyes widened. There on the hospital bed was a beautiful blond lady bug—no older than eight.

A worried father stood by her side.

"Hi there, you must be Mallory...is that right?" I asked, walking closer to the small girl.

"Yes," the young girl said, holding her left arm against her body.

"Do you know how much longer we will need to wait for the doctor?" the father asked. He pressed his fingers to his temples, and then stared at me for an answer.

"It should just be a few minutes more, Mr.-"

"Brown, David Brown." He looked at his daughter.

"Okay. Well, let me just get some information and I can make sure to get it to the doctor as quickly as possible. Mallory was hit by a vehicle tonight?" I asked.

My heart rate quickened. The little girl moaned in pain. I fixed my eyes on Mr. Brown, but he wasn't the one to answer.

"I was running...to see my friend Lauren." Mallory answered. Her sweet voice was soft, but strained. Her face twisted in pain.

My chest felt like it was twisting, too.

This reaction was unfamiliar to me. I was good at my job. I was good at being a professional.

I was even better at being numb.

"We were in a busy trick-or-treating neighborhood. Kids were on both sides of the street, but there were also cars driving kids to each block. It all happened so fast. One minute she was in front of me...the next she was crossing the street to walk with Lauren. The car came out of nowhere," Mr. Brown said. His face was full of guilt.

I swallowed hard. I knew that look.

I took a deep breath, turning my body away from Mallory completely. A burning sensation simmered in the depths of my core, threatening my ability to focus. I only needed to think about the facts, nothing else.

This is not like Anna.

Logically I knew that, but logic had lied to me before.

Logic had told me the storm wasn't that bad.

Logic had told me not to turn back.

Logic had killed Anna.

I shook my head to clear my thoughts again. "Can you explain to me where she was hit? Do you have an idea of how fast the car was going?" I asked.

"It couldn't have been more than ten miles per hour. She hit the bumper on the driver's side...and rolled onto the hood before she was thrown down on the road. She landed on her left arm and hip," Mr. Brown said, moving to touch his daughter's hair.

My eyes followed him and the movement. Suddenly, I was seeing the hair of a very different little girl. It was an image I wouldn't soon forget, one that had been permanently stamped in my mind's eye.

I blinked several times.

Mallory was in focus again, moaning in pain.

I swallowed down the thick ball of molasses that had formed in my throat. My hands started to shake. Somehow though, I found the words to speak, "I'm going to see what I can bring her for the pain. I'll be right back to examine her and get the doctor."

I left the room, pulling the heavy door closed behind me. My breathing was heavy as I clutched my hand over my heart and closed my eyes. I just needed a moment to calm the panic inside me. The thought of easing the child's discomfort propelled me forward through the hall.

Get a grip!
You can't lose it, not here.

After many deep breaths and pep talks, I returned to administer her IV. She was frightened, crying as she pulled her good arm away from me. I leaned down next to her. A shiver raced through me as I took in the fragility of her body. She stopped crying as her eyes met mine.

"I know a trick, can I tell you about it?" I asked her.

She nodded, shifting her body a tad closer to me.

"If you sing the alphabet song and close your eyes real tight, I can be done with this part by the time you get to the end of the song."

Her eyes held no suspicion in them as she stared at me.

"Okay," she whispered.

Mr. Brown smiled at me from the corner of the room. Mallory gave me her right arm, willingly. The gesture caused my heart to ache as I held her tiny wrist in my hand.

Then she started to sing; I had never heard a sweeter voice.

The only thing that kept me sane in that moment was the fact that I would do anything to ease the pain of this child. She trusted me...I couldn't let her down.

When the needle poked through her skin on the letter "H", she squeezed her eyes shut a little tighter, but by the time "W" came around, her IV was secured. She smiled at me as I laid her arm down gently.

I knew by the swelling of her left arm, that her wrist was probably fractured. There was a lot of swelling near the joint of her elbow, too. Peeling back the layers of her lady bug bloomers, her hip was a tie-dye of purples and blues. Hematoma was likely. Though she would be able to walk, it would be months before the deep bruise would heal completely.

Elvis—or Doctor Hernandez as I knew him—came in just minutes later. He confirmed that she would need x-rays along with an MRI. Mr. Brown gasped when he heard that surgery would be the most probable outcome tonight after they confirmed the lab results. Dr. Hernandez then explained that the elbow was a very sensitive area to operate on. Even with the most skilled surgeon, a full range of motion was difficult to guarantee.

Mr. Brown looked like he was going to pass out from the news.

"I...I need to make a phone call, please. Her mom is out of town. We have split custody and she needs to know what's going on here tonight," Mr. Brown said.

Dr. Hernandez looked at me. "Can you stay with her a minute while he steps out?"

"Sure," I said, instantly feeling sick to my stomach. I needed to *get out* of this room—not babysit. I pulled up a chair to her bedside as Mr. Brown stepped out into the hallway.

Mallory seemed completely relaxed now. Her medicine had kicked in and she was no longer moaning, even though her injuries were still very apparent. She turned her head to look at me.

"My mom's never missed Halloween before. We always did trick-or-treating together," Mallory said. The tears in her eyes made me want to touch her head, the way I had seen her father do only minutes before.

But I couldn't do that.

Touching was the *opposite* of numbing.

I pushed the desire away.

"I like your costume choice. I always liked bugs," I said.

Mallory's eyes lit up, her tears momentarily forgotten.

"You do? Daddy says I'm a tomboy 'cause I love bugs—all bugs."

"I guess I was, too. I liked to collect bugs when I was your age. My sister always thought it was so weird, but I loved to make them special habitats in jars and things, and to learn what they ate and how they lived."

She smiled thoughtfully. I noticed then that she was shivering, most likely from the cold liquid pumping through her IV. I stood and carefully pulled another blanket over her.

"Do you like to read about them?" I asked, distracting myself from her nearness.

"Yes, I love to read! I got some big picture books on bugs and reptiles for my birthday last month."

It was then the lab tech opened the door to take her away. A part of me was relieved. Dr. Brown had just ended his call as the tech began to roll her out the door. He was careful not to bump her arm or hip. I followed them out, about to turn in the opposite direction, when I saw her reach back to me.

"Don't you get to come with me?" she asked.

There was something desperate in her eyes—a pleading. I felt all the air rush out of my lungs.

She wants me to go with her?

Before I could answer, Dr. Hernandez answered for me. He told me to go ahead with her and that he would let Nurse Holt know. Mallory grabbed a hold of my finger then, her tiny hand gripping around it tightly.

I looked down at it.

I was no longer numb.

Touching had won.

****

It was almost midnight when her surgery was confirmed. Though I knew she would be well taken care of by the fourth-floor nursing staff, she refused to let go of my finger. I didn't argue. We traveled that way through the halls, in the elevator, and into the room that she would recover in post-surgery.

Finally though, it was time.

I felt her tense. "You'll do great Mallory. You'll sleep the whole time and when you wake up you'll have a really cool cast. All your friends will get to sign it when you go back to school."

"Will you sign it?" she asked.

Another stabbing pain tore through my heart at the sincerity of her question. Tomorrow was my day off, but I couldn't say no. Nothing would have made me say *no*.

"I'll come back and sign it tomorrow."

"Promise?" she asked.

"I promise," I said. She squeezed my finger one last time before dropping her hand. I watched her dad kiss her face and reassure her again.

Then, she was rolled into surgery.

Mr. Brown was speaking to me—thanking me I think—but I couldn't hear him. All I could hear were the sweet words of a precious little girl. A little girl who reminded me so much of the one child I would never get a chance to hear.

****

As I pulled into the driveway my phone rang.
"Hello?"
"Hey, gorgeous...where ya at?" Kai asked, yawning.
"Hey, I actually just pulled up to Stacie's house. I'm sorry I forgot to call you, I stayed late tonight," I said.
"That's alright, I'm just glad you made it home okay. It's brutal out there tonight—accidents are everywhere," Kai said.
I exhaled, thinking about his statement.
Was that what they said the night of my accident? The night of the bad storm? Was I just another accident—another sad statistic of a fatal car crash?
"You there, Tori?"
"Yeah, I'm here. I'm just really tired. It was a long night...I think I just need to get to bed."
The clock on my dash read 1:30am.
"Is something wrong, Tori? You sound different tonight... did something happen?"
I thought for a second. "Can you ask me again tomorrow?"
There was a long pause on the other end. I wasn't trying to push him away, but I couldn't talk right now. I was too raw.
"I promise you I will, but I need to know you're safe tonight before I can hang up."
"I'm safe," I said softly.
Safe.
Such a simple word...such a complex meaning.
Another pause
"Okay. I get off at noon. I'll call you. Goodnight, *Pele*. Sleep well."
"Goodnight," I said.
I looked at the dark phone in my hand—thinking.
Why haven't I ever thought about the man who called 911 after hearing the collision? Or those who were dispatched to the scene that night?
I knew I had purposefully kept myself from thinking about the EMT who had carried Anna's body to the stretcher—knowing she wouldn't wake up. I was glad I couldn't remember the faces from that night. It was easier that way. I didn't want to know if there were others who were tormented with memories from the night

Anna died.

    Sorrow was not something I wanted to share.

I could hardly deal with it on my own.

TWENTY-ONE

I stood outside the door to Mallory's hospital room and took a deep breath. I had tossed and turned all night thinking of this little girl, hoping she wasn't in too much post-surgery pain. I tightened my grip on the gift bag in my left hand, and knocked. Instantly it was met with a greeting to enter.

Just. Keep. Breathing.

I walked into the room and saw her sweet face. Her smile was bright and eager—welcoming. The full-length cast and sling that now adorned her small frame caught my eye. From her left shoulder to wrist, she was positively bombproof.

"You came!" Mallory said.

"I promised, didn't I? I never break my promises...especially to cute little lady bugs about to have surgery," I said smiling.

Mr. Brown updated me on Mallory's prognosis and the care she'd received so far. It was extremely rare for me to see a patient once they left the ER, but so far nearly everything about my experience with Mallory was that way. I walked over to her bedside and handed her the gift bag as I picked up the marker and signed my name on her cast.

She squealed in delight at the sight of the present. With her free hand she carefully pulled out the sparkle tissue paper. I held the bag steady as she reached inside to take out the bug habitat and magnifying glass. She placed each on her lap, looking at them with wonder.

"This is the best gift ever," she said smiling.

"I hope you can go on many bug hunting adventures as soon as you're feeling better. I'm sure you have some friends who will hunt with you," I said.

"Definitely, thank you, Miss Tori," she said reaching out her hand to me.

"You're very welcome," I said.

As I gave her my hand she tugged on it, bringing me closer. She leaned in as if to tell me a secret. It was then I felt my body weaken.

"I want to be a nurse just like you when I grow up," she whispered, "I want to help people."

And then it was all too much: the touching, the nearness, the whisper, the smile. I had to get out. I had to get out...*now*.

With each passing second, my body relinquished control to the tidal wave of panic that was threatening to consume it. It was all I could do to smile as I let her hand drop from mine. I muttered a weak goodbye to them both, and then I was outside of her room, floating down the hall in a sea of colorful blurs.

****

I don't remember getting on the elevator, or pressing the button for the 6th floor, but soon I was there. As I walked toward her door, I fought to take in one full breath. Everything felt so tight: my skin, my chest, my airway. There was nothing in my body that seemed to function without a direct command.

I could see her just on the other side of the couch room. Her door was ajar as she wrote in a file on her desk. She looked up as if she sensed me and stood immediately.

"Victoria? Come in—come sit," Dr. Crane said, ushering me into her office and closing the door behind me.

"I know we don't have an appointment, I just...I just-"

"Slow down, its fine. I was just about to take a lunch break; I don't have any appointments right now. Please, sit. Tell me what's going on?" The kindness in her eyes broke me. I told her.

I told her *everything*.

I told her about Mallory.

I told her how she had reached for me, how she had talked to me, how she had wanted me with her before surgery. All the while Dr. Crane nodded, saying nothing in return. I went on.

"She...reminded me so much of *her*," I said, refusing to say her name, though I didn't know why.

"And what about Mallory reminded you of Anna?" Dr. Crane asked.

I stared at her, lost in the depths of my memories.

"Her hair, her age, her size..."

"And what do you feel?" she asked me.

"What?"

"Connect this event with Mallory to a feeling...what do you feel?"

What do I feel?

I took several deep breaths as I searched for the answer to that.

"I feel...*sad*," I said. With that admission I bent forward at the waist and let my head fall into my hands.

"And why does seeing Mallory make you sad, Tori?"

If her voice hadn't been so soft when she asked it, I would have laughed at the obvious connotation of her question. But...it wasn't the obvious she was after. She expected something different than the obvious, something more.

I pushed at my temples with my fingertips.

"Because I can't pretend anymore that Anna wasn't real."

Thinking about how Anna had lived prior to that horrible night was just something I didn't do—something I couldn't do. Sometime during this last year, she had become almost like a fictional character to me. Though I knew she had been real, I had never *known* her alive. I may have seen her, touched her, held her in my arms...but there was *no life* to recall from those memories.

But Mallory was alive, and she was a living, breathing contrast of a girl I had remembered—the girl who was gone forever.

The couch cushion shifted next to me. I could feel new warmth at my side, though she didn't touch me.

"In order to accept Anna's death, you must first accept her life—she *was* real, just like Mallory is. Accepting that...is taking one giant step away from the land of denial."

I looked up at her face.

"How will I know when I've accepted it?" I asked.

A faint smile crossed her lips, "When you stop looking for someone to blame—in this case, yourself."

Dr. Crane stood up and grabbed a water bottle out of the mini fridge next to her desk. She offered it to me.

"You've shown tremendous progress today, Victoria. Not only did you connect to a person, but you connected to a *feeling*, one that is crucial to your recovery. Don't let that go unnoticed."

I rolled the water bottle in my hands back and forth. This didn't feel like progress, it felt awful. *Feeling* was awful, but I wanted to believe she was right. She pulled her chair up and sat down across from me.

"I want you to think about how you would have responded if you had met Mallory in Phoenix."

I nodded slightly. She knew I would have run. So did I.

"Today, you chose to come here. You shared, you felt, you

experienced, but I think there's something else you should process in regard to all this. You now know a little girl who thinks the world of you—who wants to be like you because of how you cared for her. If you're going to let your mind play the comparison game between Anna and Mallory, then I want you to imagine what Anna would have thought about *you*. If she could have known you were trying to save her life, what would she have thought? Be fair to yourself, you need to bring that comparison full circle."

The tightening in my chest was back. The air was pressed out of my lungs in one hard exhale as I leaned against the stiff leather sofa. Though she had spoken the words so gently, they had cut me deep.

Would Anna have felt for me what Mallory claims to?

****

On the way home I took a detour. I passed the bridge on Elm where I had met Kai a few days ago, and pulled into the parking lot by the playground. I zipped up my hoodie as the wind blew against my face. I walked the path to the giant tree and sat against it, bringing my knees to my chest. Leaning my head back to rest against the rough bark, I closed my eyes.

What if Anna could have known I was trying to save her?

I thought again of Mallory: her bright smile, her sweet laugh, her gentle spirit.

The truth was, there was so much I would never know. Dwelling on the impossible seemed useless. I stared out into the field as the strong breeze rustled the leaves and stung my eyes with its force. I inhaled deeply.

The cool, crisp air filled my lungs over and over.

I love you, Victoria.

The words floated through my mind like a whisper on the wind.

I looked around…no one. Goosebumps prickled my skin.

Then, unmistakably, I heard it again.

This time the words thundered in my chest. I looked up.

I love you, Victoria.

Why?

You are mine.

I was still—silent, too scared to move. It was too much to believe that God could be speaking to me, or moreover, that God would *want* to speak to me.

The crunching of leaves snapped my head to the left. I was eye level with large black boots. I tilted my head upward and found a familiar face staring down at me.

"Hey there," Kai said sweetly.

"Hi." I raised my hand to him as he pulled me up, steadying me on the uneven ground.

"Hope I'm not interrupting anything," he said.

"Nope, not at all. How did you find me out here?" I asked.

"Easy, your car's pretty visible from the road. I was just on my way home from the station."

I took in his uniform; he was a sight to behold, no doubt about that. I had never understood why women went gaga over men in uniform—until I met Kai. I was willing to bet he could make anything look good, though.

"I've been worried about you, *Pele*. What happened last night?"

Apparently, he didn't forget anything, either.

I leaned back against the tree as he moved toward me. I didn't know if I would be able to articulate much of anything if he remained so close to me. I took a deep breath trying to focus.

"I took care of a little girl last night and I went back to see her this morning…"

I looked away from his eyes to stare off into the distance, letting my mind escape. It hurt too much to say the words. Even if I convinced myself I could trust him with this—with talking about Anna—that fact alone could only cushion the pain so much.

I felt his hand under my chin as he gently turned my face back to him. He searched my eyes.

"Don't go away, Tori. Stay here with me, please. *Talk* to me."

I stared into his eyes. His look was not one of pity, instead it was…*empathy?*

"She reminded me…of Anna—of what I thought she would have been like. She asked me to stay with her, Kai. She held my hand and wouldn't let it go. She made me…*feel.*"

My last word was so full of emotion that it was hardly audible. Though I had no tears to cry, there was an unrelenting burn behind my eyes.

Without further comment, Kai pulled me into his arms and held me. I exhaled as I let my body relax into him. When had this gesture become so comforting? I didn't know, but I did know that in his arms I had found my safe haven.

After a moment he pulled away slightly, looking down at me. Slowly, he tilted my chin again and lowered his lips to mine, claiming my mouth and my heart simultaneously. When our kiss ended, he exhaled.

"I'm so crazy about you, Tori," he said softly. He dropped his hands from my face and stared at me with desire. I was frozen in that gaze for what felt like a year. Finally, he raked a hand through his hair and took a deep breath, breaking the spell between us.

He took a step back and held out his hand to me, smiling as I took it.

"How do you feel about going to Camping World with me this afternoon?"

I laughed at the immediate change in atmosphere. This was his not-so-subtle way of breaking the tension between us. Though we had spoken about the boundaries in our physical relationship, it was easy to get carried away, especially with someone as incredible as Kai.

"Sounds good to me," I said.

I wanted nothing more than to be with him, even if that meant shopping at Camping World.

"Great. I'll pick you up in an hour...let's get outta here."

****

The afternoon turned out to be really fun, even if I was surrounded by every piece of outdoor equipment known to mankind. Kai was excited about *everything* he found at the camping store. If I had thought my mom and Stacie were nuts in the baby stores, this was a whole new level of crazy. By the time he was done, I feared for his checking account. He assured me, however, it was fine.

We were hand in hand all afternoon and I found myself not wanting to let go, not even for a second. This man had become something very special to me in the last two months and all I desired was more time with him.

"Hungry?" he asked.

"Always," I said.

He stopped and looked me up and down in a dramatic manner.

"You don't say? The women in my country wouldn't let you leave the house like that. They'd call you a *skinny little thing that needed to eat more and get more healthier*," he mocked, in a high-pitched islander accent.

I laughed so hard I snorted.

"'Get *more healthier*, huh?" I asked, laughing.

Kai laughed too, although he told me over and over how *dead serious* he was. That only made me laugh harder.

At the Mexican restaurant he stared at me with eyes full of mischief. I knew something was up.

"What? Why are you looking at me like that?" I asked, throwing a chip at his forehead.

"Well, after laughing at my Samoan culture, I think we both owe it to them to eat a real Samoan meal together," Kai said, dipping a chip into the salsa and scooping up half the bowl.

"What do you mean, Kai?"

"I mean, I want you to meet my mom. She already knows all about you, but I want you to know her, too. She is a killer cook," he said smiling.

His mom?

"And don't for a minute think she's not going to like you—that's crazy thinking. What about this Thursday? The night before we leave for camping?" he asked.

I only worked tomorrow and Wednesday of this week, and then had a whole five days off after that. I had no excuses. If Kai loved his mom so much, I knew I would too.

"Yes, Thursday will work," I said, trying to calm my growing anxiety.

"Great it's a date then."

Great.

****

The white cottage we pulled up to on Thursday evening was a sight to behold. The house was simple, the size conservative at best. It wasn't the house that awed a visiting guest; it was every square inch of the property surrounding it. Her garden included: bushes, plants, flowers, shrubs, vegetables and berries. I simply couldn't take it all in with just one glance. Kai had mentioned that he helps his mom with her yard work—but this wasn't a yard, it was a masterpiece.

A giant white trellis stood at the path's center, inviting us to her front door. I walked as slowly as Kai would allow so I could see all that laid inside the picket fence. It was impossible to identify each type of seed she had planted.

"Kai...this is amazing," I said, as we walked onto her porch.

He smiled, but before he could knock his mother was there, opening the door and welcoming us inside.

"Mom, this is Tori. Tori, this is my mother, Sia," he said.

She hugged Kai, her arms wrapping around his waist. After she released him, she came over to me and clasped my hands together in hers.

"It is so good to finally see you, Tori. You are even more beautiful than Kai could describe to me," she said, her thick accent blending her words together like a song.

I could feel Kai beaming at me as she spoke. I did not look at him.

"Thank you. It's so nice to meet you, too, Ms. Alesana. Kai didn't tell me what a spectacular garden you have here. I'd love to see it later," I said.

"Please, call me Sia, and yes, I would love to show you after we eat," she said, winking at her son.

Inside, her home was cozy. Every room could be seen from the kitchen and everything had its place. There were no large empty spaces or furniture that didn't get used. Photographs were hung on the walls, mostly of Kai or her late husband, but decor was limited other than that. Some might see this home as too simple, but in my eyes, Sia had chosen a home like herself.

It was simply perfect.

Sia worked busily in the kitchen finishing up her cooking preparations while putting Kai and I on drink duty. I watched her as I filled the glasses up at the sink. Her dark hair was put up into a thick bun and there were several streaks of silver framing her face. I had a feeling if she let it down it would fall to her lower back—at least. Her features were soft, feminine, yet "healthy", to quote Kai's words from his culture. The roundness of her face gave her a youthful glow and there was no question where Kai's good looks had come from. Sia was beautiful.

"Okay, come and sit, please. Dinner is ready. Kai, you can say the blessing tonight," Sia said.

We sat down at a table spread with several dishes I couldn't name, but with aromas that made my mouth water. Kai took both our hands and bowed his head. I followed the manner, hoping I wouldn't be called on for any specialty prayers during the remainder of the night. Kai blessed the food and then prayed for each of the "special women in his life". Sweet warmth spread throughout my body at his grateful expressions.

Sia and Kai explained each of the main dishes and why they were significant to their island. Each food was prepared in similar ways—coconut milk a common theme. The mango-spiced chicken was outstanding, as were the coconut cream yams. The fish salad, called *Ota*, was also amazing. I worked to finish what was on my plate; my eyes had been larger than my stomach. These new combinations and flavors would be worth the over-stuffed feeling in my gut.

Kai still hadn't come up for air since starting his second round.

"Sia, this dinner was wonderful. Kai told me you were an excellent cook, but I didn't know that he meant *this* excellent," I said, pointing at the dishes on the table, half of them still untouched.

"Thank you, I'll cook for you any time," she said smiling. "You need to get more healthier—you're so skinny, Tori."

At that, Kai was gone.

He was rolling over in hysterics, oblivious to all else around him. Tears streaked down his face as he covered his mouth with his hands. If I thought kicking him would have brought him back to his senses, I would have gladly done it. Poor Sia was left baffled at her son's sudden explosion, and apparently I was the one who was left to explain. I bit my cheeks, working hard to control my own bubble of laughter rising inside my throat.

I didn't want her to think there was a joke at her expense, but it had been *exactly* what Kai had predicted would be said. I had to give him props for that.

"What is he laughing at?" Sia asked me.

"I think he must agree with you, Sia. I'd eat this food every day if I could, don't worry about him," I said, glaring toward Kai who was still lost in his own world.

At the end of the meal, or Kai's third round, he gathered the plates and took them to the sink while Sia told me about her journey to America. Kai had been twelve at the time. She told each story with such vivid detail: getting Kai enrolled in American school, applying for her job at the arboretum, plugging into her community, and finding her church home. I listened as she described the obstacles she'd had to overcome, primarily expanding her English.

She had learned English as a second language as a child, but as a housewife for many years she had primarily spoken her native Samoan tongue at home and with friends. Once she moved to America, she had to focus on re-learning and strengthening her vocabulary so that she could work and be involved with Kai's schooling.

I tried to imagine what it would be like to leave the only country I called home, based only on the *hope* of a better life. Kai was right; she was a very brave woman indeed. Kai came into the room then, a towel on his shoulder.

"Mom, you should take Tori outside and show her your garden before it gets too dark. I'll finish up in here," he said, winking at me.

"That would be great, I'd love to see what you've created out there," I said.

Sia grabbed my hand and led me outside. Small spotlights lit the perimeter of her house as we walked into the garden. Perfectly placed stepping stones marked a path near each bordered bed. Each step we took introduced a new flower, spice or plant. My mind was overloaded with questions to ask her: how much time she had spent on each plant, where she had learned her techniques, what her next projects were?

She was happy to oblige my endless curiosity.

As we rounded the corner to the side yard I gasped.

"You have Dahlias? In Texas? I thought they only grew in cool climates," I asked.

Sia looped her arm through mine as I stood gawking at what I considered the most beautiful flower on earth. She had at least a hundred Dahlias staked in the ground.

"You are a *learner* Tori—just like my Kai. Yes, I do grow Dahlia's here," she said.

"But how? How do they grow in such extreme heat?" I asked.

She knelt down, taking me with her.

"Put your hand on this soil. How does it feel?" she asked.

I laid my hand down and rubbed the surface feeling the cool, grainy soil beneath it, "I'm not sure, Sia. I'm not an expert like you," I said.

"The secret is to use mulch. When it's hot outside, the water will stay in the mulch and keep the roots cool. Otherwise, they would fry in the sun since they grow right under the surface," she said, scooping up a handful of damp soil to expose the mulch underneath it. It molded to her fist like clay. "Dahlias remind me to hope. There are many things in our lives that seem impossible, yet somehow, we can still overcome. Just like these Dahlias."

A shiver went through me as she spoke, goose bumps rising on my arms. Sia was unlike any woman I had ever known. There was something different about her, something that made me want to stay up until the wee hours of the morning just to listen to her speak.

As we walked back to the front porch, Kai was sitting there quietly observing us. My cheeks grew warm as I looked from him to his mother.

"Hey Mom, I saw you were holding out on me?" Kai said.

"What do you mean, my son?" she said shaking her head—a teasing smile tugging at the corners of her mouth.

"I saw what was in the oven for dessert," Kai said, patting his tummy and lifting his eyebrows.

I was still so full from dinner, but I knew passing on dessert in this house would not be an option.

"You sneaky little rat—stay out of my oven," she laughed, reaching for my hand again and pulling me inside. "You'd better come get a plate before he eats every last piece."

I also better serve myself. Oy.

Sia served us *Fausi*, a Samoan dessert usually made from Taro root, but stateside it was made with pumpkin. It was served warm and topped with caramelized coconut cream sauce. The taste was truly divine. Kai had two helpings in the same time it took me to finish half of one.

I looked at Sia.

She sat on the couch with Kai next to her. Even though they didn't speak as they ate, the love and respect they had for each another was obvious. I envied it.

When the evening drew to a close, Sia pulled me in for a hug. *What was it about Samoan hugs that made me never want to let go?*

"You come back and eat with me soon, Tori. I would love to have your help in the garden, someday," she said.

"I would be honored to help you, although, I'm sure I'd just slow you down," I laughed.

"Nonsense. You have a gardener's heart, you just need to discover it," she said.

Kai leaned down to kiss his mom on the cheek, before putting his arm around me. We walked down the path toward Kai's truck. I could feel her gaze on our backs and secretly wished we didn't have to leave her alone.

"Doesn't she get lonely?" I asked Kai once we were driving.

"Maybe sometimes, but she has a lot of friends in this neighborhood...she's a bit of a mother to the whole street actually," he said, looking at me. "You like her?"

"Yes, quite a bit. She was just like you described her: strong, brave, an incredible woman."

I watched the city come into view as we headed west onto Hwy 75. I still remembered the words he had spoken about his mom when we were at the lake a few months ago.

He squeezed my hand gently. "Yes, she is. Do you see the similarities?" he asked.

"What?" I asked, turning to look at him.

"I see those same qualities in you, *Pele*," he said. He intertwined our fingers and rested our hands on the middle seat between us. I thought about his statement.

We rode quietly for the next several minutes. No words were needed. I focused on the touch of Kai's hand. His thumb easily traced an imaginary pattern just below my index finger, leaving a trail of warmth behind.

It was his hands that spoke of his character the most, I'd decided.

The firm grip which showcased his strength, also showed his

restraint. He was never overpowering. The calluses on his knuckles were rough and hard, but so were the jobs he had taken on. He was both willing and able to do whatever was asked of him. And yet, somehow, these same hands had shown kindness, love, trust, safety and protection. With each caress of my face, each hold on my hand, each rescue from harm…they told his story.

I hoped I could be a part of that story, too.

As we pulled into Stacie's driveway, Kai turned toward me in his seat.

"Don't forget to pack a warm jacket and several layers of pants for the evenings, Tori. The days will get to the mid-sixties, but the evenings will be cold."

"Okay, Kai. I have gone camping before you know," I said, rolling my eyes at his reminder.

"Well, camping in the hills can be a little more challenging than a campground with hookups," Kai said, blocking my punch to his arm.

"I'll pack a coat, don't worry, and I have a sleeping bag that Stacie found for me in the garage, too," I said, remembering he had offered me one of his earlier in the week.

"Okay. I'll pick you up around nine. It should take us just about three hours to get there, so we'll have plenty of daylight to set up and explore with the rest of the bunch," Kai said, opening his door to get out. I grabbed his arm and pulled him back into the truck.

"You don't need to walk me to the door every time, Kai. Go get some rest, I'll see you in the morning," I said, kissing him quickly on the lips before jumping out of the cab.

He rolled down my window as I ran up the porch steps.

"Consider that the first and last time you win that particular argument, *Pele*. I will always walk you to the door. See you in the morning."

Morning could not come soon enough.

TWENTY-TWO

"So you're really doing this, huh?" Stacie asked, hands on her hips.

"Yes, Stacie. For the millionth time, I'm going camping and it won't kill me!" I said, pushing her aside to zip my bag.

"Okay, but don't you remember those times Dad tried to take us and we always ended up coming home in the wee hours of the morning? I just hope that doesn't happen to you with all those big, burly firemen out there; that would be embarrassing," she said laughing.

Thanks Stacie.

"I have everything I need and most importantly, Kai will be there. He does this all the time, unlike Dad, who took the pop-up camper out once a year and called it *camping*," I said.

"Like father like daughter I suppose..."

Stacie answered the knock at the door before I could comment further on that little jab.

"Hey, Stacie! How is it you look more beautiful each time I see you?" Kai asked, stepping inside.

Stacie laughed, thanking him as she closed the door, rubbing her belly instinctively.

"Come right this way, Kai. Our own *Bear Grylls* is just about ready," Stacie said while pointing at me.

I glared at her. Kai covered his mouth to suppress his laughter. It didn't work. I straightened and pulled the duffel bag over my shoulder. Stacie's grin at my effort was less than encouraging.

I rolled my eyes at her and headed outside. On my third attempt to launch my duffle bag into the back of Kai's truck, he caught it from behind me and placed it inside easily. My sleeping bag and pillow were next. He smiled at me without saying a word.

I always knew he was a smart man.

"Have a great time, Tori," Stacie said, hugging me before adding, "And I hope I won't see you back at two in the morning."

I rubbed her belly and simply said, "You won't. Goodbye, ye-of-little-faith."

After filling up at the gas station, Kai threw a brown bag full of snacks into the cab. If I'd judged him off his physique alone, I'd have guessed he only ate salads, lean protein, and whole grains, but that, I was learning, was definitely not the case. He had a metabolism for which every girl in high school would have sold her soul for. He munched now on something in the *cool ranch* variety.

"What?" he asked, shrugging his shoulders at me as he put another chip into his mouth.

"Do you have anything in that bag that has less than twenty ingredients listed on the package?" I asked.

"Hmmm...nope," he said, smiling. "I thought you didn't care about all that diet nonsense."

"I don't really, but I also don't want to live on junk food alone, either," I said.

"Well...welcome to camping, *Pele*. You ain't gonna find anything organic, gluten-free or low sugar around for the next few days," he said.

I couldn't help but laugh at him. He was quite adorable...chip breath and all. As we drove, Kai told me about each of the men that would be there and the women they were connected to.

Briggs was the only one who would be flying solo this time around. Apparently, he was taking a break from the dating world. Kai didn't go into too much detail about it. He seemed to be a lot more guarded when it came to Briggs, never revealing too much at one time. It was obvious he regarded Briggs as a brother. I could respect that.

Kai's chief, Max Lexington, whom they all referred to as "Chief Max", would be there with his wife Mrs. Julie. Apparently, she was the only reason we would have real meals on this trip. I was already grateful for her as I watched Kai unwrap his second cream-filled pastry.

Chief Max had hired Kai eight years ago and was the one who had pushed him to become a paramedic after his initial EMT certification. Then of course there was Mike, my infamous ambulance driver who was newly married to Carla. As Kai spoke about each camper who would be joining us, I tried to keep their names straight in my head. I hoped once I had faces to match, that would be easier. There were at least three other guys who would be joining us, but not until the second day.

"What are you thinking about over there? You've been awfully quiet while I've been blabbing away," Kai said.

"I'm just thinking about your station," I said.

"What about?" Kai asked.

"About when you became a paramedic. Do all of you have your paramedic certification?" I asked him.

"No, not even close. All of us have at least our basic EMT certification so we can assist with the basic needs of people in crisis like CPR, or administering asthma treatments, or giving out glucose...that type of thing. Really the simple difference is that paramedics can break the skin and a basic EMT cannot," Kai said.

"That makes sense. So you can call a paramedic an EMT, but an EMT shouldn't be called a paramedic if he or she isn't certified? That's kinda like how it is with nurses, too. A lot of medical assistant's or CNAs can look like an RN, but our job descriptions and responsibilities are very different," I said.

"Exactly. Hey...you've never told me about your graduation from UT Southwest—that must have been a great night for you and your family," Kai said, smiling at me.

I looked out the window, my stomach clenching with unease.

Hardly.

"I don't remember it that well, really. It was just your average graduation," I said flatly.

I could feel Kai's gaze on my face, but pretended not to notice it. I kept my eyes focused on the trees that filled the miles around us. The hills were in full view now and beauty surrounded us on every side. I could see a lake, which from our current vantage point looked more like a puddle, but I guessed we'd be seeing it up close soon enough.

"Tori?"

"Hmm?"

"Why don't you ever want to talk about your family?" Kai asked.

"I talk about my family—I talk about Stacie all the time," I said defensively.

"No, you *tell* me about living at Stacie's house, but you don't tell me about your parents or really anything of significance," Kai said.

I took a deep breath, exhaling slowly.

"I don't have what you have, Kai. My family life is complicated," I said, returning my gaze to the window.

"Complicated? Like moving to a new country, or learning a new culture, or losing your father at ten years-old?" Kai said, driving his point home.

I felt my cheeks flush. He was right. He hadn't had an average childhood, either.

"I'm sorry, I didn't mean to imply your life hasn't had complications. You've had a lot of big obstacles to overcome, but *your* mom chose to stick by you. She did what was best for you and that really shows," I said.

"And what? You're parents haven't stuck by you? Every time I was over there for dinner last year, *you* were all they talked about. They talked about their daughter who was a nurse, their daughter who had worked so hard, their daughter that they were so proud of."

"And what about their daughter who was *wrecked for life*...did that come up, too?" I said, anger pulsing through me.

"What? No. What are you talking about?" Kai asked looking at me, concern etched on his face.

"Nothing, I really don't want to talk about it."

I should have just kept my mouth shut.

This is pointless.

"It's too late now, Tori. Why would you say that? You don't really think-"

"It's not what I *think* Kai, it's what I heard, okay? I *heard* my mom say those very words to my father a week before my graduation. It wasn't exactly the celebration I had hoped for when I passed my boards," I said.

Kai went quiet. I knew it must have been shocking to him, coming from a home where there was open communication and enough love to travel to the moon and back. But that wasn't my home; that wasn't my family.

Our love was conditional.

"I'm sorry, Tori."

"Yeah, me too."

It was a memory I truly hated. Those words had cut me to the core, leaving the dagger inside to continue its damage. Sure I had learned to "play nice" with my mom since coming home, but there was nowhere left for her and I to go. I knew the truth.

I would never forget her words; they had represented everything I had feared and more.

Even though I knew she was right, somehow hearing it from her had cemented my fate. There was no glass-half full to that one. It was just *fact*.

I felt the truck come to a stop as Kai pulled us over onto the shoulder.

"You know that's not true," Kai said, offering me his hand.

I didn't take it. I stared ahead at the dash instead.

"Sure, fine...whatever, let's just go."

"No, not fine whatever. Look at me, Tori. This is important. You *can't* believe that. What good is all this work you're doing if you believe trash like that?" Kai said, frustration mounting on each word he spoke.

About as good as trying to bring back the dead?

"You're going to have to confront her, you know that? Someday when you're ready...it simply has to be done. You'll have to tell your mom what you heard her say," Kai said.

Now I looked at him, mouth gaping.

Was he serious? Did he know my parents at all?

That was way too open for a family like mine—way too real.

"I'm dead serious, Tori. That kind of thing will eat you alive. I'd go with you...you know that, right? If you needed support, I'd be there for you," Kai said.

I felt my throat thicken with emotion at his offer.

Why does he care so much about this?

"Thank you, Kai. You overestimate me, but I do appreciate your offer...you're a good friend," I said, taking his hand in mine, hoping that would be the end of this conversation.

"I don't *overestimate* anything. I call it like I see it, Tori. You're strong, you're beautiful inside and out, and you *deserve* to be loved. My only wish is that you would see that, too."

He raised my hand to his mouth and gently kissed it before cranking the truck engine back up and pulling onto the road. I told myself to breathe, but Kai had made that utterly impossible. He was my too-good-to-be-true boyfriend, and I would never give him up. I could never be *that* strong, and I hoped I'd never have to be.

****

The last twenty minutes, on what seemed to be a never-ending gravel road leading to nowhere, caused me a bit of unanticipated nausea. Kai reassured me we were *almost there* several times. I kept my eyes closed and my head glued to the back of the seat. I was kicking myself for not bringing my Dramamine.

I seriously could have kissed the ground when the truck finally lurched to a complete stop.

Kai came around to the passenger door and opened it for me, "Let's get you into the fresh air, *Pele*. You can sit over here on this rock while I start getting us set up. Looks like Chief Max, Mrs. Julie and Briggs are already here," Kai said.

I nodded, trying to keep the nausea at bay. He helped me over to a nearby rock. I knew I would be embarrassed when I was feeling better, but I couldn't even think about that right now. I put my head in my hands and focused on my breathing.

I could hear Kai speaking to a female who I was fairly certain was Mrs. Julie. When I tried to confirm my suspicion, though, I almost lost my lunch. I closed my eyes again and breathed out slowly.

"...Let me at least get her some ginger ale, Kai. Poor thing, that road is brutal."

"That would be great Mrs. Julie, thank you," Kai said.

About five minutes later I heard Mrs. Julie, again. She sat down next to me on my rock and offered me a tin mug filled with ginger ale and ice. I lifted my head, feeling a bit more centered.

"Thank you, I'm Tori by the way," I said, making eye contact with the pretty red-head that looked to be about my mother's age.

"I've heard all about you, Tori. It's a pleasure to finally meet you, sweetheart. I'm so glad you could come with Kai on this trip, although I'm sorry the journey was a bit rough on ya," Mrs. Julie said.

"I'll be fine in just a few minutes I'm sure, I'm already feeling better," I said, taking a sip of the icy beverage.

"Good, until then feel free to ask me for anything," Mrs. Julie said.

"Thank you, Mrs. Julie. I will."

In just under a half hour, Kai had set up both of our tents. They were about twenty feet out from the fire pit and just a couple feet apart from one another. I had guessed that the circle of tents would continue to grow as others arrived.

Kai was now helping Chief Max set up the cooking station. I could sense the anticipation in the air for our upcoming evening of *Camp Firemen*. My nerves started to wreak havoc on my insides—as if I needed one more thing to make me nauseous. I rolled my neck to the side, stretching it out before standing up. My legs wobbled unsteadily under my weight, it was then that I felt a giant hand grip my arm.

"Hey old friend, you alright?" Briggs asked.

I eyed him wearily as he withdrew his arm. "You don't look so good, pal," he said, drawing his eyebrows in to study me.

"I'm just a little car sick, but I'm starting to feel better now," I said.

"Well here, let me help. You up for a little walk to stretch your legs?"

"Uh...sure," I said.

He offered me his arm again, after assuring me he wouldn't bite. I took it, gratefully. It was slow going at first, but every few yards I felt stronger, more balanced.

"I wanted to talk to you, Tori. I hope...I hope you understand what I meant at the fireman's ball."

I stopped, and pulled my arm away from his. "Despite what you think, I'm not heartless. I'm not trying to play games with Kai, and I never was. You can relax, alright?"

"No, that's just it. I was wrong not to trust you, Tori. I realize that now, and I'm sorry for implying anything other than that," Briggs said, pushing his hair away from his eyes.

"Why now?" I asked.

"At first, I didn't think Kai was being very realistic. Things seemed to develop so quickly with you two and I guess I just couldn't believe you were all that he said you were," Briggs said.

"Okay...so where does that leave us now?" I asked, still confused.

He smiled sheepishly. "I hope it will leave us with you accepting my sincere apology. I never should have doubted what Kai sees in you...because I see it, too. You are what he says you are. I'd like to be friends, Tori. Kai is...he's the brother I never had. He always has my back, and I just wanted to do the same for him. In this case, though, I was wrong." Briggs held out his hand to me, "Friends?"

I smiled as I reached for his hand. "Friends," I said.

"Am I allowed in on this secret handshake?" Kai asked, wiping the sweat from his forehead as he walked toward us.

"Oh hey, I was just making nice with your girl, bro," Briggs said slapping Kai's hand in some sort of mutual understanding.

I smiled at Kai, reassuring him that Briggs was speaking for the both of us. He came over to me then and wrapped his arms around me, kissing the top of my head.

"Glad you're feeling better; want to come and see our new digs for the next couple days?"

"Absolutely."

TWENTY-THREE

After showing me our *new digs*, Kai took me on a walk to the lake; Briggs joined us. The walk was nothing shy of incredible. The dirt path was sandwiched between three large hills and pine trees. It was close to five o'clock by now. The sun cast a light that was bright and focused as it filtered down through the branches above us.

"Tomorrow we hike that," Kai said, pointing to a narrow pathway up the side of the farthest hill.

"Oh...wow."

Briggs tapped me on the back as he walked past me, "That ain't nothing for you though, Miss I-can-run-ten-miles-a-day." He laughed heartily.

"*Whatever*, running is not the same as hiking," I said, kicking some loose rocks in Briggs' direction.

Kai laughed at the two of us.

"So last year there was a contest involving this lake," Kai said, as we approached the water.

"A contest? Why do I get the feeling that something inappropriate happened?" I asked.

"You're in trouble Kai, she's already figured you out," Briggs said, jogging over to us. His shaggy blond hair blew in the breeze as he ran. It was then I noticed how truly handsome he was. He was tall like Kai, but leaner. His eyes were a piercing dark brown, and his smile was nothing short of swoon-worthy. He was a flirt for sure, but he was also good-hearted, I never doubted that for a minute. I wondered about his story...why didn't he want a girlfriend?

Kai laughed, "Well each man that participated had to stand on one of those rocks out there and balance on one leg. He also had to hold the American flag up with his right arm," he said.

"What on earth was the purpose of that?" I asked.

"Whoever won didn't have to swim in the lake—in their boxers—at midnight," Briggs said.

"What? You've got to be joking! Who would ever agree to that?" I laughed, looking at each of them.

They both busted up laughing. The answer was clear as day.

"And who won?" I asked incredulously.

"Chief Max," Kai said.

My mouth hung open. A man twice their age had not only played this ridiculous game, he had beaten them in both balance and stamina? *Impressive.*

"Hey, that guy is a stud, Tori. Don't let his age fool ya." Briggs laughed as I shook my head.

A loud clanging sound rang out in the distance.

"What's that?"

"Dinner!" The boys yelled in unison. They pushed each other as they made their way back up the path. I walked behind and rolled my eyes.

Brothers?

Yep…that is exactly what I'd call them.

****

By the time we made it back up the path for dinner, the night's camping crew was all accounted for: Mike, Carla, Chief, Mrs. Julie, Briggs, Kai and myself. The other three guys were still on track to be here by noon tomorrow.

"Hey, it's nice to see you again, Tori," Mike said, shaking my hand and introducing me to his new bride, Carla.

"Nice to meet you both, officially," I said, smiling.

We were each handed a plate as we stood in line to be served by none other than Mrs. Julie herself. Ladies were pushed to the front of the line, no argument allowed.

"Here ya are, sugar. I'm glad to see you up and around," she said as she plopped a giant piece of fried chicken on my plate, along with pasta salad and a slice of watermelon. "You've got to get your dinner before the rest of these thugs; otherwise you won't get to eat."

That, I could believe. I had seen the way Kai ate and I could only imagine what it took to feed this entire crew. But in the end, there was more than enough food to go around. I sat back and watched the interactions of this closely bonded group. Everyone seemed to have a story to share regarding a past camping trip or some other kind of group adventure. Mike and Carla's wedding came up a few times as well.

"How long have you been married?" I asked Carla quietly. The guys were wrapped up in some hunting expedition story.

"Just about six months." She looked at her husband and smiled.

"Congratulations," I said.

"How about you? Are you and Kai pretty serious?" she asked, her voice filled with innocent curiosity.

"I uh...it's still pretty early, but he's...pretty amazing."

I looked at Kai from across the fire. It glowed bright in the early darkness of the evening, casting a light on his perfect face. He was laughing at some joke Briggs had just told, but seemed to sense my gaze. He winked at me, and then went back to his conversation.

"I guess that's how it starts though, right?" Carla asked.

My stomach dipped at her words.

Only a few months ago I'd been convinced I would never find love, least of all get married. So much had changed after meeting Kai. Notions that were once solid and unyielding were now soft and pliable. Boundaries which had held no room for expansion had completely caved under his charm.

I had let him in, totally and completely.

"Can I get your plate for you?" I asked her, standing.

"Oh, sure. Thank you," she said.

I gathered the garbage from around the campfire and threw it all in the large hefty bag which hung from a low hanging tree branch. I worked to clean up the mess that had been created by cooking, when I heard a soft, familiar voice behind me.

"You don't need to do that, the guys always clean up after dinner. Go back and sit down. Enjoy yourself," Kai whispered to me as I put lids on open containers.

"I'm fine, I want to help out. I need to earn my keep around here," I said, half-jokingly.

He stopped my hands by wrapping his arms around me from behind, holding them to my middle.

"You have more than earned your keep, now go sit down. We will do the rest."

I knew by his tone that arguing was pointless. I dusted off my hands and walked back toward the fire. Chief Max called the guys to their clean-up duties only seconds later, and in an instant, it was just the three of us ladies who remained at the campfire. I was amazed at how quickly they had moved.

"Thanks again for dinner, Mrs. Julie," I said.

"Oh, it's my pleasure. This is a trip I look forward to every year, such a beautiful area," Mrs. Julie said.

"Is this your first trip out here, Carla?" I asked her.

"No, I came last year when Mike and I were still engaged. It was a really great time, especially the campfire singing," she said, eyes glowing bright in the light of the fire.

"Oh, there's singing?" I asked.

Mrs. Julie and Clara looked at each other and grinned.

"Oh yes darlin', there's lots of singing," Mrs. Julie said.

Chief Max and Briggs both carried guitars over to the circle. Mike and Kai followed as soon as the last plate was tossed. Kai came over to me on the tree log I was sitting on and wrapped his arm around my shoulders. I was wearing a sweatshirt, but the instant the sun had set behind the hill, the temperature seemed to have dropped twenty degrees. I rubbed at my arms.

"Where's your coat, *Pele*?" Kai asked leaning in close.

"I think it's still in the cab, I'll go-"

"Stay. I'll be right back," Kai said.

In a minute he was back with my coat and a blanket for my lap. I was grateful for the immediate warmth they provided. Chief Max started to strum and sing an old country tune that I'd never heard before, and Briggs and Kai both joined in. Soon the whole group was singing. It was a magical moment. Singing in the great outdoors was exhilarating.

A few more songs were played, some silly, some fast and rockin', some simple and fun. Briggs played very well and seemed to compliment whatever Chief Max strummed. It was impressive to watch. The chief soon pointed to Kai.

"Okay Mr. Hot Shot contest winner, let's hear from you now," Chief Max said.

"What?" I asked, looking at Kai.

"He won the contest at the fireman's ball. You better slug him for not telling you, Tori, or I will," Briggs said.

I stared at Kai in surprise; he smiled sheepishly and shrugged his shoulders.

"Oh, so now you're going to play modest?" Briggs said.

"You'd better stuff it before I jump you over this fire pit," Kai said to Briggs, who apparently got the not-so-subtle-hint.

"Congratulations," I said, patting his knee.

He grabbed my hand and kissed it, asking for forgiveness without uttering a single word. I smiled back at him. He was forgiven.

Kai looked again at the Chief.

"Let's do a few church songs, Kai," Chief Max said.

"Sure thing, sir. What do ya have in mind?"

I looked around at the rest of the group anxiously. All seemed to be nodding in agreement. I stared down at my hands, picking at a non-existent hang nail. Soon, the guitar started up again.

Kai led the group in a few songs that sounded familiar, yet had words I didn't know, not that I would have sung them if I did. I listened as their voices rose above the crackling of the fire. Kai's strong voice sent chills up my spine. When the last song ended, Kai asked for Briggs' guitar, which he willingly handed over.

Kai began to pluck and strum. Again, I was surprised. He winked at me before his face grew thoughtful, pensive.

The chords of this song I did know.

I had heard it last at Anna's funeral. My heart began to pound hard inside my chest, while Kai's voice registered on every note with exact precision.

"Amazing Grace, how sweet the sound
That saved a wretch like me
I once was lost, but now I'm found
Was blind, but now I see"

I could hear Mrs. Julie's beautiful harmony rise and fall as Kai bellowed out the strong notes, holding them for long seconds at a time before changing chords. After several verses, a new melody flowed; he sang without missing a beat. The words he sang were of redemption, love and freedom.

Words I could not relate to.

The voices that accompanied him were strong and rich. They matched the strength of Kai's strum until the very last line where no music played at all. It was simply and indisputably angelic. No one moved for what felt like an eternity.

The fire held the gaze of everyone in the circle, except for mine. I looked around at each face, curious why this song had felt like more than a just a tune, but rather some intimate declaration that I didn't understand.

Chief Max stood and reached for his wife's hand.

"Well you young pups, Mrs. Julie and I are going to retire in our quiet resort back yonder. I'll see y'all in the morning for pancakes and coffee. Boys, can you figure out shifts to keep the fire going?" Chief Max asked, exaggerating his Texan charm just a tad.

"Yes, sir," the guys said in unison.

Next, Mike and Carla left the group claiming they were *tired*. Briggs guffawed as they exited. I shot him a look of disapproval and he immediately straightened, calling out a polite "goodnight" to them both.

"Well, I'm gonna hit the sack and let you two love birds do your *thang*," Briggs said.

"You don't need to go anywhere, Briggs. Sit down, hang out with us," I said, sounding a bit like a bossy, younger sister.

"Nah, I actually had a really late night last night, so I'm pretty beat. Maybe we can play some cards tomorrow evening though—after the old marrieds head to bed?"

"Sounds like fun," I said.

Kai handed Briggs his guitar back and we watched him walk out of view to his tent. He wrapped his arm around my shoulder again as I leaned my head against his chest.

"You have an amazing voice, Kai," I said.

"Thank you...and I'm sorry I didn't tell you about the contest."

I sat up, remembering.

"Why didn't you?" I asked.

"Honestly, I forgot at first, and then...I guess I didn't want you to think that's why I sang that night," he said.

"Why would that matter? It was special no matter if you were in a contest or not, no one had ever sang to me before," I said, laying my head back down.

We sat watching the fire together for a while, Kai playing with my hair. "What did you think of the campfire tonight?"

I knew what he was referring to. My usual instinct of avoiding this subject at all costs stayed dormant. I didn't know what that meant exactly, but I decided I would play along...at least until it woke up again.

"It was nice," I said.

Kai waited for me to say more, his silence pushing me on. I

pulled the blanket on my lap higher, and clasped my hands over the top of it. Kai's hand remained in my hair as I took a deep breath.

"I don't know...I feel very disconnected from people like you and the others here, Kai, maybe even envious at times."

Kai stopped playing with my hair. I turned to face him.

"Please explain what you mean."

Great, how do I explain this without sounding completely pathetic?

"It's hard to explain."

"Try."

"Faith looks so easy for y'all. You sing these songs with conviction, you listen to sermons you trust in, you pray and actually *believe* God can hear you and talk back to you...it's not like that for me," I said.

"Faith isn't easy for anyone, Tori, even the strongest believers I know struggle at times. If it was *easy*, there would be no alternative religions or people who claim God doesn't exist. Faith is *faith* because it takes active belief to trust that God is who He says He is," Kai said.

"Then maybe that's what's so hard for me to believe. If God is good like He says-"

"Then why do horrible things happen? Why do little girls die in car accidents?"

I turned my head to stare into the fire again.

I trust him...I can do this. I can talk to him about this.

"God is loving, just, and kind. Because of that, He offered us freedom in a world that was doomed with failure and imperfection. He gave us freedom to choose how we would live, instead of dictating our every thought and move like some mythical Zeus-type god." Kai picked up my hand and intertwined our fingers, causing me to connect to him as he spoke.

"This world is full of pain and darkness. There's cancer, death, sickness, heartache...but God is not the *cause* of our suffering. He does not rejoice in our pain here on earth, this was never how He intended it to be. Instead, he mourns *with* us. Despite what you want to believe, He *loves* you Tori...and He *loved* Anna, too."

My chest ached with longing. I wanted to believe him, I just...*couldn't.* Anna's death was on my hands—not his. I knew Kai had seen horrible tragedies in his line of work, but it was not the same as being the cause of one. The sad feeling I had felt in Dr.

Crane's office came over me again, but this time it was more than just sadness, it was *hopelessness*.

"I'm really tired," I said. Though my body wasn't yet exhausted, my mind was.

I was done thinking.

"Tori, you can *know* God. If there is hope for me—there is hope for you, too. And that's a promise I'd stake my life on," Kai said. "Now, let's go get you settled in for the night."

He took my hand and helped me up. I appreciated how Kai knew when I'd had enough. He had never pushed me further than I could go, but he also didn't let me off the hook without a challenge. He was a good balance for me, even if we'd never see eye to eye on that particular topic.

In reality, Kai's tent was only a few feet away from mine, but in the dark, it felt as if the Pacific Ocean was in between us. He had laid a thick mat down for me before putting Stacie's sleeping bag and pillow on top. The temperature was dropping at a rapid rate. I pulled an extra pair of socks on my feet before he carried his lantern out of my tent, along with himself.

"Goodnight *Pele*, if you need anything…please wake me."

With that, I laid my head down on the pillow. In complete darkness, I zipped my sleeping bag up to my chin and willed myself to fall asleep.

TWENTY-FOUR

I woke up in a puddle of ice water—not really, but you sure could have fooled me. I opened my eyes in a panic; everything around me felt wet to the touch, even my face and hair. The air hurt to breathe and my nose ached from the frigid exposure.

I pulled my hood tighter around my head, but there was no noticeable difference in warmth. The silky cool of the sleeping bag acted like damp Saran Wrap against my body and legs, causing me to shiver uncontrollably. I thought then about what I had packed in my duffel bag.

Maybe I could layer myself with all the clothing I brought?

The one gigantic problem with that strategy was I would have to *get out* of my sleeping bag to do it. That thought alone was enough to make me want to cry frozen tear drops. I shivered again.

Reaching back behind my head, I searched for my phone. I needed to figure out what time it was. That would determine whether or not I was willing to climb out into the frozen tundra. If it was close to morning, I would wait it out, will myself to sleep. If not, I would have to risk the cold and go for my bag.

2:24 a.m.

No way! I've only been asleep for three hours?

I counted to ten in my head and then made the mad dash, which consequently, was more like a slow, awkward stumble. Using the glow of my cell phone light, I searched for my duffle. The cold hit me like an arctic wave the second my foot hit the floor of the tent.

My breathing came only in short, rapid gasps as I fumbled with the zipper on my luggage. Each time I pulled at it, it slipped through my fingers. I couldn't grip.

I tried again.

This time I was able to move it several more inches before it slipped out for a second time.

"Dang it!"

My body shook with spasms now. My hands were aching painfully and my eyes felt as if the air was slicing them open each time I blinked.

"Tori...are you okay?"

My head snapped up in attention. Darkness consumed all space around me, but I knew it was Kai's voice I had heard. He was outside my tent door.

"Kai?" My teeth were chattering so hard I wasn't sure if he would hear me.

He unzipped the door and held his lantern up to my face. His eyes narrowed.

"You're freezing," Kai said.

He went over to my sleeping bag and held the lantern up to it, throwing his head back in aggravation.

"What's...what's...wrong?" I chattered.

"This bag is not for camping, Tori. It's only rated down to 50 degrees! That's barely good enough for *indoor* sleeping. Go get in my tent," he said.

"But...but I-"

"Tori, do you want to stand here and freeze, or do you want to get warm?"

His voice was no longer soft, but tense, and maybe even a little annoyed. He grabbed my pillow and "indoor" sleeping bag and in a second we were in his tent. I shivered as I watched him zip our two bags together, laying them down on the floor mat.

"Get in," he said.

I followed orders immediately. I was too cold to think, let alone argue. I felt him curl up behind me, putting his arm around my waist as he pulled the sleeping bag up past my shoulders. A good five minutes passed before my body had calmed enough to speak without shuddering.

"Why were you awake?" I asked.

"It was my turn to stoke the fire. Why didn't you come find me?" he countered gruffly.

"I thought if I put more clothes on I'd be fine," I said.

"And what? Stand in your tent without a coat while you got dressed in thirty degree weather?"

Was he angry at me?

Had my stupidity caused him to compromise by having me in here with him? Is that why he's upset?

"I...I'm sorry for putting you in this position. I didn't mean to."

I felt like a child in time-out, only it was my boyfriend who was punishing me—not my parents. How embarrassing.

He signed heavily. His arm moved from my waist to brush back the hair off of my face and tuck it behind my ear. Even though he was still lying behind me, I could picture his eyes, his mouth, and his rumpled hair. The thought caused my heart to pound.

"I'm not upset about that, *Pele*. I would never be upset with you for needing help. I just don't like to think about you hurting or in pain—especially when I can do something about it. You have to stop thinking of yourself as some kind of burden when just the opposite is true," he said. "Besides, we have about ten inches of clothing between the two of us—I feel pretty confident that nothing inappropriate will happen in here tonight, don't you?"

At the mention of the many layers of clothing we both had on, I started to giggle. I tried to stifle my laugh in the sleeve of my jacket, but that only reminded me again of how ridiculous this night had become. Of all the times I had pictured being alone with Kai, this *vision of romance* was definitely not among them. He started in too, and soon we were a mixture of both laughing and *shh-ing*.

Finally though, through some sort of miraculous intervention, we managed to regain control of our hysteria.

"Goodnight, Tori."

"Goodnight, Kai."

Within minutes of settling I was asleep, dreaming of the warmth that had not only surrounded my body, but my heart as well.

****

The clanging of the pot caused me to sit up with a start. Kai put his arm back around me, pulling me down to his side again.

"Kai...Kai...its breakfast time. I need to get out of here before anyone thinks...well, thinks that something else went on in here last night," I said, whispering as softly as I could.

His eyes barely opened and he shook his head with a groan. I wasn't sure what that was supposed to mean, so I moved his arm aside and crawled out of the sleeping bag. I straightened my coat and untwisted my sweats to be centered on my waist.

Good golly, what must I look like right now?

I touched my hair briefly, feeling the work of braided knots beneath my fingers. I grimaced. I needed to locate a mirror soon, if just for the sake of my dignity alone.

Carefully, I unzipped Kai's tent door. Putting one socked foot out onto the cold, hard ground at a time, I shivered. I squatted down as I re-zipped it, hoping to duck into my own tent unnoticed.

"Good Morning, Tori," Briggs said from some unknown location behind me.

I cringed, frozen in place with my eyes closed. Of all the moments to have the super-power of *invisibility*, this would be it! Slowly I turned to face him.

"Hi...this isn't what it appears to be," I said.

Briggs' smile could have been pictured in the Guinness Book of World Records—no doubt. My face flamed, burning hotter by the second. Beyond him I could see everyone, and I was fairly certain that *everyone* could see me.

I had two choices in that moment: the walk of shame to get breakfast and sit with Kai's friends, or to duck into my tent and only come out after Kai awoke from his coma. I chose the second option, proving my cowardice. I had barely made it to the door when Briggs grabbed my arm, pulling me back with a gentle yank.

"Oh come on, we know nothing happened. Let me guess...you were freezing because you didn't prepare for *arctic camping* which then led to bunking-up with this punk in the middle of the night?"

Briggs crossed his arms over his chest, gesturing toward Kai's tent with a quick jerk of his head.

I nodded, feeling the gaze of everyone on Briggs' back as he spoke.

"Okay, well that's settled then. No scarlet letter's gonna be handed out around these parts. Go grab your shoes and let's get you some breakfast, okay? The least we can do is feed you after a night like that," Briggs said, amused.

With my face still flushed, I grabbed my Nikes from just inside my tent. I tried in vain to smooth out my hair as we walked over to the breakfast table.

Mrs. Julie was the first to speak to me.

"It was a cold night, wasn't it dear?" She handed me a plate full of steaming pancakes. My stomach growled in response.

"Yes, thank you Mrs. Julie," I said.

I sat and stared at the food, feeling the awkward eyes of the world on my face. It was in that moment though, that I heard Kai come out of the tent. He looked around a bit dazed and then found me, walking over to sit at my side.

"Good morning...how did you sleep?" he asked.

I closed my eyes and waited for the laughter. I knew it would be led by no one other than Briggs himself. Sure enough, I was right. Not even a full second later, every person around the fire was in hysterics, looking at Kai's unknowing face.

"What...what did I miss?" Kai asked. His sweet, innocent face only caused more laughter to ensue.

I laughed too, feeling just a tad guilty that Kai hadn't caught on to the fact that our arctic rendezvous was no longer a secret.

He finally smiled in understanding, and then helped himself to breakfast, completely unabashed.

****

Hiking was the big event of the day. I dressed in jeans and a long-sleeve shirt, tying a zip-up hoodie around my waist. I never wanted to be caught unprepared in the cold again—ever.

It took me several minutes to brush my hair out before eventually pulling it into a loose braid. I didn't want it falling in my face during the hike. I'd also managed to wash my face and brush my teeth with some drinking water. All of that resulted in a much fresher, much happier, Tori.

I followed Kai and Briggs up the trail.

The others were behind us, walking at a tad slower pace. The three guys who were joining us were to arrive in just about an hour, but they knew where to find us.

The largest of the hills had a trail that seemed to zigzag its way to the top. I was grateful we wouldn't be climbing on our hands and knees, though I'm sure the guys would have been up for it.

The further we walked, the more difficult the trail became, and the steeper the cliff's edge. Kai didn't seem to care about heights, but I stayed clear of that side of the path altogether. The boys both wore a water bag on their back. About an hour into our trek, I was grateful that Kai had planned ahead in that way, I had taken many sips from his. I had also pulled on my sweatshirt a while back. It was surprising how much cooler it was near the top than down at the lake.

The scenery was breathtaking. From this vantage point I could see a large stretch of forest below. There was so much green, so much natural beauty. I hadn't ever really cared about outdoor living much, but since moving back to Texas, I'd found myself drawn to nature. Somehow being near land, trees, lakes and hills caused me to feel more alive.

"I'm going to go back and check on the rest of the group. I don't see them behind us anymore," Briggs said.

"Do you want us to wait for you?" Kai asked.

"No, go on ahead. I'll catch up."

Briggs turned to jog back down the trail as Kai took my hand. We kept our pace for awhile more.

"Are you glad you came?" Kai asked.

"Yes, apart from our sleeping scandal, it's been really great," I said.

"Well, don't tell anyone…but I kinda liked our sleeping scandal," he said, winking at me when I caught his eye.

A few more steps and I felt something sharp and uncomfortable.

"Ow, I think I have a rock in my shoe," I said.

"Let's take a breather, then. I can use a water break myself."

I found a flat rock to sit on near a large tree by the path's edge. I worked quickly to untie my shoe and dump out the pebble, wanting to get away from the steep cliff side as soon as possible. Kai stood near me, drinking his water. I glanced up at him once as I hurriedly tied my laces. He was swatting his hand in the air in front of him before throwing his water bag back over his shoulder.

As I stood, my world began to crumble…in slow motion.

"Kai?"

He was stumbling—arms out—fighting to regain his balance. I reached for him, trying to steady his frightening movements and hold him back from the edge, but his body collapsed. In less than a second he was gone.

His body barreled down the hillside at a rate that seemed impossible. I screamed his name over and over before forcing myself to the same fate.

I slid on my backside feet first, trying to dodge the branches and tree stumps as they came at me. There were hidden rocks and roots that I couldn't see under the brush, but that didn't stop them from making contact with my body as I passed over them. I knew I could only be a help to Kai if I survived this fall—I had to survive.

Even with careful maneuvering, the burn of my skin and the

tearing of my flesh were unmistakable.

It didn't matter though, nothing mattered but finding Kai.

I passed yet another large tree during what felt like a never-ending plummet-to-death. I had no way to gauge how far we had traveled down the side of the cliff, but once I finally came to a stop, my eyes spotted something bright in the distance. There, next to the base of a large tree, I could see his orange sweatshirt—or at least a small part of it.

I frantically flung myself around each obstacle in between us, tripping several times as I tried to get to him. Nothing I did seemed fast enough. I dropped down to my knees the second he was within my reach, carefully rolling him onto his back to check his breathing. It was there—but very labored. I looked him over, trying to figure out what had happened.

A cold calm came over me, sharpening my senses.

A bee.

He's been stung.

I suddenly remembered how he had swatted his hand in the air just seconds before he stumbled. I checked his exposed skin for a mark.

Hands? No. *Face?* No. *Neck?* Yes.

A panic ripped through me.

The neck was one of the worst places to be stung for a person with a severe allergy to bee stings. He was in anaphylactic shock; I was a hundred percent certain of that. His neck and lips had already begun to swell, and his breathing sounded more labored with each passing second.

"Please, please, please, have your EpiPen on you Kai."

Why didn't I ask him where he kept it when he told me about his allergy?

I started at his ankles patting him carefully in an upward motion. Working my way up his legs I hoped to find it in a front pocket, no such luck. I felt inside the pocket of his sweatshirt near his waist—not there either. My stomach lurched then, nausea hitting me hard as the reality of what this missing Pen would mean for him—*for us.*

Is it in a back pocket?

I pulled his right arm out straight and then bent his left leg, rolling him over with ease the way I did in the hospital when someone outweighed me.

Right back pocket? No. *Left back pocket?* Yes!

There wasn't time to rejoice, every second was critical. I rolled Kai back over and jabbed the first of two EpiPen injections into his right outer thigh. I was careful to inject all the fluid inside it.

There was no immediate change in his breathing. I checked his pulse again—*way too fast*. I waited the five minutes necessary by counting in my head, and then gave him the second dose.

It was then he took a deep breath.

I no longer heard the labored wheeze of seconds earlier. For a moment I was elated.

I went to his head then, kneeling over the top of his. A large bump on the side of his temple indicated that he had hit something hard on his way down. I pulled off my sweatshirt and braced it around his neck, trying to keep him in alignment as best I could.

He was fortunate to have been wearing long pants. They had most likely protected his legs from any major cuts and gashes during his fall. I scanned the rest of his body. Noting only bruises and scrapes on his hands and face, I found no other trauma I could treat.

He just needed to wake up.

I nudged and prodded him trying to get a response, patting his cheeks with my hands, but he didn't stir.

Hopelessness ripped through my heart like a rogue bullet, forcing it's shrapnel to explode in every cell of my body. I screamed out in anguish, the pain and fear overwhelming me as my echo reverberated through the silence. I was all alone; no one had heard my cry for help.

Kai could be dying, and I could do nothing more for him.

My body ached and burned, thawing itself after its adrenaline rush down the hill. I stroked Kai's forehead gently, ignoring the painful throbbing of my own body. Wishing he would open his eyes and know what to do, I continued to stare at him.

Nothing changed.

I thought briefly about going for help, but I couldn't leave Kai, not like this. I called out over and over, until my voice grew hoarse. There was no reply. Watching the slow rise and fall of Kai's chest, I finally bowed my head.

For the first time in over a year and a half, I prayed.

"I know we aren't close, but you know Kai. He believes in you…and he needs help right now. Please help him! Help us get out of here so he can get back to safety. Please…just let him wake up." I looked again at Kai and whispered, "Just let him wake up."

With my head still bowed over Kai's face, I felt a sensation that was almost as unique to me as prayer: hot, streaming, tears. I couldn't stop them. They rolled down my face and picked up speed as they hit Kai's forehead.

I sobbed over this man who had become closer to me than anyone ever had. I couldn't lose him. I *needed* him. I *loved* him.

Please don't take Kai; please don't take him away from me.

I am with you.

My tears kept falling as I focused on that voice inside me. I put every shred of energy I had into one word now: *hope*. There was nothing else. I could either put my hope in a God I wasn't sure existed…or I could put it in myself.

I was all out of ideas.

I wiped Kai's forehead dry, though my tears still fell. Running my fingers through his hair, I began to sing, quietly.

> "Amazing Grace how sweet the sound
> That saved a wretch like me
> I once was lost
> But now I am found
> Was blind, but now I see"

I sang it again and again.

On the fourth time through, I saw his eyelids start to flutter.

"Kai? Kai, can you hear me?" I asked.

"Wh…What happened?" he mumbled.

"You're okay. You were stung by a bee. I found your EpiPen…and you're going to be *okay*," I said, tears streaming down my face.

"You're….crying?" he asked, eyebrows narrowing slightly.

"Yes," I laughed nervously. "Congratulations…after a year and a half of having no tears to cry, you brought them back to me."

I leaned down and kissed his forehead. He smiled for just a second before closing his eyes again.

Please let someone find us soon!

I called out again for help, but still heard nothing in reply. If I had to guess we'd already been down here for close to an hour. I hoped someone would figure out we were missing sooner or later.

I hoped for sooner.

Please Briggs, please notice we're gone.

Kai's eyes opened again after some time had passed—how much time? I had no clue. He was much more alert now, and his breathing was steady and strong.

I finally exhaled. It felt like the first time I had really taken a full breath since Kai fell. Kai looked at me.

"How long have we been down here?" Kai asked.

"A while, over an hour for sure, maybe closer to two. It's hard to say."

Kai's face was calm, no traceable panic to be found.

"Briggs will come for us, don't worry," he said.

"Okay, I won't," I lied.

"Did you...did you *pray* for me?" Kai asked, as if looking back at a distant memory.

I nodded. "Yes, two big things for me today: prayer and tears."

Kai reached his arm up and pulled my face down to meet his. Though brief, this kiss held new meaning for both of us.

As I raised my head back up he said, "You're my hero, Tori. You saved my life today."

My eyes grew blurry again, because I knew it hadn't been me at all.

TWENTY-FIVE

I could see that Kai was getting stronger, but I also knew the standard protocol of treatment for reactions like his. He still needed an additional dose of antihistamine in his body. That would help to prevent any longer lasting allergic reactions.

Judging by his current state, the two doses of epinephrine he had been given had done their job. He was recovering well, but there was no way to be certain he was in the clear while on the forest floor. I wasn't willing to take any chances.

"I feel well enough to get up and start the climb to the top," Kai said.

I stared at him, mouth gaping.

"You're telling me, that if a patient of yours had just been in anaphylactic shock, that you'd let him climb up the side of a mountain two hours after treatment?"

Kai's mouth became a tight thin line, his eyebrows narrowed at me.

He wasn't used to feeling helpless, or being a patient. That much was obvious.

"I didn't think so," I said crossing my arms over my chest.

"I know Briggs will find us, Tori. I just think we could be a little more proactive than just sitting down here, waiting," Kai said.

"Then let me go...I'll start the climb up," I said, zipping up my hooded sweatshirt that Kai had forced me to take back from him.

"Absolutely not. If I don't go, you don't go," he said.

I sat down hard, wincing as my sore backside made contact with the ground. I pulled my knees up to my chest. Kai turned slightly now to lie on his side. Apart from some bruising, his slide down the mountain hadn't seemed to affect him much. I was grateful he didn't have any broken bones, that would have made our rescue much more complicated. I laid my head down on my knees, feeling Kai's hand wrap around my ankle.

"I still can't believe you flung yourself off the side of a mountain for me?"

I lifted my head, "Well you were going down it pretty quickly yourself, there fireman."

He laughed softly. "I was unconscious. You did it willingly and you *hate* heights," Kai said.

I looked out again at the forest that was our makeshift home and thought about his words. I knew *why* I had done it, and nothing short of God himself could have stopped me.

I could sense he wanted to say more, but I wasn't sure I was ready to hear what *more* was. *More* would complicate things, *more* would come with expectations. *More* would change us.

I pulled out of his grip and walked to a place with good footing, calling out again for help. Finally, it was met with an answer.

"Briggs! Briggs! We're here...can you hear me?" I called.

I heard a faint reply and tried again. Soon the sound drew closer, cutting the tension in my body with the sweet knife of relief. About five minutes later, Briggs appeared with Andrew, Skyler and Caden.

I ran to him and hugged him the second he was steady, dismissing my usual inhibitions.

"Hey there good lookin', glad you called out. We passed this place on the trail several times already," Briggs said, lowering me down and looking at Kai.

"What happened to you, bud?" Briggs asked, going to Kai's side and kneeling down beside him.

"Bee," Kai said.

Visibly alarmed, Briggs turned to look at me. He swallowed hard. "Did you use his EpiPen?"

"Yes, but we need to get him some Benadryl, or some other kind of antihistamine back at camp. He was in full anaphylactic shock by the time I got to him," I said.

Briggs looked to Kai again, "Must be nice having a trauma nurse for a girlfriend, eh pal?"

"She's a hero, Briggs. She threw herself down the cliff after me and then had to figure out what had happened. I was unconscious," Kai said.

The three guys with Briggs all had a comment or two regarding Kai's statement, but I busied myself, trying to find a good walking stick for the climb up. I didn't respond to their praises. There wasn't time for that.

"How should we move him?" I asked, looking at Briggs.

I tried to ignore the look in his eyes when he answered me, "We'll do our best to carry him. There are four of us, so it will just be a matter of footing issues, not strength."

"Okay...well let's go," I said, standing with my new walking stick in hand.

"Alright gentlemen, you heard the lady, let's get on with it."

****

Kai argued and grumbled all the way up the cliff, not wanting to be carried or helped. This was a side of him I had never seen. Finally, though, Briggs put an end to it. He threatened to drop him right then and there if he didn't shut up and let them do their job. Kai was quiet after that.

My new walking companion proved to be a great help and I found myself almost enjoying the climb up—almost. My backside, which had taken a beating on the way down, burned something fierce with each step.

Finally, we were at the top.

Kai stood on his feet then. He seemed to be pretty steady now, but he remained supported at all times as we headed down the trail to camp. I walked behind them.

After Briggs rotated out of the mix, taking a break from bearing Kai's weight, he waited for me to catch up. We walked together quietly for some time. As we passed the lake, Briggs finally spoke.

"You saved his life. You know that, right? He would have died if you hadn't done...if you hadn't done what you did for him," he said.

"You would have done the same, Briggs," I said.

Briggs stopped me, his grip firm on my shoulder. Looking at my face, his eyes grew intense.

"What you think someone else *might* have done doesn't matter. They weren't there...*you* were. You chose to go after him at the risk of your own life and it was you who saved him."

I wasn't sure what to say to that. I swallowed hard, refusing to cry any more tears now that Kai was safe. I stared at the ground waiting for the moment to pass.

"Thank you, Tori. If there is anything I can ever do for you-"

"You're a good friend, Briggs. He's lucky to have you, and we're both lucky to have *him*," I said.

We walked to the end of the trail and into the campground.

All kinds of chaos was unleashed the moment Kai was spotted. Mrs. Julie cried out in relief at the sight of him, busily working to prepare a spot for him to rest in his tent. I found something even better than the oral antihistamine I had hoped for in the first-aid supplies—these EMTs didn't mess around. They had the steroid shot that Kai would have received at the ER. I was more than relieved.

He was propped into a sitting position by several donated pillows, when I entered his tent. He smiled as I went inside. He rolled his eyes at the sight of the steroid shot, but was a good sport as I administered it. I nestled into his chest and listened to the strong beat of his heart.

It was the best sound I had ever heard.

"That's gonna knock me out for the night," he said, regret filling his voice.

"It's better that way, you need to rest. We'll still have some time left here tomorrow." I wrapped my arms around him and squeezed him tight.

"True, are you going to sleep in here again tonight?" Kai asked.

"I don't think I have another option, everyone else has a tent-mate...except Briggs-"

"You won't be rooming with anyone else but me, *Pele*. I want you here. I'll be passed out, so you might have to fight for space once you're in here, but at least you won't be cold," Kai said.

"I'm never cold when I'm near you."

He lifted my chin and kissed me deeply. All my anxieties of the day, all my worries, all my fears were released in that one kiss, and I never wanted it to end. Kai held my face, pushing his mouth away from mine, gently. He moved his lips to kiss my cheek instead, then my forehead, then my chin. My pulse quickened as my desire for his touch intensified.

I opened my eyes to search his face. I wanted to memorize it, to burn this moment into my mind forever.

He was alive. He was safe. God had given him back to me and I'd never forget it. I scooted away from him, determined to let him rest, when he reached for me again, catching just the tips of my fingers.

"Tori...I-"

"Shhh...just rest, Kai. I'm gonna go help Mrs. Julie with dinner. I'll come and check on you in a bit," I said.

He nodded reluctantly.

He was asleep within minutes.

I helped with the massive taco feed at dinner, serving each man and woman as they came through the line. I had to beg Mrs. Julie to let me assist her. I continued to keep myself busy with tasks during the dinner conversation. I didn't want to hear it—much less be a part of it. I had received enough validation for the events of the day, and I was more than done being the focus of questions and commentary.

Due to Kai sleeping in a nearby tent, the regular campfire festivities were cancelled. Poker however, was plan B. It had been set up on the two large picnic tables which were now lit by heavy lanterns on each end.

"Come have some fun with us, Tori," Briggs said.

"I should probably go check on Kai again," I said, avoiding his gaze.

"Yes, because a man heavily doped up for the night might suddenly be in need?" Briggs asked, raising his eyebrows at me.

I sighed, "Fine, one game only though, Briggs."

He smiled and said, "As you wish."

Briggs was likely the wittiest person I knew, but that also made him fairly annoying at times. He dealt to our table of six and called for Texas Hold-em to be the game of the hour. He knew I had played before as I waved off his entry-level instructions, but what he didn't know was that Jack had spent a good two summers teaching me everything *he knew* about the game.

I was no lightweight when it came to cards.

The first two rounds I folded. But on the third round I held out to the bitter end, taking the pot and earning the respect of the men Kai called, his *brothers*. Three more times I won and three more times fists slammed down on the table in exasperation as I laughed.

"Weren't you only going to play *one* game?" Briggs asked me, his tone flat.

"Oh? So now that you know *I'm awesome* you don't want to play with me anymore," I said.

"I already *knew* you were awesome, but yeah...you're kinda crampin' my style," Briggs laughed.

I stood up from the table and stretched, twisting my back to release the tension. I grabbed a flashlight and walked out past the fire into the inky darkness beyond. I could hear an owl up above and somewhere nearby a group of cicadas hissed. They quieted each time I shifted my weight.

I was alone, and yet my heart was heavy.

Shouldn't I be happy?

Kai is alive, safe. So why do I feel this way?

Stop Running.

The words finally had a source; I *knew* that voice.

"Why do you keep saying that? I've stopped! I'm getting help now—*treatment*, even! Isn't that why Kai's in my life? To help me *trust* again—to help me trust in *you*?"

I kicked some bark near my feet, silencing the cicadas for a minute more.

I searched the sky.

"I don't know how to know you, God. I've...I've been on my own for so long that I've forgotten how to *need* you."

The words were true, but the meaning was far from simple. If I had experienced *faith* in God this afternoon, then maybe that was the spark that would start the fire.

Maybe there was *hope* for me after all.

TWENTY-SIX

Kai had slept through the night and was awake before I was. I heard him walking around inside the tent; I snuck several glances his way. I watched as he fished through his bag for a clean set of clothes and a toothbrush.

I kept very still.

I knew I wouldn't be able to fall back asleep, but I wasn't quite ready to let him in on my secret. The warmth of my cozy cocoon was far too appealing, and so was the sight of Kai this early in the morning.

"You can stop pretending, Tori. I saw you peeking over here a few minutes ago," Kai said.

"Oh, uh...good morning," I said a bit sheepishly. He laughed.

"Good morning, beautiful."

Butterflies took flight in the base of my belly. I'd never grow tired of hearing him say that.

"Are you feeling completely restored today?" I asked.

"Yes, as it turns out I had a very persistent and somewhat annoying nurse yesterday who saw to that."

"Hmm...She sounds like an excellent professional," I said.

"Something like that." He grinned at me and winked.

After stealing a few more moments of bliss, I crawled out of my happy place and stepped into the brisk morning air. Reality was unkind. Zipping up his tent behind me to let him get dressed, I went and did the same.

Mike and Carla had already packed up and were leaving shortly after breakfast. The three guys that had helped carry Kai yesterday—Andrew, Skyler, and Caden, were already fishing at the lake. Mrs. Julie was preparing coffee and eggs as I walked over to the fire, waiting for Kai to join me.

"Good Morning," Briggs said, handing me a cup of coffee and sitting down beside me.

"Oh, thank you, good morning to you, too," I said, "Looks like the place is almost deserted. When are you heading back?"

"Probably late afternoon if the weather holds out. I might join the guys fishing down there. I bought all my gear...I might as well use it," Briggs said with a shrug.

Kai walked over then, bringing me a breakfast plate with eggs and toast.

"Oh, you already have coffee?" Kai asked me.

"Yes, thank you. You have nice friends," I said, smiling at Briggs.

"Guilty." Kai slapped Briggs on the shoulder before sitting down next to me.

****

The plan was to head out a little after two o'clock. Kai had to be back at the station fairly early in the morning. I re-packed my bag and helped him tear down our tents. When I pretended to chuck Stacie's *indoor sleeping bag* into the fire, he ran over and ripped it from my hands.

"This, this right here is my new *favorite* piece of camping gear, but only when it's brought by you," he said, winking at me, "Don't ever get rid of it."

I blushed and kept working till Kai's truck was packed and ready to go. Mrs. Julie had made us all sandwiches before she and Chief Max had left for home. Kai and I took one last walk to the lake where we met up with our fishermen friends—Briggs among them.

After many good laughs and stories, it was time for us to go. Kai helped me into the truck and we were off, leaving behind a weekend full of memories—*our* memories. This camping trip had forever marked my life.

"So I heard you have a few tricks up your sleeve in poker, huh?" Kai said.

"I swear you guys are worse than sorority girls, is there nothing you keep to yourselves?" I asked, laughing.

"Uh, no, not really, especially when it comes to our hot girlfriends."

I rolled my eyes and shook my head. He laughed, of course.

We drove again on the same horrid gravel road, but this time I had prepared. I cracked my window and closed my eyes, focusing on the cool wind in my face and hair. I was relieved when I felt the tires hit the smooth, quiet highway.

"Looks like there's a storm up ahead," Kai said, pointing out into the distance.

The distant sky was dark and gray—eerie. It was a glaring contrast from the sunshine we had left just an hour prior. My stomach grew uneasy with anticipation. As the wind started to howl, I rolled up my window and shivered instinctively. I hadn't been in a storm—a Texas storm—since the night of the accident.

"You okay?" Kai asked, taking my hand.

"Yeah...fine."

"You know, Thanksgiving is less than two weeks away and I was thinking..."

I knew he was talking—probably even asking me questions—but I couldn't focus on his voice. The clouds ahead were forming into monstrous black masses, and soon they would be overhead. I nodded, trying to stay engaged with him, but after a few minutes, the cab went quiet.

The rain started only seconds after I heard the first crack of thunder. There were no light sprinkles of warning, just hard unforgiving sheets of rain. The force of it was so intense I feared the windshield might shatter.

Kai slowed the truck in order to regain visibility. He glanced back at our gear which was now getting soaked as I clung to the door handle with white knuckles. I could feel my mind shifting.

No, not now. I don't want to see it...I don't want to see her!

Out of the corner of my eye, I could see Kai gripping the steering wheel with both hands. The truck's cab had grown dark, the sun, nowhere to be found. I thought I heard him say my name before the hail hit, but I was in a one way tunnel with no way out. I didn't want to close my eyes; I didn't want to give in to the memories that were pulling me under, suffocating me.

I was helpless against them.

My chest tightened, restricting the oxygen to my lungs.

I can't breathe!

My pulse throbbed in my ears, drowning out everything but the relentless beat of the hail. I contemplated my next move as my palms started to sweat. I eyed the lock on the door.

I can do it. I can get out.

I have to get out.

Somewhere deep inside, under piles of literature and printouts from Dr. Crane, was the voice of reason, but it was too quiet now. It was too weak.

There was no going back.

I saw the overpass, or at least the shadow of what I hoped was an overpass, and made my move. As Kai slowed his truck even more due to his decreased visibility, I unlocked my door and jumped out. In one quick, self-sacrificing motion, I flung my body to the ground...and ran.

My feet slid and slipped over and over again as I raced across the shards of ice, almost losing control completely. I didn't care. I just kept running. The dark mirage I had seen from a distance was indeed an overpass. Without hesitation I ran underneath it, climbing to its highest point of shelter.

I pulled my knees into my chest, panicking.

I can't breathe.

I can't breathe.

I can't breathe.

My breathing was shallow and rapid—I couldn't calm it. I was no stranger to this kind of panic, I had felt it once before, wishing then that death would be its end. It was the same end I wished for now.

I shuddered as I saw her.

I could see Anna, lying in the grass, body soaked with rain.

I felt something shift next to me. Something solid, yet warm was pressed to my side, but it was too late to be rescued.

The memory had already overtaken me.

Her beautiful hair was matted down by mud, I had touched it. I had held her in my arms, trying to take away her pain, trying to patch it. I wanted her to breathe, to cry, to speak...but nothing came.

Anna! Anna! Please wake up! I need you to know I'm trying to save you. I need you to know I would do anything to trade places with you. Please don't leave me like this...please don't die.

I was sobbing now—shaking violently.

"Why didn't she wake up?" I screamed.

"Oh, Tori," Kai's voice was strong, yet broken.

His arms wrapped around me as I wept into his chest. My body still felt separate from me, held captive by a prison of shame.

"Why did God take *her*? It should have been me. I tried..." My voice broke again to a sob.

"I know, I know you tried, *Pele*," Kai said, pushing the wet hair off of my face.

"But *she* never knew! She never knew I tried," I said, and then the painful truth was on my lips before I could stop it. "I wasn't good enough to save her."

Kai shook me, his hands strong and firm on my shoulders as he positioned himself in front of me.

"Yes you were, Tori! You did *everything* that could have been done for that little girl...do you hear me?" Kai said, yelling over the loud echo of the hail.

He gripped my face in between his hands, forcing me to see him.

"You did *everything*," Kai said, again. A desperate plea marked his voice.

I searched his eyes. "You don't know that," I whispered.

Grazing his thumb over my scar, he stared at me, unblinking. "Yes...I do."

Exhausted, my eyes struggled to stay focused.

But it was there, on his face.

The answer to all the looks I couldn't place, all the emotions I couldn't understand, all the words that had been left unsaid. Anguish filled his eyes as his unspoken revelation washed over me.

I gasped, shaking my head in disbelief.

"No!"

"I was there, Tori. I was a first responder on the scene that night. I *saw* you. I saw the compress you made from your shirt; I saw your cut-up, bloody legs from crawling across that road; and your hands that worked triple-time trying to keep her alive. You did *everything* there was to do!"

I stumbled back, breaking free of his touch. I slid down the overpass wall. Panic had overwhelmed me again. The tremors that shot through my body were explosive.

Chaos was closing in on my world. The safe, untainted world I'd found in Kai had just been assaulted by death's thievery.

I shook my head, trying to grasp it, trying to comprehend what he had just revealed. "You...you were there? You were at my accident?"

"Yes. I've wanted to tell you so many times, Tori, but I didn't know how. I was too afraid you'd push me away…and I couldn't be without you, not once I'd found you, not once I *knew* you," Kai said.

And then…there was *nothing*.

No fight.

No anger.

Just. Hollow. Space.

He took a step closer. I couldn't move.

"It was your empathy that captured me that night, Tori—your *compassion*. I've never seen anything like it. I work with men and women every day that are supposed to care like that, and nothing holds a candle to what I saw in you that night. What you did for Anna—a stranger—was nothing short of heroic," he said, staring at me intently. "I went to the hospital several times, asking about you. And then one day…you weren't there. I thought about you all the time and then-"

"*Jack*," I whispered, my brain finally catching up.

"Yes, but he doesn't share your last name, Tori. I didn't know he was your brother-in-law until I met your parents and then I put the pieces together. I came…I came to your coming home party to-"

"To what, Kai? To see if I was as *wrecked* and damaged as my mother thinks I am? You may have seen me cradle a dead child in my arms, but that does not mean I need to be rescued—not by *you*!"

Rage.

Hot. Burning. Rage.

"No! I went to understand *why* I couldn't get you out of my mind. I wanted to talk to you, to be your friend and then…I fell in love you," he said, taking several more steps toward me.

I backed away, pushing my hand out to stop him.

"Don't, please don't touch me," I said.

"Victoria, I *love* you! I never knew the meaning of those words, until *you*. I'm sorry I didn't tell you sooner, I never wanted to hurt you," Kai said, gripping his head with his hands, pacing.

"I know you'll need time to process this, but please…please don't doubt that it's you who owns my heart, *Pele*. I love you."

And then a memory from a different time and place, with a

different boy, flooded my mind.

Just. Like. Ian.

Kai's words were tainted, devalued, and compromised by guilt.

Would that phrase ever mean something real?

Sorrow stained his face with tears, tugging at my heart. I had the sudden urge to forget my pain and fall into his arms, to wipe away his tears. But the urge passed, and the pain spread deeper.

I stood motionless.

"Please, just let me take you home...we can talk more in the truck," he said, holding out his hand to me.

His hand.

I stared at it.

Was it Kai's hands that had pulled me off her?

I didn't move. I couldn't move. My eyes focused on a place beyond him, a place empty and void of all life. A place I begged would swallow me whole and leave nothing behind.

There was a flash of light, blinding me momentarily. Kai pulled me back, away from the center of the overpass we stood under. The light grew brighter. I blinked rapidly, willing my eyes to focus. An old Chevy truck finally slowed to a stop.

The face of the driver I knew, I'd shared a coffee with him only hours before.

Briggs.

My body sprang into action. I ran to his window, rain soaking me through, again. Briggs' eyes met mine with curiosity and surprise.

"Tori, what's-"

"Did you mean it when you said I could ask you for anything?"

"Yes, but wh-"

"I need a ride home...*right now.*" I was nothing short of desperate. By the look in his eyes, he understood that.

"Okay...get in," he said, obviously bewildered.

I did so, immediately.

Briggs opened his door and stepped out into the rain as I secured my seatbelt. Apparently, he was seeking some sort of silent approval from Kai. I tapped my foot anxiously. I wanted to leave.

Before I had time to react, Kai was at my door, rain streaking down his face as his eyes met mine. Despite the war raging inside me, I couldn't look away from him.

His eyes were haunting.

He put his hand on my window, "Please don't do this, Tori. Please don't leave like this."

I turned my head away, refusing to cry another tear in front of him; I had shed too many tears already.

A second later, I heard him say, "Just get her home safely."

And then Briggs was in the truck and we were driving away.

Away from Kai.

Away from hope.

Away from love.

But not away from death, that was inescapable.

I closed my eyes and laid my head on the window. The cold glass acted as an ice pack to my puffy eye and cheek. Briggs was quiet. I was grateful.

There was nothing to be said.

He knew this ugly truth, of course he knew. I would be willing to bet he had known it from the very beginning, but there were levels to betrayal. Briggs had hurt me, but Kai had crippled me.

The drive home was long. I feigned sleep.

The only words spoken were when Briggs needed to stop for gas about thirty minutes out. He'd asked if I wanted anything from the store. I shook my head, closing my eyes once again.

What would I tell Stacie?

The thought alone was exhausting.

Briggs took his time in the store, finally coming back to the truck with a banana and a water bottle. He handed them both to me. Instinctively I took them, but they remained in my lap until we pulled into Stacie's driveway.

He made a move to open his door.

"Please don't get out, Briggs. Thank you though...for this, for helping me tonight," I said.

He nodded, a painful expression appearing on his face. "Tori?"

I turned to look at him as I opened my door.

"He really does *love* you. Process through this however you need to, but don't let it be the end to what you have with him. What you *feel* right now is different than how things really are."

"Unfortunately, I know that...all too well." I closed the truck door behind me and walked up the porch steps.

As I pushed open the front door, it was met with resistance. My wet camping gear was sitting in the entry way.

Kai's already been here.

Stacie stood just beyond the soggy pile. As she opened her arms to me, my body went limp.

Together, we sobbed.

Kai had told her.

TWENTY-SEVEN

The only marker of time that existed was Stacie's impending due date, now just over ten weeks away. She'd been gone Christmas shopping for hours, picking things up for Jack's arrival after the new year. Like usual though, I declined her invitation to "come with".

Things at the hospital had slowed down substantially, my on-call hours all but gone. That fact was ironic since I now had more time on my hands than ever before. I'd found new ways to fill the empty hours in my day though, besides my running, which had increased considerably.

One new time-killing hobby was *baking*.

When I'd refused to leave the house for nearly a week after "the event" with Kai, Stacie had called a mandatory meeting with Dr. Crane. It was at that meeting, that this new, mind-numbing outlet was suggested for me. I'd never done much in the kitchen, nor cared much about sweets, but as Dr. Crane put it, "the holidays are a wonderful time to give back".

So here I was now, giving back.

I had learned to bake: cupcakes, pies, cobblers, cookies, sugar cut-outs, and jelly thumbprints (those were Stacie's favorites). Stacie and I had a list of organizations to deliver them to around Dallas every week. Though I didn't find much joy in making them, giving them away was the highlight of my week. As long as I could keep my day full, it was one more day I had moved forward.

One more day I had chosen to overcome my heartache.

With the increased visits to see Dr. Crane, my feelings had started to thaw. I was breaking them out of the ice boxes they'd been trapped in for well over a year. There wasn't much that I wouldn't tell her now. I had a whole new perspective on secrets, and I refused to let them take me down.

One nearly had, just six weeks ago.

Dr. Crane called it my "healthy anger", but I knew the root wasn't from a place of health at all. It was from hurt. Kai had hurt me, deeply.

We didn't talk much anymore about the night in the hail storm with Kai. We had ridden that Ferris-wheel to the ground and back and there was nothing left that hadn't been said already. Her feelings were different than mine on the subject, but I knew I couldn't love a man who could keep such a secret from me, no matter what his intention.

The challenge now was making my heart believe that, too.

Those first weeks had been dark, frighteningly similar to a darkness I could easily recall from my not-so-distant past. Kai had called me of course, but Stacie had played the role of mediator. I was beyond grateful to her for that. In the beginning she had urged me to meet with him, to hear him out. She soon realized, though, that her efforts to convince me were futile.

Eventually, she stopped persisting.

Apart from what I considered an unforgivable lack of integrity and judgment, I knew he'd never force his presence on me, unless I asked for it. He wasn't overbearing or disrespectful. He was a gentleman—always.

My view of God had been yet another element of change in my quest to move forward, perhaps the most surprising to date. Though I wouldn't say we were *close*, I could no longer deny His existence. I also couldn't deny that He'd heard me, on a very desperate day, crying out on the floor of a forest.

Despite the fact that our future together was no more, I'd never wish for a different outcome. Kai had lived, and God had revealed himself. Why He would choose to save Kai and not Anna I still questioned. But that was one battle I had grown weary of fighting.

I was not in control, nor would I ever be.

I was currently in the kitchen making my second batch of peanut butter balls. Stacie planned on delivering them to the school staff she volunteered for tomorrow. I shut the pantry with my foot after grabbing another cup of powdered sugar, when I heard a knock at the door.

At only a week before Christmas, the amount of neighborhood activity had increased tenfold. Everything from middle school students selling their last roll of wrapping paper, to dedicated church members trying to get the message of baby Jesus out, all had stood on our doorstep as of late. I dried my hands on a towel and walked to the door, pulling it open.

I blinked a thousand times before my eyes could *believe* what I was seeing.

"Hey, Sister."

I jumped into his arms as he twirled me in the air, hugging me tight. Jack was home three weeks early! I screamed in delight, feeling happier than I had in weeks. His deep jovial laugh echoed down the street.

"Is she still out?" Jack asked.

"Yes, come in quick. She should be home any minute," I said.

He came inside the entry way and I couldn't help but squeal again. Stacie had better be sitting down for this surprise or she would have that baby much earlier than planned.

"It's so great to see you, Tori," Jack said.

"It's wonderful to see you too, Jack!" I said. "Now, where do we hide you?"

Jack quickly put his luggage in the closet, out of view from both the garage and the front door. He stood near the pantry, ready to escape into it at the first sound of Stacie's homecoming. I grew anxious as the minutes ticked, but finally, I heard the familiar purr of her car engine as she rolled into the garage.

"Ah, you would not believe how crazy it is out there. Why do I always wait to shop? The lines and the traffic…it's all horrid!" Stacie said, waddling into the kitchen, arms over-loaded with bags.

"Stacie, here…let me take those. Go into the living room and sit down, let me get you something to drink," I said.

"Uh, okay?" She was looking at me like I had four heads.

"What? I can't offer my *very* pregnant sister a cup of hot tea? Go in there and sit, you shouldn't have been out so long," I said, sounding more like a nurse than a sister.

"Huh, you're probably right. My feet are *killing* me," she said, waddling to the couch.

When she was out of sight and I heard her shoes clunk down on the coffee table, I opened the pantry door to let Jack out. He grinned wide and I bit my cheeks trying not to laugh with giddy anticipation. I walked into the room before him.

"Stace?" I said.

"Yeah? Where's the tea…are we all out?" Stacie asked, looking at my empty hands.

"No…Not exactly, but I did find something else in the pantry," I said.

"What? Not a mouse I hope…" she said, eyes growing wide.

"No…I'm afraid I'm slightly larger than a mouse," Jack said, stepping around the corner into full view.

At first Stacie did nothing.

She was a statue, jaw unhinged and open. It wasn't until Jack took a step toward her that her trance was broken. Squeals and tears came non-stop. The reunion was perfect; a Christmas present she'd never forget.

The next several hours were filled with Jack's stories of the sights and sounds of Australia. Though his weekdays had been filled with office work, he had spent nearly every weekend adventure-seeking in the land down under. Stacie and I were caught up in gut wrenching laughter as he told the story of his first time snorkeling in the ocean.

"...before I realized, I was way out past the buoy marker...just caught up in my own world of tropical fish. The problem was the tide had gone out and I had to make my way back over about two hundred feet of reef," Jack said. "By the time I finally reached the beach, my chest, belly and legs bore the scars of that sharp sea demon."

Jack was a fantastic storyteller. I could listen to him for days on end, but I also knew he and Stacie needed their time alone as well. I finished my tasks in the kitchen and bundled up to head outside. The air was crisp, not yet cold enough for ice or snow, but a coat was much more than a casual accessory these days.

I walked the length of their street, looking at the light displays on the houses and yards in the neighborhood. Stacie's house was the only one without the outward twinkling of *Christmas spirit*, but I was sure Jack would change that soon enough.

What else would change?

The question in one sense had little to do with Jack's return. I couldn't be happier now that he was home with Stacie and the baby. Yet, in another sense, I couldn't help but feel a bit lost. My purpose in Dallas had been to keep Stacie company during her pregnancy while Jack was overseas. To support her, help her, take care of her, although in truth, she had done far more of that for me. I stuffed my hands down inside my coat pockets, my fingers aching from the cold.

As surprising as it was for me to admit that I had really enjoyed living with Stacie, I knew it couldn't last forever, nothing ever did. With the arrival of the baby quickly approaching and Jack's return home, I needed to start making plans, immediately. The last thing I wanted to do was cramp a growing family. A family who had already given me more than I could ever re-pay, they had given me the chance to start anew.

****

As I checked-in at the nurses' station, a huddle of women stood at the bulletin board discussing New Year's Eve plans. I rolled my eyes.

It's two weeks away ladies, seriously?

But as I rounded the corner to grab my first chart of the day, I stopped short.

Kai's face.

A huge poster on the bulletin board stared back at me. It was surrounded by a group of nursing staff.

"Hi, Tori, looks like your boyfriend's got a pretty big gig on New Year's Eve, huh? You must be so proud of him," Bev said.

"Uh...he's not...he's not-" I started.

"Oh, that's right. I think I heard about that, you guys broke up, right? Bummer, and right before the holidays, too," Bev quipped, coming to my side, her fire-red nails stroking my arm.

Yeah right, 'think I heard about that…'

Of course she had heard, she was the leader of all things gossip related.

"It's fine, really," I said.

"Well, the whole hospital's been talking about it—the New Year's Eve Party, not your breakup, of course," Bev said, laughing without a smile.

"Everyone I know has already bought tickets. It should be quite a night from the plans I keep hearing about. Too bad you'll miss it," she said, sticking her bottom lip out.

"Who says I'll miss it?" I asked, heat coursing through me.

"Oh...well, I assumed because-"

"Well you know what they say about a person that *assumes*, Bev."

With that I walked down the hall, chart in hand, leaving her to gawk and gossip all she wanted. I would not be anyone's charity case, however fake and misguided Bev's intentions were.

My skin crawled at the thought of her little nurse posse talking about Kai. If not for the sake of my professionalism at work, I would have said much more than I had. Of course, I had absolutely no intention of going to that party, but Bev's comment had just made things a bit more complicated.

Pride sucked.

Why do I even care what she thinks? I'm not going—that's it.

Each evening after eight o'clock, Meg Holt had allowed Christmas music to be played throughout the main hall, as long as it was kept at a minimal volume. The mood changed almost instantaneously.

The night had been fairly low key and few staff were needed, most were caught up in the hallway talking about Christmas plans. The others were doing paperwork so they could exit the second their shift was over. Not feeling much enthusiasm to join in on another yet holiday discussion, I watched the clock.

"Hey there, Tori," Meg said.

"Hi, slow night, huh?" I asked.

"Yeah, kinda nice though for a change, except for the slow tick of that clock," she laughed.

"Yes, exactly," I said.

She turned to the desk and riffled through a folder.

"I don't know if you've heard about the nurse's abroad program yet, but I have a flier here if you think you might be interested."

She handed me a bright yellow piece of paper with the words "Consider Africa" centered at the top in bold lettering.

"What is it?" I asked, studying the page.

"It's basically a twelve-month opportunity to be on a mobile medical team. They focus on taking vaccines and nutritional care to villages all around Africa. Because it's mobile, you don't stay in one place for longer than a week at a time, so you would really get to experience a lot. If I didn't have a husband and kids I'd be all over something like that," she said.

I continued to read it, examining the pictures that bordered both sides of the page, "Huh...well, thanks."

"The deadline to sign up is February first, team leaves March one," Meg said, strolling away in her Birkenstocks.

Africa.

The clock finally read ten till midnight.

I started my walk to my locker to collect my keys and phone. I was anxious to leave. Standing around in a hospital with no work to do was the thing I liked least about nursing; thank goodness it was a rarity in my particular department. I bundled up and headed out the main emergency doors. At this time of night all the other doors were locked and armed for security reasons, this made the walk to my car much longer.

"Tori?"

I jumped at the sound of the male voice behind me, dropping my phone, keys, and the Consider Africa brochure to the ground. Adrenaline surged so strong through my body that the hairs on my neck stood up straight. The man knelt down instantly, gathering up my scattered belongings.

"I'm sorry; I was trying to figure out a way not to startle you, but couldn't think of any. Here, let me help," Briggs said.

"What on earth are you doing out here, Briggs?" I snapped.

He handed me my phone and keys and then slowly the yellow brochure, reading the words on the front. I snatched it from his hand.

"What's up?" I said, growing increasingly impatient.

"Look, I know I'm not on your top-ten-favorite-people-list right now, but...but Kai's-" Briggs started, his face tentative.

My stomach dropped, knotting instantly.

"What about Kai? Is he sick? Is something wrong?" I asked, my words rushing out.

His face seemed to change with my last question, as if he was considering it carefully or maybe considering *me* carefully.

"What? Just tell me, Briggs!" I stomped my foot.

"Maybe not sick in a *conventional* way exactly, but-"

"You know, I have heard enough lies from the two of you. Ironic, isn't it? Look who the game players are now—Batman and Robin, both."

I turned from him quickly and continued to walk in the direction of my car.

"Stop, Tori, please. You're right. I did know that he was at your accident that night. What I didn't know—or rather, what I didn't understand was why he was so *impacted* by you that night. That is, until I met you for myself, until I saw you save my best friend's life at the risk of your own," he said, getting in front of me, causing me to stop mid-stride. "Don't you find it the least bit odd that out of this whole huge city he meets *your* bother-in-law who just happens to attend his same church? Then only months later he realizes that the girl he'd prayed for...the girl he had cared for in the back of his rig, was you? He couldn't have planed all that, Tori; he's not some creepy stalker. He *loves* you."

The word was a physical blow, causing me instant pain all over.

"*Love*...really? That's what you think *love* is Briggs? Because all I hear is *deception*, and last time I checked that wasn't the best foundation to build a relationship on," I said.

"Tori, he is beyond regretful for not telling you sooner. I've never seen a man so broken." Briggs paused and looked at me, a new resignation in his voice. "Answer me this, can you *honestly* tell me that you would've given him a chance if he had told you all that up front?"

I stared into his hard eyes, knowing the answer.

No.

I said nothing.

"So that's it, then? You just go on with your life and pretend you never knew each other?" Briggs took a step closer to me, gesturing with his arms in the air. "Or maybe *you* never really did care for *him*...maybe losing him isn't a big deal at all-"

"Shut up! I love him..."

I slapped my hand over my mouth the instant the words were spoken. Regret loomed over me.

A large smile spread over Briggs' face.

I've been played.

"Sorry about that. I knew you'd never admit it if I didn't coax it out of you. Think about what I said Tori, before you make the biggest mistake of your life." Briggs nodded to the yellow brochure in my hand.

Instinctively, I put it behind my back, knowing full well I was hiding nothing that he hadn't already seen and read.

He took another step toward me and in a voice as soft as a whisper asked, "Is there anything you'd like me to tell Kai for you?"

Without missing a beat I stared him right in the eyes and said, "Yes...tell him *baking* helps."

By the time I got to my car, my tears were unstoppable. I laid my head down on the steering wheel, waiting for my sobs to subside.

"Why did this happen, God? Why would you let me fall in love with a man I can't trust? Why does the pain of my accident get more and more complex every single day?"

No answer.

"And why do you speak at the times I'm *not* trying to hear from you? Urgh!"

No answer.

TWENTY-EIGHT

I may have been running more often, but the duration was get shorter each time I went out. The white puffs that replaced my breath reminded me again of how cold Dallas could get in the winter. I was careful to watch for ice, but so far there hadn't been any to navigate around.

For the last seven weeks, I had taken a route that wouldn't lend itself to thoughts of Kai. But today, for reasons unclear to me, I ran up Elm Street bridge and into the park. It was a little past nine in the morning, and there wasn't a soul around. I kept my pace steady, running along the sidewalk that bordered the swing set. From there, I could see the tree. While keeping it only in my peripheral, I passed by it twice, before finally deciding to go to it.

Why those few steps were more difficult than the miles it took me to run here was obvious, but why I felt compelled to torture myself, was not. The tree was as big and bold as I had remembered. It's rough bark snagged on the dryness of my hand as I brushed over it reverently. The memory of Kai's thoughtful words gifting me his *special spot* burned vividly in my mind's eye. Then, a much more intimate memory took over, one that forced me to remember the kisses we'd shared together, standing right here.

Dr. Crane's latest push for me was to find a way to bring "closure" to Anna's death. To somehow find a way to express to her the thoughts, feelings, regrets, and most definitely the guilt, I had buried deep inside myself. Closure from Anna's death was the inevitable end for me to be granted freedom from PTSD—Dr. Crane had made that abundantly clear. But here I was, the pending closure of a death looming over me, when I hadn't even faced the closure of my most recent loss.

It was a loss that *lived* and *breathed* just miles from where I stood, a loss that I fought to treat like a death, permanent and indisputable.

I could feel it building in me, the need to let go, but I wasn't brave enough to face that, not yet. A chill came over me as my sweat began to cool, freezing onto my skin.

I saw the frost on the ground, the weight of the tiny blades of grass that were bent under its pressure. I looked over the roots of the tree that stood inches above the earth's surface one last time, saying a silent goodbye to a tree that had once brought me indescribable hope. As I turned from it, a gleam of white caught my eye.

I looked again, reaching down for it.

Paper.

It was curled now, weathered, but unmistakably a message to someone.

The pen had bled and smeared over its trusted companion: the note card. Most letters were still intact however, and to a patient eye, even *legible*. I fell back on the tree with a thud as I read the first word.

Pele.

It was from Kai...*to me.*

Tears filled my eyes as I read on:

Pele,
I was wrong to wait so long to tell you.
I thought losing you would be the worst pain I'd ever feel, but I was wrong about that, too.
Knowing I was the cause for your pain is far, far worse.
If you are reading this now, then maybe there is still hope...
Maybe there is a chance for forgiveness?
I love you Tori.
Until then...I'll keep waiting.
Kai

His name was just a dark glob of ink, but I could read the letters clearly, as if they shouted directly into my thoughts. I re-read the card over and over, until I'd memorized it, stuffing it deep into the pocket of my heart. I curled the note card back up and carried it in my hand as I ran back to Stacie's.

When had Kai written this?

Only moments before I had been dwelling on closure, but was that what I really wanted? Was it enough that Kai was sorry? That he had admitted wrong-doing and wanted my forgiveness? Were we supposed to be together?

I meditated on those questions with each step that pounded the pavement, my mind spinning in circles again. God seemed so distant when I prayed about Kai. The more passionate I became about the matter, the further away He felt. I was confused by the lack of direction.

It seemed easy enough, this question in my mind. A simple *yes* or *no* would do the trick. How hard could it possibly be for me to hear, or for Him to speak?

And then, a new thought occurred to me.

Is that not the right question?

I stopped, breathing heavily now. I looked up into the sky, waiting.

"What *is* the right question?"

Where does forgiveness start?

The prompting was deep and rich, overwhelming my senses with its power.

I searched for the answer, scattering my confusion into a million pieces. I replayed it again, focusing on each word, saying it out loud.

Was this God's idea of a riddle?

Was there even a right answer?

Would I continue in this constant circular pattern of pain and self-destruction forever?

And then it was clear.

Forgiveness starts within.

It wasn't just an answer, it was a priority.

And Kai was not *first* on that list.

I was.

****

"It's hard to believe this is our last session for the year, Victoria," Dr. Crane said.

"Please, call me, Tori. You've earned that right by now," I said, smiling at her.

She laughed lightly and handed me a box wrapped in shiny red paper.

"I wouldn't normally give a Christmas present to a patient, Tori, but I felt this was appropriate. You have worked so hard over the last four months and you've grown tremendously since our first session together. I hope you can see that, too. Don't get stuck on what's left to overcome, there will always be more to do, for all of us," Dr. Crane said. "I would be out of a job pretty quickly if *perfection* were possible."

I smiled at her and unwrapped the pretty paper. It was a beautiful spiral-backed journal.

"Thank you, Dr. Crane. This is very thoughtful of you," I said.

"It's not just a journal to keep track of your days, Tori. This journal has a purpose. Its spiral back is essential to that purpose," she said, looking at me, willing me to conclude her thought.

"So I can choose what to keep in it and what to tear out?" I asked.

"Exactly. Closure of grief, especially grief that bears guilt, can be a tough task. Writing may prove helpful to you, but not all of it should be held on to. Some things we write need to be released in order for healing to come. Clinging onto harmful words, even those we write about ourselves, will never get us far. Think of it like a dog that spends his days chasing after his tail, satisfaction will never find him."

Though she had never spoken the words, I had a sense there was more to Dr. Crane's understanding of healing than her schooling alone could take credit for.

There was something ultimately more divine at work in her.

"I will use it, I promise. I will see you after the new year, then?" I asked.

"Yes, Happy Holidays," she said, hugging me gently.

"Happy Holidays to you, too, Dr. Crane."

I looked again at the journal as I left her office.

Yes, something ultimately more divine indeed.

****

After another long and dreadfully slow night in the ER, I headed home. December 23rd had held no real significance to me, other than being the day I wrote my first journal entry. The list I'd begun had proven longer than I first had anticipated. Due to my aimless meanderings in the hallway at work, though, I had found plenty of extra thought time. I added names and offenses accordingly.

Tomorrow I would test it.

****

Jack was awake when I walked into the house. His jet lag hadn't quite worn off yet, as he was often awake during normal sleeping hours. He was in the kitchen now, pouring a giant bowl of frosted flakes.

"Greetings, how was your day?" he asked.

"You mean my night?" I said, laughing.

"Oh yeah, right, *night*," he said.

"It was fine, painfully slow, but no major complaints," I said, taking my shoes off.

Jack shoveled the cereal into his mouth with a spoon designed only for serving casseroles, and gestured for me to sit down. We had talked several times since he'd been back, but most of those talks were covering major bullet points of the things he'd missed, and vice versa. I slumped into the leather recliner, drawing my legs underneath me. I rested my head on my hand.

Jack drank the last of his milk like a child on a Cheerios commercial, and then smiled at me. Likely he already knew my thoughts regarding his breakfast-at-midnight-display.

"So, let's hear it," he said.

"Hear what?" I asked.

His eyebrows narrowed at me and he shook his head, waiting.

"Jack it's midnight. I'm not up for a Jeopardy round of whatever discussion you might want to have with me at this particular hour," I said.

"Okay party-pooper," he said, measuring me for a moment before speaking, "I want to hear about what happened with Kai. I mean, what *really* happened," he said.

"I'm sure Stacie told you all there is to know-" I started.

"Yes, and that's Stacie's version. You have your own perspective...and that's the one what I want to hear," he said seriously.

I shifted on the chair uncomfortably.

"Well, it's a pretty short story, Jack. He told me I could trust him and I believed him. I told him everything about me: my shame, my pain, my brokenness, and he kept his secrets to himself all the while," I said.

Jack nodded. There was no judgment on his face. He was purely seeking the facts, that was his way. He was not a reactor; he was a gatherer only.

"Listen, I know you and Kai are good friends and I don't want that to change for you—either one of you. I don't hate him...I don't even *dislike* him, we just aren't..."

"I'm waiting," Jack said, looking at me inquisitively.

"I don't know. I just don't know, anymore," I said.

"Anymore?" he asked.

I thought for a second and then reached down for a pillow, slowly bringing it to my lap before making my move. It was glorious; he was as unsuspecting as possible when I chucked it right into his face. He startled back, but only for an instant. Then, he was gathering up pillows in a fury.

"Oh, game on!" Jack said.

I jumped behind the recliner, heart pumping fast. This may not have been my greatest diversion plan. I pulled pillows left and right from around the front room, throwing them over my barricade.

Jack was *much* quicker, though. He managed to throw *five* pillows for every *one* that I threw at him. Jack threw pillows like they were Chinese throwing stars; how soft fabric and cotton stuffing could hurt was beyond me. My hair was matted all over my face as he was now standing on top of the recliner pelting me with a new stash he'd hoarded. I lay helpless on the floor trying to shield my head, laughing so hard I was gasping for air.

Jack had a great laugh when it really got going. It was mix between a teenage girl screaming, and a wheezy asthma attack. It was absolutely contagious, too. We were both in hysterics—a million throw pillows all over the front room, when the stair light flicked on and we were caught, red handed. We both froze, a silent kind of horror coming over us: the fear of the woken pregnant lady.

Stacie looked around the front room and then back to us. We waited for our punishment, but instead she simply said, "Merry Christmas Eve, *children*." And then she headed back to bed.

We each grabbed a nearby pillow and laughed into it for a good five minutes before deciding we should probably clean up and head that way ourselves.

Jack slung his arm around me as we trudged up the stairs

together.

"See ya in the morning, Sis," he said, "It's nice to have you back."

I stared at him, puzzled, "*You're* the one who just got back," I laughed, thinking his jet lag had fogged up his mind, again.

"No, you've been gone a lot longer than I was...and it's really nice to have you back, Tori."

Jack hit me on the shoulder and walked into his bedroom.

I stood there for a second more.

"It's good to be back," I whispered.

TWENTY-NINE

I stared at the list.

It was the list I had scratched onto the first page of my new journal. With my phone in hand I paced my bedroom floor. Several deep breaths later, I dialed the name at the top.

After just three rings, I heard her voice.

"Hello?"

"Hi, Dr. Bradley...it's Tori," I said.

Silence.

"Hello?" I said again.

"Tori...I'm...it's a surprise to hear from you," she said.

"I know and that's actually why I'm calling, do you have a minute?" I asked.

"Yes, of course," she said.

"I've been angry at you for a long time, feeling betrayed and hurt that you'd set up therapy for me without my permission," I confessed.

"Yes, I thought that might be how you felt, and I'm sorry-"

"No, please, let me finish. I'm the one who needs to say I'm sorry...to *you*. I don't think I would have ever sought help if it hadn't been for you caring about me—about my future. I owe you an apology and would like to ask for your forgiveness?" I said.

Silence again. This time I waited.

"You sound...you sound *so* different, Tori. Even just on the phone I can tell you're not so...closed off," Dr. Bradley said.

"Yes, a lot has happened here. Dr. Crane has been a great support for me, and so has my sister and...*others*. I really do feel different," I said.

"Tori I'm so glad you called today. I accept your apology and of course I forgive you. I hope you can start to move forward with your life and the amazing opportunities that are in your future, and in your career," Dr. Bradley said.

"Thank you, that means so much to me," I said, thinking of a topic right along those lines. "Have you ever heard of *Consider Africa* before?"

We talked for a while longer. She gave me a few contacts of friends who had done similar nursing abroad programs in the past. She encouraged me that all of them had only positive things to say about their experiences. Excitement stirred in me. Susan was not only a medical professional that I respected, she was also a friend—a true friend.

I was grateful I had started with her; the others would prove much more difficult.

****

Jack had been up on a ladder hanging lights on the house since early this morning, Christmas Eve. I told him he was probably better off just holding out for New Years decor at this point, but he waved me off and kept right on hanging. Stacie had been busy decorating the artificial tree that Jack had brought in from the attic while I was out on my run.

I came in through the entryway.

"Hey want to help?" she asked.

I looked at the boxes of ornaments all around her and laughed.

"What would you have done if I had said no?" I asked.

"Sat down in the middle of all this and taken a nap." She rubbed her hand on her greatly expanded belly.

"Okay, let me change and I'll be back down to help in just a minute," I said, laughing at her.

****

When the tree had come to life with color, shapes, and lights, Stacie and I stood back to examine our handy-work. We were quite satisfied.

"Glad it will be up for tomorrow," Stacie said.

"Yeah."

How different this holiday would be from last year. My parents had wanted to fly me back to Dallas of course, but I had refused. I told them I had to work the Christmas weekend because I was the lowest on the totem pole. Stacie had been beside herself, calling me to announce that her and Jack would be joining me Christmas morning. Naturally though, I had wiggled my way out of that net as well. I claimed I'd be at the hospital for over 14 hours, so it wouldn't be worth their efforts. She had finally conceded.

Though I had worked all day last Christmas, I had volunteered for it, trying to tell myself it was *just another day* of the week. I had also tried to pretend that not having family—especially at the holidays, didn't bother me.

"I was thinking we should leave by six tonight to secure good seats, the Christmas Eve service is always so jam-packed," Stacie said.

My stomach dropped, "Oh...I'm not sure about that, Stace," I said.

"Well, I am. Last year people were standing in the lobby! Parking was a total nightmare-"

"No, I mean...I wasn't planning on going," I said.

Putting her hands on her hips, she stared at me in disbelief.

"I thought you were past all that nonsense of not fitting in at church, Tori. You've been making so many efforts to-"

"No...That's not it at all, Stacie. Yes, things are going better now in that department, but there's a reason why I've only gone to the early services lately," I admitted.

"Oh. Kai." She sighed. Though her voice was soft and thoughtful, hearing his name from her lips caused my heart to ache. I hated that he still had that effect on me. I hadn't even seen him in nearly two months.

"Yeah," I said, swallowing hard.

"Tori, I don't want to tell you what to do, but I think you need to decide to either move forward and go on with your life—despite a possible chance meeting in a crowd of thousands—or decide it's not over yet," Stacie said.

I looked at her, an edge of rebuke on my lips. "It *is* over. It's been decided, Stacie."

Her face remained unchanged.

"If that's true, then you won't let him hold you back from a Christmas Eve service with your family."

I bit my bottom lip. She had a point. Still, I couldn't shake the sinking in my gut. The odds felt stacked against me; our relationship had been one unlucky coincidence after another.

I hoped tonight would prove that theory wrong.

****

The borrowed short, black skirt and tights coupled with the red, cowl-neck sweater, came from no other than Stacie's closet. It had become habit now to ignore my own closet which housed dull, bleak neutrals and go directly to the free boutique. The one that was located just down the hall.

Stacie and Jack had both dressed up for the evening. They looked like they could be featured on a Hallmark holiday card. My folks had called us on our way, already having saved us seats. Stacie was relieved, as we, of course, were running behind schedule.

The parking lot of the church was just as Stacie had described—a nightmare. The line of cars was at least two blocks long. From there, we were directed by one of the numerous parking attendants who wore a hat of festive blinking lights. Stacie moaned that she had to use the restroom, even though she had gone just fifteen minutes earlier at home. Jack gave me a wayward glance in the rear view mirror. We kept our mouths shut.

The candlelit stage was a sight to behold. Children dressed in their Christmas attire had lined the stage. They stood quietly, waiting for instruction as people filled the dim auditorium. The large, open-concept room felt strangely intimate in light of the special events to come. After only a few minutes of searching, we found my parents.

As the starting time approached, a soft hush fell over the audience. A small boy took the stage. He opened the evening with the passage in Mathew which spoke of the birth of Christ, his sweet voice resonating within the room. When he was done speaking, the choir behind him started to sing. There were many songs celebrating the birth of baby Jesus, along with several well-choreographed numbers. Jack and Stacie exchanged warm glances, as if thinking of their own Christmas performers someday.

The pastor shared a few words on the true meaning of Christmas and instead of tuning him out like I had tried to do months earlier, I listened. He spoke of ending the year without regrets, without offenses, and most importantly, without bitterness.

"Bitterness," he had said, "Will only serve to rob the joy that is the Christmas spirit."

My heart sank. It was yet another confirmation.

My list was not delusional—it was *right*.

The service ended with each person holding a candle and lighting it for another. Down each aisle, down each row, until every section of that entire room was lit by the start of single flame, it was beautiful. My eyes stung with tears at the sight. We sang one last song, and then we were dismissed.

The crowd was massive, yet even amongst all the commotion, I had the unmistakable feeling I was being watched. I fought the sensation to turn my head for what felt like an eternity. But finally, the temptation was too great. My eyes confirmed what my heart already knew.

Kai was there, standing just a few feet away from me.

My breath hitched.

Instantly, I was trapped in a world where only Kai and I existed. The distorted sound of music and chattering people faded away. It was only us. Nothing could tear my eyes away from him.

The magnetic pull that gripped my heart was too strong for me to break on my own. Within seconds, I was walking toward him and him to me. A deep ache resonated in my chest as I studied his face.

His eyes were a tortured kind of beautiful. I knew the look well; I had seen it in the mirror for the last two months.

As we stood now, just a few feet apart from one another, I had to remind myself that I couldn't reach for him. He was no longer mine to touch. I balled my fists, pressing my nails deep into the palm of my hands.

"Hi," he said.

"Hi." My words were barely audible.

"It's...it's good to see you, Tori."

I stared at him, refusing to cry, while the warm ache of tears throbbed behind my eyelids. They fought a battle against me. It took all my energy and focus to deny their release.

"You too."

The note from the tree burned a hole in my purse, as if it could identify its author. I wouldn't reveal it, though. I wouldn't give him a false reason to hope, or allow him to believe that something more was possible.

"Briggs said he saw you the other night," Kai said.

"Yes, he did."

The ache had spread throughout my chest, causing tiny tremors to escape each time I exhaled.

"He said you have a lot of stuff going on these days, some...some new interests?" Kai said, hesitantly.

Was he asking about baking?
I can't believe Briggs really told him about that...how lame.

"Uh, yeah, I suppose I do," I said.

He stared at me a long minute more and then ran his hand along the back his head. The movement made his hair rumple and stray, causing me to flush. I loved that rumpled hair.

"I'm glad you're doing well...that's all I ever wanted for you," he said.

This is unbearable!

"Merry Christmas, Kai," I said.

"Merry Christmas, Tori."

As I turned to break away, a thought flashed in my mind.

The list...my list.

But even as I thought it, I knew I couldn't do it.

Not here. Not like this.

I wasn't strong enough tonight.

I had taken no more than five steps when I heard his voice behind me. I stopped. A shiver crept down my spine. Unwilling to be caught in yet another agonizing trance, I didn't turn around. I couldn't face him again so soon.

"Will I see you on New Year's Eve? At the benefit?"

His voice was nothing short of desperate now, and something physically broke inside me at the sound of it. One stay tear slid down my cheek.

That was it, the opportunity I needed.

It was the last day of the year, a last chance to reconcile the loss of what we had.

I nodded and simply said, "I'll be there."

****

I watched my mother clear the dishes after Christmas supper. The morning had been filled with stockings and gifts, followed by a visit to my parent's house where the meal was exquisite enough to feed a royal family. Of course, the main course had all been pre-ordered and catered, but it was delicious just the same. I'd brought several plates of baked goods to add to the mix—my therapy working overtime.

Though I fought to wear a face of good tidings and joy, inside I felt anything but. I had struggled through most of the day, pushing aside the picture that kept trying to make its way to the front of my mind: Kai's eyes. Despite the many distractions around me, it proved an impossible task.

I picked up a rag and quietly helped to dry the serving dishes that lay on the counter. I could hear Jack telling a story about his parasailing experience as my dad and Stacie enjoyed their decaf coffee near the fireplace in the den. My mother's hands, delicate and prim, washed the dishes, her manicured fingers, sudsy.

I swallowed hard, thinking for a moment about the list that lay on my dresser at home. Her name was second from the top. I hadn't actually imagined ever crossing it off, but there was no time like the present—holiday or not.

My heart hammered against my chest.

"It's been wonderful to have you back home, Victoria," my mother said.

"Thanks, it's been...a nice Christmas," I said.

Laying down her final pot, I took in a deep breath. Conjuring up every last bit of bravery I had, I opened my mouth.

Just start...then I'll have to finish.

"Do you think we could take a walk, Mom?"

My mother looked at me, her perfectly-aged face shadowing with apprehension.

"Just you and I...right now?"

"Yes, if that's okay," I said.

"Sure...I'll go get our coats."

****

The air was crisp, our scarves, gloves and thick wool coats protecting us from the bite in the wind. Stepping out, my mother immediately filled the silence with her next home improvement plan. This one consisted of a play-cottage and swing set for her future grandchildren. After describing in detail the area to which she thought best for such a feature, I interjected, cautiously.

"Mom, I've been doing a lot of thinking lately...about the past," I stammered.

She turned her head toward me, but kept her eyes low, contributing nothing to my unexpected announcement. I went on.

"It's been easy for me to think that this last year and a half had only affected me—that I was the only one who'd been struggling," I said.

She nodded now, slowly.

I continued, "But, I am starting to realize, that might not be entirely accurate."

She stopped walking. It took me a second to realize she was two steps behind me when I turned around to face her.

Her eyebrows set into a deep pensive stare before a reply was offered.

"Victoria...you're right, that's not accurate at all," she said.

I felt a spark of heat in the base of my stomach and pushed it down. I took a deep breath.

Stay calm; this is an apology, not an argument.

"Well...I've been in a rough place for a while now, Mom, and I know I haven't done a good job at communicating-"

"No, you haven't. Your father and I have never had a more difficult year in our almost thirty years of marriage. We've been worried sick over you, never knowing where you were or how you were...never able to get a straight answer from you. All we ever heard were excuses and conversations about anything and *everything*, but yourself...and that's all we've ever been concerned about," she said, a new passion filling in her voice—strong, yet pained.

I could feel my insides ignite again, this time they burned dangerously close to the edge, an edge that threatened my safety—*my truth*. I bit the inside of my cheeks, feeling my face grow hard.

But she continued on, unaffected.

"You treat us like we don't *care* about you, like we aren't the parents that have watched you grow up...nurturing you, providing for you, *loving* you. And yet, you keep pushing us away every chance you get. I've prayed so much, Victoria. I keep asking God to reveal to me what has caused this callousness in you. I am still so uncertain. When you left us without a goodbye it...it *broke* my heart. Do you have any idea what that did to me as your mother?"

The fire was unleashed. It jumped over every boundary, every restraint that I had put in place.

"Well, let me clear it up for you, *Mother*. I left because I knew no one could understand me or-"

"How could we, Victoria, you never gave us the chance?"

I stared at her, fear momentarily choking my earlier resolve.

"What?" she asked, hands gesturing broadly in the air.

"You never *gave* me a chance," I said, my voice low and hard.

"What do you mean? What are you-"

"I *heard* you, Mother! The week before my graduation, I heard you tell Dad that I was 'wrecked for life!'"

Pain ripped through me, as if I was hearing it again for the first time. Her hand flew to her mouth, eyes panicked. I looked down at the road.

My heart was going to explode.

"Victoria...you...I...," she started.

Tears stung my eyes. I wanted to run away, I wanted to be alone. I wanted to be anywhere but here, stuck in this raw moment of weakness.

"I never meant that, Victoria. I was in pain-" she said, shaking her head.

"You? *You* were in pain? I had just been in an accident! I had just taken the life of a six year old girl! I was the one in pain, Mom...ME!"

The volume I had managed to keep low only seconds earlier was back now with a vengeance. She stumbled back a few steps as if shocked by my tone, shocked by my words, shocked by my *truth*.

She covered her face with her hands.

"I'm so sorry you heard that, and I'm even sorrier that I said it. I was grieving, Victoria—*for you*. I wanted so badly to take away your pain and I knew nothing I could do would fix it. I was scared for you, but I was wrong...I was so wrong to say that," she said, staring at me, "I wasn't trusting in God."

Her last words cracked me, breaking the hardened shell that had quickly grown back around my heart against her. I couldn't look at her face; it was too raw, too filled with regret. I took several deep breaths in the silence, drawing from a place within, a place that I'd only recently invited in for the first time.

"I forgive you, Mom. But...I was wrong, too. I cut you out. I didn't want you to know what I was dealing with. I couldn't stand the thought of anyone's pity. I know that I hurt you, and I know now that I hurt our whole family with my choice to leave. I need to ask for your forgiveness, too."

She reached for me, hugging me in the cold of Christmas night. This embrace not only fought to let go of our past, it also revived a need that had long been silenced: a need for my mother.

THIRTY

The bright yellow flier caught my eye as I got into my car, the words bold and insistent. I thought again about the opportunity I'd spoken to Dr. Bradley's colleague about. Though the work would prove arduous, the experience would be one I knew I'd never forget. The reward for serving people in such great need would be incomparable.

Why wouldn't I do it?

The answer was there like the nagging presence of a hangnail, his face burned in my memory.

Soon I'll have closure...with everything.

After New Years, I would begin the necessary paperwork with the agency. Just a couple of weeks after the baby was born, I'd be starting over again, this time in a new country. I debated when the best time to tell Jack and Stacie would be, as well as my parents.

I'd made an unspoken promise to keep my family more apprised of my life decisions, but this proved to be my first real test. Though I didn't want to hide it, I knew the close timing of the baby's arrival was the priority. I didn't want to distract from it or be insensitive to Stacie's ever-growing hormonal complexities.

Driving through the farmlands on the old country highway brought my mind back into focus. I hoped my recent revelation would bring the clarity I needed to move forward. I meditated now on the words of Dr. Crane and then on the words that had echoed over and over in my heart as of late. There was only one way to find out. I slowed the car, parking just a few miles out. Taking a deep breath before surveying my surroundings, I stepped out.

Outside the car, I braced myself against the heavy steel door behind me. Reminded of the task at hand, I zipped my sweatshirt higher, pulling on the hood and tying it tightly around my ears and face. I started my run then on a road I'd seen a thousand times in my mind, a road that had haunted me for far too long. I was exactly one mile out now and could visualize what was up ahead, even without the sight to see it.

Closure. This is part of my closure.

I slowed as I approached the grassy bank, my body reacting with dread. A hundred feet out, I stopped completely. The scene before me was already in motion. Every detail was exact, a perfect fit to the memory that had held it captive. My body knew this land, this road, this setting, better than any place it had ever been. Though yesterday it was still tainted by death, pain, and resistance, today I hoped that would change. Today I hoped I would change.

The ground was hard and cold, frozen beneath me. My knees grew numb as they touched the very spot where they had once knelt to pray for a child, a child I'd held in my arms. The last time I'd been here, I believed my skill and effort alone could save her, but today I knew differently.

Today I knew I was powerless to overcome on my own.

God, here I am. I don't know how to find closure in all of this, I don't even know how to move on, but I want to. I need to. I've been stuck here too long, in this place of death. How do I find closure so I can live again?

And then…I knew.

****

Stacie rested on the couch as I cleaned up the Christmas aftermath around her. Her baby bump had grown again. Within this last week I could see the toll it had started to take on her energy level and her overall demeanor. Though she was still Stacie in so many ways, I could sense a difference in her.

She often sighed as she rubbed her tummy, seemingly off in another world, one that I couldn't get inside of no matter how I tried. Jack's early arrival home had resolved her issues of anxiety, and now she just wanted to hold her daughter.

She wanted to be a mother.

I watched her from the dining room and smiled. Stacie, my older sister, Jack's beautiful wife, would become a mother in just shy of eight weeks. The thought alone was perfection. There was no woman better suited for motherhood.

Stacie had always played the role of bride or mom in our make-believe games as children. She had carried the dolls and pushed the strollers. She had babysat during her summers in middle and high school, on speed dial for the whole neighborhood.

This was simply her destiny, perfect and complete.

There had been no names decided as of yet. Both parents lacked the ability to compromise. Jack had recently started drawing names out of a bowl in the kitchen, claiming he would just let the odds of the lotto system decide. Stacie pretended not to hear his crazy antics.

I chose to stay out of that altogether. It was one thing to be a tie-breaker when I could voice my opinion and then go on my merry way, but it was entirely another when I lived in *their* house. I'd keep my opinions to myself on that one.

After putting the last of the indoor decorations away while Stacie napped, I grabbed my journal and headed to the recliner near the window. Looking over my list once more, I focused on the final names for just a moment. Then, I turned to a fresh page.

On my lap was something foreign to me. Something I had only referenced, but had never known intimately: a Bible. Stacie had given me one for Christmas and had even gone through and highlighted the passages that she thought I'd find most helpful and encouraging. I ran my hand over the cool cover and cracked it open for the first time.

Her letter on the front page cover read:

Sister,

Words cannot express the love I have for you, or the hope I have for your future, but they would only fail in comparison to those God has already written for you. So rather than attempt it, I have highlighted some passages. Your journey has inspired me, Tori. He is faithful. Let Him restore you in His perfect timing and in His perfect way.

Love you,

Stacie

I looked through several highlighted passages, always coming back to the same theme: God promises were hope-filled, not hopeless.

I picked up my pen and started what would be the most difficult letter I would ever write. The words were far from flowing, but each touched the page with a powerful determination that seemed outside my control. The sentences turned into paragraphs and soon I had filled both sides of the page. At its completion, I carefully tore it out and folded it, tucking it inside an envelope. This letter was not for now, but for a time that was quickly approaching. It burned in my hand as I held it, my heart pounding at its revelation inside.

Today I'd been given a glimpse of hope.

I could only pray the same for tomorrow.

THIRTY-ONE

"Where you off to this morning?" Jack asked me in the hallway.

"Work."

"Work? It's New Year's Eve...and it's not even eight a.m.," he said, looking at his watch.

"The hospital doesn't observe holidays, Jack," I said, punching his arm. "I was able to change shifts, though. I'm starting earlier so I can get off earlier."

He nodded approvingly, "Lucky girl."

"Hardly," I murmured, walking past him to head downstairs.

"What?"

"Nothing. Happy New Year, Jack. Hope you and Stace have a great night."

****

The graveyard shift had just rotated when I arrived at work a bit after eight. The first hour was always busy transferring the patients from one shift to the next and getting caught up on the events of the prior evening. A large banner hung on the nurse's station proclaiming a wish for a *Happy New Year*. Nurse Stormy sat directly behind it.

Well, that's an oxymoron.

She barely lifted her head as I walked by, but I didn't mind. Stormy might have been an old grump, but after my last few shifts with Bev, I was grateful for her presence. At least she wouldn't be talking much to me today, which was all I could ask for.

I headed down the long hallway to greet my first patient of the day, an older gentleman with a sinus infection. I worked busily, asking him questions of drug allergies and symptoms, all the while thinking of the countdown before me. My countdown had nothing to do with the turn of the year and everything to do with the hours just before it.

There was a steady flow of patients all day, which helped the slow-ticking clock seem to speed up with each new face I saw. As the end of my shift approached, uneasiness washed over me.

My movements became robotic: clocking out, grabbing my bag from my locker, walking to my car.

The night sky was dark, the sun having said its final goodbye of the year, just as I would do all too soon.

Jack and Stacie had already been gone for hours when I arrived home to shower. I found a simple black dress and paired it with a plum cardigan and black pumps. I readied quickly, not wanting to spend extra time on primping. I wore my hair down and applied the basics to my face. I focused for a moment on my scar.

What had once been the reminder of so much shame, now represented something entirely different: mercy.

My scar also reminded me of something else, the lone trace of a thumb that had known its shape almost as well as I did. Though Kai must have seen it in its original state of trauma—bloody and exposed—he had a rare way of making me feel *more* beautiful with it than without. I knew now that it had been his *connection* to me. His connection to the broken woman he had seen that night long ago. I still couldn't understand it, but I couldn't fight it anymore, either.

It was time to let it go, time to let him go.

****

I arrived at the stadium at half past nine. The valet met me at the curb and parked my car in the very overcrowded lot. The amount of people who had chosen this venue to ring in the New Year was overwhelming to say the least. As I walked inside, however, I realized my expectation for the evening was far from accurate.

Kai would not be easy to locate.

A Christmas pageant was one thing, but here, where the lights were low and people danced and congregated in pods all over this gigantic room, chances seemed low.

I'll have to find him after he sings.

I didn't want to hear him sing, or see him sing, or feel him sing. I had one purpose: to find Kai, talk to him, and be done. That, however, did not prove realistic. I made my way down the stairs to the bottom floor.

Looking out into the crowd, I searched. It was hopeless. I couldn't even see the back wall from where I stood.

The perimeter was seemingly endless.

Skylights, which were a hundred feet above me, hung metallic streamers that reflected glints of silver and gold around the room like a disco ball. The band on stage seemed miles away from where I stood, yet the music carried effortlessly over the crowd. Dancing was well underway, and it was hard to fight my way past the couples who were sandwiched together all over the floor. I finally made it to a far wall. Feeling flushed from my exertion, I leaned back against it and scanned the room again.

No Kai.

The irony of the moment hit me then. After all the effort I had placed on avoiding Kai these past two months, after all the ways I had been careful to dodge an accidental run-in…it had come down to this. I was now seeking him out.

I stood there for almost an hour watching people dance, laugh, and drink. Three different men had approached me, but I had declined their offers. I had a plan, and they weren't a part of it.

The music started to fade. A well-dressed man, who looked like he could host the MTV music awards, took the stage.

"Ladies and Gentlemen, may I have your attention, please? We are just over an hour away from bringing in the New Year and we have saved the best for last. We have with us tonight a local celebrity and hero. Our evening entertainer is a paramedic in Dallas County. He is also one hunk-of-a-Samoan, one that I'm certain every lady here will remember after tonight. I'll let his talent speak for itself. Please welcome to the stage, Kai Alesana!"

The crowd cheered, clapping as he approached the main stage, microphone in hand. A bright light captured him in its orb, lights dimming to a soft glow all around the room. I stood motionless, caught off guard by his presence. My breath hitched, and my stomach took a nose-dive at the sight of him.

Anticipation shot down through my toes.

When the crowd quieted down, all that was left was the pounding of my heart. The music started.

I was compelled to move. My feet no longer felt attached to my body. I was powerless to control them.

Kai.

His name was so familiar, so comfortable, yet so distant at the same time. It hurt just to think it. I walked toward him, to a place where I could easily hide behind a group of rowdy women. I could see the buttons on his long-sleeve cobalt shirt and the laces in his shoes. I was close. Peering over a shoulder in front of me, I stayed hidden from his view.

He sang two upbeat songs on the current Top-40 play list and executed each perfectly. His tone matched every note, creating full swells and dips along with the melody line. His body swayed naturally to the rhythm of the music and with the crowd. He would be the talk of many after these performances; his talent was showcased at its peak tonight. The crowd applauded him again at the end of his second set, shouting for another.

He walked out of the spotlight for a second, only to return to it again with a guitar strapped over his chest. I peeked out, seeing him as he sat on the edge of a stool, strumming lightly. The band behind him played softly, matching his tempo.

He looked out into the crowd for a long moment, moving his eyes over the floor. Before tilting his head toward the microphone, Kai closed his eyes. A familiar ache traveled through me as I moved several inches to the left, veering further away from the ladies that were now calling out his name in drunken slurs. Kai didn't seem to hear them.

He was lost in the haunting tune that echoed throughout the building.

Then, he started to sing:

"I knew your face before your heart,
I saw your pain right from the start
A stunning sight I won't forget,
Tears that flowed out of regret,

So take your time and take your space
I'll be here while you navigate
My love for you alone will wait
My love for you alone will wait

You captured me before I knew
A rare reward, a heart so true
How could it be with just one look,
My world was changed, my love unhooked

> So take your time and take your space
> I'll be here while you navigate
> My love for you alone will wait
> My love for you alone will wait
>
> I only want to see you freed
> Outside the walls you cannot see
> So break away from debts not yours
> Receive the grace that's been out-poured
>
> So take your time and take your space
> I'll be here while you navigate
> My love for you alone will wait
> My love for you alone will wait"

Kai lifted his head to a room silenced by the hallowed sound of emotion. The song had been so raw, so vulnerable, yet so unbearably beautiful. I was under its spell, too. Fresh tears blurred my vision before I could blink and re-focus.

A single clap started, and one by one the room exploded into a roar of encores, but Kai simply bowed and thanked the Emcee before exiting the stage. I made myself move, made myself run after him before he was lost to me forever.

"Kai!"

He stopped.

"Kai," I said, as I approached him from behind.

He turned slowly, face still somber. He looked at me with disbelief.

"You came?" he asked, the surprise in his voice cutting me deep.

"Yes, I said I would. I meant it," I said.

As he stared at me, a pained smile spread across his face. The ache was back again, tossing in me like the choppy waves of an ocean after a storm.

"Can we talk somewhere, please?" I asked.

He nodded, leading the way in silence.

We walked in perfect stride to a courtyard just outside the main complex, the breeze crisp. Goose bumps spread down my arms in an instant. Though we never touched, Kai's hand was dangerously close to mine, the heat of it calling to me for warmth.

As we stopped at the circular fountain, Kai slipped off his suit coat and offered it to me. He was careful to keep his distance. I thought to refuse it at first, but knew without it my lips would be too frozen to speak.

And I needed to speak.

The jacket provided much more than warmth. It also seemed to provide strength and courage as well. I wrapped it tightly around my middle, crossing my arms to keep it close to me.

"Thank you," I said.

Kai nodded, again, staring at me.

"Your song...was beautiful," I said.

He turned toward the fountain, "I wrote it for you."

I followed his gaze, too caught up to respond. I knew the song had been for me. The words were far too intimate not to have been his own, but the admission was still overwhelming.

I took a slow breath in, the cold evening air chilling me deep. I pulled the jacket closer. It smelled of Kai, and that was all I wanted in this moment: more of him.

The sound from the fountain was strangely calming as the five water peaks changed levels and volumes, hitting the rock wall below. It was a nice distraction to watch as we stood there together, both knowing there was much left to be said. Finally, he turned and looked at me.

His face was full of torment.

"Tori, I have imagined this moment so many times, but now that you're here in front of me..." Kai shook his head, as if unsure what to say next.

I met his eyes, willing him to go on.

"I know after we speak tonight, my wondering will be over and I'll be left to deal with facts, not just assumptions and feelings," he continued.

My stomach flipped as a new wave of sorrow washed over me, this time pulling me under, taking my breath with it.

Does he know?

Does he know this is goodbye?

He held my gaze. I knew my face most likely mirrored his in this moment. It was marked by the undeniable heartache that had settled between us.

"I know you must be here for a reason, but I need you to know how truly sorry I am that I deceived you, how deeply I regret keeping the truth from you for that long...for being a *coward*. There is no regret I suffer from more in all my life," Kai said, still looking at my face.

In that moment I was sure, certain of my next move. I had thought the words, I had even written them down time and time again in my journal, but speaking them had been the question that had hovered in my mind for weeks.

Could I say them and mean them?

The answer now was a resounding *yes*.

A surge of courage brought life back to my frozen body.

"Kai...I forgive you. I'm sorry I couldn't say it sooner, but I mean it now. I forgive you."

Kai's entire countenance lifted at my words. His eyes seemed to sparkle again as a heavy sigh escaped from his lips.

"Thank you, Tori," he said, choked with emotion, "I've been so afraid you hated me."

I closed my eyes, the sting of his words burrowing deep, words that couldn't have been farther from the truth.

"I could *never* hate you. Even at the peak of my anger I still believed you were a good man."

The gap between us closed before I knew he had even taken a step. He touched my shoulder, sending a blaze of fire radiating through the thick fabric of his coat.

"And what do you believe to be true now, *Pele?*" The deep strength in his voice had returned, yet *I* was consumed with weakness. The flame worked its way down through my core. My bare legs ignited the cold that enveloped them.

I was a pawn to its warmth.

"I believe...I believe you didn't mean to hurt me, that your intention was *never* to hurt me," I said.

"And do you believe that I'm *in love* with you? That I *need* you? That I can't fathom my life without you in it for even one more second? Because all of that is true, Tori. I can't live without you anymore; it hurts too much to not be with you. I *love* you." His hand moved to my face, warming my cheek with his fiery touch.

I lifted my hand to rest on his and melted into it. I wanted this moment to last, to stretch until morning. I wanted every morning after that, too. I wanted to tell him I felt the same way.

I didn't want to walk away from him...but that's what had to be done.

I'd made a promise to myself; I didn't break my promises.

"I believe you, Kai, but-"

"But *what*? Can't we move past this, Tori? I'm willing to do whatever it takes to regain your trust, to show you I can be the man you need me to be-"

"But that's not what I *need* from you, Kai," I said, my heart pounding a thousand beats a minute.

He lowered his hand with mine, gripping it tightly in his. He stared into my eyes with desperation. Tears filled and blurred my view of the only man I'd ever loved.

A man I was hurting.

"I need you to let me go. There are things I have to do on my own. I've come too far, worked too hard to stop this process before I can finally find a sense of freedom. You...you started it for me, Kai. You stirred the desire for me to want to live outside of Anna's shadow, but you can't finish it for me. I have to do it," I said.

He pulled me into his arms and held me in a way that no other person ever had. I wanted to weep, yet I wanted to hide at the same time. I wanted to be led into his refuge, away from the sadness, away from the pain. Minutes passed before I felt the soft shudder of his body, no sound to be heard.

And then I felt it on my cheek: a tear, foreign to my own eyes. And then I felt another and another. Silence hung between us and I burrowed myself deeper into his chest, deeper into his hold on me.

I would not be the first one to let go.

I was the coward.

"I can see a change in you. It's like you've been transformed. I saw it even from across the church last week at the pageant," he said.

I listened to the sound of his heartbeat as I rested my ear against his chest.

"I've prayed so much for that, Tori. I prayed that you would find God and that you would *stop running*."

I lifted my head at those words.

I had heard those words countless times before, just as loud and clear as the heartbeat I was hearing now in his chest.

"I wish this wasn't the end, Kai," I said.

Holding my arms in his hands firmly, he pushed me back slightly to look in my eyes. Our bodies were still close—still touching.

"It doesn't have to be." He paused as he searched my face. "Do you really feel I'll hold you back…from healing? Is this really what you need from me?"

I swallowed hard. "Yes, it's what I need."

He closed his eyes. A single tear slid down past his jaw and dropped onto my arm, absorbing at once into the jacket I wore.

"Then I won't argue…even if…"

He couldn't finish the sentence.

I knew what it meant and it would hurt too much to hear him say it.

An explosion of sound filled the air around us: screams, shouts, fireworks and music. The reality of the moment we shared broke into our intimate conversation.

It was midnight, on New Year's Eve.

In the same exact instant our eyes met, a desperate intensity sparked between us. This was our last chance. This was our goodbye.

There was no leader; the kiss was desired equally by us both. There was no beginning, just a relentless passion that multiplied itself with each passing second. He held my head in his hands as heat blazed down the back of my neck. I strained forward to keep his lips on mine. I'd missed him, more than I ever dared to realize.

With him my heart felt whole, restored and complete.

I love him.

My arms moved from his chest to his shoulders, pulling him toward me, willing him to keep me close. When I felt his grip start to loosen in my hair, I stood up on my tip toes, tightening my arms around his neck. I forced him to lift me off the ground and continue what I couldn't bear to end. His hands were now tight around my waist, supporting my body as I refused to acknowledge the truth about this kiss.

This kiss was to be our last.

His lips stopped moving after a moment more. His breath was labored and quick as he pulled away from me. My name he whispered softly in my ear, bringing me back to my senses, to my reality, to my promise. As he lowered me onto to the ground I felt dizzy, intoxicated from his touch. I stabled myself on his outstretched arm, finding my footing once more.

"I'll let you go for now, *Pele*, but not forever. Whatever you have to do, wherever you have to go, I'll keep loving you. I'll keep waiting for you...praying for you," he said.

His face shadowed again with pain.

I love you, Kai. I love you!

"Goodbye, Kai."

He shook his head, refusing to say it back to me. A new set of tears filled my eyes as I stared at his stubborn resolve. I took off his jacket and held it out to him. He refused it as well.

I shivered, bare, and exposed without the warmth it provided. He stood looking at me, unmoved. I didn't want to leave like this, without the closure I had come for. I needed something concrete, something more than a passionate kiss shared on New Year's Eve. I needed something more than an unconditional declaration of love.

Those words had only bred new hope, not finality.

Not closure.

"Please, Kai. I need to hear you say it...please just tell me goodbye," I pleaded.

He exhaled slowly, and with a look that could chill a flame he said, "Until then, *Pele*."

With that, he turned and walked away.

I stood alone, holding his jacket in my arms, trembling in the cold. I put it on again, watching him until he was completely out of sight. There was no point in trying to stop the tears now.

Making my way through the parking lot to the valet booth, the world around me hummed. A new year had begun. I stuffed my hands into the pockets of Kai's jacket and felt something crinkle beneath the weight of my fingers.

The lyrics to his song—*my song*.

I placed them on the dashboard once inside my car. Reading them through slowly, the last verse and chorus came alive with new meaning.

> I only want to see you freed
> Outside the walls you cannot see
> So break away from debts not yours
> Receive the grace that's been out-poured
>
> So take your time and take your space
> I'll be here while you navigate
> My love for you alone will wait
> My love for you alone will wait

Kai had known. In his own way, within his own words, he had known.

I wished that fact alone would bring me comfort, but I couldn't feel anything but the cold.

THIRTY-TWO

Two weeks had passed, bringing the coldest January known to Dallas in over forty years. The air had been frigid, but it was the increased precipitation that was the concern of many. Black ice and freezing rain had meant more automobile accidents and slips and falls by unassuming folks, especially the elderly. The ER had been packed, the majority transported by emergency vehicles. I had worked several extra shifts to help lighten the load, always searching the faces of the EMTs who delivered our patients.

I had not seen Kai since New Year's Eve.

Dr. Crane had returned from her holiday vacation, but her schedule was working overtime. My appointment had been bumped to the end of the week and I found myself looking forward to meeting with her—only more proof that change was indeed taking place. Since I'd begun my therapy last September, this was the longest break I'd had from seeing her. It felt strange that several significant events had transpired without her knowing.

I walked down the hallway past the nurse's station to a tiny workspace in the corner. I'd been inside only once before, the day of my job interview with Meg Holt. She was working on the department schedule as I tapped lightly on the framed glass. She waved me in.

"Hey Tori, everything okay?" she asked.

"Yes, thank you. I just had some paperwork I wanted to turn in for the Consider Africa program," I said.

Her eyes lit up and her smile grew wide, "That's wonderful Tori, how exciting for you. It must be nice, having no strings attached. A lot of gals your age are already so tied down. I'll fax this over ASAP. They should be sending you some additional information to explain the rest of their procedures, along with your acceptance into the program. I know you'll have a phone interview for sure, along with a list of vaccines to schedule. Wow, in just six weeks, you could be in Africa!"

I swallowed hard before responding, "Thanks Meg, I look forward to hearing from them."

I handed her the papers, feeling a rush of nerves hit my gut at once. I tried to shake the unsettled feeling as I left her office, but it continued all the way out into the parking lot.

I heard her words again in my head and cringed.
'Must be nice, having no strings attached...'

If only I felt the same.

Careful to navigate my way back to my car and avoid the ice, I imagined the heat of Africa and the children I would get to help. I thought of the team I'd work with and the techniques I'd learn. There were many things to be excited about, many new challenges and discoveries that awaited my arrival.

I just needed to figure out how to tell my family; the clock was ticking in more ways than one.

****

I awoke to the strong smell of cleaning supplies. A lemon scent mixed with the menthol of mouth wash filled the air as I made my way down the stairs. Stacie—hair in a headband with blond curls flinging left to right—was cleaning the stove top. She was in Jack's sweatpants and an oversized t-shirt that read *Go Organic* on the front. I stifled a laugh at the site of her.

She had been in quite a mood lately and joking about her attire wouldn't bode well for me. I waited to speak till she saw me. I didn't want the charge of sneaking up on her added to my rap sheet.

"Hey Stace, how long have you been cleaning, this morning?" I asked.

Stacie glanced behind her at the clock on the wall, "A couple hours. I'm not sleeping well these days and there is *a lot* that has to be done around here."

I looked around at the practically spotless house and decided not to argue with her. Instead, I asked how I could help.

"I actually made a list last night. I'm going to check things off as I go. Most of it I should probably just do myself," she said.

I nodded, uncertain of my next response.

If I told her I'd like to help anyway, she might think I felt she was incapable, which of course, wasn't the case. However, if I agreed to let her work alone, she might think I was uncaring. It was a precarious situation for sure. I tried a mixed approach. At least that way she'd have to think about *which* offense she'd grab a hold of.

"You know, that's a really good plan. You're so detail-oriented, Stace. I'm sure you just want to get everything right. I'd love to help with anything you need though, so just let me know."

She stared at me for a long second. I braced for the fall-out. She smiled then, and put her hand on her hip, "Thanks Tori, I'll do that. I appreciate your offer."

Phew. Close one.

I made myself a pot of coffee and sat down at the counter, watching her scrub with her made-from-the-earth products. I'd made a goal to tell Stacie about Africa today, but the reality of the moment was much harder than I'd anticipated. Instead, I brought up her baby shower this coming Saturday. Hard to believe her due date was less than four weeks away now.

"Are you getting excited for your shower?" I asked.

"Yes and no. I feel like a whale...and I'm kicking myself for not pushing Mom to do it before the holidays," she said.

"Oh, Stace...you still look really great, no one is going to think you look like a whale."

She shot me a death glare that almost knocked me off my stool.

What did I say?

"I didn't say I 'looked like a whale'...I said, I 'felt like a whale'! But I guess I should worry about *that* now, too," Stacie huffed.

Shoot.

"Stace...that's not what I...I mean, you look beautiful," I said, smiling to cover my panic.

She turned and opened the cabinet drawers, dumping out the cooking utensils to organize them by size. I took my leave then, glad I chose to abandon the conversation about Africa. Maybe I should wait for Jack to be present; it would be safer that way, for everyone.

****

I layered my shirts, doubled my socks, and pulled on a down-vest over my hooded sweatshirt. Due to the road conditions, I couldn't run on the pavement. Jack told me another ice storm was on its way over the weekend, so I knew I needed to get out today. I headed to the local high school track. The dirt and grass were much safer than the roads.

I ran the giant oval three times before I started to feel warmth return to my legs and chest again. My cadence was sluggish at first, labored due to the intensity of the chill in the air. I emptied my distracted mind in order to focus on each step, pushing myself forward, relieving the stress in my body.

The fog was low and the visibility poor, but in a strange way it brought me comfort. There was no sound other than my breath to be heard on the track. In this silence I found peace—no distractions, no voices, no impending announcements to be made.

After another three times around the track I quickened my pace. I stared out into the field, watching the fog roll by. While staying clear of Africa and clearer still of a certain Samoan, I let my mind wander.

An image seared itself into my mind: the letter.

I had seen it every day since the day I had written it, and every day I made a new plan for its delivery. But just like the Africa conversation, it too, had been aborted time and time again for some reason or another. It was worn now, crumpled from being smashed inside my purse by keys and protein bars.

Someday soon.

I thought about my upcoming appointment with Dr. Crane. Would she be disappointed that I hadn't done it yet, or were my other stories of progress enough for one appointment? Maybe she could offer me some inspiration. I needed it.

The most difficult words I'd ever speak were on those pages.

I ran around the track another time, contemplating my options. Regardless of my excuses, there was but one timeline that would have the final say—*Africa*. I wouldn't leave without doing it; I couldn't leave without doing it.

By the time I got back to my car, I had made my decision. After the baby shower on Saturday was over, I'd have my date with the letter.

And then, the last two names would finally be crossed off my list.

THIRTY-THREE

The difference was noticeable.

I'd wondered when Dr. Crane gave me the journal before Christmas if something had changed in our relationship. Now I was sure. Her gift had *softened* me that day. No longer was I the broken mess she had met months ago, and no longer did I despise her office.

When I looked at Dr. Crane now, only one word came to mind: *friend*.

She would always hold the respect of a doctor in my eyes. She was a wise woman by anyone's standard, but there was a new sweetness that now stretched between us today. I was grateful for it.

She asked me several questions regarding the holidays, to which I offered light answers. Those were some of the hardest days I had faced to date. She shared briefly about her trip to the Caribbean with her kids and grandkids and then grabbed her notepad, indicating it was time to get down to business.

Before I began, I realized the majority of what I was about to share I hadn't told anyone. I felt a pang of shame go through me as I thought about each topic on my mind. My promise to keep my family in the loop had waned considerably since before Christmas. I had felt justified in my with-holdings due in part to Dr. Crane's extended holiday, but that was a weak excuse for the truth.

How can I really think I'm making progress if I'm hiding again?

The question made me shiver. I didn't want to think about going backward, it was too overwhelming. Dr. Crane looked at me puzzled, waiting for me to share. I cleared my throat and began.

I started with the phone call to Dr. Bradley. As one of her personal friends, I realized Dr. Crane might already know about this conversation, but she listened patiently like usual. She complimented me on my bravery and willingness to step out and make amends. Her encouragement felt good. I moved on.

Recounting the confrontation with my mother was more involved. She let me share the entire conversation before asking any questions—some more direct than others.

"How are things between you two now, Tori? How are you walking forward in this resolve?"

I thought for a minute before answering, "We've talked briefly on the phone a couple of times and I'm making four dozen cupcakes for Stacie's baby shower tomorrow which my mom is hosting. I guess I'm just trying to be more understanding," I said, honestly.

"That's good. I would challenge you, though, in order for a relationship to progress, you must invest more than just a few *brief* conversations. You need to show some more vulnerability with her at some point," she said.

I swallowed hard.

Why was that still so hard for me?

"What are you thinking about right now, Tori?" she asked.

"I...I'm wondering why that still seems so foreign to me...why I'd still rather process everything on my own," I said.

She smiled knowingly, "Because you're re-learning how to connect with people, how to trust them, how to let them trust you. That's all normal. It shows more progress than you might think. You wouldn't have even asked that question a few months ago."

She was right, I wouldn't have. I nodded, hoping she was right about the rest as well.

"What else happened...you seem to have lots on your mind today," she said.

Geesh, she would be great at poker.

"I talked to Kai...*twice*."

Her eyebrows rose in surprise, but she said nothing.

"We talked on New Year's Eve and I told him that I forgave him, and that I believed his intention was never to hurt me," I said. As I spoke his name, the old familiar ache came back. I took a deep breath.

"And what happened, what was his response to that?" she asked.

I hesitated, a war waging within me. There were many things about that night I replayed: his song, his jacket, our kiss. But recalling his words to me was the most painful of all, without a doubt. To share them meant to relive them.

I rubbed my palms on my knees. The pressure seemed to trigger a response.

"He told me he loved me, that he wanted to be with me, that he would wait for me to figure out whatever I needed to...and then I told him goodbye."

Empathy.

A face full of empathy stared back at me. I looked at the ground trying not to react, trying not to feel anything at all. It didn't work.

"*Why* Tori? Why did you tell him *goodbye* if you could forgive him?" she asked, the words soft and meaningful.

"Because...because I have to do this on my own. He may have helped me find faith, but he can't be what helps me find closure with Anna or myself. I'm not going to be around for much longer anyway..." I let my voice trail off.

She looked at me in surprise. I bit my cheeks.

"Excuse me? What are you referencing?"

"I signed up for the *Consider Africa* program. If I'm accepted, I'll leave March first," I said.

If the recounting of my conversation with Kai had been a surprise to her, this was a shock. She took a deep breath, closing her eyes for a moment before speaking. It was the first time I'd seen her physically tense, the first time I'd seen anything but professionalism from the woman sitting across from me. Her eyes lacked their usual pleasant curiosity when she opened them. Instead, they were narrowed and hard.

"Please explain this to me, Tori. *Why*, when you're having so many breakthroughs, and gaining back *valuable* relationships in your life, would you think it was a good time to move continents?"

I was taken aback by her tone and her pointed question. This wasn't her usual prompting to get me to share or be more introspective about my underlying motivations. No, this was something else altogether. I worked to gather my thoughts, to find an answer worthy of retaliation, an answer that would prove I had done right. Then she hit me with another.

"Can you honestly tell me that moving to Africa is not about running away again? That it's not about running from the happiness that's waiting for you right around the corner?"

Her words stung. I *wasn't* running away. I was moving on, gaining ground. This wasn't about self-sabotage, it was self-discovery. There was a difference.

"Who says I won't be *happy* in Africa? I'll be working with people who need what I have to offer. I didn't go to school or gain all this experience in an ER just to throw it away and be tied down.

I'm moving on, not running away. I'll finish up my *closure assignment* before I leave, so you can't accuse me of running away from that," I said.

She shook her head slowly, disappointment in her eyes.

"*Closure* doesn't work on your timeline, Tori. There's a give and take, an ebb and flow. Authentic closure happens when it happens; sometimes you have to *wait* for the right moment. Timing is just as important as the words and actions themselves," she said.

I slumped back on the couch, exhausted. The *right moment* would have to present itself within the next five weeks. I was moving to Africa, that was a fact. I decided then it would be a bad idea to tell her that my family didn't know about my decision.

I was grateful when the chime cut the tension between us. I stood to make my exit. She stopped me at the door.

"Please consider what I said. I care about you, Tori. You're a beautiful, talented, young woman, and I don't want to see you throw away what could be an amazing future all because you're too afraid to *stay*. Be honest about your motives, if not with me...then with yourself."

I nodded, leaving her office.

If we couldn't agree on this, than what would be the point of coming back here?

A sad resolve filled my heart.

There wouldn't be one.

****

Downstairs the ER lobby was chaotic. I could hear the sound of many voices even before the elevator doors were opened. Gurney after gurney whizzed by me as crying seemed to come from every corner. I threw my bag behind the empty nurse's desk, sanitized my hands and ran to help in receiving.

Through a collection of broken conversations, I'd gathered these were victims of a multi-car crash. My pager buzzed on my hip indicating a Code Yellow alert: mass casualty incident. I could see Meg Holt in the bay closest to the main doors working alongside a trauma surgeon. She was calling up to the O.R.

Along with the distinction in trauma codes, patients were also separated into two tiers based on the severity of their injuries.

Some would not make it into either.

I could see four ambulances parked out front now and knew more were on their way. The distant sound of sirens and the increasing number of staff who ran to get into the rotation mix caused adrenaline to surge in my veins.

There would be nothing *normal* about today. No standard protocol for trauma nurses specifically. Instead, we would take direct orders from the code team and doctors as we worked to serve each patient, doubling and tripling up if necessary.

It would be rough, organized chaos.

I met the ambulance in the receiving bay with a MD resident who I had recognized from the day shift, he nodded at me and together we raced to the howling ambulance. It came to a halt just a few feet away from us. The doors flew open and Briggs jumped out. My heart sank knowing that Kai was most likely out there somewhere, too. He was probably on his way now with patients who were near death or worse.

Briggs nodded at me, lowering the gurney to the ground. He rattled off the patient's stats quickly as we rolled through the lobby and hallway together.

She was in bad shape—critical condition.

"And the driver?" Resident Anders asked Briggs.

Briggs looked at us and shook his head. His answer was understood—DOA, dead on arrival.

We rolled her into the first bay where Meg Holt, an EKG tech, and a trauma surgeon, Dr. Nelson, waited to make the next call. I scribed the drugs and labs called out. Everyone moved at lightning speed. Her internal bleeding was cause for immediate action. In an instant she was headed into surgery—no time for extra lab work.

I called up to make sure a circulator RN was on the floor ready to receive her and knew the updated information I had gathered. Her fate did not look good.

Released to assist another patient, I jogged back to the receiving bay, Briggs on my heels.

"What happened out there?" I asked, breathless.

"A semi spun-out on black ice. He was going around sixty five miles per hour, it's laid out flat across all four lanes of traffic on I-75. Caused a twenty two car pile-up...most of them spun into the side ditch, some buried on top of others. The cars that hit the semi are in the worst shape, though," Briggs said.

My chest was heavy with grief, the unimaginable misery of all those victims at the forefront of my mind. I shook my head as his gaze seemed to penetrate to my soul. He put his hand on my shoulder as we neared his rig, "I miss you, Tori, take care of yourself today."

As he opened his door I yelled out the one question I could no longer contain, "Where's Kai?"

His face filled with understanding. He was no longer the joker I knew outside of his job; there was nothing amusing about a tragedy of this magnitude.

"I'm sure he's on his way here, don't worry. He and Mike were called out first...last I saw him he was assisting with the Jaws of Life. There are some pretty mangled cars out there."

He closed his door after saying a quick goodbye, knowing he'd most likely be back within the hour.

It was one thing to see these victims strapped to a board with basic care having already been given to them, but quite another to see them suffering in a twisted piece of metal on an icy highway. I cringed at the thought and went to assist with my next patient.

The emergency bays were packed with injured, hurting people. The total count of fatalities was up to seven and many more were undergoing surgery or in the ICU. A few were lucky enough to walk away with only minor injuries, but the average patient that had survived this horrific accident would bear the scars—both physical and mental—for a long time to come.

Hours had passed. I had still not seen Kai.

I'd seen Briggs multiple times within that time frame, and though I tried to remain focused on each patient, my nagging thoughts were hard to ignore. The recovery rooms upstairs were filling up with patients who had made it through surgery. By early evening, the trauma pods were finally starting to clear as patients were moved for overnight observation and care.

It was after seven when I finally saw him.

Relief filled me from head to toe when I saw him through the large glass doors of the lobby. He sat on the back bumper of an ambulance, staring off into a distance unknown. He looked tired, worn and dirty. But through the grit was the heart-wrenching portrait of a man who'd just given his all for the sake of others.

He was the portrait of a hero.

I walked toward the doors without giving myself permission and grabbed a staff jacket from the hall wall. I zipped it up before the cold could take me hostage. He didn't move an inch as the automatic doors opened and closed behind me, his eyes were so focused, so pensive.

I approached him slowly, shoving my hands into the pockets of the oversized coat. I sat down next to him on the bumper saying nothing, but knowing enough. He turned his head toward me, seeing me for the first time, but remained silent.

I knew this kind of tired. It wasn't about lack of energy or lack of sleep. It was the kind of exhaustion that only came from trying to save lives—lives that couldn't be saved. I knew *that* exhaustion well.

I realized in that moment why I hadn't seen him all day, why he hadn't brought any patients into the ER. He had done his days' work out at the scene. Briggs had said he'd seen him working to free someone trapped inside a vehicle. My guess was that he'd stayed to work on every last one of the seven that had perished, unwilling to give up the fight.

I leaned my head onto his shoulder in understanding. After a moment I felt his arm wrap around my waist, as he laid his head on top of mine. We sat there staring off into the distance together, not speaking a word.

There was nothing to say.

Meg came outside holding my bag, the one I had thrown behind the nurse's desk hours ago. I stood then, breaking away from the embrace I shared—embarrassed. I had let time get away from me while I was still on the clock. She put her hand out as if to calm me.

"You did great today, Tori, but I want you to get outta here. Several interns have come in within the last hour. They can take over your last couple of patients. With all the chaos today, it's important to decompress and to rest. I already sent Bev and two others home for the night, please go and do the same," Meg said, handing me my bag.

I took it, not quite sure how to respond. I'd never been sent home early, not even on the days that had been slower than molasses. I nodded, thanking her. She winked at me before turning to leave.

I stood in front of Kai, his sad eyes resting on my face.

"Please let me drive you home, Tori. I can't—I need to know you'll get there safely," he said.

I couldn't argue with him, not after a day like this, not after the things he had witnessed. Together we walked through the parking lot, careful to step only on dry pavement. It hurt to be so close to him again, to smell him, to feel him. We didn't speak on the drive; it was enough just to be together.

It was a little after eight when he parked my car in front of Stacie's house, the lights from the inside reflecting in the driveway.

I turned to him, recognizing his despair. I bit my lip, fighting back the question I had been rolling over in my mind.

Be a friend.

"Please come inside, Kai. Let me make you some coffee. I'm sure Jack and Stacie would love to see you, too," I said.

A hint of a smile began to spread across his face as he pondered my words.

"I'd like that, thank you."

THIRTY-FOUR

Kai showered and changed into an extra pair of workout pants and a t-shirt that Jack had loaned him. When he was finished, I did the same. I was convinced that clean had never felt so nice or smelled so good.

Jack handed me a cup of coffee as I joined Kai on the couch, tucking my legs underneath me. I was careful to keep my distance. Stacie lay across Jack's lap after he sat down, pulling an afghan over her legs and propping her feet up on a stack of pillows.

"So, what are the family bets on delivery day?" Kai asked, life returning to his voice.

Stacie smiled casually, rubbing her very round abdomen.

"Hmm...We don't really have any bets, but now I'm wishing we did. I could have started a college fund that way," Stacie said.

Kai laughed, making me smile.

"Let's see...you're about thirty-six weeks?" Kai asked.

"That's right," she said, impressed by his memory.

"I say you deliver early, maybe around week thirty-eight," Kai said.

"Oh I could just kiss you for saying that! All the old ladies love to tell me their horror stories of carrying way past their due dates, and I'm telling ya...I'm about done with this whole thing!"

We all had a good laugh. I set my coffee mug down on a coaster near me.

"I'll tell you what, any day after tomorrow is fine by me," she said.

"What's tomorrow?" Kai asked.

"Stacie's baby shower," Jack and I said in unison.

I jumped up with a sudden panic, leaping to my feet.

"What on earth?" Stacie said.

Kai stood too, waiting for me to articulate my sudden spastic attack.

"The cupcakes! I have four dozen cupcakes to start and icing to make before we leave at 10am! I totally spaced it," I said, biting my lip.

"Just go buy some, who really cares anyway?" Jack asked.

Stacie and I looked at him with horror. We both knew what would happen if I showed up bearing store-bought cupcakes to a catered event my mother was hosting. It was simply out of the question, especially since I was currently working toward restoring that particular relationship.

"I'll help you," Kai said.

Everyone stopped and looked at Kai, including Jack, who smirked at the suggestion. I stared at him, contemplating his offer. I weighed the risk/reward of a late night spent with him in my sister's kitchen, baking with me. It was quite possibly more idiotic than Jack's comment only a moment earlier.

But what were my options really?

I didn't let myself think of any. I agreed, and minutes later I was taking out the supplies and laying them on the counter top. Jack stopped in the doorway, leaning his body against one side of it.

"How were you planning on getting home?" Jack asked Kai.

"Hmm...Well, Briggs said he'd pick me up, but I better let him know it's going to be later than I thought. I forgot I didn't have my truck here," Kai said.

"Well, why don't you just stay over? The roads are only going to re-freeze tonight and I have to take off in the morning anyway. I can just drop you at home. Stacie's already laid out a pillow and blanket for you on the sofa bed," Jack said.

Kai looked at me, unwilling to answer such a question without my approval. I swallowed hard, trying to calm my nerves as both men waited for me to speak.

"That's fine with me," I lied.

"Great, I'll plan on leaving here around eight, will that work for you?" Jack asked him.

"Sure, that's sounds great. Thanks, Jack."

For the next hour we mixed and measured, turning Stacie's immaculate kitchen into a floury mess. Kai was a great help, always reaching for the next ingredient to add before I asked for it. As he put the last pan in the oven, I started on the icing.

I felt myself growing delirious in the late-night hour. I laughed at silly concepts, depicting the names and usages of all the herbs and spices Stacie had stacked in her pantry. Kai was no better. After the stress-filled day we had shared—each in our own way—laughter had proven the best remedy.

"I think we should add this to a portion of that icing, make it like a secret taste test. The winner can get a prize or something if she guesses it right," Kai said, holding up a small jar of turmeric.

I laughed till my eyes watered. Batting his hand away as he hovered dangerously close to my perfect vanilla icing, I was a crying mess of giggles.

"The only prize for that poor *winner* would be a barf bag, Kai. That would be so disgusting!"

He laughed too, pulling himself up to sit on the counter near my mixer. His face grew serious as he watched me add the pink food coloring drops to the mix. I glanced up only once and then determined to keep my eyes away from his face. My late-night filter remained uncensored, however.

"This is so odd," I said.

"What is?"

"Baking *with* you," I said, "I only started all this to get over you."

He stopped the whisk in my hand, careful not to touch my skin.

"And how did that work out?" he asked.

"You already know how it *worked out*, Kai."

"No, I only know how I *hope* it will work out, Tori...that's all." He hopped off the counter and walked toward the window.

I leaned onto the counter and took a deep breath, trying to slow my heart rate.

This was a bad idea.

I whisked for a minute more, alone in the kitchen.

I nearly jumped out of my skin when I heard his excited whisper break through the silence.

"Tori come here! Quick!"

I dropped the whisk in the sink and hurried to his side. He grabbed my hand and pulled me out the front door. My mouth gaped open as I felt the large soft flakes hit my hair and face. My t-shirt was certainly not the best attire for this sub-freezing event, but for once I didn't care about the cold. The snow was breathtaking. Ice was fairly commonplace for winters in Dallas, but snow was a rarity, one that was met with the excitement of many.

Kai's smile was huge as he held out his hand to catch the snowflakes. I shivered, laughing at the sight of this large Samoan man catching snow in Dallas, Texas.

"I've only seen snow a few times. In Samoa there was nothing to compare it to...I couldn't even understand the concept, until I felt it for the first time," he said, joy exuding from him.

I smiled, as I shivered harder. He looked at me, a realization coming over him.

"I had nothing to compare *love* to either, before you, before I felt it for the first time," he said.

He scattered the snow in his hand, wiping the remaining moisture onto his pants. I stared at him. I knew he wanted to kiss me. I knew, because I wanted to kiss him, too. The moment was too beautiful to ignore.

But instead, he took my hand and led me back inside, grabbing the afghan from the chair and wrapping it around my shoulders.

"I'll clean up...you should head to bed," he said.

"But you've had an even longer day than I-"

"No. Please, let me do this. Go get some sleep. I'll see you in the morning."

With that, our evening had come to an end. I crept up the stairs feeling a mix of relief and disappointment. I snuggled into bed, thinking of him downstairs.

The picture of Kai holding snow in his palm was the last thought I had before drifting off to sleep.

****

The morning brought with it a whirlwind of *busy*. I frosted cupcakes and arranged them on two large serving platters. Due to the frosting I couldn't wrap them. I prayed they would survive the drive, and not end up a mess of pink frosting and fuzzy floor mats. Each tray held twenty-four cupcakes.

Jack had offered us the use of his Jeep. It had more room in the back to carry the cupcakes and shower gifts Stacie would be receiving. It would also have much better traction for ice.

The only disadvantage was it was parked out front on the street, while Stacie's car would have meant a warm and toasty walk into the garage.

Both Jack and Kai were concerned about letting us drive to our parent's house with the re-freeze last night. They went over the road reports in detail, researching the best route online with the department of transportation. We had to promise to stick to their approved route—we both gave our girl scout's honor.

The city had been working overnight to de-ice the well-traveled roads and highways to avoid further catastrophes, like the one yesterday. I would be driving since Stacie was too round to fit behind the wheel comfortably.

"So, where are you off to today while your wife is being pampered in pink?" I asked Jack who was drinking a cup of coffee.

"I'm gonna head to Fort Worth, to a pro ice hockey game. An old college buddy has a brother in the league. He gave us free tickets. There's some Guinness World Record attempt going on before the game starts, too. Should be fun," Jack said.

"What kind of world record attempt is it?" I asked, pulling my tall boot on by the door, noticing Kai's eyes on me.

"To break the world's longest conga line on an ice rink," he said.

Kai and I busted up laughing. Only Jack would find this so entertaining.

"And you think that's more fun than eating cupcakes and playing baby shower games?" I asked.

Jack rolled his eyes at me, tipping his coffee cup toward the ceiling as he emptied it.

"Are you ready to go?" Jack asked Kai.

"I'm ready to get into my own clothes, yes," Kai laughed, looking down at his borrowed wardrobe.

Kai blocked Jack's friendly jab to the gut and they both headed toward the garage door at the back of the kitchen. As Jack went into the garage, Kai stayed behind.

"I had a really good time last night, Tori. Thank you for being a friend. I really needed one," Kai said.

He was so handsome, even in Jack's borrowed clothes. His hair was still ruffled from sleep, making him more adorable than ever. I wished it was possible to only be his *friend*, but I knew better.

"Thanks for your help with the cupcakes, you saved my bacon," I said.

He smiled wide, "I'd save your bacon any day of the week, Victoria Sales. Have fun with your sister today. Call if you need anything and *please* drive carefully."

I nodded, refraining from rolling my eyes, "I will, enjoy your day off."

A minute after Kai closed the door, Jack was back with a pile of mail in his arms.

"Stacie's been hoarding mail in her car again. I keep telling her that I can't pay the bills if I don't know we have them...I don't think she believes me," he laughed, shaking his head. He threw the pile on the counter before leaving again.

I made a pot of oatmeal, being sure to make enough for Stacie, too. It was a new obsession of hers, although I wasn't sure if it was the brown sugar or the oatmeal that was her latest craving. I poured the last of the coffee and sat on the bar stool at the counter. A large yellow packet caught my eye. Within the mix of envelopes that Jack had brought inside was the packet I had been waiting for.

I lifted it from the pile, opening the tab in the back and sliding out the contents. An acceptance letter was on top. I scanned it over, suddenly feeling my appetite disappear. I dropped my spoon back into my bowl, pushing it aside to read through the pages.

I had met all the criteria. All there was left to do was submit my completed immunization record with the required vaccines and a phone interview. I was so engrossed in the reading that I didn't hear Stacie enter the kitchen.

"Whatcha reading over there?" Stacie asked, walking toward her bowl of oatmeal.

A cold sensation crept over me. I felt ill. I didn't want to lie, but I didn't want to tell the truth either, not today. I gathered the papers up quickly, pushing my stool out as I stood.

"Oh...nothing much," I said.

Stacie's face was inquisitive; she looked from the stack of papers in my hand to my face and back. She was not a skeptical person by nature, but my face must have given something away. Without taking her eyes from me, she snatched the large empty envelope from the counter, reading the words aloud.

"Consider Africa—a nursing exchange program."

I swallowed hard. Caught like a deer in headlights I was frozen, waiting for impact.

Her face grew dark, shadowing her delicate features. She lay the envelope back down and picked up her bowl, walking into the living room. I was suddenly nauseous. There was no way out, no excuse that could fix this. I took a deep breath and walked into the room.

She sat staring into her bowl, taking slow bites.

"I was going to tell you, Stace. I just didn't want to distract from the baby," I said, realizing how stupid it sounded the instant I spoke it aloud.

She looked from her bowl to my face. Her eyes were hard.

"Don't. Don't you use my baby as an excuse, Tori." She set down her bowl with a clank "When? When are you leaving this time?"

Her sharp tone was startling. I hesitated to answer her. This conversation was quickly plummeting from bad to worse.

"In five weeks," I said quietly.

"Five weeks? You are moving to Africa in *five weeks* and I am just now hearing about it? How long were you planning on keeping this a secret, Tori? Was I just going to wake up one day and you'd be gone, halfway around the world?"

"No. I wasn't sure when I was going to tell you exactly, but I was going to tell you. I just got accepted. It wasn't even for sure until I got this today," I said, raising the paperwork slowly.

She shook her head. "I thought we were past this...I thought we had finally gotten to a place where we didn't hide secrets from each other, where you felt you could be *honest* with me. I guess the joke's on me, huh?" Stacie stood, bracing her back with her hands to counter the weight of her belly.

"I...I'm sorry-"

"You're always *sorry*, but nothing ever changes! Don't you care about your niece, or are you too selfish to realize that other people might actually want you around?"

I closed my eyes. That hurt.

"It's only for a year," I said.

She looked at me again, this time with sadness. As she walked past me into the kitchen I heard her say, "Perfect, that's just perfect."

Stacie milled around the house for the next hour, saying nothing. Picking up pillows and dusting off tables, she was in nesting-mode, again—angry nesting mode. I went upstairs to grab my purse, throwing my phone inside it. I heard something crinkle in the bottom of it.

The letter.

I'll do it after this stupid shower.

Then I'll have nothing left hanging over my head.

But even as I thought it, I knew that wasn't the truth. I'd have plenty left hanging over my head.

I walked back into the kitchen seeing only one tray of cupcakes on the counter.

Weren't both right here a minute ago?

I did a quick glance around the room, thinking I was losing my mind. Jack's keys were missing from the counter, too.

Stacie must have taken one to Jack's jeep already.

I grabbed the second tray and slowly guided the front door open with my foot, careful not to drop a single frosted treat. I walked slowly down the sidewalk, inching my feet along the slick cement that was covered with a light dusting of snow. It was hard to see over the top of my tray, but as I neared Jack's Jeep I realized it wasn't running, nor was Stacie inside it. I opened my mouth to call her name, but saw something strange out of the corner of my eye. Three pink cupcakes were lying on the ground.

I stopped, turning my body to see over the platter that obstructed my view. I gasped as my eyes focused on the icy ground below.

My hands broke away from the tray, pink cupcakes flying everywhere.

THIRTY-FIVE

Stacie's lifeless body lay near the back of Jack's Jeep, on the cold, hard asphalt. My world was quickly spinning out of control. She was on her back, obviously having slipped, but I had no way of knowing how hard she'd landed. I knelt beside her, the tights I wore soaking through in an instant.

"Stacie, Stacie!" I cried.

Her eyes fluttered as a moan escaped her lips. I reached for my phone, calling 911. Stacie moaned again, but I concentrated on the dispatcher. I had to get the information to her clearly. I was familiar enough with emergency protocol that I knew the highlights they were after and the questions I needed to ask of them.

"What's their ETA?" I asked the dispatcher.

"Between ten and fifteen minutes, ice has made for more of a delay today."

"Okay, I need you to call her husband for me, I have to make another call *right now*," I said.

"Ma'am I would like to stay on the phone with you-"

"I'm a nurse; I know what I need to do. I just need help to do it. Call her husband, please. He's over an hour away. Have him meet us at the hospital," I said.

I gave her Jack's number and hung up, immediately dialing out again.

"Hey...miss me already?"

"Kai?" I said, letting myself panic for the first time.

"What's wrong? Where are you?" Kai said.

"I'm at Stacie's...she fell outside. I need your help."

"I'll be there in less than five minutes, I'm already out."

I yelled down the street for help, my voice echoing through the hollow space. A man who was picking up a newspaper from his driveway looked over at me. I yelled again, he waved. As soon as he was close enough I asked him to go and grab me some blankets.

He reacted immediately, shocked at the sight of Stacie on the ground. She was shivering already, even with her coat zipped all the way up. I continually checked her pulse and said her name, trying to keep her alert, awake. Her breathing was labored, but I knew that was partly due to pregnancy and the frigid air.

"Tori?" Stacie's eyes were frightened. She tightened her grip on my arm.

"You're okay, Stacie. Everything's going to be just fine. We're going to get you to the hospital."

"I feel something warm," she said.

"What? Where?" I asked, looking her over.

"I think my water just broke."

Kai was parking as the neighbor man shuffled down the sidewalk, blankets in hand. Kai intercepted them, thanking the man and asking him to standby in case of another need. He agreed.

Kai knelt beside me, assessing Stacie the same way I had.

"Stacie, how do you feel? Does anything hurt...your neck, your legs, your back?" Kai asked.

"I don't think so...maybe my lower back a little. It's starting to throb a bit, but-"

"She thinks her water just broke," I said, cutting to the chase.

His eyes narrowing in concern, Kai glanced at me quickly.

This was not a good scenario. At thirty-six weeks pregnant, Stacie was practically full-term. The risk to delivering a baby at this stage was minimal, but the fact that a trauma had induced the labor was not. Kai helped me scoot Stacie's body onto a dry blanket, covering her with the other.

"The ambulance is still another five to ten minutes out, the dispatcher said there were delays from the ice."

"Call them back, find out exactly where they are. We may need to take her in ourselves," he said.

I dialed emergency again, my hands starting to shake. The delay was confirmed—only the projected time had lengthened. The new estimate from dispatch was over ten minutes due to all the wrecks. I told Kai.

There was a calculated risk to taking Stacie ourselves. Kai would do his best to get us there safely, but the advantage to lights and sirens was huge. The hospital wasn't far, five miles at most, but with the current road conditions there was no telling how long it could take today. The fact that Kai had just come from that direction, gave me hope.

"We need to move her into the Jeep. My truck won't fit us, she'll need to lie on the back seat," Kai said.

He looked to the neighbor man who was already in motion to

help us. Stacie moaned, holding her lower abdomen. I recognized that face from my year in labor and delivery, she was having a contraction.

After finding the keys on the ground and opening the back door to Jack's Jeep, Kai nodded at me. The three of us lifted her, the blanket acting as a support underneath her body. Once she was secured, I scooted in beside her. She lay propped on the seat, her knees bent as she held her tummy. The blanket underneath her was already completely soaked. I wasn't sure if it was caused by amniotic fluid or melted ice. I asked Kai to grab some towels from inside.

Stacie began to cry.

"You're okay, Stace. Everything is going to be okay. Jack is on his way to the hospital right now. Do you want to call him?" I asked her.

She nodded, taking a deep breath, trying to calm herself. I bent down and reached for my phone. That's when I saw it, a pool of blood. There was blood mixed in with the amniotic fluid—a lot of blood.

A chill ran up my spine as I handed Stacie my phone after dialing Jack's number. Kai was back before I could hit send. I heard Jack answer and Stacie's muffled cries filled the Jeep again. He reassured her, telling her that he was on his way and that he was excited to have a baby with her today.

Good ol' Jack, always able to say the right thing.

She calmed then, getting lost in the idea. Today she would hold her baby girl. Kai's eyes found me in the rearview mirror. I communicated my concern to him the best I could, using only my face. He seemed to understand. We were off a second later.

Stacie laid the phone down twice, breathing hard through contractions, moaning in pain. I took her pulse over and over, watching her every movement. We pulled into the emergency drive. Kai ran to grab a wheelchair, moving Stacie into it carefully.

They were waiting for us.

The minutes that followed were some of the scariest minutes of my life.

The ultrasound machine was able to diagnose what I was afraid I already knew. Stacie had marginal placenta previa, and she was in labor. A part of her placenta had detached during her fall, most likely when her water broke from the impact. That was also the source of the bleeding which had now soaked through the towels she sat on top of. She needed an emergency C-section, and quite possibly a blood transfusion.

I held her hand as we made our way to the eighth floor. They prepped Stacie quickly. Within minutes she was rolling into an O.R. I kissed her forehead as she passed me. She was crying.

I wanted to be in there with her, to hold her hand, to reassure her, but there was no place for an extra body in an emergency C-section. It would be over soon. The second she was out of sight, I felt my body crumble beneath me.

Fear had suffocated me in its grasp.

Kai lifted me up, walking me to a chair and letting me cry into his chest while we waited. He brushed my hair away from my face and spoke gentle words of reassurance. Then he prayed. He prayed for Stacie, for Jack, and for the baby. I began to pray too, feeling a new strength come over me.

He called my parents.

A delivery nurse came out just minutes later. She told us that the baby was healthy, but that Stacie would need a blood transfusion. Between the fall and the surgery itself she had lost far too much blood.

"We need to monitor the baby for a little while longer, but if you'd like to see her we can bring her into your sister's recovery room," the nurse said, smiling at us.

"Yes, please. Her husband should be here soon, too," I said.

"Okay, great. Her room number will be 824, just straight down that hall to the right. The baby should be there in about twenty minutes, as long as all her monitoring goes well."

Kai wrapped his arms tighter around me and together we thanked God for the precious life he had spared, followed by yet another prayer for her mother.

****

As the nurse wheeled the newborn into the recovery room, I was certain I had never felt anything like I did that first time I saw her. How could a baby so new, so small, evoke such a strong emotion? It was uncontainable. She was the most beautiful thing I had ever seen.

At just 5lbs. 10oz, she was tiny, but her face had the same delicate features and the same fair skin as Stacie. I leaned over her, touching her small fingers and toes and feeling a love for her I couldn't explain. It was as if I'd always known her.

I wanted to hold her—I ached to hold her, to let her know her mom was going to be fine and that her dad would be here soon. The nurse started to lift her up to me, when I looked at Kai in a panic.

"What's wrong?" he asked.

"I don't think I should be the first one to hold her...I feel like I'm stealing a moment from Stacie and Jack if I do," I said, my eyes filling with tears.

Kai shook his head and smiled, "You helped save her mother's life and her dad is not here. You're the next best person in line for such a job. No one will think twice about that."

I took in his words and sat in the rocking chair near the bed. I held out my arms as the nurse brought her to me. She was swaddled in a pink blanket.

"Do you know her name?" the nurse asked me.

"No, they hadn't decided yet," I said.

The nurse smiled and walked over to the counter in the room, filling out paperwork. Kai and I were in our own private world, staring at my precious baby niece. I was overcome with love, for both the hearts that beat near me.

****

Jack ran into the room fifteen minutes later, breathing hard. He saw me holding his daughter and his hands flew to his head, bracing them at the base of his neck. He was working hard to regain his sanity.

"She's here Jack...she's *perfect*. Stacie's still in surgery, but she should be out soon," I said.

I stood up, offering him my seat and laid his baby daughter in his arms. Kai and I backed up, giving him room for a moment much deserved. He wept grateful tears over his daughter, rocking her, and kissing her sweet face. When he recovered, he held her up to me again, asking me to hold her so he could check on his wife.

I happily obliged; I wanted an update, too.

Stacie was wheeled into the room an hour later, groggy and tired. My parents were still on their way, stuck in slow moving traffic. The roads had been much worse than they had anticipated.

I knew Jack and Stacie needed some time alone. They needed time to meld as a family before our parents arrived. I gave Stacie a quick hug and left her holding her daughter. In the hallway Kai stood, leaning against the wall, just inches away from me. I smiled at him, my heart bursting with gratefulness. He touched my face softly.

"You're so beautiful, *Pele*—inside and out," he said.

My stomach clenched with longing.

"Thank you so much for today, Kai. I can never repay you..."

He leaned in and kissed my forehead as a familiar warmth spread through me.

Why...why does this have to be so hard?

Why when I'm leaving do I have to feel this way?

Stop running.

I saw my parents round the corner, my mom's hand moving to cover her heart as our eyes met. She hugged me close and then grabbed Kai, kissing him on the cheek and thanking him profusely for his help.

"You're welcome, but it's this lady here who should get the credit," Kai said looking at me.

My mom hugged me again and then knocked on the door to Stacie's room. She and my father entered together. A moment later I heard Stacie call for me. I reached for Kai's hand and headed for the door. Kai hesitated, pulling his arm back gently from my grasp.

"Come on. Let's go in." I stared at him confused.

He shoved his hands into his jean pockets, his face pensive. "I don't think I should go in, Tori. This is *your* family. It's a special day for all of you. I'll just hang out here for a bit."

It was easy for me to forget at times that Kai had feelings, too. So often I thought only of the way our breakup had affected me. I was selfish to think like that. The things that had transpired between us *had* affected him.

I could see that now, in his eyes.

"I'm sorry Kai...I don't know what to-"

"Go on...go enjoy your special moments with your family. I'll wait out here."

****

The picture inside that hospital room was beautiful. Parents, grandparents, and an auntie all surrounded this precious little life. We took turns holding her, swooning over her every sigh. This baby girl had stolen all our hearts in just a matter of hours.

This little girl had brought us together. I looked at Stacie. She was still so weak and frail, but her face was overcome with love and adoration.

I had spent so much time and energy questioning God's goodness, questioning His will, but today I saw Him with fresh eyes. God didn't *cause* pain. God didn't *cause* tragedy, but God could make beauty from the ashes of our lives. My niece was just one example of that.

"Is Kai still here?" Jack asked.

"I think so, he said he was going to stay out in the hallway for now," I said.

"*What?* Go get him, Jack. He's just as much a part of this celebration as we are, plus we need to tell ya'll her name. We finally agreed on one," Stacie said, laughing lightly.

Kai walked into the room with Jack. He stood several few feet away from me. My heart ached to be closer, but I knew he was trying to keep his distance. I had to respect that. I had given away my right to wish for anything more.

I remained near the head of Stacie's bed. She looked from me to Kai.

"You both deserve a *thank you* that's bigger than anything we could ever do or say..." She grabbed Jack's hand, shaking her head as tears streamed down her face. Jack smiled and took over for her.

"What she wants to say, is that we are so grateful to you both and because of that, we'd like to name our daughter in your honor. We have chosen a name that is a part of you both," Jack said.

My mother burst into tears as my father wrapped his arm around her shoulder, smiling proudly. I looked over at Kai who appeared just as surprised as I was.

"Her name is Kailynn Grace- Kailynn after Kai and Grace after Tori's middle name," Stacie said.

Until that moment, I had never cared about my middle name or its defined meaning. Today that changed. It was by *grace* alone that Kailynn was born healthy, to a mother that suffered no long-term effects of her birth.

Jack carried Kailynn across the room, laying her in Kai's arms. His smile was unmatched. Stacie's touch on my hand pulled me back to reality.

"I need to apologize for what I said before, and how I said it."

I looked at her puzzled.

"Back at the house—the Africa stuff. I'm still not happy about it and I don't want you to go, but I wasn't kind. I'm sorry for the things I said, Tori."

I nodded, feeling my blood turn cold inside my veins.

The room was a tight fit with all the bodies we had crammed into it. The odds that our conversation had been ignored were not good. I could feel my mother's gaze on us and I knew it was only a matter of seconds before the truth came out. Nausea hit as I looked from my parents, to Jack, to Kai.

All attention was on me.

"What's going on? What's Stacie talking about, Tori?" my mother asked.

I exhaled hard, gripping the side of Stacie's bed rail.

"I...I've just been accepted into a nursing exchange program," I said.

"But we've just got you *back*," my mother said.

"Phoenix is hardly *Africa*, Mom," Stacie said, pointedly.

"*Africa?*" My dad and Jack said the word together in unison.

My mom's hand flew to her face. "You're seriously considering going to Africa, Tori? Please tell us you're kidding!"

Trying to seek refuge, I looked to Stacie. There was none to be found there. She might have been sorry for her careless words earlier, but now she was quiet, waiting for me to speak.

"It's a great opportunity for my career and it's just for a year-"

"A *year*? Heavens, Tori-" my mother cried.

"When do you leave?"

Kai asked the question quietly, participating in my family drama for the first time. All attention in the room went to him. I heard my mother gasp, surprised he was learning this information along with the rest of them. I couldn't will the words to come out, they were stuck somewhere between my shame and my humiliation.

"She leaves in five weeks," Stacie announced.

THIRTY-SIX

Uproar exploded from all corners of the room, the birth of Kailynn momentarily ignored. Stacie and my mother were talking rapidly, asking questions left and right. Jack was digging for more detail and facts about the program, and my father was silently shaking his head, eyes diverted. I watched Kai place the baby into my father's arms, excusing himself from the room.

It was then I felt a whack on my side.

"Well, go...go after him!" Stacie said, cords dangling from her arm as she hit me a second time.

I ran out the door following Kai's long stride down the hallway. I caught up with him in the waiting room.

"Wait, Kai, please."

He stopped, turning to face me.

Regret drowned every other sense I had.

When will I stop hurting this man?

"My sister told me today that my apologies are worthless, that I say them, but never change. Maybe she's right, but right now I *feel* sorry, Kai. I'm so sorry you found out that way," I said.

"Me, too."

I stood waiting for him to say more, but nothing more came.

"Is that all you're going to say to me?" I asked, feeling the knife of panic slice into my heart.

"What else can I possibly say that I haven't already said, Tori? That I love you, that I want to be with you, that I'll wait for you? All of that is still true. Only now the waiting has become way more real, hasn't it?"

I stared down at the floor, too afraid to see what was in his eyes.

"I never asked you to wait for me."

"You never had to, Tori." Kai said, taking a deep breath. "You do realize the irony here though, right?"

I looked up at him, confused.

Realization dawned on me only seconds later. I had once felt so justified in accusing him of a similar kind of deception, yet here I was now, guilty of the same. I had withheld information from him out of fear, out of selfishness, out of pride.

Ashamed, I nodded. I understood the irony and I could do nothing to change it.

"You should get back to your family, sounds like there's a lot left to discuss in there. I need to go," he said.

"How will you get home?"

"I'll manage. See you around, Tori."

With that, he walked away.

****

A full week had passed. Kailynn and Stacie were home resting peacefully while Jack worked from an upstairs bedroom. He wasn't ready to leave his new family for his office downtown quite yet.

The drama from the hospital room had settled to a dull roar. After many debates, online reviews, and geography research, there was an unspoken mandate over the topic of *Consider Africa*: agree to disagree. They were all tired of the fight and I was tired of fighting.

****

I pulled my running shoes on, needing a reprieve. Though having a new baby in the family had brought so much joy, I couldn't ignore the ticking of the clock. Every day that passed reminded me of what I was leaving behind, of *who* I was leaving behind. Every day I told myself that I had made the right decision—the *only* decision.

As I ran down Stacie's street, I passed the familiar houses, pond and park. I felt a pang in my chest. It was the same desperate tug I had been discounting for weeks.

I pushed on, fighting the resistance in each stride.

I just needed my *fix*—however temporary it was.

But it never came.

By the time I got to the bridge, my legs felt like lead. It was the first time in nearly two years that I hadn't been able to escape…*from myself*. I couldn't take one more step; the heaviness in my chest was too unbearable.

I had spent so much time and energy trying to forget, trying to right the past, trying *not* to feel. And now, as I stared at the bridge in front of me, the *truth* was overwhelming. All along I had looked

for a way out, but that was never the answer.
Stop running.
Though I had done the work, though I had made some progress, the gap between my future and my past wasn't yet bridged. I sank to my knees and wept.

It was time to stop running.

****

My palms grew sweaty as I gripped the steering wheel. Today I would deliver the letter. I was one stop away from closure, one stop away from peace. I had thought for weeks—months even—that in order to find healing I had to do it alone. That support had to come from within.
I was wrong.

Breakthrough rarely happens alone; mine was no exception.

The people who had been a part of my journey were catalysts to my growth and advocates in my recovery. *Gratitude* was far too simple a word for what they had helped me see.
Going to Africa may have been a dream for some, but it wasn't my dream—it was my *escape*. It wasn't moving forward; it was leaving the only future I wanted, behind. I was done chasing after escapes.
No matter how far I could run, it was never far enough. My problems, my hurts, my fears, my failures, all came with me.
Every. Single. Time.

I wasn't fixed, I wasn't whole, but I was ready.

I was ready to bridge the gap.

I was ready to move forward.
It had been more than two months since my last flashback and longer still since I was frozen in my guilt and isolated in my shame. God had sought me and He had won me. There was still much I did not understand, much my heart still could not fathom, but I

knew the taste of freedom and I wasn't going back. What God had asked of me was nothing short of everything, but what He had given back was the promise of a future.

I pulled my car in, overwhelmed at the enormity of my decision. The letter remained on my passenger seat. This was not its home; this was not its recipient. I grabbed the box out of my trunk, securing its lid and walked forward, each step easier than the last. My heart thudded hard inside my chest and my hands shook with nerves.

There were at least twenty men I could see as I approached the large open door. I scanned the room, feeling faint as one by one the eyes of the firehouse were on me. I saw Briggs tap Kai on the shoulder, causing him to turn, causing him to blink me into focus. I took five more steps, stopping just a foot from the floor inside the station.

I waited there for him, making certain he was willing to see me. In record time, we were standing face to face. I held out the box to him.

"This is for you," I said.

Perplexed, he took it from my hands, opening the cardboard lid.

"Shoes?" he asked, looking from them to me.

"Yes, my running shoes. I'm done running, Kai. I'm done running from God, from life...from *you*. I'm not going to Africa. I want *this* future, I want you," I said, my voice thick with emotion. "I love you, Kai."

"Oh, *Pele*," Kai said, dropping the box and lifting me up off the ground hugging me tight.

We kissed, holding onto each other with no intention of ever letting go. The men inside the station went wild. Their whistling and clapping continued even after our kiss broke, laughter escaped from us both.

I could not contain my joy.

"I may share a piece of your past," Kai said as he dropped to his knee, "but *you* are the only future I could ever want. Will you marry me, Tori?"

Without a single doubt, I yelled my response for all to hear, "Yes! I'll marry you, Kai!"

Kai rose, grabbing me around the waist. Pulling me close to him, he kissed me again, this time with renewed fervor and passion.

Our story may have begun in the midst of heartache and loss, but our future would forever be rooted in hope and love.

EPILOGUE

Hand in hand we walked up the grassy hill. Her grave was marked with fresh flowers and a bench seat that had been cleared of all debris. We sat, Kai wrapping his arm around my shoulders as I opened the letter.

I took a deep breath before I began:

"Dear Anna,

I never knew you, but there were many days it felt as if you were more alive inside of me than I was. I used to dream of what your laugh would have sounded like, how your eyes would have sparkled, how your hair would have looked in the sunshine. There are many things I'll never get to know about you, but even in your absence you have managed to teach me. Your mom talked about your love for God, your hope in Him, your salvation. I didn't understand those things. I didn't think I could ever believe in Him that way—the way you did.

I tried to be your savior, Anna, and I thought all this time that I had failed you. I thought that I had contributed to your death, that I had taken your life away from your family. But I realize now that I was never in control of that.

I did try to save you. I wanted more than anything to see you alive, to feel your heartbeat, to hear your breath. But I can no longer accept the blame for your death.

The forgiveness your mom offered me is the same forgiveness I must offer myself every day that you're not here. I've found faith, Anna—in your Savior. You helped me find Him. You helped me know Him for the first time. Thank you for that.

I will never forget you.

Goodbye, Anna."

I wept into Kai's arms as he rocked me slowly, feeling the release I once never believed possible. My letter turned to ashes in the wind as a tiny spark took it away in an instant.

Anna would always be a part of me and I knew in some way I was a part of her, too.

The End.

John 16:33 (NLT):
"Here on earth you will have many trials and sorrows. But take heart! I have overcome the world."

Author's Note: Recovery

Recovery.

A necessary evil.

Often it feels like a hike that's uphill both ways, in the snow, while wearing a swimsuit and no shoes.

Sound familiar? Whether you need recovery for something you did to someone else, something done to you, or something you are currently doing, recovery is hard and always painful.

Though Tori's journey is purely fictional, her recovery from shame and guilt is far from unique. I, too, have battled with those issues as I have explored the depths of my addictions and coping mechanisms.

Though my addiction was easy to mask and hide from others—even those closest to me—my body and mind bore the scars. Listening to the lies, believing them, and acting on them have a heavy price to pay, but thankfully, it was a price that was already paid for me.

My need for a Savior came in the midst of my recovery. Though I had claimed to know Christ all my life and had grown up in a faith-based home, I had no idea the magnitude of my need *for* Him. It was in a dark pit of despair where He found me, a pit I was certain I would never climb out of. I believed I was a lost cause. My addiction was a weed, choking out all hope in the pit that surrounded me.

And then...I cried out.

It was not the cry of countless years prior, the one that was full of empty promises which led me back to my old ways. Instead, it was a cry that marked my desperation; I could not go on without Him.

That is where my Savior found me.

That is where my Savior won me back to Him.

Often people think *recovery* is a journey of self-reflection and healing. With that being true, it is also about others: those we have wronged, those we have hurt, and those we have lied to and manipulated in order to keep our masks on tight.

Without the process of "making amends" just like Tori did in this story, recovery is only surface deep. God desires our heart—our whole stinkin', rotten, black-as-night heart.

And then, only then, change can happen.

Isolation is the *enemy* of recovery. I continue to learn this lesson over and over. Every time I thought I could handle it on my own, I was knocked down. Truth finally took root in my heart once I became vulnerable enough to be held accountable by those who loved me. Re-learning how to think, how to deal, how to live, is difficult, but sharing with others can lighten that load tremendously.

I am not fixed, but I am far from the pit that once consumed me in darkness.

If you are in the pit, it is not too late for you. You are not too far from God's reach, or too far from His redemption.

There is hope for you.

Cry out. Your Savior awaits.

Psalm 103:2-4 (NIV)
Praise the Lord O my soul, and forget not all His benefits. Who forgives all your sins and heals all your diseases, who redeems your life from the pit, and crowns you with love and compassion.

Special Thanks:

God: Your relentless pursuit of me, your unfathomable grace, your endless forgiveness, your all-consuming passion, your boundless love, your unreachable depths, your constant faithfulness.
Without You I am nothing.

Husband: You are a rare gift, Tim Deese. Your love for me is a reflection of your heart for Him. You have pursued me, you have fought for me, and you have won my heart for all of eternity. It is yours and you are mine. Thank you for letting me stay up until the wee hours of the morning to write. Thank you for pretending not to notice when I stole your energy drinks in order to stay up, and for your forgiveness when you did notice! Ha! Thank you for believing I was great before I ever typed a word. Your support was the anchor I needed...as it always is. I love you.

My Boys: Preston (7) and Lincoln (4). Though you were often sound asleep while I typed, there were plenty of times that my story was a distraction in our day to day lives. Your patience has not gone unnoticed. God has blessed me with two smart, independent, loving, sensitive, active and overall *amazing* boys. I am more grateful for you with each passing day. I love you both to infinity and beyond.

Family: My life is made up of many wonderful people and so many of those I'm privileged to claim as my family (whether by blood or by marriage). I wish I could list you all by name.
I love each one of you so very much!

Dad and Mom: Thank you to my amazing parents who read my *entire* manuscript aloud to each other despite my utter disapproval and humiliation...haha! Thank you for showing me how to love and how to be loved. I am blessed to be your daughter.

Aimee Thomas: Thank you for thinking our "reading parties" are cool—even when other people may find them weird. You are an endless supply of passion and dreams; you are an inspiration.
I love you, sister.

Ashley Brahms: Thank you for reading my original "sloppy-copy" and for loving it just the same. Your many phone calls and texts over this last year have reminded me that *home* is relevant only to love, not location. I love you, sister.

Friends: Without your love, support and continual encouragement, this book would have ended around chapter five. I am SO blessed for the diverse friendships God has given me. To all my friends in the Pacific Northwest…all the way over to my friends on the East Coast (and especially to all my cyber friends!), please accept my deepest, most heartfelt *thank you*. You have enriched my life.

Kacy Koffa: You are a tangible representation of faithfulness in my life. Our friendship has withstood the trials of many seasons, yet our bond continues to strengthen with time. I am undeserving of such loyalty and devotion. I love you.

Kim Southwick: You are the older sister I never had, the bosom buddy I always wanted, and the other half I never knew was missing…until you found me. Your friendship is matchless. I love you.

Lara Brahms: You are my little ray of sunshine. Thank you for the countless hours you have spent in "fiction land" with me and for pretending it was *totally normal*. Thank you for reminding me to laugh—a lot. I love you.

Nicki Davis: Let us never underestimate the bond that can form over purses and books! I value our many forms of techy-communication in a day. I love you friend.

Rebekah Zollman: Your friendship has been such a sweet answer to prayer this year. Your honesty, empathy, and love continue to challenge me to be a better wife, mom and friend. I love you.

Renee Deese: I find it quite funny that you can fit under all three categories: family, friend and **editor**. Words cannot express how grateful I am for you little sister. Your "Renee-ness" has blessed me beyond measure. Thank you for the MANY hours you have poured into my manuscript, for your opinions, and for your constant affirmation. You are a rare gem; I treasure you greatly. I love you.

Beta Readers: Many, many thanks to all my beta readers. You inspire me to write from my heart. I love each of you: Ashley Brahms, Aimee Thomas, Bill Deese, Bethany Deese, Cara Dyson, Helen Deese, Irina Owens, Kacy Koffa, Katie Karin, Kim Southwick, Lara Brahms, Meredith Hall, Nicki Davis, Rebekah Zollman, Renee Deese.

Community Girls: Irina Owens and Katie Karin. Thanks you for your prayers, your love, and your encouragement. My life has been fuller because you are in it.

Cover Design: Thank you Sarah Hanson at Okay Creations! You are brilliant. I am in love with your work! Check out: *http://www.okaycreations.net*

Georgia Varozza: Your words changed my life. I cannot thank you enough for your time, your critique, and your *belief* in me. I am forever in your debt.

Regeneration Ministries: I found my "voice" during ReGen. Thank you Watermark Community Church for providing such an amazing recovery ministry…my heart and life will never be the same.

Thank you.

All for Anna is the first in a series of novels.

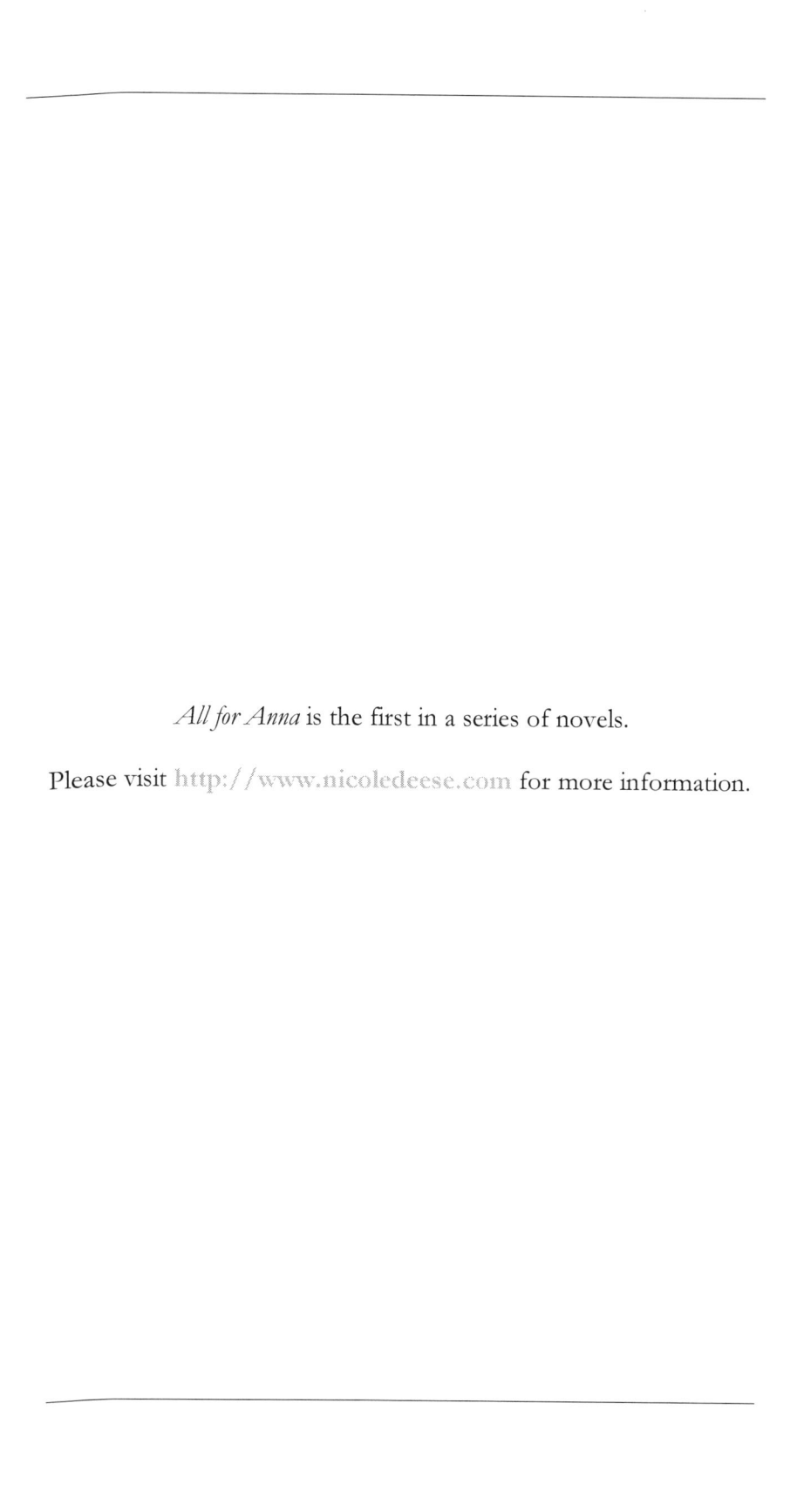

Please visit http://www.nicoledeese.com for more information.

Printed in Great Britain
by Amazon